Crocodiles and Angels

Carolyn Belcher

First Published in 2015
by GWL Publishing
an imprint of Great War Literature Publishing LLP

Produced in United Kingdom

ISBN 978-1-910603-16-1 Paperback Edition

GWL Publishing
Forum House
Stirling Road
Chichester PO19 7DN
www.gwlpublishing.co.uk

Carolyn was born and grew up in South Lincolnshire in a small village called Holbeach Hurn. Her Aunt Margaret introduced her to the power of drama and theatre when she was twelve.

In 1970, with her first husband, Barry and their three children, she moved to Knotty Ash, in Liverpool. When the last of her three children started school, she took a Bachelor of Education degree in drama, dance and education. Her first teaching post was at Page Moss Comprehensive, and as a performance arts teacher, she was invited to be on the Board of trustees for The Everyman Theatre.

It was at Knowsley Community College, in 1984, where as Course Coordinator for performing arts she began writing seriously, developing scripts from student improvisations. Some of the pieces were performed at the Edinburgh Fringe Festival and two were Pick of the Day in The Scotsman.

She was one of the Founder members and first artistic director of Icarus Allsorts, a performance arts company set up to help Knowsley graduates of the performing arts, to achieve an equity card.

She took early retirement when she was fifty, and moved with her second husband, Colin, to the Maine et Loire in France in order to have more time to develop her writing.

She now lives in Suffolk where, until recently, she supplemented her pension by becoming an examiner for GCE and GCSE drama practical work. She is a volunteer at Oxfam and belongs to Write Now, the Bury St Edmunds Writers' group.

She has had several stories and poems published in magazines and anthologies, both in England and The United States, and a monologue, which was chosen to be performed at a new writing festival, in Reading.

Theatre still plays an important part in Carolyn's life, as do dance, gardening and entertaining family and friends.

Dedication

To my husband, Colin, for all his patience and tolerance

Prologue

Once upon a time there were four friends, Einna, Maggie, Angela and Debbie. When they were together, they laughed and laughed until they wet their knickers. Like dominoes, they tipple-toppled into laughter.

There is a mirror in a cathedral. It is there to help visitors look at the stained glass windows without hurting their necks. Four women stop, look, sigh and move back a few paces.

"It's time. Now I know," Einna whispers to the angels in one of the exhibition windows. "I shall tear up all the prose and poetry that constitute my attempts to understand my life, burn the fragments and throw the ashes up into the west wind "

Chapter One
Crocodile Teeth

My bears have been eaten by a crocodile
who gnashed her terrible teeth.
She grabbed them off my bed
And tore off their heads
That horrible crocodile.

I wrote this poem when I was eight years old. Annie, my sister, didn't actually eat the bears; she gave them away. But she might as well have eaten them, for they were dead to me. I was only six when it happened.

My name is Einna. This is my story.

There were a lot of women in my immediate family and only one man. There used to be three men, but my father and Uncle Arnold died in the second world war. My father's name was Gilbert, Gilbert Huckle. I never met him or Uncle Arnold. Uncle Arnold was married to Amethyst. She was my mother, Pearl's sister. I wish I'd known my father. I often wondered if I was like him, if he was nice, what he looked like?

I've got one of his handkerchiefs. Neither Annie nor Pearl knew about it. It was one of my secrets. I'd found it in a drawer in Pearl's bedroom when I was eight; she'd asked me to fetch her headache pills, because Annie was still at college; Annie liked waiting on Pearl.

Pearl kept the pills in her paraphernalia drawer; that's what she called it, and there were these white handkerchiefs by the side of her embroidered ones. I saw the initials on the top one, *GH*, and knew they were my father's.

I hid the handkerchief in the treasure-box that Jean gave me. Jean was one of my angels, a guardian angel; that was how I saw her. She gave me sanctuary when I was running away from Annie and Pearl. But I hadn't met Jean when I was six.

I can't remember if I first learnt about angels in school, or in church. I remember the bible in our class library; it had lots of illustrations in it, some of them included angels. The one I liked best was of Jacob wrestling with an angel. In free time, I painted a picture of that wrestling match, only I changed Jacob into a crocodile, because the angel put Jacob's hip out of joint. I didn't really understand what it meant then, but it looked as though Jacob was in pain, so I thought the angel must have won. Our teacher asked me why I'd chosen to change Jacob into a crocodile. I didn't know what to say, because I couldn't tell her about Annie. I made up a story about crocodiles being very brave and fierce.

"That's how Jacob is," I said, "because he fought the angel."

She put my picture on the wall.

I hid the treasure box between the bed springs and the mattress at the foot of the bed; I knew no one would find it there. I had to crawl under the bed to push it in. Pearl and Annie wouldn't have found it; they never looked under beds. Mrs. Foreman, who was Pearl's cleaner, swept under the bed, but she wouldn't have been able to see it. Sometimes, when Annie hurt me, I took the handkerchief out of the box and held it against my cheek.

I knew the one man in our family. His name was Uncle Charles. He was married to my Aunty Ruby. She was also Pearl's sister, her youngest sister. I made up a fairy story about Pearl, Ruby and Amethyst, and put it in the treasure box along with the poem.

Once upon a time there were three sisters. The eldest sister was called Amethyst, the middle sister was called Pearl and the youngest sister was called Ruby.

The three sisters were as beautiful as flowers and as kind as angels. They lived on strawberries and cream and drank homemade lemonade. Princes came from far and wide to play croquet with them.

That was fairy tale truth. Neither Pearl nor Amethyst were beautiful or kind. Pearl was very thin. She had permed brown hair in a style like Queen Elizabeth: our queen, not the one who lived a long time ago. Pearl didn't smile very often. Her face was frowny. I thought the name suited her. Pearls are cold gems.

Amethyst was plump, like a saggy cushion. She also had brown hair, but it had grey strands in it. She smelt of lavender. I had to kiss her when she came to see us, or when we went to Wisbech to see her. I remember her talcum powder wafting up my nose and making me sneeze. She always said, "I hope Einna hasn't got a cold. You know how susceptible I am to catching colds."

Of course I didn't know what 'susceptible' meant, and I didn't dare ask, so when we got home, I looked it up in the dictionary, 'easily affected', it said. Then I had to look up 'affected'; I knew what 'easily' meant. Dictionaries aren't fair to six year olds who want to know what difficult words mean. They use more big words to describe the one you are looking up. In the end, I asked Mrs. Aymes, my teacher. She told me it meant you caught colds and other ailments easily.

Ruby wasn't skinny, like Pearl, nor fat like Amethyst. She was beautiful. Not beautiful like Elizabeth Taylor was beautiful; beautiful like a ruby, all glowing and smiley. I remember wishing I could like look like Elizabeth Taylor when I grew up. She had dark hair and blue eyes; so did I. But my hair was straight; the crocodile always cut it like a German helmet. I knew what German helmets looked like, as well as angels. I'd seen pictures of Second World War German soldiers in a history book in school. There were lots of books in my school.

I loved Uncle Charles and Aunty Ruby and I think they loved me. I always liked calling them 'Uncle' and 'Aunty' because I wasn't allowed to call Pearl 'Mummy', except in public when it would have looked odd if I'd called her 'Pearl'. When you're six, it's hard to remember something like that and sometimes I got in a muddle, then Pearl asked Annie to punish me.

I didn't see Uncle Charles and Aunty Ruby often, because they were very busy. Uncle Charles was an auctioneer. Aunty Ruby told me that meant he sold things with a hammer. I thought it sounded funny, selling things with a hammer. I couldn't help imagining a lady who wanted to buy a chair and Uncle Charles saying, *"You can buy the chair if you take a hammer as well."* I thought there must have been an awful lot of hammers at the selling place; that was what I called it, a selling place. Later, I learnt it was called an auction room.

What Aunty Ruby did all day was a bit of a puzzle; she didn't do any housework or cooking. Pearl had Mrs. Foreman to do the housework, but she only came once a week. Aunty Ruby had Audrey to help her and she came every day, to clean, do the laundry and cook. Uncle Charles said she made the best short crust pastry in East Anglia. It melted in the mouth. Ice cream and ice lollies melt in the mouth. Pastry crumbles, it doesn't melt, but I didn't tell him he was wrong, that would have been rude. Aunty Ruby always asked Audrey to make strawberry jam tarts and American lemon pie when I stayed with them, as they were my favourites.

When Pearl was being nasty about Aunty Ruby, she would say, "She swans about pretending to be a great lady." I hadn't ever seen a swan, except in stories like *The Ugly Duckling*, but I remember thinking they were probably like ducks in the way they moved. In the pictures of them, they looked like big ducks, only with longer necks. Ducks waddle. I couldn't accept that great ladies waddle. I used to watch Aunty Ruby to check how she walked. She didn't waddle, she sort of trotted. Uncle Charles said she tripped about. I thought it odd the way adults described things. In my mind a trip was what you did when you fell over, and Aunty Ruby didn't fall over.

A trip could also be a sort of journey. Pearl called people who went on day-trips 'trippers'. She didn't like them. "Oh dear, it's the season of the trippers again," she would say. It was the, 'oh dear', that told me she didn't like them. I wondered where the trippers came from? They always seemed very jolly and, as far as I could see, they didn't trip over anything.

In a book that Pearl had on her coffee table in the lounge, there were photos of the royal family. At the coronation of King George VI, they all had to wear crowns, even the two princesses. Some of the photos showed them waving at the crowds in the streets from one of the balconies at Buckingham Palace. I wondered if they had to practise walking with books on their heads so that the crowns didn't fall off. I'd seen people's hats blow off in the wind and they had to run after them. Sometimes they blew into the sea. That was funny. Pearl always put a hatpin through hers. She wouldn't have run after it if it had blown off; she would have made me do it. Crowns looked as though they were too heavy for the wind to whisk them away, but I imagined they could topple off, especially if you moved your head about. Sometimes, in my bedroom, I pretended to be a princess and I practised walking with a book on my head. It was very difficult

The photos I liked best of the royal family were the ones in their garden where the two princesses were playing with Corgi dogs. I wished I could have a dog. I would have liked a spaniel, not a King Charles one; I thought they were ugly. I'd have liked a Cocker spaniel.

Aunty Ruby didn't wave at people from balconies, nor did she have a Corgi dog. Aunty Ruby didn't have any animals because she was allergic to them. I had to ask her what 'allergic' meant. She said that the dust from their fur made her sneeze. Talcum powder made me sneeze, so I was allergic like Aunty Ruby.

She did have a garden. I liked her garden. It had croquet hoops in the lawn. Croquet was a game for posh people. Uncle Charles and Aunty Ruby were posh. They were nice posh. Not all posh people were nice posh. Pearl and Amethyst weren't nice posh. Poor people didn't play croquet because their lawns weren't big enough. Some poor people didn't even have gardens. They played marbles out in the street. My uncle and aunt played croquet with their friends. Uncle Charles had made me a special mallet, so that I could play with them, as the ones in their set were too big and heavy for a six year old.

I lived in Norfolk. So did the King and royal family in a big house called Sandringham. But they only lived there in the summer, because they also lived in Buckingham Palace and a castle in Scotland. I thought it was a bit greedy having three houses, but Aunty Ruby told me that lots of rich people have more than one house. Our house had four bedrooms. Sandringham house must have had at least seven. Aunty Ruby and Uncle Charles's house had five bedrooms. They kept one of the bedrooms specially for me.

They gave me a teddy bear for my first birthday. He was a golden bear and, when I was big enough to talk properly, I called him Golden Syrup because I thought the colour of his fur looked like Golden Syrup. I loved Golden Syrup, but not treacle. I thought it tasted burnt. If I had a cocker spaniel I would have called it Golden Syrup, but Pearl would never have let me have a dog. Sometimes Pearl made drop scones for tea and, if Annie thought I'd been good, she allowed me one with butter and Golden Syrup on it. She always had two. A lady in our street had a golden cocker spaniel. She called him, Josh; the name didn't suit him.

By the time I was six, Uncle Charles and Aunty Ruby had given me six bears; one at each birthday, Golden Syrup, Cocoa, Fudge, Hazelnut, Coffee, and Ice Cream. No one in our house knew their names, only me.

When I went to stay with Uncle Charles and Aunty Ruby I always took one bear with me. I gave them turns, because I could only get one in my case. Annie always packed my case. After she'd finished and left the room, I would open it and sneak in one of my bears. It was risky, but I did so want one of them to have a holiday with me. The first thing I did, after Annie had left for the railway station to go back to Hunstanton, was to unpack my case; Aunty Ruby helped me.

"Which bear have you brought with you this time?" she would ask.

"Ta-da!" I would say, like a magician, and whisk whichever bear it was, out from his hiding place. We would both give him a cuddle and lay him on my pillow.

Visiting Uncle Charles and Aunty Ruby was the most wonderful treat ever, but I had to pretend I didn't care about going. I would make my face grumpy so that Pearl wouldn't phone Ruby and say, "Einna can't come to stay with you this holiday, Ruby." It had happened once. Annie had caught me smiling as we were about to leave the house to go to the station. She'd told Pearl I was being sly. Pearl had lied to Uncle Charles and Aunty Ruby. She'd pretended I'd got a cold. I was always smacked if I lied.

There were so many things I liked about staying with my aunt and uncle. Sometimes I thought that the food was best. Sometimes it was all the things we did, like listening to *Children's Hour* while I drank a mug of cocoa. Uncle Charles and Aunty Ruby drank something called 'gin and it'. Sometimes it was the stories they told me. But really, the best of all were the hugs and kisses. Annie always hugged me after she'd punished me. Uncle Charles and Aunty Ruby never punished me, they just hugged and kissed. It wasn't nice being hugged by a crocodile; I was always scared the hug might turn into snapping teeth.

The year I was six, I was invited to stay at my aunt and uncle's for two weeks in the summer holidays. I'd overheard Pearl say to Annie, "Ruby thinks Einna's old enough to stay for two weeks now. What do you think, dear?"

"Well, it would mean we could have more time to ourselves without her round our feet. We could take the bus to Wells-next-the-Sea, and Sheringham, maybe."

"What a lovely idea. We will, if I feel up to it."

"Mind you, it'll depend on how Einna behaves over the next few weeks."

I crept upstairs, excited and nervous. It was very difficult to know what would make Annie gnash her teeth. Two weeks seemed like forever heaven. How was I going to stop myself from laughing with joy?

On the first morning after I arrived, when I was practising hitting the croquet ball through the hoops, so the next time I played Uncle Charles I would beat him, I saw Aunty Ruby coming across the lawn to find me.

"Einna, if you're not too wrapped up in your game, your uncle would like you to help him with something," she said.

I could ask questions at my aunt and uncle's that I couldn't ask at home, like, "Can I just do one last hit, please?" At home, if I didn't do things straight away, Annie smacked me or boxed my ears.

"Of course," said my aunt. "I'll watch."

The ball swerved into the roses. Aunty Ruby picked it up and placed it on the edge of the bed. Then she stood behind me so we could hit it together. It rolled to the front of the hoop.

"You can do it on your own now," she said. "Just a little tap, sweetheart."

"Are you women coming?" My uncle's voice interrupted us.

I tapped the ball through the hoop, dropped my croquet mallet, and we ran into the house together. "Where are you?" I called.

"Here, pet, in the hall. Would you like to help me wind up Thomas Gardner?"

"Who?"

"Our old man." He was standing by the grandfather clock. "Didn't you know he was called Thomas Gardner?"

"No. I've been to visit you lots and lots, on my own and with Pearl and Annie—"

"Pearl?"

"I mean Mummy. Sometimes I call her Pearl because..." What could I say? I couldn't think of anything to say. I couldn't tell Uncle Charles about Pearl and Annie; he would be angry with them and then they would know I'd said something.

"Um." My uncle let it go, but he looked sad. He put his arm round me. "Thomas is named after the man who made him. Don't be nervous. Hold the key firmly. He wants to be wound up."

"But how will I know when to stop?"

"The key gets harder to turn. We'll do it together, this time. When we can't turn it any more, you can nudge the pendulum."

"I love Thomas Gardner."

"Do you? Why do you love him?"

"Because his tick-tocks make me feel safe. I think he guards the house, like an angel."

Uncle Charles kissed the top of my head. I could feel his bristly moustache through my hair. It tickled. "I know just what you mean. Aunty Ruby calls him our guardian angel."

"Are guardian angels different from other angels?"

"Maybe. There are all sorts of angels in the scriptures."

"I know. I've seen them in our class's bible. I think my bears are my guardian angels."

"One day you shall have Thomas Gardner."

"Me? Have Thomas Gardner?"

"Yes. When you get married. Your aunt and I will give him to you as a wedding present."

"When I get married? You have to have a boyfriend first, don't you?"

"Yes."

"I don't like boys. The boys in my class are naughty. Martin Scrimshaw's alright but I don't want to marry him because his nose runs. It's disgusting."

'Disgusting' was my new word. Our teacher, Mrs. Aymes, used it all the time. "That's disgusting, Martin. Go and wash your hands immediately." "That's disgusting, Melanie. Where did you get it? Put it in the bin right away and then wash your hands." "That's disgusting, Faith. You must never use words like that."

"I don't think I shall ever get married, Uncle Charles."

"Silly Billy, of course you will."

"I will if I meet someone like you." He ruffled my hair. "Will Annie get married?"

Uncle Charles snorted, then tried to hide it with a pretend cough. "Who knows?" he said and gave me a big, Uncle Charles, bear hug. I loved being hugged by Uncle Charles, but it squeezed all the breath out of my body. "Come on, I expect it's elevenses, time."

I looked at Thomas Gardner. "The big hand's on the three and the little hand's on the eleven. That's a quarter past eleven"

"Is it. Whoops! Do you think your aunt will be cross with us for being late?"

"Aunty Ruby's never cross."

"No she isn't, is she? She's an angel."

I looked up at Uncle Charles. "Can you have lots of guardian angels?"

"I don't know, poppet. Why?"

"Because, if you can, I'd like to have you, Thomas Gardner and Aunty Ruby as my guardian angels, as well as my bears."

Uncle Charles laughed, but the laugh sounded a bit sad, like a crying laugh.

When I went to Ely, to stay with Uncle Charles and Aunty Ruby, Annie took me on the train because Pearl didn't have a car. On the way there I felt as fizzy as lemonade. All my bubbles were trying to escape, but I knew I had to keep them in until Annie left to go back to Hunstanton.

She pretended to be nice in front of Uncle Charles and Aunty Ruby. But when she said goodbye, she squeezed my arm hard and whispered in my ear, "You make sure you behave. You know what you'll get if I hear you've been naughty." The squeeze hurt, but I didn't cry out. If I had, I would have been punished when I got back to Hunstanton. Of course I knew I wasn't in danger of Uncle Charles and Aunty Ruby telling Annie I'd been naughty. In Ely, there weren't rules like there were in Hunstanton.

On the way home there were no fizzy bubbles, only unfizzy pop and unfizzy pop is disgusting. Sometimes I made a mistake and told Annie about the things I'd been doing. Mostly, she didn't listen, but if she did, she frowned. I think it was because she didn't like to hear about me enjoying myself.

I knew I oughtn't to have told her about winding up Thomas Gardner but I didn't seem to be able to keep the news to myself. Perhaps it was because when I was with my aunt and uncle I could say anything, so I'd forgotten to be careful.

"What did he want to let you do that for? You might have broken it," she said showing her crocodile teeth.

"Him, Annie. Uncle Charles says grandfather clocks are hims. And I didn't break Thomas. I was very careful. He said I can do it every time I stay with them." I nearly told her that Thomas Gardner would be mine when I got married, but the frown on her face warned me to be careful.

"Don't be stupid, Einna. A clock can't be a he."

"But Uncle Char—"

"That's enough. I'm not sure you'll be going to stay with Uncle Charles and Aunty Ruby any more. Aunty Ruby told me you'd been naughty, and she doesn't want to have naughty girls to stay."

The railway carriage tilted. I felt as though I was going to fall off the seat. I hadn't been naughty. I knew Aunty Ruby and Uncle Charles loved having me to stay. Sometimes I dreamt of living with them. My eyes filled with tears and the crocodile's frown changed to a smile.

"You're a liar," I shouted. "I hate you."

"You just wait until we get home," she snapped.

As the train pulled into Hunstanton station, she grabbed my hand and marched me down the street. Punishment waited behind the blue front door, a beating with my hairbrush, no sweets, no biscuits, no Sunday serial on the wireless, no going to the beach. I knew all the punishments off by heart, and what she said while she punished me:

"Children should be seen and not heard."

"Don't you pull that face at me, young lady. The wind might change and you'll be stuck with it, then you'll be sorry. I'm going to give you something to be sorry for. No Children's Favourites on Saturday morning."

"You're lying. I've told you what happens when someone lies, haven't I? They get spots on the tongue. No sweetie after tea."

"This is hurting me more than it hurts you." Whack, whack.

It wasn't true. She enjoyed hitting me. I could see it in her face. It hurt. It hurt a lot. Later, she would cuddle and kiss me and I would have to hold my breath because the cuddle hurt my back.

As soon as we got home, she called out, "Mummy, Einna's been naughty again," and she yanked me upstairs.

"Oh, poor you. Come and see me when you've dealt with her, dear. She has to learn."

"Okay, Mummy." She shoved me through the door of my room. "Now, am I going to beat the nastiness out of you, or…?" She looked around. Her eyes rested on my bears. They were asleep on the bed, waiting for me to wake them and give them a hello cuddle.

"You're too old for cuddly toys, Einna. Go downstairs and ask Mummy if there's a jumble sale soon?"

Jumble sale? "Please don't sell my bears, Annie. Please beat me." I didn't know what a jumble sale was, but I guessed my bears were going to be sold.

"I'm not going to sell your bears, Einna. I'm going to *give* them to a good cause."

"You've got a cuddly toy and you're much older than me."

"We're not talking about me, are we? Stop answering back."

"But they're mine. It's naughty to give away things that don't belong to you. A policeman will come and…"

Annie grabbed the bears, and marched out of the room. I ran after her, screaming.

"What on earth's all this noise?" Pearl emerged from the lounge.

"Einna's too old for these. I'm going to give them to the Salvation Army for their next jumble sale. Is there one soon, Mummy?"

Annie held the bears up in the air so I couldn't get them. I was sobbing and sobbing.

"Next Saturday, as it happens. Here, give them to me." Pearl took them. "Stop yelling, Einna."

That was the last I saw of Golden Syrup, Fudge, Ice Cream, Coffee, and Hazelnut. Cocoa was still in my case. I had to find a place to hide him. In the case? It lived under my bed. He'd be sad without his friends, but safe. I always unpacked my case and put my clothes away. No one would know I'd left Cocoa in it.

Annie beat me anyway, for I deserved two punishments because I'd been naughty twice. With each stroke of the brush, she said, "It's for your own good. I don't enjoy this, Einna. I have to beat the nastiness out of you. You mustn't tell people you hate them. Go on say it, 'I don't hate you Annie'. I shall carry on beating you until you do."

How could I have said, 'I don't hate you Annie', when I did? I tried to stifle my sobs. Usually, when she beat me I closed my mouth so tight it hurt my teeth. I wanted her arm to ache before I cried.

Later, lying on my tummy as my bottom and back were too sore to lie on, I pictured her dead in a coffin. I pictured the accidents leading to her death. I pictured me laughing, and Pearl crying.

Shove! I pushed Annie down the stairs. Shove! I pushed her under a bus. That I was six and Annie a big fourteen-year old crocodile made no difference to my story book strength. I was the angel of my picture.

Chapter Two
Matilda

Changing Pearls into Rubies
is very hard to do.
It's as hard as killing a croc,
and flushing it down the loo.
Pearl, Ruby, Pearl, Ruby.
Annie down the loo.
Pearl, Ruby, Pearl, Ruby.
Annie down the loo.

I was running down the street, past the pier, past the pitch and putt, past the lighthouse, down Sandy Lane, over the golf course. I heard the golfers shouting. Grasshoppers scattered before my flying feet. Little blue butterflies flitted away. I dived under the wooden balcony of the last hut along the beach. I was safe, safe from Annie.

On my eighth birthday, four months earlier, Pearl and Annie had given me an alarm clock with a very loud tick. As soon as I saw it, I thought about the ticking crocodile.

"Now you're eight, you can get up by yourself without me waking you," said Annie. "I've set the alarm for seven. Don't alter it. Also…" She didn't say anything for a moment. This was Annie's way of delivering news, both good and bad, when she wasn't in a temper. I had to be quite still, for if I moved she gave me a slap. "If you're good," another pause, "Mummy will give you sixpence pocket money each

Saturday. I shall take you to the corner shop so you can buy sweets and a comic."

"Can't I go on my own, Annie? I go to school—"

She gave me a clip round the ear. "One more word from you and I shall tell Mummy I've changed my mind. Go to your room."

I knew what sweets I wanted to buy, pear-drops and a gobstopper. I saw them in their tall glass jars in the corner shop window, when I walked past on my way to school. But every week, Annie made me buy jelly babies. Jelly babies were alright, but they weren't exciting like pear-drops and gobstoppers.

One Saturday morning, before I could stop the words from pitter-pattering out, I said, "I'd like some pear-drops and a gobstopper today, please Annie."

She grabbed my arm and squeezed; it hurt. But I knew that if I said, "Ow!" if I wriggled, she would march me home and give my pocket money back to Pearl.

"How many times do I have to tell you? Mummy says gobstoppers are vulgar, and I don't like pear drops," she said. She yanked me round to face her. "Well, do I?"

"No, Annie."

Her grip loosened a little. As I felt the blood flowing back into my fingers, I coated all the sweets she would eat with poison so that I could watch her writhing on the pavement in pain.

Inside the shop, Annie said, "Einna would like tuppence worth of jelly-babies and *Girl* comic, please, Mrs. Jones. Give Mrs. Jones the money, Einna and say thank you."

Mrs. Jones was a big woman with three wobbly chins. I counted them as I watched her measuring out the sweets.

"You're a lucky girl, you are," she said, as she gave me the white coned bag and the comic. "I hope you know what a lovely sister you have."

Annie smiled her crocodile smile and I wanted to tell Mrs. Jones not to smile back, because you should never smile at a crocodile. Then Annie grabbed my spare hand and didn't let it go until we were in the house.

"We're back, Mummy," she said. "Give me the sweets, Einna." She took out two jelly babies, a red one, her favourite, and an orange one for me. The ones I liked best were the black ones. "You can go to your room now and read your comic. I'll call you when lunch is ready."

I knew she was going to put my sweets in the tin on top of her wardrobe. I wasn't allowed to keep them in my room.

Annie never bought anything for herself at the corner shop. Once a month, she went to Kings Lynn with one of her friends, leaving Pearl to look after me. This meant I had to entertain myself and keep out of Pearl's way. I stayed in my room until it was time for her to make the lunch, then I crept downstairs to play my spying game. It was a bit like Grandmother's footsteps, and very dangerous. If she caught me, she would tell the crocodile.

When I heard, "Lunch is ready." I ran into the kitchen where Pearl's mouth in a thin, straight line greeted me. It curved upwards when she spoke to Annie. "Have you washed your hands, Einna?"

"No, Pearl."

"Then go and do it, while I dish up."

Saturday lunch was always sausages, mash and peas followed by semolina. I wished I could have had tomato ketchup on my sausages, like I did when I stayed with Uncle Charles and Aunty Ruby. Pearl said tomato ketchup was vulgar. I wondered why having a cigarette hanging out of your mouth, when you cooked, wasn't vulgar? The mashed potato often had grey streaks in it.

At the table I had imaginary conversations with Pearl.

"Can we play monopoly this afternoon?"

"Of course, darling, and I'll read you a story if you like."

"Will you take me to see a film next week? I think Hans Christian Anderson is on."

"That would be fun. Now, are you going to help me with the washing-up? You can wash and I'll dry."

One Saturday, after Annie had returned from Kings Lynn, Pearl told her I'd made a noise clomping down the stairs.

"It gave me one of my migraines."

"No sweet after tea," snapped the crocodile.

"But I didn't—"

Quick as a flash, she boxed my ears and sent me reeling. "Room – now. Shall I get you a pill, Mummy?"

It was then I decided the time had come for me to be in charge of my sweets. I hadn't clomped down the stairs, I'd tiptoed. I always did. It was the start of my spying game. One stair had creaked, because I forgot to step in the right place. A creak isn't clomping.

The next day, I ran home from school, eager to put my plan into action. "Steal my sweets. Steal my sweets… No, they're mine. *Take* my sweets," I muttered, all the way home.

"Have you been a good girl today, Einna?" Pearl said as she opened the front door.

"Yes, Pearl." My feet, of their own accord, did a dance in the hall.

She frowned. "Do you want to go to the lavatory?"

"No, Pearl."

In school we said, 'toilet'. But at home I had to say 'lavatory'. The word 'toilet' was vulgar.

"Then stop jiggling. There's a biscuit and glass of milk in the kitchen. After you've finished, wash up the plate and glass and put them away."

I muttered the words with her, under my breath. I knew them off by heart.

I didn't want the biscuit or the milk but I did as I was told and then tiptoed upstairs whispering the Einna enchantress spell:

> *"Changing Pearls into Rubies*
> *Is very hard to do.*
> *It's as hard as killing a croc,*
> *And flushing it down the loo.*
> *Pearl, Ruby, Pearl, Ruby.*
> *Annie down the loo.*
> *Pearl, Ruby, Pearl, Ruby.*
> *Annie down the loo."*

On the landing I did a twirl and fizzed my arms into the air. Sparks flew out of my fingers.

I knew Annie wouldn't be home until five-thirty. I had enough time to creep into her bedroom and take some sweets. By the window was a chair. On it sat Cuthbert, Annie's furry, toy cat. I picked him up and rubbed his soft body against my cheek before putting him on the windowsill.

"You're a lucky cat, Cuthbert. You're not hidden away in a case, like Cocoa. Now, you won't tell Annie what I'm doing, will you?" I imagined he meowed, *'no'*.

I took the chair over to the wardrobe and climbed onto it to feel for the tin. *Ah, I have you.* I opened it, snatched a handful of sweets, closed the lid, put the tin and the chair back where they belonged and ran to my room.

After tea, Annie marched ahead of me up the stairs, as usual. By now, I was feeling very nervous. Had I taken too many sweets?

She got the tin down, opened it, and frowned. "I'm sure…" She looked at me. I stared at my feet. Suddenly she seized hold of my arm. "Why is Cuthbert sitting on the windowsill, Einna? It couldn't be that a thieving little girl needed the chair to get her sweets, could it? I shan't let go of you until you tell me the truth."

Cuthbert had given me away. How could I have forgotten to put him back?

"I had a cuddle with him, that's all." I tried to wriggle out of her grasp.

Her face drew closer to mine. I smelled her 'beans on toast' breath. "No you didn't," she hissed. "How many times have I told you, you'll get spots on your tongue if you lie? Go and get your hair brush."

"No," I screamed. "It's not fair. They're my sweets."

She marched me into my room, snatched up the hairbrush and forced me onto the bed, face down. Then she pulled up my jumper and blouse, tugged down my knickers, held me with one hand and hit me with the other.

"Naughty, wicked, girl," she said with every stroke. "No sweets for the rest of the week and no pocket money next Saturday."

"They're *my* sweets," I screamed. "They're *my* sweets."

"For that, six more smacks. Thief. Liar." When she left the room, she forgot to put the sweets back on the shelf. I lay still for a few seconds, gritting my teeth to stop the hiccupping sobs from jumping out of my mouth. Then I rolled off the bed, rearranged my clothes, grabbed a black jelly baby and tiptoed down the stairs. In the kitchen, I saw two cups and saucers, ready for Pearl and Annie's bedtime drinks. I spat in each cup, wiped it all over so it couldn't be seen, then escaped out of the back door.

The last hut along the beach was brown, not brightly coloured like most of the others. It reminded me of the shed in our garden, which my daddy had built before he was killed in the war. I slid under the balcony and lay face down in the sand and Marram grass, because I was too sore to lie on my back. All the tears I'd refused to let out while Annie was beating me rolled down my cheeks. "I wish she'd die," I sobbed. "I wish they'd both die, then I could go to live with Aunty Ruby and Uncle Charles. I wish my spit was poisonous."

I couldn't have been lying there for more than a few minutes when some legs appeared by the steps. They were covered in navy blue trousers. I tried to stop crying so the legs would go away, but another sob escaped. The legs bent at the knees and a lady peered under the hut.

"Hello," she said.

I couldn't answer for I heard Annie saying, "You must never talk to strangers. They might kidnap you and do horrid things."

Annie wasn't a stranger and she did horrid things to me, all the time. Strangers, according to Annie, were murderers, kidnappers or gypsies. I liked the idea of being kidnapped by gypsies. I'd seen pictures of them and their decorated caravans in books, and one of my favourite songs was *The Gipsy Rover*. I would have liked to run away with the gypsies. I bet they would have been kinder to me than Annie and Pearl.

"I expect you've been told not to talk to strangers," said the lady. "This is my hut. You'd be doing me a great favour if you'd come out. I'm getting a sore back, crunched up like this."

My back was sore. I didn't want the lady to have a sore back. I liked the sound of her voice. It was gentle. I crept out.

We looked at each other. I saw a slim lady with dark hair speckled with grey strands, pushed into an untidy bun. She was wearing navy trousers and a red jumper. She must have seen a child with dark brown hair and a tear stained, sandy face, wearing a grubby blouse and skirt.

"I've been for a walk along the beach with my terrier, Nelson," she said. "Now I'm going to make a pot of tea and open a packet of chocolate digestives. Will you join me? Nelson's very partial to chocolate digestives, but he mustn't have more than one: they're not good for him."

She didn't wait for an answer. She climbed up the steps, took a key out of her shoulder bag, and opened the door. "This is my hut, Matilda. Matilda, meet…?"

"Einna."

"What an unusual name! My name's Jean, very ordinary. Matilda meet Einna, Einna meet Matilda. I think Nelson's chasing grasshoppers. Fortunately he doesn't catch any. Can you hear those creaks, Einna? They mean Matilda likes you."

At that moment, Nelson flung himself up the steps, jumped up at me and licked my hands.

"Down, boy. Einna doesn't need a bath. Do you think you could open the packet of biscuits while I make the tea?"

She poured hot water from a thermos flask into a small, enamel kettle and lit a primus stove which flared yellow and then settled to a steady, blue flame.

"I always bring hot water with me. This old thing's so slow. One for you, one for me and one for the pot," she said as she put three teaspoons of tea into small brown teapot. "What do you think of Matilda?"

I looked around. The hut was small but cosy. There were deck chairs and a table in the corner by the door. On one wall there were two shelves with picnic things on them and there were shrimping nets leaning up against the back wall.

"Matilda's nice," I said.

"She knows lots of stories. Perhaps she'll share some with you if you ever visit us again. Oh, kettle's boiling." She poured the water into the teapot. "Why were you crying?"

"Huts are like garden sheds, aren't they? My Daddy made a shed in our garden."

"Is it his hidey-hole? Lots of men use garden sheds as hidey- holes."

"I don't know. He was killed in the war, before I was born. I'd like to hide in the shed when…" I pulled my lips into my mouth for I saw the crocodile gnashing her terrible teeth.

"Are you being bullied at school?" Jean put her hand on mine, it was soft and warm. "You don't have to tell me if you don't want to."

And suddenly I did. "I want to hide from Annie."

"Who's Annie?"

"My sister. When I was born, my Mummy didn't want me, so she gave me to Annie. My name's 'Annie' spelt backwards. I'm not allowed to call Mummy, Mummy. I have to call her Pearl. When I was six, Annie gave all my teddy bears to the Salvation Army jumble sale, except for Cocoa. Cocoa was in my case because I hadn't unpacked yet. I'd been to stay with…" I told Jean everything.

She looked at me for a long time.

"Do you think I'm naughty because I took my sweets?"

"Well, it's against the law to steal but, strictly speaking, you can't steal what belongs to you, and it doesn't sound as though you had much choice. Can you keep a secret?" I nodded. "Matilda's going to be your sanctuary."

"What's that?"

"A safe hiding place."

"You mean, I can hide in Matilda instead of under her?"

"Yes. I'm going to lend you a key. We'll put it somewhere safe and, when you need to hide, you'll know where to find it. Nelson and I might be here sometimes. Do you like brown shrimps?"

"I've never had them."

"What? You live in Hunstanton and you've never had brown shrimps? One day, when we're both here, we'll go shrimping." She looked at her watch. "Time to go, Einna. But before we do, we have to decide where to put the key. We can't bury it because the sand shifts in the wind and we'll never find it again... I know, Alfred's hook." She went outside. On one of the balcony supports was a hook. She popped the key on it. "There," she said, "the key to your sanctuary."

I wondered who Alfred was, but I didn't ask. "Can Cocoa live in Matilda, so he's safe from Annie?"

"Of course he can," she said, and gave me a hug. "I wish... no matter. I can't make my wish happen."

It wasn't long before going to see Jean, Nelson, Cocoa and Matilda was something I did every week, sometimes twice a week, not just sanctuary. They were always glad to see me. I wondered if Jean was a guardian angel? If she was, maybe she could do magic and make Annie and Pearl... no. I knew they would never love me. I didn't think angels, even guardian angels did magic. That wasn't what they were supposed to do. They made you better for a while.

Most angels had wings. They were huge and white. Jean, Uncle Charles, Aunty Ruby and Thomas Gardner didn't have wings, unless they were hidden inside their bodies. Perhaps guardian angels didn't need wings because they lived on earth? I wondered if my teddy bears were being guardian angels to the children who had bought them? Cocoa couldn't be a guardian angel while he was in the case.

I pretended I'd been invited to play at a friend's house. It wasn't a 'spots on the tongue' lie: Jean was my friend. But Pearl didn't really care where I was, as long as I wasn't being a nuisance. I always made sure I was home before Annie got back from college. She was doing a course in typing and shorthand at Kings Lynn Technical College because she wanted to be a secretary.

One day, a high tide day so we couldn't go shrimping, Matilda gave a loud creak.

"I think she wants me to tell you a story," said Jean.

I'd become used to her talking about Matilda as though she were alive. "A real story or a pretend one?"

"A real one. All Matilda's stories are real. It's about a man called Alfred."

"Alfred? The hook for my key, Alfred? Is he your husband?"

"No, when I was seventeen, he was my secret boyfriend."

"Why secret?"

"He was a gardener. My parents would have disapproved. He was working class."

"What's working class?"

"I keep forgetting you're only eight."

"I'm nearly nine."

"Whoops, sorry, Miss nearly nine years old! In England, people are called working class if they have a job working with their hands. My parents, and many others, think they aren't well mannered or intelligent. It's very silly and insulting. I think everyone knows how to behave and we all know different things. Anyway, Alfred and I met here, in Matilda. But when I turned eighteen, I was presented at court."

"What's that?"

"In the class I was born into, you had to curtsey to the King before you could go to balls or parties." Jean laughed. "I was terrified I'd do something wrong and disgrace my parents. All the debutantes, that's what we were called, were dressed in white. We were like brides tripping down an aisle to greet our husbands, only it wasn't a husband waiting for us, it was the King.

"In the following months I began to lose interest in Alfred. I enjoyed flirting with the young men I met at parties. My parents approved of them. Suddenly I realised my infatuation with him was over, for that's what it was: I liked him, but I didn't love him. Now, of course, I know the subterfuge, sorry, the secrecy was as thrilling as the romance itself. Hindsight's a wonderful word, Einna. Do you know what it means?" I shook my head. "It means recognising the truth of something after it's happened. I was too cowardly to tell Alfred to his face, so I wrote him a letter. Do you know what he did? He left his clothes on Matilda's balcony and disappeared. It was assumed he'd gone for a swim and drowned." She sighed. "His body was never found."

We gazed out over the Marram grass dunes, out over the rippled wave sand to the sea and the North Lincolnshire coast beyond as though they might give up their secrets.

"How can anyone drown here, and their body not be found, Einna?" I wished I could tell her, for she looked so sad. "I've always been suspicious that Alfred wanted to hurt me because I'd hurt him. I think he wanted me to believe he'd drowned. But I suspect he ran away to war and was killed."

"My daddy's war?"

"No, the First World War."

"Don't you get a letter if someone dies in a war? Pearl did when my daddy died, Annie told me."

"A telegram? Yes, but it would have gone to his parents, not me. For a while I kept hoping he would reappear so I could apologise, but he didn't."

"It's horrid being hurt, isn't it?"

"Yes. But we can learn from being hurt."

"Learn what?"

"To try not to hurt others, and when others hurt us, to put it behind us." It was then that she told me about writing a hurt away.

"Einna, before I forget, I've got something for you." She fished in her pocket and brought out two, dark red stones. "Mr. Tiedemann, in the jewellers, polished them for me. They're the cornelians you found on the beach earlier in the week. I thought you could keep them here in a treasure box, this one, if you like." She took a flat, wooden box off the shelf. "Alfred made it for me."

"And I can have it?" She nodded. "Can I put the little pink shells in it, and the dog-fish skeleton?"

She laughed. "Of course you can, it's your treasure box. Whoops! Look at the time. You'll be late home if you don't scoot."

That night I dreamt about Jean and Alfred. Dreams are funny. They have people in them you don't know and they take you to places you've never been. They do magic. I'd never met Alfred. I didn't know what he looked like, but there he was, in my dream, and I'd made him into the one eyed man who worked in the candy-floss kiosk on the pier. I told him Jean wanted to see him. He looked at me with his good eye and, before I could blink, turned into a huge fish.

"I can't," he said, blowing word bubbles. "I have to swim to Skegness and back, every day."

The next time I ran to Matilda, neither Jean, nor Nelson were there and I never saw them again. I went to the hut as often as I could and sat alone inside or on the balcony.

It was from Pearl I learnt the truth, one morning at breakfast. "Goodness," she said. "Lady Cornwallis has died. She can't have been much more than fifty."

She held up the local newspaper for Annie to see. I got a glimpse of the photo. It was Jean. I couldn't stifle the gasp. Luckily they were too busy reading to notice. My friend, a Lady; my friend, dead. I wanted to ask why, but I couldn't. I dug my nails into the palms of my hands to stop myself from crying, and chewed my toast into a soggy blob which I managed to push into my cheek.

"May I leave the table?" I whispered.

Annie looked up. "Don't forget your PE kit."

Once I was safely away from the house, I spat the soggy mess into the gutter. Somehow I got through the day without anyone asking me what was wrong. How could I have told them? After school I ran to Matilda, collected my treasure box and Cocoa from the shelf, and curled up in a deckchair, hugging them to me. I wished I could have stayed there forever. When I left, I placed the key in the box and popped it in my satchel. I knew it wouldn't be safe there, because Annie went through it every day, to see if there were any letters from school. Before she got in from college I had to find a proper hiding place.

Pearl let me in. She left me in the kitchen with the usual glass of milk and a biscuit. I rummaged through the newspapers on the kitchen table until I found yesterday's *Sentinel*. The announcement was on page six.

'Lady Cornwallis died at five am on Wednesday morning. She had been diagnosed with bowel cancer earlier in the year.'

What was cancer?

'Lady Cornwallis was fifty five. She had no children.'

"She did," I whispered. "Me. Me and Nelson."

All newspapers were used to light fires in our house. I doubted anyone would miss one page, so I tore it out. When I was in my bedroom, I put it in my treasure box, slid under the bed and pushed the box between the mattress and the springs. Cocoa I put back in my case.

On the night of Saturday, the thirty-first of January, nineteen fifty-three, there were floods in East Anglia, the combination of a storm and an unusually high spring tide. Matilda was swept away.

Chapter Three
Can't, Not Won't

A spider called Arry
climbed up my wall.
She hid behind a picture frame,
and no one saw her at all.
Except for me.

There was a spider in my bedroom. I called her Arry, short for arachnid. She, or her ancestors had been in my bedroom since I was nine. Her web was behind a picture of an elf in a garden. Annie chose the picture. I never liked it. You couldn't see Arry's cobweb unless you moved the picture. I checked, from time to time, to make sure she was still there. Flies and daddy long legs got stuck in the web; she wrapped them up to eat later. I didn't know this; it was a guess. Why else wouldn't she have eaten them right away?

I could never understand why people were scared of spiders. Arry fascinated me and, in some ways, became my friend. I talked to her and pretended she talked back. Watching her gave me the idea of how to deal with Pearl and Annie. Like Arry, I spun webs. They were word webs of lies and secrets; each one intricately fashioned to protect. Angels and Arry helped me to survive childhood and early adolescence.

The years ticked by, like Thomas Gardner, no, not like him; his tick-tock was steady, comforting. It would be more truthful to say the years hiccupped by in Annie and Pearl insecurity, for even with webs and angels, I never knew, was never sure. Thomas was one of my secrets, a secret guardian angel in Ely. Arry, Cocoa and my treasure box were yet more secrets.

On the cusp of leaving home to go to a music college in London, a boy asked me out. I'd never had a date before. Adrian was in the sixth form, like me, and could have had his pick of any girl, or that's what I thought. I accepted the date, and spun a web. *An end of school party. Everyone was going. It was expected. Expected? Why would it be expected? Erase expected. All my friends were going.* Annie and Pearl wouldn't be curious about friends. They'd never encouraged me to bring anyone home. *It wasn't just an end of school party. It was a leaving do for... for those who had college places.* That would appeal to Pearl's elitism.

I almost broke the web in shock at Annie's response. "I'm not your keeper, Einna," she said. "Mummy and I know you have to go out. After all, you'll be in London in October. I hope you have an escort to this do, I don't want you traipsing home on your own."

I was so eager to go out with Adrian, who looked like Adam Faith, I fell for it. I saw the crocodile smiling and forgot to be wary.

"All the girls have escorts," I babbled. "Mrs. Drummond insisted. Our names were put into a hat and—" *What am I saying? Names put in a hat?*

"I don't need the ins and outs, Einna. Just make sure you're back by eleven."

"I will, Annie. I promise."

Hidden in my treasure chest was mascara, eyeliner and Tangee lipstick. Whenever I could, I practised different styles of make-up, ready for when I went to college. On the night of my date, I secreted them down my bra. I wouldn't have put it past Annie to search my bag before I left. I was meeting Adrian outside *The Golden Lion* at six-thirty. We were going to see *The Parent Trap*. I ran to the public toilets and gave myself what I believed was my Audrey Hepburn look.

The rhythm of the wheels on the tracks seemed to echo my sister's words.

It's a quarter past.
It's a quarter past.
It's a quarter past.

I was running away and the words were running with me. I closed my eyes. I'd like to have put my fingers in my ears, but the man opposite, immersed in his newspaper, might have noticed. Why couldn't I turn off the scene, like you switched off a projector?

I saw Annie opening the front door as Adrian was about to kiss my Tangee lipsticked lips.

I heard, "Do you know what the time is? Inside, young lady. As for you, how dare you keep Einna out until this hour? Some escort you are."

The mouth that had been so near to mine opened and closed. Adrian didn't know what Annie was talking about. I took two steps and fluttered like a moth drawn to a bulb.

"Our mother's been worried sick. She hasn't been able to get any sleep and some of us have to go to work in the morning. I shall be writing to Mr. Drummond about this."

I didn't dare look at Adrian's face. I ran upstairs, not caring that my feet thudded on the ungiving lino, and flung myself face down on the bed. I knew how it was. I'd known for some time. She couldn't punish me with beatings any more. I was bigger, stronger than her. She used words to beat me now, words and sanctions. She'd allowed me to go out, so she could humiliate me when I came home and my web had given her the ammunition she needed. I put the pillow over my head.

I wasn't allowed to wallow. Annie stormed into my room and snatched up the pillow. "What did you think you were playing at?" she hissed. "I let you stay out till eleven, on the understanding you were back on the dot."

"I was."

"No you weren't. It was a quarter past when I came downstairs."

"Oh come on, Annie. I was back at eleven. I was saying goodbye to Adrian, that's all, and you—"

"Don't you play games with me, Einna. You were not inside this house. And from what I saw, you were behaving like a little tart."

"There's nothing wrong with what I did. It's normal behaviour. You wanted to show me up."

"You showed yourself up. How old are you? Come on, tell me, how old you are?"

"I'm seventeen. You know how old I am. What's that got to do with anything?"

"You're not of age, that's what. You're seventeen and you're grounded." She said this with such a look of delight on her face that I wanted to haul her into the bathroom and scrub it off.

You're seventeen.
You're seventeen.
You're seventeen.

The train slowed down, and the words slowed with it. It drew into Downham Market station. The man opposite me folded up his newspaper, put on a trilby hat and got out. A woman got in. She sat by the door, opened her bag and took out a novel. I closed my eyes.

I was hoping Uncle Charles and Aunty Ruby would be at home. After my seventeenth birthday, they'd tried to get me to drop the 'Aunty' and 'Uncle', but I liked calling them that; after all I didn't have a mother I could call 'mother'.

I was sure they'd let me stay with them, as long as they were at home. They might have thought it odd I hadn't contacted them first, but... what would I have told them? What was I going to tell them? That I'd had enough of Annie's bullying? I'd never told anyone about the abuse I'd suffered at Annie's hands, except for Jean and she was dead.

I've had enough.
I've had enough.
I've had enough.

The train gathered speed.

"Did you hear what I said, young lady?"

Of course I'd heard. Did Annie think I'd gone deaf all of a sudden? What difference did being grounded make? There wasn't any point in going out. Adrian wouldn't want me as his girlfriend now.

Annie was hissing like a boiling kettle, all spit and steam. "You don't care about anyone but yourself, do you?"

"And you do, Annie? Just how long do you think you can go on controlling me, hey? I may be seventeen now, but I'll be eighteen next month, and in October I'll be going to London, for God's sake." Even saying it gave me a thrill. London, a college of music, freedom from Annie's tyranny and Pearl's indifference. A place without webs.

"Whatever age you are, you're not too old to have your mouth washed out with soap and water, and don't think I won't do it."

"Try it, Annie. You know I'm as strong as you now. I'll say what I want, and in case you didn't hear, in October I'll be out of here, thank God, bloody thank God. You won't know what time I get back to my digs. You won't know who my friends are. You won't know anything about me."

I'd never spoken to Annie like that before. I shivered with pleasure. But why, oh why, hadn't I found that courage, that defiance, on the doorstep?

Her face sagged. For a second I saw the elderly woman she would become. Fleetingly, I felt sorry for her. I was about to put a hand on her arm when I remembered that crocodiles weren't just savagely dangerous. They were cunning. They lay in wait for victims and, snap, their jaws closed.

Pearl came into the room. She was holding a cologne soaked handkerchief to her forehead. "What's all this shouting for, Einna? Annie will have to put a stop to your going out if you make all this noise when you come in. Do you know what the time is? You woke me up."

Annie had lied. Pearl hadn't been lying awake, worried sick. After all, I was the nuisance she'd rejected.

"Einna, now you're about to start school, I want to make sure you understand that I'm your mother, in name only. Do you understand?"

"You're Pearl."

She was staring at the form she had to fill in. "I have to put that I'm your mother, on this form." Impatience made her voice ragged. "I've told you, many times, that when you were born, I gave you to your sister as a Christmas present. You're a very lucky little girl. She told me it was the best Christmas present she'd ever had. She's been a good mummy to you. Now, repeat after me: Pearl, Mummy in school, Annie, Mummy at home. Pearl, Pearl at home."

She made me repeat it many times. Annie was thirteen when I started school; she was eight when I was born. To all intents and purposes, I was an orphan. I'd lost two parents, one to the Second World War, and the other to indifference.

"I think I've got a migraine coming on, Annie. Could you get me a drink of water? I'll have to take a pill."

"Of course, Mummy. You go back to bed." Pearl exited to the strains of violin music for tragedy queens.

Annie leant forward, staring me straight in the eyes. "You're not going to be free to come and go as you please when you go to college, young lady. I've had a word with Mrs. Hallam. She's going to keep an eye on you and report back to me." She got up and marched out of the room; another dramatic exit. They would make a grand stage duo, my sister and mother.

I wanted to shout after her, jump off the bed, rush out of the door and pummel her back. I wanted to push her down the stairs. Instead, I put the pillow back over my head and plotted.

The next morning, I waited until Annie left for work, then I scrabbled under my bed for my case and treasure chest. My violin was on the shelf in the wardrobe. As I had grown, so had my case. I packed it and left. I assumed Pearl was in the lounge reading a magazine, or lying on the couch with her eyes closed. She wouldn't have thought I would run away. But that was what I was doing.

34

Ely. I'd go to Uncle Charles and Aunty Ruby's until I went to college. I would find new digs. My aunt and uncle would help me find digs where no one spied or controlled.

I knew that the only reason I was being allowed to go to music college was the status it gave Pearl and Annie. I'd heard them talking about it in church. I was Pearl's daughter, then.

"My daughter has got a scholarship to a music college in London."

Sick. Finger down the throat sick.

Report to me.
Report to me.
Report to me.

"Excuse me." I opened my eyes. The woman, sitting opposite was staring at me. Her face showed concern. "I couldn't help noticing, you look very pale. Are you okay?"

"I'm fine."

"Would you like a drink? I've a flask of tea in my bag."

"No, thank you."

"As long as you're sure; how far are you going?"

To sanctuary. "To Ely."

"Well we're nearly there. Good thing I woke you up. You might have gone past your stop."

I got up and heaved my belongings off the rack.

"That case looks heavy, dear. You must have everything bar the kitchen sink in there." She smiled.

I knew she was just being kind, but I wished she'd be quiet. I wasn't feeling all right. I was feeling sick.

"You ought to get a porter to help you with that," she said.

I didn't reply.

"Well, goodbye, duck. Take care. You look really peaky."

I stepped out of the carriage. The woman waved to me as the train picked up speed.

I'm nearly there.
I'm nearly there.
I'm nearly there.

Nearly where? I couldn't do it. I couldn't go to Uncle Charles and Aunty Ruby's. What could I have said? I didn't even know if they were at home. I couldn't go to college. I couldn't go anywhere. I plonked my case on the platform and sat on a bench. I had to go back to the place I least wanted to be. I balled my hands and rubbed my eyes. I looked down at the rails, rails leading to the future, rails leading to the past. At least I had a return ticket. I sighed. That's why I'd bought it. I knew I would take a railway journey to nowhere. There was a train at ten. I glanced at my watch. It was due in seven minutes' time. I twisted the pearl earrings in my ears.

'Leave them alone, Einna. You'll loosen the butterflies and lose them.'

Annie's voice was so loud, I was convinced she'd leapt out of my head and appropriated the station tannoy. I would have liked to twist the earrings off, throw them on the rails and see the sparks fly as the next train crunched them. Instead, I picked up my case, and walked over the bridge to the other platform.

Of course Pearl hadn't noticed my absence. During a silent evening meal, I said, "I'm not going to music college. I shall take a secretarial course at Lynn Tech." *Like you did, Annie.*

A look passed between my mother and my sister. I couldn't decipher it. Had I expected them to try to dissuade me? After all, whatever kudos they'd derived from my going to college had evaporated with those words.

I knew keeping my violin safe would be difficult. I couldn't trust Annie and Pearl not to sell it out of spite, thwarted kudos. Uncle Charles and Aunty Ruby would take care of it. They too would be disappointed that I'd given up the idea of going to college but not for the same reason. Uncle Charles had paid for my lessons; I was letting him down. I knew he was too generous a man to see it like that, but... maybe I could tell them I was deferring for a year or two; I didn't feel mature enough to tackle London. It was a only a little white lie. On Ely station platform, any confidence I'd had, ran away with the rails.

But, hang on, Einna. You love playing your violin. It's a way to escape. You lose yourself in the music.

'Got to practise, Annie.'

'Got to practise, Pearl.'

Annie knows this. She could easily take the violin and sell it before you have the chance to talk to your uncle and aunt. Got it! Sometimes you do show you've got a brain.

I glanced at their impassive faces. "I'm going to look into joining the local chamber orchestra. They have a very good reputation. If they accept me, you'll be able to come and watch me playing in concerts." I was weaving. They had never attended school concerts. But they could use the chamber orchestra as a sop to their damaged pride. As long as they had something to boast about, my violin would be safe.

I could just hear them. "No, she's deferring her college place for a year or so because she wants to get experience of playing in an orchestra. The chamber orchestra fell over backwards to give her a place. She's very talented."

I lasted one term at Lynn technical college. That was all it took for me to know that the life of a shorthand typist was not for me. Annie shouted. Pearl sniffed.

"I'm not going to keep you any more, Einna. Your sister pays her way. You'll have to get a job. Scratching away on that old fiddle isn't going to pay for your food, clothing, shoes and toiletries."

'Scratching away' was home talk. 'Playing like a virtuoso' was church talk.

The Kardomah, where I worked on a Saturday took me on part time. I gave all the money I earned to Pearl, except for ten shillings. My free days were spent in the library, or if it was fine, walking along the beach to where Matilda had stood before the storms took her. Sometimes I found a cornelian, sometimes a special shell. Sometimes I saw Jean striding towards me, Nelson flying ahead, ready to jump into my arms and cover me with licks.

I passed the chamber orchestra audition. Uncle Charles and Aunty Ruby came to the performances, so did Pearl and Annie. At church they boasted with knowledge.

"It was an evening of Chopin. Such lovely music. We're not sure Einna needs to go to college now. This little chamber orchestra and her job will do just as well."

Escape. I had to escape somehow... If I didn't... I could see my future. Pearl dead. Annie and I spinsters in the blue door house; an adulthood full of petty tyranny.

In the late summer, of nineteen sixty two I met John Carter from Liverpool. He and his friend were on holiday. They came to one of the summer concerts and then, by coincidence the Kardomah Coffee Bar, the following afternoon.

"I know you," he said.

"Well, I don't know you," I replied. I was used to dealing with young men trying to pick me up.

"You were playing in that concert yesterday evening. I didn't want to go to it. My friend bullied me. He's into classical music. I prefer The Beatles. I'm glad I did go, now."

"I like classical music *and* The Beatles," I said. I found it interesting that he hadn't been put off by my snub. Nine months of long distance courtship later, it was the eve of our wedding.

Bathed, hair washed, I was sitting at my dressing table, staring in the mirror. *HELP!* I wrote in the mist on the glass. John. I'm going to marry John, tomorrow. Why did the words, 'marry John', haunt me like the furies in a Greek tragedy? I didn't want to feel like this, wishing I were not about to be married, wishing I'd taken up my place at Music College, wishing I'd never met him, wishing... *Come on, Einna, you're about to marry the man who is going to take you away from Annie and Pearl. You are going to float down the aisle... help!*

Annie came in. She didn't knock; she never knocked. In my new home, she wouldn't be there to knock or not to knock.

"What's the matter with your face? You look like a wet week," she said.

"Nothing."

She sat down beside me. "I'll blow dry your hair for you, if you like. You're not putting rollers in are you?"

I shrugged. "I think I'll just put it up in a chignon tomorrow."

"'Just put it in a chignon?' That's careless talk. This is the most important day of your life."

Was it? Should such an important day make me feel so apprehensive?

Annie got up and went over to the wardrobe where my wedding dress was hanging. She stroked it. "Guipure lace and satin, it's a dream dress. Mrs. Guthrie's done us proud."

Us? A thunderbolt thought thumped me in the guts. Us? It was Annie who wanted to glide down the aisle in that dress, not me.

"Pre-wedding nerves, is it?"

Was it? Was it pre-wedding nerves to rehearse the service over and over, in my mind, and each time get sucked beneath the waves at my cue, 'Do you, Einna Huckle take this man, John Carter, to be your lawful wedded husband?'

I pointed to the cupboard. "The hairdryer's in there."

"I know where the hairdryer is, Einna."

Of course she did. She knew where everything was in my bedroom, no, almost everything. She'd made it her business to pry into all the caves of my life, but she didn't know that, when I was nine I'd learnt to spin webs. I had safe secrets, one of which was my treasure box. It and Cocoa were tucked safely away in my case, ready to go on honeymoon with me, and afterwards, west to Liverpool. Yes, escape, but escape to what? John was... I didn't know what John was.

When she turned on the hairdryer, my hair flew away from my ears revealing the pearl earrings she'd given me the Christmas after I'd had my ears pierced. The same pearls I'd wanted to see crunched under the wheels of the train at Ely. As I only had three and a half pairs of earrings – I'd lost one of the gold studs the jeweller had inserted – I didn't have much option. I couldn't wear the gold hoops Pearl had given me for a wedding present. They were hers. My father had given them to her on the leave before he was killed in action, the leave I was conceived. Her giving them to me confirmed what I'd always felt; she'd rejected my father as she rejected me She ought to have kept them always.

I couldn't wear the cornelians. How would I have explained their provenance? I'd asked Mr. Tiedemann to make them into earrings after I saved enough money from the ten shillings a week I kept out of my wage packet.

"For goodness sake, Einna, you didn't wash your hair with those earrings in, did you? You could have lost them down the plug hole. They cost me an arm and a leg, you know."

Of course I knew, she'd told me often enough along with, *"Pearl earrings, Einna. A lovely reminder of our mother."*

I lifted my hands to take them out.

"Keep still or the brush will get caught in your hair. You mustn't wear those earrings in church tomorrow. They could bring bad luck. I told you, you were daft to go for a pearl engagement ring. How long did you have it, a fortnight? Only you could lose an engagement ring in the dunes. Most men would have been really upset. Not John, he's a treasure. You don't deserve him."

"I didn't realise you gave me earrings to bring me bad luck." How I'd have liked to add, *'Wasn't being saddled with Pearl for a mother and you as a sister enough bad luck?'*

"Pearls are only bad luck for a wedding."

"I didn't choose a pearl engagement ring, Annie." I would never have chosen a pearl anything. "John chose it. He said it looked pure and chaste."

"He was right there. He can't have known about the bad luck, then. Wear the gold hoops Mummy gave you. That will please her so much."

Pearl, pleased with me? An oxymoron, surely? Nothing I'd ever done had pleased Pearl. The boasting about my prowess on the violin wasn't because she was pleased with me. The earrings had seemed like the final nail in the coffin of our relationship. How could I wear them? They would burn my ears.

"I'll look after the pearl ones until you get back from your honeymoon. I can bring them with me when I come to Liverpool to help you settle in. John and I thought it would be a good idea. After all, he'll be far too busy with his new job to do anything in the house."

What? How dare they? I glared at the floor and swallowed the bile clogging my throat. If I'd started spewing, I might not have been able to stop. "I don't know whether there's going to be a honeymoon, Annie. I'm not even sure…" What was I doing? Surely I wasn't going to tell her? *Crocodile, bears.*

"Silly Billy, of course there's going to be a honeymoon. John's shown me the tickets. I can't tell you where you're going, though. He's sworn me to secrecy."

I wished she were going with him. I was sure she was in love with him.

When I first met John, it seemed as though I was being swept along like a pile of leaves, with Annie in charge of the broom. She had stars in her eyes from the moment she saw his tweed jacket and cavalry twills.

"John's so polite. Mummy thinks the world of him," she'd said after his first visit to our house.

He was polite and persistent, but he was an autumn wind and I always felt slightly chilly.

"I don't think I love John, Annie." *Fool! Now you've done it.*

She switched off the dryer. "Just as I thought. Pre-wedding nerves. It's quite normal."

How did she know what *normal* was? She'd never had a boyfriend, let alone a proposal of marriage, as far as I knew.

"I tell you what, I'll go and make us a nice cup of cocoa. It'll help to calm you down."

I put my hand on her arm to stop her leaving the room. Now I'd started, I had to continue because… because… "All I've done today is think how wrong it would be for John and I to go through with this marriage."

"You can't back out at the last minute. What about all the arrangements? What about the expense Mummy's had? This is so typical of you, Einna. No thought for anyone but yourself."

The waves of her annoyance threatened to engulf me. Now I'd started, I had to try to make her see. "I can't make him out, Annie. He doesn't like… you know. And surely, if he were normal, he'd want to."

Her knuckles went white as she crushed the handle of the brush. Was she going to hit me? "Are you deliberately trying to provoke me? There I was all concerned for you, and what do you tell me? That John doesn't like… sex? I assume that's what the, 'you know' is. No decent girl wants sex before marriage. Poor John, I'm surprised he hasn't broken off the engagement. And don't look at me as though you've swallowed a lemon. I know what I'm saying… *sex* indeed."

"It's nineteen sixty-three, Annie. Lots of people have sex before they're married."

Her face twisted. "Not my dau… sister. John was right to push you away."

"I'm not even talking about sex, Annie. I'm talking about petting. He just keeps his hands still, on my back or shoulders, and… all we've ever done is kiss." I heard the defeat in my voice. Stupid! It was stupid. I'd given her a dramatic scene on a plate.

"I hope you're not lying. Just you remember what happens if you lie, spots on the tongue. If the sun shines tomorrow, I shall know you're a virgin. If it rains…" She flung down the brush and flounced out of the room.

I picked up the hair-dryer, switched it to very hot and tried to Sahara wind my doubts away.

Chapter Four
Floating, Not Drowning

*From east winds
to west winds
I moved.
From cold indifference,
and tyranny
I moved.
Who is the man
I've married,
to be here
in this windy city?
Why did I move?*

Liverpool isn't as far from Hunstanton as John O'Groats is from Lands End, but it was far enough for me to feel a stranger and anonymous.

The house John had bought, with the help of a loan from his father for the deposit, was in Mosseley Hill. It was a three bedroomed Edwardian semi. When I walked through the front door, I thought, *east to west, Victorian to Edwardian; the suffragette era. Will I be emancipated?* If the honeymoon was anything to go by, no. One deflowering, on the first evening and one sore thrusting on the last evening. It was definitely 'lie back and think of England' sex; nothing emancipated about it.

The house was sparsely furnished. John's mother and father had given us a three piece suite for a wedding present, and John had picked up a double bed, two bedside cabinets, a chest of drawers, a dining table and chairs in a second-hand shop on Smithdown Road, one of the spokes of the umbrella, leading down to the docks.

In the kitchen, there was a gas cooker with an eye level grill, left by the previous owners. They'd also left a blanket chest, in the back bedroom. The wood was beautiful. Both John and I were puzzled as to why they had left it, until we opened it. It stank of moth balls. I wasn't convinced we would ever get rid of the smell, so we certainly couldn't put blankets or spare bed linen in it. Luckily we had an airing cupboard in the bathroom.

We didn't have a fridge or a washing machine. There was a larder, which was pretty cold in winter, apparently, but even in early summer, which it was when we moved in, I could tell we would have to keep the milk from going off by putting the bottle into a bowl of cold water. May, John's mother, said she would teach me to make scones from any milk that went sour.

The furniture seemed to sit forlornly in the rooms. The suite begged for cushions, the walls for pictures; as long as they weren't of elves, or poplar trees. I was hoping that when Thomas Gardner was in place in the lounge, it and I would feel some sense of belonging.

Thomas was due to arrive on Friday, two days before Annie would descend. I tried to tell her that Sunday travel always took much longer than any other day, and that there were fewer trains, but she didn't want to listen.

"I finish work on Friday, and I need Saturday to sort things out," she said. "I can't leave Pearl without doing the shopping, you should know that, Einna." *'Self centred, thoughtless'*, zinged down the line even though she hadn't spoken the words.

I'd thought about ringing her and telling her not to come. I'd picked up the phone, only to put it down again. She wouldn't take any notice, and John would be cross. At present, the phone was situated in the hall, on the floor. I was staring at it, wondering if we had enough money to buy a small table, when it rang. I squatted down to answer it.

"Mother's ill. I can't leave her." It was Annie.

Oh my god! Was this a case of 'be careful what you wish for' being contrary to the warning? I could scarcely take it in. Pearl, a good fairy, not the snow queen? I mouthed platitudes and, when I put down the phone, rushed upstairs, took Cocoa out of my case, gave him hug and danced round the room. The Liverpool air suddenly seemed to be full of summer possibilities. "No Annie," I yelled, throwing Cocoa up in the air and doing a twirl before I caught him. "You, my one and only bear, can now live on my bedside cabinet." My treasure chest was already hidden inside it.

If I had a baby, and I hoped I would have a baby, I would give Cocoa to him or her. No crocodile would take him away. He would be able to live in safety in the baby's room.

Thomas did bring a friendly warmth to the house. Vibes? Whatever it was, I felt that Uncle Charles and Aunty Ruby were here, in the house, with him.

I was alone when he arrived. John was at work and wouldn't be home until late as he was on the rugby club's committee and was going to a meeting. So, no-one was there to see me stroke him, wind him up until he told me to stop, nudge the pendulum and shed a tear as the familiar tick-tock filled the silent house. I phoned Uncle Charles and Aunty Ruby to tell them he'd arrived safely. They had given John a cheque for a wedding present. I believed it was to signify that Thomas Gardner wasn't a present for us both. John had bought a second-hand Vespa with it, saying it would enable him to leave the house at eight-fifteen instead of seven-forty-five, to get to school on time.

John was and wasn't the person I first met. He was and wasn't the man I got to know on his subsequent visits to Hunstanton, during the nine months of our courtship. The honeymoon proved to me that my sexual fears were justified. For John, sex was penetration. I'd tried to tell him the dry, chafing sex hurt, but all he'd said was, "All virgins say that, Einna. It'll get better when you're used to it. I'm not like most men, you know."

I didn't know what he meant by 'like most men', and I didn't get used to sex. I got used to coping with cystitis.

Sunday morning, after breakfast, was the time when John wanted sex, if he wanted it at all; sometimes he was too hung-over from post match drinking. There were no cuddles, no kisses, no lazy arm snaking across the bed to pull me close. John woke. He stretched. He spoke. "I'm going to get our breakfast now, Einna." It was his one household duty; his suggestion, not mine, but only on days when he hadn't drunk too much the evening before.

After we'd finished eating, he would push my nighty up to my waist, take off his pyjama bottoms, fiddle about with his penis to make it erect, and then shove it inside me. He would bounce up and down, while I tried not to squeak with the soreness of it. After he'd ejaculated, he would pull out and roll off. Then he'd go to the bathroom to have a soak in the bath. I couldn't help feeling he was washing me away. I'd roll out of the wet patch and lie on his side of the bed until I heard the water draining down the plug hole.

I put up with 'it'. 'It' was how John referred to sex. I tried to console myself with the fact that, 'it' only occurred every so often. But my body kept telling me there had to be more between people who loved each other. We did love each other, didn't we?

As yet, I had no friends in Liverpool. But what real friends had I ever had in Hunstanton? I had school friends, none of them close. Annie and Pearl hadn't encouraged closeness. I had acquaintances at work and in the orchestra. One friend, a real friend, had been snatched from me by cancer. Uncle Charles and Aunty Ruby were my friends.

John's mother was very kind. I hoped she might become my friend. I was a little bit scared of his father, James. But I could hardly talk to them about 'it'. Nor could I ring Aunty Ruby. My mind spiralled at the very idea of talking about sexual matters to her. She was a delicate romantic. I wasn't sure that she and Uncle Charles even had sex. I suspected that I would have been able to talk to Jean. For the few months I knew her, I could talk to her about anything to do with me and my childhood and I'd never forgotten her Matilda stories.

I wished I didn't feel as though I was colluding in my sexual misfortune. I was sure it didn't have to be like this; it was the sixties, not Victorian England. Books I'd read, where romance was an element, suggested that there was a fizziness between people who were physically attracted to each other. Sometimes, when John smiled at me, I felt that. I wanted him to touch my breasts and… and I didn't know what else I wanted… kisses, lots of kisses all over my body, not this shove in, pump, pump, spurt.

In Hunstanton, I used to borrow Annie's magazines. The stories were romantic, the agony columns real life. *'Sex can be beautiful. Women can take charge,'* wrote the agony aunts. Could I take charge? A web? It might work. I'd nothing to lose, had I?

Nervously, I began to look forward to Sunday. I ate breakfast, taking quick glances at John, trying to gauge his mood. Was this an 'it' Sunday? He didn't look hung-over. Of course he wasn't, he only got breakfast if he was feeling fit. As he picked up the tray, I whipped off my nightdress.

"John, put the tray down, please," I said.

He obeyed, oh my god he obeyed. *'Language!'* I heard Annie snap. I took hold of his hand and guided it towards my nipple. He jerked it away, as though he'd been scalded.

"It's all right," I said. "We're married; it's allowed. I want you to do it."

I slipped my hand through the slit in his pyjama bottoms. His penis was small and limp, no bigger than a shrimp.

"Whoa!" he shouted. "What on earth's got into you? You're behaving like a whore. Annie warned me you were oversexed."

Annie? When did she do that? At our wedding, because of what I'd confided in her the evening before? Yes… yes. I'd seen them in a huddle just before we left. I almost fell out of bed in my hurry to escape. I grabbed my nightdress, made for the bathroom and locked the door. John's – I didn't know what he called his penis, something euphemistic, no doubt – todger, willy, ding-a-ling, could dangle limply forever, for all I cared. Or, he could, jerk himself off. That's what men called masturbating, didn't they? As I sluiced my face with water, I wondered if there would be repercussions? Experience of childhood defiance had taught me that there were always repercussions. I heard down the years:

'You're old enough to choose your own punishment now, Einna. A beating, no sweets for a week, no wireless, or no being allowed to go to your friend's after school. Which is it to be?'

Never, not going to Matilda. Never that.

I needed to get out the house. It wasn't far to Otterspool Promenade. Perhaps the Mersey wind would blow my bleak thoughts away. I'd moved from east to west, from a seaside town to a large port, but as a person I hadn't moved at all. I'd exchanged two tyrants for one, that was all.

In Hunstanton, locals said that the bitter east winds came straight from Moscow, but they weren't persistent. In Liverpool the wind was a persistent westerly; on the whole mild, but an every day wind. Today, Liverpool's westerly took my bleak thoughts and whipped them up into a flurry along with the street's litter. It was at this moment I got a whiff of paraffin. Paraffin... paraffin... I nearly jumped over the railings into the polluted river with excitement. Paraffin was a fuel, but there were other paraffin products. I'd been forced to swallow liquid paraffin, once a week, when I was a child, *'to keep you regular, Einna.'* Wasn't Vaseline made from paraffin oil? I turned my back on the Mersey and headed for the chemist's shop on Rose Lane. There, I learnt about a lubricant which could be used internally.

When I got home, John told me he was going to have a drink with some friends from the rugby club. I was grateful not to be facing a tirade or a sulk.

On the following Sunday, when John went downstairs to get our breakfast, I smeared myself inside and out with gel. 'It' was no more enjoyable but at least I might have solved the cystitis problem.

Ignorant of my chafing cure, John continued with his spasmodic Sunday ritual until I became pregnant. Then, just like that, Sunday morning sex ceased. "We can't risk bruising the embryo's head," he said.

I had an odd feeling that he was relieved. As for me, even though it sounded like Annie rubbish, I was grateful for the hiatus.

The first person I rang was Ruby. "This isn't our day," she said. "What's wrong?"

"I know it's not our day, Ruby." She rang me every Monday evening, considerate of our phone bill. "I'm pregnant."

There was a shriek of joy. "Oh darling, how wonderful. You'll make a super mother. Now, what can we buy you? Or at least, what can I buy you? I'm sure Charles will want to send you a cheque. I know, there's a darling little crib in Vivienne's. Charles and I will bring it over when we visit next month. It's so kind of John's parents to invite us. They're sweethearts, aren't they? Of course we'd much rather stay with you, and when you get a spare bed, we will."

She prattled on until she remembered it was my bill, then she said, "It's a good thing Charles isn't here. He'd have cut us off."

"Yes, but you'd have rung me back, wouldn't you?"

"Of course I would have, darling. Hugs and kisses."

The next person I rang was May. She didn't shriek. "Oh my dear, how wonderful," she said calmly. But I could hear the delight in her voice. "Are you going to have the baby in hospital, or at home?"

"At home. I hate hospitals."

"Why?"

"Because of what happened when I had my tonsils out. I was ten. There were more children than there were beds, so some of us were on mattresses on the floor. I was terrified, May. Children were being sick all around me and nurses were telling them off, telling them they ought to have made it to the toilet. Whenever I think of hospitals, I can smell sick and disinfectant, and I'm back on that floor."

"Ah. Well, I'll help you in any way you want."

"Thank you."

"No need to thank me, poppet. It'll be a pleasure. It's so exciting… my first grandchild."

Her first grandchild. Pearl's first grandchild. I didn't ring Pearl. My happiness was too fragile to risk her indifference. As for Annie, I knew John would want to tell her. It was a relief that I didn't have to bother. I didn't want to listen to endless clichéd advice.

As the days passed, John became more and more like my sister. He seemed to want to control every hour of my day.

"You must rest. If you don't, you could lose the baby."

"You have to eat for two now."

"Don't stretch. Don't bend. Don't lift. Don't drink any alcohol. Don't, don't…"
The words piled up around me until I couldn't see over them. If it hadn't been for the common sense talked by my midwife, I would have become an obese, somnolent blob.

When Uncle Charles and Aunty Ruby came to stay, May, Aunty Ruby and I went to The Walker Art Gallery. Uncle Charles and James went to watch John play rugby. Of all the paintings there, I was drawn to the pre-Raphaelites and the one I liked best was *Isabella*.

"If you like these paintings, I must take you to The Lady Lever," said May. "We'll go tomorrow, if you like. James loves the Wedgewood collection there. We'll all go. You ought to see Port Sunlight, in any case."

"Is there a nice pub there? We could treat everyone to lunch," said Aunty Ruby.

As soon as I saw the picture called *Pandora* I felt as though I'd seen her somewhere before, but I couldn't think where.

The very next week, at antenatal exercise class, I realised where, for there she was. It was the hair more than anything, like an energy field around her head. Deliberately, I placed myself next to her and when we did the exercise that Becky, the woman who took the class, called 'the farting exercise', I felt sure we could be friends. All round the room there were little explosions. Pandora snorted. I snorted, and soon we were helpless with laughter. After class she introduced herself. Of course she wasn't called Pandora; her name was Maggie, Maggie Harvey. She was a scouser. I loved her accent. I wondered if my child would grow up with a scouse accent. As soon as we started at a mother and toddlers group, he or she would be mixing with Liverpudlians. John didn't have any accent, but then he had gone to Liverpool College, a fee paying school.

"Where do you live?" Maggie asked me as we were putting on our coats.

"Ferndale Road."

"Not far from me, then. I live just off Lark Lane. Do you fancy coming back to mine for a cuppa? I can still drink tea... coffee, yuk."

"I'm the same."

"What do you do?"

I told her that I was just a housewife because John was a bit old fashioned where women and work were concerned. "Before I met him, I'd thought of going to music college, but... oh, it's a long story. I won't bore you with it just now."

"What does John do?"

"Teaches PE. He's a rugby fanatic."

"Trevor's a musician. He wants to be a well known contemporary composer, like Steve Reich. Have you heard of him?"

"Yes. I prefer the romantic composers, like Richard Strauss and Bruch."

She also told me that she was a drama teacher. "Our school is divided into houses. The Head likes competition. Our house Head is a man called Clem. He's a Welsh anomaly, a stuffed shirt, oddball. He litters his speech with poetic metaphors, which is endearing, like when there's going to be a fire alarm practice he tells us we have to abandon ship, and then in the next breath he criticises my informality with the pupils. He can't cope with my bump. I think he feels I ought to hide it under one of those hideous smocks. He tells me I ought to put my feet up at break or my ankles will swell."

"He should get together with John and my sister. I'm being driven mad with their clichés. *You must eat for two. Don't lift, don't stretch. You could damage the baby.*' I feel as though the don'ts are going to smother me."

"Trevor just expects me to get on with things, thank goodness." She unlocked the door. A man with floppy, dark hair sat at the dining table, surrounded by manuscript paper.

"Hi love," Maggie said. "You want a cuppa? This is Einna. Our babies are due the same week."

"Unusual name." He got up. "I've just got to finish this, so if you'll excuse me—"

"You'll go into the bedroom while we have a natter."

"Yes. I've just had a cuppa." He planted a kiss on the top of her head and left the room. *John would never do that*, I thought.

"Plonk your coat on a chair, Einna. And that reminds me, I meant to ask you before, why 'Einna'?"

"Are you sure you—"

"Don't tell me if you don't want to."

Matilda, Jean, same response years apart. "No, it's okay. I'll do the short version…"

"Shit," she said, when I'd finished. "And I thought I had a dragon for a mother. Her name's Edith. I always think of her as Edith, never Mother. Hey, I've got to change the subject. Talking about our mothers is depressing. You know your problem with your husband's attitude to your pregnancy? Why not invite him to your next appointment with your midwife. Is it Bev?"

"Yes."

"Well, she's lovely. You can confide in her. She'll be up for it, and next week I'll introduce you to my college friends, Debbie and Angela. I call them that even though we're no longer at college. Debbie's a little brown mouse and Angela's a mermaid. You'll see why when you meet them."

"And you're—"

"Lizzie Siddal."

"I knew you were going to say that. As soon as I saw *Pandora* in The Lady Lever, I felt like I'd seen her, live, somewhere."

When I left Trevor and Maggie's flat, I felt a as though I was in a bubble of warmth. It was similar to how I used to feel when I went to stay with Uncle Charles and Aunty Ruby, or visit Jean and Nelson at Matilda. Not only had I made a friend, she was going to introduce me to two of her friends. I felt sure I would like them. I might stop being a no-where, no-person, woman.

The following evening, with several fingers crossed, I tackled John. "I'd like you to come to the ante-natal clinic with me, so we can both chat to the midwife."

"Why?" John asked

Because I'm going to drown in old wives' tales if I can't get some common sense into you. "She suggested it." This small web was partly true. In one of the exercise sessions, she'd told us that the more a couple shared the pregnancy, the more in tune they were at the birth and after.

"You haven't thought this through, Einna. How am I going to get time off work to come with you?"

"There's a Friday afternoon clinic. We could see her at four-thirty."

Grudgingly, he agreed.

Our doctor's surgery was on Garston Old Road. I popped in to change my appointment when I did my Wednesday shop, leaving a note for Beverly to explain why.

On the Friday, she winked at me as John closed the door. "It's good to see you looking so fit, Einna and I'm glad you could make the appointment, John. I like to get to know husbands."

Before I could open my mouth, he said, "I hope you'll support me, nurse. Einna does too much. I keep telling her to rest. It's not good for her or the baby. Her sister——"

"The best thing for Einna to do, is to keep active. Her muscles need to be strong, not flabby; that's why we run exercise classes. And please call me Beverly or Bev." She looked at my notes. "Any morning sickness, Einna?"

I sneaked a glance at John. I wasn't sure if he was looking annoyed or astonished. "Not so far," I said.

"That's good. There's an effective new drug on the market called thalidomide, but obviously it's better not to take drugs. Drink plenty of water and don't eat for two. That's the advice I give to all pregnant women."

"Not eat for two? But…"

"Babies get all the nourishment they need from a normal, healthy diet, John. It wouldn't be sensible for Einna to be overweight. The fitter she is, the better able she'll be to deal with the birth. It hurts and I'm not going to pretend it doesn't."

"Is it necessary for Einna to attend two exercise classes a week? Surely she has enough to do…"

"The ante-natal classes are vital. Later on, she'll be shown how to breathe during the birth cycle; which reminds me, are you going to watch your baby being born? We've moved a long way from husbands running up and down stairs with pans of boiling water, you know."

"I can't stand the sight of blood. I'd faint or something and be in the way. Annie, Einna's sister, is coming to stay. She's like a mother to her, very no nonsense if you know what I mean. My wife can be such a drama queen."

I couldn't stifle the gasp. Beverly glanced at me. How could he talk about me in this way to a comparative stranger? Why had he said that? *A drama queen?*

"I've always found Einna to be calm and sensible," said Beverly.

I would have liked to hug her, say thank you.

"Well she's not always, believe me. Any little thing can set her off. Annie will help."

Control. That's what all this was about. "I don't want Annie with me. She…" How could I tell Bev, in a short sentence, about my relationship with Annie? I just hoped he hadn't already rung her. I could see, only too clearly, how it would be. She and John would nag me into a permanent state of tension and frustration, rob me of the joy of my baby's birth by taking over and most likely plunge me into post-natal depression. The very thoughts were threatening to turn me into a drama queen.

"Einna will be fine with me," said Beverly. "And even though you don't feel you can be in the room with her, she'll know you're in the house, supporting her."

I wondered if diplomacy, or husband handling was part of a midwife's training?

John shouted at me nearly all the way home, so as soon as we got to the front door, I muttered something about the toilet and fled. Two years of marriage had taught me that he was prone to rage patterns. If I allowed him to shout, uninterrupted, his anger almost always fizzled out. He seemed exhausted afterwards, and often his tantrums were followed by days of blissful silence.

Today the quiet lasted until our evening meal. "You have to have someone with you, other than the midwife, at the birth, Einna."

"I know—"

"Also you'll need help afterwards. You're not an organised person, are you? We don't want to risk our baby."

That was twice he'd insulted me in one day. What did he mean, I wasn't organised, or that I'd risk our baby? I'd had to nag him to decorate the small room and buy a safety-gate for the stairs.

"You'll probably panic if the baby hiccups. Anyway, it's all arranged."

And it was going to be un-arranged. The following day, I checked with May that she really did want to help and then I rang Annie.

"I notice you left John to tell me," were her first words.

With as much strength as I could summon, I banished my Hunstanton self. "You know John, Annie. He would have been so disappointed if I'd told you." I could picture her indecision: want warring with the desire to call me a liar. "Oh, and I've asked May to be with me at the birth. After all, she knows what it's like." And she would be the only Granny wouldn't she? Pearl changing, wanting to play a part in her grandchild's life? I doubted it.

"I can't pretend I'm not disappointed, Einna. You hardly know May. She can't possibly understand you as I do."

No one understands me as you do, sister. You don't understand me at all; you never did. I trust May. I know she won't bully me, and although she's older than you, her head's not full of superstitious claptrap. "You can come when things have settled down a little."

"I'm…" She dried up, I could hardly believe it. Assertiveness had floored my sister.

That evening, I spun a web. I pretended Annie couldn't come. "I thought it might be difficult for her," I said. "You never know when babies are going to arrive, especially first babies and she can't leave Pearl for weeks on end."

"She was okay about it when I spoke to her. She said she would come when your pains started."

I was astonished at the idiocy of this decision. Come when my pains started? "Think of the journey, John. Annie would never get here on time. Your mum's only fifteen minutes away."

He frowned. I seemed to have floored him as well. *Don't smile, Einna.*

"I hope Annie wasn't too disappointed."

"You know Annie. She bounced back."

Will I be found out? Will my web unravel? I didn't seem to care.

Early weeks, where my figure pretended I wasn't pregnant, turned to months of a rounded bump. I felt like a sleek, well-fed cat. Then the last month arrived. It was almost impossible to cut my toenails, I had a permanent problem with flatulence, and sleep was a transient affair as the baby chose to exercise at night.

"You're getting me used to your routine, aren't you?" I crooned. "You're going to turn night into day and visa-versa, and do I care, baby? No, it's you and me against John Tyrant and Annie Bully."

Even with Beverly's warning, I was taken by surprise at the severity of pain that came with each contraction. Lower back pains came and went, each time catching me out. Pain one, as I was hanging out the washing, pain two as I was making myself a mid-morning drink of marmite in boiled water, one of my pregnancy cravings. Pains three, four, five, six; our baby was on the way. I felt fizzy with excitement. I rang Beverly, May, Maggie and then John. I asked him to ring Annie.

"I wish Stuart/Alice was on the way," said Maggie. "Can I do anything?"

I would have loved to say, "Come round. Be with me." But that would have been too many people and I knew Maggie was having problems with swollen feet and ankles. She'd made light of it, saying, "Trevor believes I have elephantitis, very reassuring. He's a very good masseur, though. I'm thinking of hiring him out."

May answered the phone immediately, almost as though she was hovering by it. "Shall I come round?" she said.

"Would it be okay if I came to yours instead? I feel so energetic. If I don't have a good walk, I'll probably clean the house again."

"I see," she said.

"What does, 'I see,' mean?"

"It's normal to have a huge rush of energy; we're all animals preparing our nest. I'll see you in about quarter of an hour. I've a little something for you."

"How exciting. Will you tell me… No, I'd rather it be a surprise."

I'd discovered that I quite liked housework; I did it to Radio Luxembourg. I'd also discovered that I enjoyed cooking, indeed had a flair for it. I didn't have a lot of housekeeping money – five pounds a week – but with the help of Marguerite Patten's *Cookery in Colour*, a wedding present from one of John's aunts, I'd learnt to be creative with cheap cuts of meat, offal, fish, and to cook vegetables without boiling all the goodness out of them. Nutmeg. I loved nutmeg. If you grated a little on some cabbage, it turned an ordinary vegetable into something special.

John enjoyed my cooking; one of his favourites was Coq-au-vin. And he appreciated the way I looked after the house, but I didn't ever feel he loved or wanted me. I was… I didn't know what I was to him, a possession, maybe?

The morning was a Disney cartoon morning. The spring blossom was pinker, whiter, than any other year, the leaves a fresher green. I bounced to May and James's house, singing, *'Spring is busting out all over.'* We had lunch in the garden, and when another pain rushed at me, May helped me control it through the breathing exercises I'd been taught. After lunch, she handed me a small box.

"I want you to have these," she said. Inside was a pair of earrings, turquoises set in gold. "They were my mother's." The next pain caught my thanks.

She looked at her watch. "Time to ring Beverly again, I think.'

The moment our daughter was put into my arms, the pain was forgotten. I fell in love: mother love. At last I knew the meaning of the phrase. How could Pearl not have felt it for me?

John and James came into the bedroom, one with his arms full of a huge teddy bear, the other with a bottle of champagne and a bunch of roses. I was touched, but all I needed was to be left alone with Claire. I wanted to fall asleep watching her. May noticed my fatigue. She allowed them one drink, then bustled them out of the room.

As I drifted off, I knew I was floating, not drowning.

Chapter Five
Mona Lisa

There is a painting in Paris
of a woman with an enigmatic smile.
Through the ages people have puzzled
over it, all the while
coming up with explanations
that make no sense, to me.
I know why she is smiling.

Some people find routines boring. But everything connected to looking after Claire pleased me. I caught myself wanting to eat my baby daughter. I suspected that this was a cliché, but one, nevertheless, true for me, but not one to share with John or Annie. I heard *'drama queen'*. I knew my Liverpool friends would have understood.

Whilst there were routines that pleased, gave comfort, equally there were routines that annoyed. When Thomas Gardner chimed five o'clock and I heard the key turning in the lock of the front door, I wanted to grind my teeth with frustration. John's coming home routine hadn't varied for almost two years; not since the birth of our daughter. I would wait, counting the footsteps in the hall, 'one, two, three…' the door would open.

"Have you got the kettle on?" John would say.

"No, it doesn't suit me." We would laugh, although it was no longer funny.

He would kiss Claire on the top of her head, and give me a peck on the cheek. He had been distantly affectionate since her birth; no tantrums in front of our daughter. I could almost feel secure in his pride. I was a good housewife, a good mother, but not a desirable sexual partner; no change there.

Greeting over, he would make himself a mug of instant coffee and repair to his den, lair, indoor shed, until it was time to eat. Sometimes I wondered how often we would perform this ritual before he retired.

Although it was the beginning of April, the weather in Liverpool was still behaving as though it were March, with persistent westerlies. Wind, from whatever compass point, seems to make people unpredictable. Liverpudlians, I discovered were no exception.

Claire and I were cosy in the kitchen. I was preparing our evening meal while she was playing with her post-box, trying to shove the round shape into the triangular hole. Her small face was set with determination. We heard Thomas Gardner chiming five and there it was, the key in the lock. "One…" I began.

"April in Paris…"

'Two' and 'three' froze in my mouth.

"Daddy?" Claire's voice sounded as puzzled as I felt.

There was no measured tread down the hall. We heard running. He flung open the door. Claire dropped the round shape and crawled behind my legs. Clutching my jeans, she peeked out.

"Guess what this is?" He brandished an envelope in the air. Before I could say, 'I've no idea,' he added, "It's our holiday tickets."

"Holiday?"

"Yes, an April break in Paris during the Easter holiday. I put some of the money your uncle gave us when Claire was born, into a deposit account. Aren't you pleased?"

"Well yes, of course I am. I just can't take it in, that's all. Let me get this straight, you've booked us a holiday, in Paris?"

"Yes, yes." He sashayed around me, scooped Claire up onto his shoulders and danced about the room. She squealed with delight. "I've booked Mummy and Daddy a holiday: five days in Paris. Annie can come to stay and look after you."

"No Annie," said Claire, patting his head.

Too right, Claire. "I don't think Annie would be comfortable on her own here with Claire. She doesn't know anyone. Liverpool's a huge city and Hunstanton——"

"You sort it then. I just thought… It doesn't matter."

"I'll ask your mum and dad. They'll be thrilled to have their granddaughter to themselves for a few days." I looked at Claire. *Even though you're a sunny, smiling angel one minute and a screaming Nero the next, you little tyke.*

"Fine. Whatever's best."

He wasn't arguing. *What's going on?*

"Daddy's been to Paris with the Rugby Club, Claire. Mummy hasn't been to Paris ever, ever. I can't wait to show her the sites. *April in Paris.*"

He continued to dance around the kitchen, not even noticing that Claire was shrieking with pleasure. Usually shrieks or squeals would elicit a look of disapproval and a caution to be quieter.

John had surprised me and, despite my refusal to seek Annie's help, he still sounded pleased and excited. Suddenly I was caught up in his enthusiasm and was spinning with the west wind. We would be going to one of the most romantic cities in the world. Perhaps he would be swept away by its influence and become the husband, the lover of my dreams. This man, careering round the room with a screaming toddler on his shoulders, was more like the John I'd met in Hunstanton. Tony, his friend, had picked up a young woman at the fair and the four of us had spent a lot of time together. The men had indulged in horseplay on the beach, and once we'd piggy-back raced up to the lighthouse. It had ended with the two men throwing us in the sea. Luckily we'd both had on our bathing costumes; I doubted that Pearl and Annie would have looked at John in such a kindly light if I'd returned home in sopping wet clothes.

Follow your dream. Follow the yellow brick road. Was Paris going to be my Emerald City?

Later, as I was giving Claire her tea, I reminded John that I was going to Maggie's. She had invited the rest of the gang round. That was what Trevor called us: an unruly, bolshie gang of women. I had no problem with being called 'a gang', indeed I treasured it; just the sense of belonging. I didn't feel bolshie. I felt as though a world of which I knew nothing had opened up. These women talked; not about women's things in particular, about a variety of subjects, like teaching, the arts, politics, world wide issues. At first I listened. Then I bought *The Manchester Guardian* every so often. I stopped tuning in to Radio Luxembourg or The Light Program, and listened instead to The Home Service.

Our talk wasn't only about serious matters. We also had fun. One day we were laughing so loudly that Trevor came through from their bedroom, where he was working. "Hey you monstrous regiment of women, tone it down a bit. I can't work."

Maggie threw a cushion at him and, before I knew it, we were in the middle of a cushion fight.

I was changing. I didn't realise how much until we went to Paris.

In the weeks prior to our holiday, I was both excited and nervous. Secretly, I wished we were going by boat and train; the idea of flying terrified me.

Our charter flight was from Lydd to Beauvais. Lydd didn't live up to my idea of an airport; it was an airfield with a building on it. There was no sense of mystery or excitement. It seemed like a doctor's waiting room with ordinary people, in high street clothes, whispering to each other. There was very little to distract a nervous, first-time flyer.

When I asked May if she and James would look after Claire, I admitted that, whilst I was excited about the holiday, I was apprehensive about the flight.

May gave me a hug. "It's only the take-offs and landings that are dangerous, Einna. Flying's safer than driving. James taught me a trick. Count to ten. If you're not off the ground by ten, you can start to worry."

As the twin engine Dakota taxied down the runway, I counted. "One, two, three…"

"Why are you counting, Einna?" John asked.

I couldn't break the sequence. "Seven, eight, why isn't it taking—?" The plane lifted off over a hedge. I saw the cliffs below and a seagull flying past our window. No one had told me the airfield was so close to the coast. John was staring at me. I didn't want the man who had courted me to change into the man who had married me.

I told him about my fear of flying and what his mother had said.

"Silly mutt." He took my hand. "I can see I shall have to keep an eye on you when we go up the Eiffel Tower."

"I'm not sure I want to go up the Eiffel Tower, John. I don't like heights. Can't we just look at it?"

Mistake. He frowned. "We have to go up the Eiffel Tower, Einna; it's what you do on your first visit to Paris. I hope you're not going to be difficult."

Difficult! I didn't want to be difficult. I wanted to be romantic. I wanted to be cultured. I wanted a new start, sexually, with satin sheets, champagne, croissants and crumbs. I didn't want to be a first time tourist who had to go up the Eiffel Tower. *Compromise Einna. Go up the Eiffel Tower and encourage John to come with you to The Louvre.* "I'm sure I'll be fine, if you look after me," I said.

He smiled. John looked so pleasant when he smiled and, despite my fear of flying, or maybe because of it, I felt a sexual frisson flirting round my body. It settled between my legs.

By the time we'd registered in our hotel and unpacked, it was barely fluttering. I'd been given a detailed description of The Rugby Club's Paris, and he'd refused to consider any alternative.

"Won't you just have a look at the guide book I bought?" I pleaded, and handed it to him.

He threw it on the bed. "I don't need a bloody guide book. I know where to go. I thought you'd agreed to my plan?"

My idea of Paris crashed with the book. For not the first time in my life I thought, *silence is not agreement.* I looked at the bed: no satin sheets. There was a nylon bottom sheet, no doubt full of static electricity and a huge eiderdown. Later, I discovered it was called a duvet.

Suddenly, John threw a crumb to the, would be, cultured tourist. "If we've time, we might be able to squash in the Mona Lisa."

Squash in? "Lovely, John. Thank you."

"Are you being facetious?"

"No!" Furious, yes. Disappointed, yes. Beginning to wishing I was back in Liverpool with Claire and my friends, yes.

He looked at me suspiciously. "I'm not unreasonable, Einna."

Really? What was it Maggie had said about leopards when we'd been talking about The Christine Keeler affair?

"The French are more sensible about affairs," Angela had said. "As long as the person is doing a good job, their private life is their own business."

Debbie had disagreed. She thought that people in the public eye should set a good example.

"He's a risk," Maggie had said. "He obviously can't keep his dick in his trousers, and you know what they say about leopards and spots."

They couldn't change them. I was beginning to understand that nothing of what I'd imagined would come to pass.

Later, as I was trying to work out whether it was better to have both the square pillow and hard bolster, or do without the bolster and have one pillow. John said, "I was wondering, as we're on our hols, maybe we could...? I know it's not when we usually do 'it', but..."

He wanted to have sex. *'It?'* Bugger! I hadn't thought to protect myself from lack of foreplay soreness. Maybe... No. The magic of Paris hadn't cast its spell on him. The humping ritual began. But why? We hadn't had sex for weeks.

That night, I dreamt I was a medieval damsel riding a white unicorn through the cobbled streets of Paris, to escape the thousands of Johns who were pursuing me with maces of intransigence whirling around their helmeted heads. The unicorn was sweating. Its back was slippery. Bending low over its neck, I clung to its silky mane and listened to the thud of its hooves. We clattered through the doors of Notre Dame, and up, up the stone steps of the bell tower.

"There are no such things as unicorns," shouted the John pursuers. "You can't escape that way."

"I can try," I said, as we teetered on the edge of the parapet. I plummeted awake with my hand between my legs.

'You'll get hairs on the palms of your hand if you touch yourself.'

"Go away Annie," I whispered. "I want to know."

I pulled up my nightdress to caress my breasts. "Oh," I gasped as tiny electric shocks raced to my groin. I pinched my nipples and nearly cried aloud with pleasure as they became hard. They wanted to be sucked. I licked my finger and drew a circle round them. I stroked my pubic hair, my labia. John, who was wrapped in sleep, provided the rhythm with his snores.

"Stroke me," my clitoris begged. "Pinch me, press me. Don't stop. Don't…" I clenched my vaginal muscles and spiralled towards a place I'd only read about.

Our bedroom wasn't en-suite. I slipped out of the door hoping the bathroom wasn't being used by anyone else. I was still swollen with desire and my urine took a long time to come. I couldn't help giggling. I'd experienced my first orgasm. What did I smell like, taste like? I sniffed my fingers, licked them. They were salty, fishy; I smelt and tasted of the sea.

On the white tiled wall, an image of Audrey Hepburn appeared. She was singing, 'I could have come all night'. I joined in as a gush of urine fell into the pan. I wiped myself and walked over to the basin to wash. If I could smell me, John could smell me.

I stared at myself in the mirror, wondering if I'd changed? A flushed face with dark blue eyes stared back. I smiled an enigmatic, Mona Lisa smile. Was she smiling because… no… maybe? If John managed to slot her in between the Eiffel Tower, the Champs Elysée, the Boulevard Hausmann, Montmartre, Pigalle and the Moulin Rouge, I'd study her to see if I could tell.

When I got back to our bedroom, he was sitting up in bed. "Where've you been?" he asked. "You look flushed. Are you ill too?" Before I could answer, he added, "I think I'm going to be…" and almost fell out of bed in his panic to get to the bathroom.

I didn't know whether to follow, or leave him alone. When I was ill, I liked to be left alone; a reaction to the years of Annie control. I followed. He was sitting on the lavatory, groaning, his head between his knees. Unbidden, a smile hovered about my mouth, for I couldn't help thinking about the difference in groans.

"Shall I go downstairs and ask the concierge to ring for a doctor?"

He shook his head. "Can you help me back to bed?"

We lay, side by side, drifting in and out of sleep as fresh bouts of sickness and diarrhoea overcame him.

The next morning I went to a pharmacy. Luckily the chemist could speak a little English. "Perhaps your husband has eaten the food… the stomach does not like?" he said.

"We had mussels for dinner, yesterday evening, but I'm okay."

"It only takes one bad one, Madame. You must telephone to a doctor."

The receptionist in the hotel phoned for me, and within half an hour a doctor arrived. He diagnosed food poisoning and gave John a prescription.

"Sometimes you feel better in twenty four hours," he said. "If longer than three days, please to ring again."

"Three days? Our holiday will be almost over," John said.

The doctor shrugged. "This is the chance you take if you eat the seafood."

After I'd been to the pharmacy again, I sat on the edge of the bed to give John all the prescribed medicines.

He groaned. "Don't do that Einna. You're making the sheet tight over my stomach."

I got up. "Do you want me to stay with you?"

"No, all I want to do is sleep."

Whoopee! Freedom… my Paris. "Can I get you anything?"

He shook his head. "You go out and enjoy yourself. Don't go up the Eiffel Tower though."

"Don't worry, I won't." Did I look like a masochist? The metal symbol of Paris could corrode, as far as I was concerned. And, despite my interrupted sleep, I went out into the bright, April sunshine with thoughts of croissants and a large coffee in Samaritaine, rumbling in my stomach.

'I'm going to Sainte Chappelle this morning.
Ding-dong its bells will surely chime.
I'll see the windows.
Glowing in the sunshine.
Because the morning is so fine.'

I sang, under my breath, for fear of being regarded as a mad English woman. The book John rejected was in my hand. It had all the maps I needed. I didn't have to take The Metro. I could dance everywhere.

Well Einna, you've come a long way from the gauche teenager who couldn't face going to music college in London, haven't you? That girl wouldn't have had the courage to dance round Paris. Thank you, whatever angels have helped me to metamorphose into a butterfly.

Samaritaine was an art deco department store. Once there, I whizzed up the escalators to the rooftop restaurant. With Paris spread out like a model city before me, I experienced another orgasm; a spiritual one. It was almost more than I could bear. My eyes filled with tears of joy as my day stretched away to evening.

But time is a flirt which is forever changing its parameters. The hours charged down the quays of the Seine and over the cobbled streets, like the unicorn of my dream, whereas I believed I meandered, absorbing the beauty of the city. The medieval stained glass of the Sainte Chappelle was awe inspiring, just as I knew it would be. The dark grandeur of the Conciergerie looked oppressive as I mooched past. I wasn't unhappy that I hadn't chosen to explore it. Why did I want to see the prison where the 'let them eat cake' queen was incarcerated before being beheaded? I needed beauty and amazement to fill my starved spirit.

I sat, for some time, in Notre Dame, listening to a rehearsal for an organ recital. My thoughts clattered up the stairs of the bell tower to the soaring notes and, in their midst, I heard the three o'clock chimes. If I were to complete my chosen program, I needed to make my way to see the Mona Lisa in the Louvre.

The room was busy. I wandered about until the crowd had moved on. When it was my turn to look into the eyes that appeared to follow people around, I whispered, "Well, you're a much smaller portrait than I expected; small but beautiful. Tell me, is masturbation what you're smiling about? Did you discover that we women don't need men, that we can pleasure ourselves?" Of course she didn't reply, but I believed her eyes said, 'Yes.'

As I was making my way back to the hotel in the rue du Grand Prieure, I realised that I could adopt another angel, a Mona Lisa angel. An angel who looked after women's sexual needs. I floated down the Rue de Rivoli, found a souvenir shop and went in to buy postcards. I wanted to tell my friends about my discovery. As soon as I saw the Mona Lisa earrings, I knew I was meant to buy them. Did the woman who served me think I was mad for smiling and smiling so, or did she recognise the smile?

When I got back to the hotel, John was sitting up in bed. He looked a little better.

"You've been a long time."

"I didn't think… No matter. How are you feeling?"

"What have you got in your ears?" he asked, ignoring my question.

"New earrings." I moved closer. "They're Mona Lisa ones."

"I can see that." He pulled a face. "Whatever made you buy them? They're tacky."

I attempted a Mona Lisa smile which said, *'well I like them'*. "How are you feeling?" I asked again.

"Better, I think. I'm starving. That must say something, mustn't it? Is there room service in this hotel?"

"I doubt it, but it doesn't matter. There are shops nearby. I'll go and get us a picnic after I've phoned your mum and dad to see how Claire is."

"Can't you get us something to eat before you do that? What are you going to do if she's not fine?"

"I don't know, John. I could talk to her. Tell her I love her." *What will I do? Oh God, what will I do? I'd have to go home. How would I do that? I haven't any money to buy another ticket. Calm down, Einna. May would have rung the hotel if Claire was ill.*

"Well do it after we've eaten, please. I'm sure Claire is fine. I bet Mum will be spoiling her. My dad won't. He's far too sensible."

"Okay," I said, having every intention of doing what I needed to do first. How could I concentrate on shopping? How could I eat? I found it alien that he didn't need to know how his daughter was faring.

"Don't buy anything too exotic."

"I was thinking of bread and water for you."

"I hope you're joking."

"No, John, I'm not. I think bread and water's about all your stomach will be able to tolerate. If we were in England, I'd have bought water biscuits. I had food poisoning when I was twelve. Several pupils at the High School had it. We never really knew why. Water biscuits and lemon barley water was all Annie and Pearl would allow me to have."

"Einna, I need something a little more appetising than bread and water, for God's sake."

Be it on your own head, Mr. Stubborn. "I'll do my best," I said, and escaped to the hotel lobby, where I bought some telephone tokens from the receptionist. Claire was fine. No tantrums. May and George were, to use May's words, "Having a whale of a time."

"I'm afraid we're thoroughly spoiling her." I noticed the, 'we'. I would delight in telling John that Claire had wound his dad round her little finger. I couldn't help thinking how it would have been with Annie. *'She's been a very naughty little girl. I've had to punish her.'* I trembled at the voice in my head.

The picnic I procured was as bland as a charcuterie and boulangerie could provide.

"You've been a long time," John said.

"There was a queue at the boulangerie," my spider replied. "It's because the French buy fresh bread twice a day."

John began to retch not long after he'd finished eating. "That doctor wasn't very helpful. I shan't have any holiday at all, if I go on like this."

Hypocritical words spilled from my mouth, when what I wanted to say was, 'I told you so.' I was sorry for him; of course I was sorry for him, but the thought of another day of my Paris had me salivating with anticipation. The lady and the unicorn, the Place de Voges, the domes of Galleries la Fayette and Printemps, lunch in the Marais; so many pleasures to choose from. I knew my thoughts were selfish, but maybe one more day would do it, for both of us.

I sent identical postcards to Maggie, Angela and Debbie. They would understand and find it amusing when I saw them and explained the cryptic message...

'Paris has given me a present. Tell you all about it when I see you, love E.'

I popped the postcards in envelopes and mailed them on my way to catch the bus. I could have walked to the Cluny Museum, but I wanted to do as much of my itinerary as possible, and walking did take time.

"Thank you," I whispered to the unicorn, for I fell in love with the magical beast as soon as I saw him in the tapestry. "Thank you for saving me from all those Johns."

We did have three of his days. And for his sake I strove to enjoy them. We didn't go up the Eiffel Tower: John was scandalised by the ticket price.

"It didn't cost as much as that on the rugby trip."

"Maybe it was because it was a group booking," I said, thanking whatever guardian angel was looking after me.

I enjoyed the walk along the Seine to the Tuileries gardens. The plant market was full of wonderful plants and flowers. I was almost overpowered by their scent. I would have liked to saunter past the art stalls on the quay of the Seine, but I soon realised that, mostly, they sold poor quality reproductions of Paris scenes. The walk had a comic element to it, for a man walking towards us was smiling at me. I thought, *how jolly* and smiled back. John grabbed my arm and hurried me on.

"Didn't you notice?" he hissed. "He was masturbating." His face twisted. "Disgusting. He ought to be arrested."

I had to turn away, for I couldn't help smiling. He was doing in public what I'd done in the secrecy of a double bed. Was that comic or tragic irony?

Montmartre was more interesting than I'd anticipated and I enjoyed walking down to Opera, through Pigalle. The prostitutes in their variety of mini skirts, low cut blouses and fake furs were exotic. John made no comment about them. Indeed, I wondered if he saw them? I also wondered if they suffered from cystitis? If I'd known the French for paraffin, I would have told them about my gel, but maybe in their profession they would have already known about it.

On the plane home, thoughts about what had happened to me in that magical city tripped about in my mind. I knew I would have to accept that John would never be the husband or lover I craved. I couldn't say, 'I shouldn't have married him', for without John, there wouldn't have been Claire. However, I needed to broaden my horizons and, once she started school I determined to go to college. I knew I might have a fight on my hands, but if so, it was a fight I was prepared to engage in to the death. I grinned. Now that was a drama queen thought. I had thought of being honest, and telling John that the Cluny, the Louvre and the Sainte Chappelle were the most inspiring places I'd visited, but I couldn't face the possible sulk. He might have a long sulk ahead, with regard to me wanting a career. Bridges to cross.

Before Paris, if anyone had asked me if I missed playing the violin, I would have said, 'no', it was a part of a life I wanted to forget. Now, I could admit to myself that I did miss it. Ruby and Charles would be delighted that I was going to train to teach music. I could hear her coos of delight floating alongside the plane.

As for the Mona Lisa earrings, they were a reminder that I had a sexual angel who would smile and smile when I touched my breasts, stroked my labia, found the secret spot to squeeze and press until I spiralled out of control.

Chapter Six
Tinsel and Tears

Hark! Can you hear the bells?
They herald the season
of good will, when
Father Christmas is a promise
to good children,
a threat to naughty ones.
"What about poor children?"
asks the child of wealth.
"They aren't naughty
but Father Christmas
doesn't come."

Time is not an 'old father', rather it is a capricious child, behaving as he or she chooses. How and when did my daughter fly out of toddlerhood and become a little girl with a life outside the confines of my wings?

As for me? I felt that my life, which had been defined by being a wife and a mother, was growing beyond its former boundaries too. I was at college and Claire was at primary school and, before we knew it, the end of the term was approaching. Christmas was in sight and, each morning, as I got dressed, I was sure I heard the Christmas bauble earrings' glittery giggle.

"Put us on," they tittered. "It's spree time. It's glee time. Time to laugh with your witchy friends. Time to cackle with laughter until you wet your knickers."

'Get em off.'

'We can't we've peed in them.'

The gang of lads outside TJ Hughes were 'gob smacked', dumbstruck. They had thought to embarrass us and we had floored them.

A gang outing, jaunt, spree that I would never forget, the first when wet knickers became the gang badge. What were we like?

Saturdays were jaunt days; a once a month outing we cherished. Debbie's husband, Bill, was happy to mind his two offspring. Grandparents looked after Claire and Stuart. "My work," being Trevor's cry. "Rugby matches," John's. Angela and Dave had decided that they didn't want children. They would enjoy surrogate parenthood through other people's offspring.

The story that had had us helpless with laughter, was Maggie's. "I was in George Henry Lee's looking at Liberty's fabric I couldn't afford, looking at furniture I couldn't afford, looking at every bleeding thing I couldn't afford, when I saw these two armchairs on a dais. They were stunning. I knew they wanted to be bought for Munster Mansions." She smiled wryly. "I knew they would never find their way to Munster Mansions. Unlike you, Einna, I don't believe in angels."

"Neither do I," I said. "I pretend they exist. People say, 'you're an angel', don't they?"

"Anyway, I had a sneaky look round. No one was near me, so I decided to sit in one. Just a little try; just to say, 'hey you lot, I'm the sort of person who could own a chair like this.' What I didn't see was, that the chair I chose to sit in had casters, and one caster was on the edge of the dais. I sat down, the chair rolled back and tipped, with me in it. We both fell off the dais. I banged my head and my elbow, but worse, I was stuck, legs in the air showing the world my pussy because the chair was wedged between the dais and the wall."

We began to laugh. "But you had knickers on," said Angela. "You didn't show your pubes."

"I might just as well have done. My knickers are skimpy to say the least, but they were clean. I almost blessed Edith for trotting out, *'Clean knickers every day. You never know when you might be involved in an accident and have to go to hospital.'* An assistant or three came running. I could see them trying to avert their eyes as they attempted to haul me up. I didn't dare look at their crotches.

"'We're going to have to get the dais shifted,' said one.

"'With all this lot on it?'

"'How else are we going to rescue the lady?'"

"They didn't know you," said Debbie.

Maggie gave her a look. "I can be a lady when I want. Anyway, they proceeded to have an argument as to how best to rescue me. *Come on Maggie,* I thought. *There are no bones broken. Think Debbie. Think dance. Think I'm a frigging turtle upended on a beach. Turtles can't right themselves.*

"The manager arrived. 'Get all the goods off the dais, immediately,' he said. 'When we've done that, two of you support the chair while Carl and I shift the dais.'

"Fifteen minutes later, I was being given a coffee and kind words, when all I wanted to do was take my exposed pussy home."

That was when the laughter got out of control.

"I've got them on today. Look." She lifted her skirt. She was wearing black bikini style knickers and a black suspender belt. "And now I'm going to have to take them off and buy some new ones in TJ's."

We had to hold onto each other we were laughing so much as we teetered on stilettos down London Road, not a dry pair between us. That was three years ago. It was my first visit to TJ Hughes. First stop, buy new knickers; second, the ladies.

Today, I wasn't feeling like cackling with laughter and even the memory of that seminal gang jaunt failed to cheer me up. I didn't know how to shake off the jolly season blues, because the day of my sister's invasion was approaching. For Claire's sake, I'd spun a web of Christmas spirit. I'd decorated the house. She, John and I would decorate the tree next week, after we'd been to Delamere forest to choose one. This was a ritual begun when Claire was two and Trevor, Maggie and Stuart had moved into The Old Vicarage. The same year John and I went to Paris and I bought the Mona Lisa earrings.

John's job was to test and arrange the lights. He would then repair to his den with a mug of coffee and the newspaper while we arranged the baubles. When we had finished, Claire would run upstairs to tell him it was done so he could inspect it.

The only Christmas I could remember enjoying, when I was a child, was the one we'd spent with Uncle Charles and Aunty Ruby. When we'd got home, Pearl had said, "Well we shan't be doing that again. The food was far too rich for my stomach."

Annie had added, "And they spoil Einna."

I'd been allowed liberties that were forbidden in Hunstanton, like two spoonful's of cream on my pudding, and brandy butter as well. When Pearl had demurred, Ruby had said, "It's Christmas, sister," and that had been that. I'd known not to smile in glee. *Never smile at a crocodile...*

Dr. Spock had been my every day reading when Claire was a baby, so I understood the necessity for boundaries. They were important for a child's security. But I wanted Claire to feel she had rights as well as responsibilities, so on the Tuesday before the Christmas tree weekend, when I discovered her in our bedroom arranging my earrings in a pattern on the dressing table, I didn't feel she had done anything wrong. Rather I was intrigued by her creativity. I wondered if they made collages in her primary school? John would have reprimanded her for touching my belongings. Annie would have punished her.

"They were in a big tangle, Mummy," she said.

Before I met Maggie I'd had no particular penchant for earrings. I'd bought some silver knot earrings on honeymoon and worn them or my cornelians until the first gang jaunt. Paddy's Market had a stall with earrings that might have been part of a Mary Quant dress show. They were extraordinary, arty and so cheap they were giving them away. Maggie had encouraged me to buy two pairs. The Annie, pearl ones were in a small cardboard box in my dressing table drawer. The Pearl, gold hoops were in a similar box in the camphor smelling chest in the spare room. The turquoise ones May gave me I only wore when we went to their house for a meal; I was frightened I would lose them.

After Paddy's Market day, I gradually amassed about twenty pairs, including the Monas and the ridiculous Christmas bauble ones.

"Well, they're not tangled now. That's a very pretty pattern," I said.

"Can we keep it, always?"

I laughed. "I do like to wear them."

"You can. But you have to put them back in their proper place."

"Claire, I've got an idea. I won't be a mo."

I went down to the shed which served as our second larder and storage space. It wasn't a wooden one like my father's shed, but brick built and attached to the house. It was big enough for John to keep his phut-phut, Vespa in, as well as groceries and other household stuff. I called it 'stuff', for it ranged from gardening implements to D.I.Y. tools, to odds and sods.

In a corner were some old cork boards John had brought home from school, thinking they might be useful, one day. That day had come for one of them. Having chosen the least drawing pin holed, I took it up to our bedroom. Together, Claire and I arranged my earrings on the board, using pins from my needlework box. Then I hung it on the wall by the dressing table.

"Pretty," said Claire, smiling. "Can I have my ears pierced soon, like Jade?" Jade was her best friend, in school.

I shook my head. John and I would be in agreement over this one, though I suspected he would try to veto the age I'd suggest. "You can have your ears pierced when you're thirteen. Annie wouldn't let me have mine done until I was sixteen."

"She's mean. Can I wear your pink dangly ones when I'm thirteen?"

Claire's favourite colour was pink, despite all the other rainbow colours I'd encouraged her to like. I resorted to parental delaying tactics. "We'll see," I said and changed the subject. "Do you know what we're doing on Saturday?" She shook her head. "We're going, to The Old Vicarage for lunch, then Delamere forest to choose our Christmas tree." The gang plus husbands and children would be there.

"Is Bill coming?"

"Yes."

"And Debbie and Dave and Angela?"

"Yes."

"Stuart?"

"Well, he lives at The Old Vicarage, doesn't he?"

"Sophie and Jacob?"

"Everyone. Maggie wouldn't leave anyone out, would she?"

"No. I like Aunty Maggie. She's funny."

I glanced at my watch. It was five o'clock. John wouldn't be in until six: a staff meeting. "Do you want to watch TV while I get our meal?"

"Is it *Magpie* today?"

"Yes."

She ran into the lounge. The phone rang just as I was about to peel potatoes.

"Why do I do it? The bloody staff are turning my hair grey." It was Maggie.

She was in the middle of the school Christmas production. Starting out as an English teacher, she had gradually taken on more and more of the drama on the curriculum.

"Never. Your hair would fight before it turned grey."

"Not true. I pulled a grey strand out this morning.'

"You shouldn't do that. They say two grow in its stead."

"Old people's tales. How are the college concert rehearsals going?"

"As badly as your play rehearsals, I expect. I've written two new carols, and I'm not at all sure that either of them works."

"Today's dress rehearsal was a fiasco. I can't think why I decided to involve the staff this year; they're far less reliable than the pupils. Mrs. Mabbot's the only one who's confident with her lines. And now Trevor's decided to add himself to my list of frustrations. Do you know what he said to me this morning? 'You're not inviting the gang again this year, are you Maggie? You do so overdo things, you look grey.' I'd told him about Delamere."

"John's wearing his pinched look that tells me he's metamorphosing into Scrooge. I know he's thinking, *Christmas, humbug, she'll want extra money for presents, food and drink.*"

"'Metamorphosing', that's a big word for a student. Does it show remarkable powers of endurance, or stupidity, that we tolerate the miserable attitudes of our two husbands, Einna? Trevor never used to be like this."

"I don't know, Maggie. I hope it's endurance, I refuse to accept stupidity. John has a nasty habit of calling me stupid. Odd, isn't it."

"You've lost me. What's odd? John calling you stupid?"

"No, you, I and endurance. We don't have the Christmas conversation with Debbie or Angela, do we?"

"No. Do you know who Trevor reminds me of?"

"Tell me."

"Eeyore. He was such a lovely man when I first met him. No, I'm not being fair. He was lovely until Stuart became a demanding toddler and he decided he had to get a job and move to Munster Mansions. He still is lovely, sometimes. I just wish… Oh, there's no point."

That was the difference between us. Maggie was in mourning for the man she fell in love with. I was never in love with John, and I don't believe he was ever in love with me. If I was in mourning, it was because I'd never been in love. The more I thought about it, the more I realised I didn't know why John had asked me to marry him, or why I had accepted.

"I reckon we should write a new fairy story, Maggie, about Grunt, who is an Eeyore and Groan, who is a miser. They and the two Grizzles, Edith Grizzle and Annie Grizzle, went for a walk in the woods."

"And the big, good wolf saw them and said—"

"My dinner, ha-ha."

"But when he'd caught and eaten them, they gave him stomach ache and he was sick."

Just for a moment our laughter was hollow.

"Is Annie Grizzle coming to yours this year?"

"Yes, on the twenty-third."

"What's your mother doing?"

"She's going to my Aunt Amethyst's. She always goes to Amethyst's. What are Edith and your dad doing?"

"I don't know. I know I find Edith easier now. I mean she loves the bones of Stuart, but the thought of her and Trevor… They find it so difficult to relax in each other's company. If it were just my dad, it would be fine." I could hear Maggie's shiver. "That brother of mine won't invite them, will he? 'Brenda gets terrible migraines, Maggie.' I am going to have to try to persuade him to have them this year. If they do come to us, Trevor will hole himself up in the attic like a catholic priest hiding from the Roundheads. It's such a shame. I'd love my dad to be with us."

The stream of laughter that was always gurgling along when we talked, trickled out of my mouth as a picture of Trevor bricking himself up, invaded my mind. An echoing giggle rippled along the wires. That's what always happened. Any member of the gang could start a ripple and when we were together it was like a waterfall.

"Oh, Maggie," I gasped. "If I don't stop laughing, I'll wet my knickers."

"So soon?" said Maggie. "I think my present to you should be incontinence panties. Do you know, I saw an advert for recycled ones the other day."

Claire stopped watching *Magpie* and stared at me with five-year old tolerance. She was used to me giggling when I was on the phone to one of my friends.

"Do you know what we need? Some, *Get out of that kitchen, and rattle those pots and pans*, time. What are you doing next Thursday?"

"Thursday? Aren't you in school?"

"The Head's given all those involved in the Christmas play, the day off."

"Can't remember, let me check." I grabbed my work bag off the floor and ferreted in it for my timetable. "It's the last day, so very little. A tutorial with Ruth."

"Thursday's Angela day off now she's doing a four fifths timetable. She and I think we need a jaunt; a wig type jaunt. What do you think?"

"I think you're a traitor, Harvey. You know you have to discuss everything with me first. I want a divorce, you've been unfaithful." I pretended to cry. Claire frowned. "I won't go on any jaunt now, not even if you beg me."

"You need a laughter booster injection to immunise you against John and Annie."

"Yes, but I'm still not going on a jaunt."

"You need a Beethoven wig."

I could feel my insides fizzing, as the laughter bubbled.

"Not a big enough incentive."

"You need to buy full face masks for John and Annie, like the ones in that shop on Ranelagh Street."

The year before we'd happened upon a shop selling a variety of imported goods from far-flung places, including huge tribal masks; some of them would have covered you from top to toe. They were amazing in their ugliness; masks to instil fear, perhaps? But they made us laugh, especially when Angela told Maggie she ought to buy one for Trevor so he could hide his miserable face behind it. Trevor saw Christmas as an unnecessary interruption to normal living. It meant he had to leave off composition, descend from his eerie and socialise. She held one up in front of her to demonstrate. It was black and white, with huge lips and a bulbous nose.

"The mouth is a bit like the mouth in the mask of tragedy," said Debbie.

"This one's better," said Maggie. "It's grinning." She held it up in front of her face. "Trevor wouldn't have to pretend he was enjoying himself."

That was it. We had to try every one they had. Elephant head masks, jackal masks, and caricatures of human faces masks. They were much too expensive for us to buy, so we each bought a packet of joss sticks.

Mask memory collapsed me into a helpless, giggling idiot. When exactly had I become this, prone to knickers' wetting person? Sometimes I had to pinch myself to make sure I was still Einna. I did used to giggle with Ruby and Charles, sometimes, but never like this, never knickers' wetting giggles.

"Oh, okay then. I'll postpone my tutorial until next term. I imagine Debbie'll be okay, because she only works Mondays, Wednesdays and Fridays." Debbie was doing an M.ED with the Open University.

"Has Angela told you the Head's asked her to take some cookery classes?"

"No, that's great. Perhaps it will encourage her to start that recipe book. She's so creative with raw ingredients."

"Just what I said. Where shall we meet?" asked Maggie.

"Since you mentioned them, the wigs, I should think."

"I'm not sure we'll be allowed in Lewis's."

"It's our right to go into the shop with the statue exceedingly bare; it's every Liverpudlian's right."

"You're not a Liverpudlian."

"I am in heart and mind."

"I don't think hearts and minds count."

"Oh all right, but you, Debbie, and Angela are. I can belong on your tickets."

"No, Debbie is not. How dare you. She and Bill are woolly-backs. As for Angela, she's upper middle class You can't be a scouser if you're posh."

"Whoops, oh sensitive scouser. I still think we could chance meeting in Lewis's."

"And run if the pink dragon appears? You did look like Beethoven, you know."

"I didn't. That was Angela. I had the Jayne Mansfield one on, and you said, 'You'll have to buy falsies if you're going to go for that wig; your tits aren't big enough.' Remember?"

"I remember you singing about the exceedingly bare statue, and putting on a pair of Christmas bauble earrings. The Pink dragon made you buy them."

"But that was fair, wasn't it? You can't try on earrings for pierced ears and then put them back. I wore them on Christmas day, hoping Scrooge and Grizzle would be amused, but they looked as though they were sucking lemons instead of eating turkey. Now that was stupid."

"What was stupid?"

"To be naïve enough to imagine John and Annie would find Christmas bauble earrings amusing, especially as I know they deplore my taste in earrings."

"At first, we thought the pink dragon was another customer, trying on wigs, didn't we? Debbie asked her if she was going to a fancy dress party as Mrs. Slocome from *Are You Being Served?*"

"That was the first pelvic floor challenge," I said. "The second was the masks. Oh Maggie, the number of times we've trailed round Liverpool carrying wet knickers in our bags."

"Do you remember the lads outside TJ Hughes?"

"Get em off!"

"We can't. They're in our bags… Their faces."

I was now crying with laughter. A small hand tugged at my jeans. "Why are you doing a dance and crying, Mummy?"

"I'll ring you back, Maggie, I need a wee right this moment." I hung up. "You jiggle about when you need a wee, don't you?" I said.

"Annie says it's rude to say 'wee'."

"Annie's wrong. And I need one right now."

"Are you unhappy, Mummy?" she called as I waddled down the corridor.

"No, why do you ask?"

"Because you were crying."

"I was crying because Aunty Maggie was making me laugh."

"It's a good trick."

"What is?"

"Crying and laughing at the same time."

When I rang back, Maggie said, "That was a long wee."

"Sorry. I got into a discussion with Claire about tears of laughter and Annie saying 'wee' is rude."

"How philosophical, and how typical of Annie."

"Do you know, Maggie, I sometimes look in the mirror and wonder who I'll see. If I'm able to be like this with you, why can't I cope with the idea of John and Annie together at Christmas?"

"The same reason I find Edith and Trevor together a potential nightmare. It's the uncertainty as to how they'll behave and the desire to make a nice Christmas for the children."

"Of course. You are so wise, my friend. Have I told you Bill wants to join us on our jaunts? He really is one of the nicest men we know; in fact, he's a saint."

"Now that's going too far."

"He's got a saintly nature. It wouldn't be a burden to have him with us," I said

"It would. Think of his trumping. No saint trumps like Bill does."

"We don't know that. I can just imagine Saint Peter enjoying a good trump. It would cheer him up. It must be pretty boring having to sit at those gates every day. And as far as Bill goes, I'm convinced it's the beans; all they ever eat are beans and pulses. Debbie takes their vegan diet to ridiculous extremes. She's getting her knickers in a right old twist over what to cook for Christmas."

"I don't think she knows how to cook anything other than beans and pulses. Do you know what Bill told me, once?" Maggie imitated his slow, Saint Helen's drawl. "'I'm thinking of going to see the doctor about this flatulence, Maggie. Debbie says I'd better do something or the bed'll lift off right through the roof one night.' I told him it was the beans, but he didn't believe me. He said, 'If it were the beans, Maggie, I'd have been trumping since I were a lad. All I ever ate were baked beans and Weetabix.' How did 'wee' make you think of Bill?"

"Wee, fart, Bill. I'm sure I didn't use to fart when I went for a wee. I think it's an age thing."

"You're only twenty-seven, for god's sake, Einna. Anyway, it's out of the question. If we let one in, we'll open the floodgates. The gang won't be safe."

"Don't worry. Debbie told him he couldn't come. He was most hurt, apparently. He looked so crumpled she almost gave in. 'But they like me,' he said."

Of course we liked him, but Maggie was right; let Bill come and we'd be obliged to ask the others. It wouldn't be the same. As soon as we started laughing, they'd look disapproving, and probably say something cutting, or John would. I caught a glimpse of myself in the mirror. A panda stared back.

"Guess what, friend? I'm a panda with a damp fanny."

"Why panda?"

"Because my mascara's run."

"Do you know, Einna, it's a wonder we're still sane."

"Did you use the word 'sane' about yourself just then?"

"If my arm could get down the phone line, I'd give you a good slapping."

"You and who's army, Edith? What are you going to give her and Grunt for Christmas?"

"I would have thought that was obvious."

"Not a mask?"

"Uh-huh."

"I shall have to give Annie and John one each, shan't I? Thinking of them hidden behind a tribal mask helps."

"I wonder whether they have the power to change behaviour."

"Oh I think so; they have to be magic, don't they?"

"In that case, Debbie ought to give Bill one."

"What on earth for? He doesn't need to change."

"You've forgotten the farts. He needs a bum mask."

"It would just make his farts echo."

"Do echo farts stink?"

"Maggie, this conversation is deteriorating into schoolboy, toilet humour. Claire will repeat the word, 'fart' at every opportunity, and John will be furious. Tell me where we're to meet, and Debbie and I'll be there."

"I think it's best if we come to you. Then we can decide what way round we're going to do things. I'll ring Angela now."

When I put the phone down, I heard a key being turned in the lock. John had arrived home.

"Is that the new fashion in make up?" he said. "If it is, I don't like it."

"Oh. Ha-ha!"

Claire got up. "Mummy's been crying and laughing. It's a good trick."

"Why?"

"Because it's hard to do. I bet you can't laugh and cry at the same time, Daddy. She was talking to Aunty Maggie."

"What a surprise. She rang Mummy, did she?"

John was checking up on who phoned who... sneaky.

"Yes. Then Mummy needed a wee. And it isn't a surprise. Aunty Maggie always makes Mummy laugh."

"Yes she does, doesn't she?"

Oh the weight of disapproval in that sentence. Claire ran over and put her arms round my legs. "Aunty Maggie makes me laugh too. She and Mummy were talking about farts. Fart's a funny word, so's poo. Fart poo, fart poo." She started giggling and couldn't stop. Her laughter was infectious. It set me off again.

"Stop it, both of you. Do you hear me, Claire? Stop it, or you'll have to go to your room. Really Einna," he mouthed, "standards."

I gathered Claire up in my arms and sat on the sofa. "Shall I tell you a rhyme Aunty Ruby told me when I was a little girl? Her granny told it to her, so it's very, very old."

"And Daddy?"

"And Daddy. Sit down Daddy and listen." John stayed where he was.

> *"A fart is a musical sound.*
> *It comes from the land of bum.*
> *It travels through the valley of trousers,*
> *and comes out with a musical hum.*
>
> *A fart's a mechanical device*
> *which gives the bowels ease.*
> *It warms the bed in winter,*
> *and suffocates the fleas."*

Claire rolled off my lap she was laughing so much. "I shall wet my knickers like you, Mummy, if I don't stop laughing."

John's face told me what he was going to say, but I was saved by a phone call. It was Tony; they belonged to the same rugby club. While he was on the phone, I poured a glass of wine for myself and some juice for Claire. Friday was wine and a square of dark chocolate. Angela often said, "Give yourself a treat, woman. If you don't, no one else will." It was sound advice.

On jaunt day, after John had left for work, I walked with Claire to school and then returned home instead of going to catch the bus to college. As I was putting spare knickers in my bag, the doorbell rang. I ran downstairs to answer it.

"What a beautiful morning," said Debbie as she gave me a hug. "I feel like singing the song." Before I met Debbie, Maggie had said she was like a little brown mouse. I could see why but I'd added, 'with character'.

It was one of those rare December mornings, a pure azure sky and, in this windiest of cities, no wind, so we took our coffee into the yard.

"What did you tell John you were doing?" she asked

"I didn't. I couldn't bear another lecture on standards. You ought to have heard the furore over my phone conversation with Maggie. Claire overheard me say 'fart'."

Debby sniggered. "Oh no, pelvic muscle action needed already." She crossed her legs. "Coffee goes straight through me. I shall have to go to the loo. What time do the others arrive?"

The phone rang. "Ten-thirty," I said as I ran to answer it. "I hope this isn't a hiccup."

"Einna? What are you doing there? I knew something wasn't right at breakfast, you were looking shifty. You're not going to college, are you? You're skiving."

Not, 'Are you ill?' Not, 'Has something happened to Claire?' Why was it that when I felt angry, heat rose behind my eyes?

Web needed. "It's not Einna," I said in a voice, which I hoped was a passable imitation of Debbie's. "It's Debbie."

John knew that I'd told Debbie she could use our house while their bathroom was being sorted. Apparently, a pipe had been leaking behind the tiling for many years; just a drip leak, but enough to cause severe damage. Bill had noticed the tile grouting had blown.

Debbie had an Open University essay to send off before Christmas, and the noise plus the interruptions were making it impossible for her to concentrate.

"Debbie? Oh, yes, your essay. You don't sound like your usual self. Nothing wrong, is there?"

"No, of course not." My attempt at a St. Helen's accent was getting stronger by the minute.

Debbie, on her way back from the lavatory looked at me in disbelief.

"The workmen just wouldn't leave me in peace this morning."

"Right," said John. "Are you sure you're okay?"

"I'm fine, John. I've got a bit of a cold, that's all."

"Well, Could you do something for me? I think I've left my keys in the shed door. Can you check? If they're there, pop them on the telephone table in the hall, will you? I'll pick them up later."

"I can't see the door from here. Just a mo." I put the phone down on the shelf and went outside. Sure enough, John's keys were dangling from the keyhole.

As I passed her, Debbie whispered, "If I sound like that, I'd better book some elocution lessons."

"Don't set me off." I whispered back, as I picked up the phone. "They were there, John."

"Thanks Debbie, and if you want my advice, you should go home to bed. You sound terrible." He rang off.

"It's a bloody good job you're going to be a violin teacher, not an aspiring soap star," said Debbie. "I don't think I can begin to describe what you sounded like."

Twenty minutes later, we were still laughing when we heard John's scooter phut-phutting into the drive. We froze. We panicked. We put our mugs down, only to pick them up again. We ran into the kitchen, only to scurry back into the yard.

"What are we doing?" I said. "This is ridiculous. I've deferred my tutorial and you don't have to be in work today."

"I know," Debbie whispered. "It's just that…"

"You're both mad. You ought to be certified," snarled John as he came into the kitchen. "I thought better of you, Debbie. I've always imagined you might be a restraining influence on Einna, like Annie is. But I can see I'm wrong." He went into the hall, grabbed his keys, and slammed out the front door. The Vespa phut-phutted away, echoing his indignation.

Laughter bubbles up in people for a variety of reasons. We laugh because we find something funny. We laugh for joy. We laugh out of relief. We laugh out of embarrassment, and we laugh because if we don't, we'll cry. I laughed now because I was near to tears; tears of frustration that I'd married a man to whom I lied for a quiet life; a man who believed one of my best friends was like Annie. Debbie sensed I was on the edge. She put her arm round me. The phone rang again. I thought I was safe to answer it.

It was Maggie. "Where are you?" I said.

"In Winnowsty Court. We saw John's penis extension in the drive, so we thought we'd better stay out the way till we had the all clear. Has he gone?"

"Yes, and guess what, I'm certifi…" I couldn't get the rest of the word out. I leant on the kitchen wall for support. I was laughing and crying.

Maggie, Angela, Debbie and I were a gang of witches, who laughed at our husbands, our children, our work and ourselves.

Chapter Seven
Why am I Crying?

*I don't want to go
in a box.
Dead and in a box.
A hard, wooden box.
A locked box.
How would I get out?*

I wished I'd known my father. It was almost as though he were a figment of my imagination. He'd had sex with my mother on the leave before he was killed, and thus I was conceived. There were no photos, nothing to prove he'd existed, except for the shed in the back garden, gold hoop earrings which Pearl had given to me as a wedding present, and the hankies I'd found in a drawer in her dressing table when she'd sent me to look for her headache pills. Neither Pearl nor Annie had ever talked about him.

Maggie's father was rushed into hospital on Christmas Day; the Christmas day after the jaunt when John had rung about his keys and I'd pretended to be Debbie. We all knew he had angina. Maggie had talked about his health and the possibility that he might die.

"I'll be as sad for Stuart as myself," she'd said. "He's a wonderful granddad. He treats Stuart as a person, not a little boy. He was the same with me when I was little. 'Children need to be told things how they are,' he would say. 'They'll cope, as long as they feel safe.'"

Why did it seem so much worse because it had happened at Christmas? Was it because the date sealed it in everyone's memory? The phone call, the rush to hospital, the waiting, the doctors' grave faces? I didn't know the precise day my father had died. Maggie wouldn't ever forget.

I knew, from experience that the fear of those we love, dying, was an incapacitating fear. I could be gripped in a vice by that fear, with regard to Claire. Every morning, when I left her at the school gate, I was terrified I would never see her again.

When I was pregnant, I didn't think about the fear of surrendering my child to the care of strangers; fear of surrendering her to Annie's care, yes, I knew what that was like.

Why was I so afraid? I'd not experienced teacher bullying during my schooling. I was aiming to be a peripatetic music teacher. Maggie, Debbie and Angela were teachers. What child wouldn't have enjoyed being taught by them? But I couldn't protect Claire from crocodiles, nor could I ensure that all the adults and children she met would be angels.

Every afternoon when I collected her was a celebration. I knew that Pearl had never felt like that about me. I wasn't sure she felt it about Annie. But I had to be careful that my mother love didn't confine and restrict Claire. Still, I couldn't help feeling, *she's safe*, once we passed through the front door.

"We did the ugly duckling song in class today," Claire said as we took off our coats. "I told Miss you always sing it to me."

"And what did Miss say?"

"She said, 'Do you know the words?' And I said, 'Yes,' so she asked me to sing the first verse on my own."

"And did you?"

"Yes. She said I did the raspberry bits very well."

Her chatter about her day at school was interrupted by the phone. It was Annie. Her voice sounded odd, as though her mouth was full of cotton wool.

"Einna, is John there?"

"No, he's not home yet. He shouldn't be long though. I'll get him to call you back, shall I?" Now what? Why did Annie want to speak to John? Was she planning another visit?

"I don't want to talk to him, I just thought it might be better if he was there."

Odd. "Why?"

"Pearl's dead, Einna."

My stomach clenched and my legs turned to jelly. I leant against the wall for support.

"Are you there? Einna, talk to me."

"How?" I squeaked. *I didn't know Pearl was ill. Cancer? A heart attack? Surely Annie would have known if Pearl was suffering from cancer? It must have been a heart attack, like Maggie's dad.* "Was it a heart attack?"

"Yes. She was very brave. But she always suffered in silence, didn't she?"

"But I didn't know she had—" *Pearl, suffer in silence!* Annie was already re-writing history.

'Annie will you fetch me my migraine tablets? I'm going to have to lie down for a while.'

'Could you make me a chamomile tea please, Annie? I think I've got one of my headaches coming on.'

"She didn't. There has to be a postmortem. The doctor can't issue a death certificate until the pathologist is satisfied that a heart attack was the cause of death. After dinner she mentioned that she had a touch of indigestion, and asked me to fetch her tablets. When I came back, she was slumped over the table. I can't describe how I felt. It was such a shock."

A post-mortem? What could I say? "It must have been." I wanted to say something else, something comforting. "Some people don't feel pain, when they have a heart attack. The doctor told Maggie that her father didn't suffer."

"Trust you to try and belittle what our mother went through."

Annie didn't want comforting words from me. *Our mother? Pearl, our mother?* "When's the funeral?"

"I haven't had time to sort out funeral arrangements, yet. I can't do anything until after the PM."

"Would you like me to come and help?" *Please don't say, yes.*

"No, I can manage, thank you."

Perversely I felt she was cutting me out.

"You'll all come?"

"I may leave Claire with May and James."

"You and John will stay with me."

"Have you told Ruby and Charles?"

"No, not yet. I'm going to ring Amethyst next."

"Do you want me to ring them?"

"Of course not. It's my job."

We said goodbye after I'd offered more empty words. Pearl would have been sixty one next birthday. Had a heart attack robbed me of the possibility of love? Why was I wondering? Pearl wouldn't have changed in her feelings towards me, if she'd lived to a hundred.

I saw Claire coming into the kitchen with her glass and plate. *'Don't forget to wash your plate and glass and put them away.'* I heard through time. Hurriedly, I wiped the tears away with the back of my hand and held out my arms. "Do you want a cuddle?" I asked.

She put down the crockery and ran over. I picked her up and carried her through to the lounge. Little children smell so fresh. Sometimes I wanted to drown in Claire's child fresh smell. We sat on the settee. She patted my cheek, intuition telling her that something was wrong.

"Pearl's died, Claire."

"Like Snowy died?"

"Yes." Snowy was the school rabbit.

"I cried when Miss told us he'd died. I don't want to cry now. Is that bad?"

I pulled her closer. About a month after Claire was born, I'd made one attempt to appeal to the grandmother in Pearl. It had ended badly.

'But can't you see? All her friends have grannies.'

'She has a grandmother. May's her grandmother, isn't she? James is her grandfather. Isn't that enough? Many children don't have any grandparents at all. Annie didn't.'

'I didn't either.' I was fed up with her insensitivity.

'I really don't see why you're making all this fuss.'

'Because...' Tears of anger, tears of distress threatened. I rang off.

Two wrongs, three, four, five; wrongs piling up over the years, and the mountain was too high to climb.

Claire put her cheek close to mine. "Why didn't Pearl like being called Nana?"

I was saved from answering because we heard the key turn in the lock of the front door.

"Daddy," said Claire. She put her thumb in her mouth.

Since college, since Claire had started school, the homecoming routine had, perforce, changed. We weren't always in the kitchen. Sometimes we weren't even in the house. Today, we heard John's formal, black shoes tapping their way down the hall, knowing he wouldn't find us in the kitchen.

"Einna?"

"We're in the lounge."

There was the sound of a tap being turned on. A few minutes later, he came through.

He was holding a jar of instant coffee. I wasn't sure how to break the news. Why did I feel so sad?

"Claire, take your thumb out your mouth," he said.

"Mummy's sad, and when Mummy's sad, I'm sad too," said Claire, thumb still in mouth.

"That still doesn't mean you..."

"Pearl's died."

"Pearl's died? Oh my... I don't understand. She wasn't ill or anything. Annie would have told us if she'd been ill. Was it a heart attack?"

"Yes. There has to be a post mortem."

"Of course. Sudden death. I'm sorry, I liked your mother." He sat beside us on the couch and removed Claire's thumb from her mouth.

She frowned and hid her face in my chest. "But... I didn't... I mean your relationship wasn't exactly..."

"I know. I think it's the shock."

The phone rang and John answered it. "It's Maggie," he said. "I presume you'll want to take it?"

Claire scrambled off my knee. "I'm glad Aunty Maggie's rung. She'll make Mummy laugh."

I got up and he handed me the receiver. "Hi, Maggie."

"I had such a weird thought, and I had to ring you. I always seem to be involved with women who have knickers' problems. There's the gang who wet their knickers whenever we laugh and Debbie who went knickerless to her college interview. What are we like? "

I smiled. Claire looked at John. "See Daddy," she said.

"Einna, before you get wholly wrapped up with your friend, there's no instant coffee left."

"Oh sorry, I didn't check. There'll be a new jar in the shed, I..."

"Right." I knew what the 'right' meant. His rule had been ignored. Whoever finished something, replaced it. I didn't remember using the last teaspoon of coffee, but now wasn't the time to discuss it. I didn't really like instant coffee. Mostly I drank tea.

"Either John's playing up, or you've gone loop de," said Maggie.

"John's unhappy about having to fetch a new jar of instant coffee from the shed. He could have ground, but..."

John gave me a look and walked out.

I killed him with a neat dagger between the shoulder blades. *He and Pearl can share the same coffin.* What was I thinking? That was sick.

"Apart from coffee, how's life?" Maggie asked.

"Odd." I told her about Pearl dying.

"And John had the gall to go on about coffee?"

"To be fair, he's a bit puzzled by my reaction."

Out of the corner of my eye, I saw Claire put her thumb back in her mouth.

"I don't understand why I cried. I still feel tearful. I mean it's not the same for me, as you. I understand your grieving for your dad, but—"

There was one of those conversational pauses where words mustn't be allowed to intrude on feelings; a natural one minute silence. Then Maggie said, "It's the umbilical cord, Einna. I mean, why do children want to return to an abusive situation rather than stay with foster parents who're kind to them? I only have to think about Lorraine to be reminded of that."

"Lorraine?"

"She was one of the cleaners at St Benedict's. I say 'was', because she moved to Sefton. We got into the habit of having a chat after drama or dance club. One day, I found her crying in the cupboard where all the cleaning materials are kept. She told me her kids had been taken into care because her partner had been abusing them. I was so shocked, I didn't know how to react. To be honest, I didn't know whether to scream at her for not realising what was going on, or hug her because she was in such distress. He wasn't the father of her children; she'd divorced him soon after her daughter was born because he sold all their furniture to feed his heroin addiction. It was her present partner, Stephen. Apparently, her ten-year-old son said something in school that alerted the teachers. She asked me if I would go to social services with her. She wanted her children back. I agreed to go and, to cut a long story short, they told Lorraine she could see her children whenever she wanted, as long as a social worker was present because her daughter had told the police and social worker that Stephen had drawn on her face with his pen.

"'I hadn't noticed, Maggie. I thought her face was sticky from sweets.' It sounded reasonable, Einna, I mean the child hadn't said anything other than that to her mum, but I felt sick. Had I offered to help someone who'd colluded in the abuse of her children? I mean I didn't really know her.

"Stephen was found guilty and sentenced. Nothing was proved against Lorraine, so the children were allowed to go home. Not their Huyton home. Social services moved them to Sefton. And this is what I still can't believe; she goes to see the shit in prison. How could she? How could she bring herself to see him? I bet she takes him back when he gets parole."

"Social Services won't allow that."

"I hope not. They did warn her that if she did, her children would be taken into care again, but things do go wrong, especially as she moved from one district to another. Social services are overstretched. Files can go missing. And what do people who are in power really care about ordinary people? They mouth platitudes before general elections because they want to win. Afterwards, they renege on promises and make across the board cuts. How many times have we heard about investment in education, and health?"

It sounded cynical, but I knew there was more than a grain of truth in what she said. "Will you grieve for your mum, when she dies?"

"I don't know. She can be such a bitch. I expect so, given what I said about the umbilical chord. Pearl and Edith cared for us for nine months, whether they wanted to or not."

"True." A biological caring. "I thought you were going to say, *dragon*." I'd met Edith. She could be charming, but she could also glower and spit fire words.

"Dragon, bitch, both words suit her. I can't remember a moment in my childhood when I enjoyed her company."

I wondered when the word, *bitch*, came to be used as way to describe a nasty woman? Bitches aren't that different from dogs, in character. I'd come across plenty of sweet tempered bitches.

"It's odd the way memory works, isn't it? I have loads of lovely memories of my dad." There was another pause. "I may grumble about Trevor, the way he seems to have changed, but I have lots of memories of good times with him as well."

I looked at Claire. Would she be talking to her friend, Jade, about me as a dragon, a bitch, when she was an adult? I felt as though I were looking through a glass into the future. If I stood still, in one spot, I could see clearly. If I moved, even slightly, the whole picture shifted, became warped. When I put down the phone, I felt slightly dizzy, out of kilter. I stood still for a moment and closed my eyes.

"You only laughed a little bit," said Claire, as I sat down beside her again. "You always laugh lots when you talk to Aunty Maggie."

"Do I?"

She nodded. "Do you love Aunty Maggie?"

"Yes, I do."

"Do you love her more than me?"

I hugged her. The idea of loving anyone more than I loved Claire was ridiculous, crazy, unthinkable. Could I explain love, so she would understand?

"Daughter love and friend love are different, Claire. Sometimes I feel like eating you, I love you so much. I don't want to eat Maggie."

She giggled. "Or Debbie, or Angela. Will you miss Pearl?"

"I don't know, Claire." That was the truth. Possibly the idea of loving her?

"If Maggie dies, will you miss her?"

"Yes I will."

"And me?"

My heart plummeted through the lounge floor. "You aren't going to die until you are a very old lady. You'll be a beautiful old lady sitting in a comfy chair, wrapped in a woollen shawl."

"No, your black baa-lamb coat. I always wear your black baa-lamb coat when I'm cold. Are all grannies cold?"

She was right. She made my friends laugh. Debbie called her a *Tsarina*. "I don't know. But you won't be cold in the baa-lamb coat, will you? Lots of old men will ask you to marry them—"

Claire shook her head. "I'm never going to get married," she said. "There's too much quarrelling. I'm going to have lots of children but no husbands. If I tell you a secret, will you promise not to tell?"

"I promise."

"Cross your heart and hope to die."

"Cross my heart and hope to die."

She pulled my head close, so she could whisper. Her breath tickled my ear. "I love you more than Daddy. Is that bad?"

It was sad, not bad. "You probably love Daddy differently. Like I love Maggie differently."

She shook her head. "I don't. When Daddy tickles me, he's too rough. It hurts. It doesn't make me laugh. I love it when you tickle me."

Was that it then? Was love dependent on tickling ability?

"And Daddy tells me off for sucking my thumb. I only suck my thumb if I'm sad or scared. He makes me scared sometimes. I don't like it when he shouts. That's two more things why I love you better. You don't shout at me or make me scared. I don't think I loved Pearl 'cos she didn't love me, or you." She frowned. "And I don't love Annie. She's bossy like Daddy and she cheats when she plays games with me. Not like you cheat, Mummy."

"I don't cheat."

"You do, you do. You cheat to lose. Annie cheats to win. Can I tell you another secret? Sometimes I hate you." She put her hand over her mouth as though she wanted to push the words back inside. "That's bad, isn't it?"

"No. It's quite normal."

"I hate you when you won't let me have a sweet." She looked at me with a sly smile on her face. "Sometimes I pinch one when you're not looking."

"I know. I've got eyes in the back of my head." *I won't ever beat you, Claire.*

"Why can't I have one when I want?"

"Sweets aren't good for your teeth, poppet." I hoped it was that and not because I enjoyed having power over her.

"Mummy, were you in Pearl's tummy, like I was in yours?"

"Yes."

"It's funny to think of being in a tummy. Can we look at my pictures?"

"I don't see why not. You stay here and I'll go and get them."

The door to the room that was part spare room and part John's den, was open. He hadn't shut himself away this evening. He was stretched out on the bed, arms behind his head, staring at the ceiling. Today's newspaper was lying across his chest.

"I am sorry about Pearl," he said.

"Thank you."

I got the photo album out of the bottom drawer of the linen chest. I was used to the smell of camphor now. It was as strong as the day we moved into Ferndale Road. We had never discovered whether the cause of the smell was mothballs used by a previous owner, or whether the chest was made of camphor wood.

"Food will be ready in about half an hour."

"Fine."

Just as I was about to close the lid, I noticed a small box. I picked it up. Inside were the gold hoop earrings, my wedding present from Pearl. I took them and the photo albums into our bedroom. I chose a black-headed pin and hung the earrings on the board.

As I passed the spare room door to go downstairs, John said, "You don't love me, do you, Einna?"

"Love's difficult."

"I knew you'd say that. Do you think we should get a divorce?"

"No. Do you?"

"Not if you don't." He looked sad. It was sad.

"I wish… it doesn't matter. I think children are better with two parents."

"If they work from the same page."

"Yes. But I can't agree with you if what you say or do is wrong. For example, it's a myth that thumb sucking pushes your teeth forward. All children grow out of it."

He shrugged.

Claire wasn't in the lounge when I went back down, she was sitting at the kitchen table and she had helped herself to another glass of milk. She opened the first album. "I like me when I was a baby. You haven't got any photos of you when you were a baby. Why not?"

"Nobody had a camera in our house when I was a baby."

There were plenty of photos of Annie as a baby, taken by a professional photographer. Pearl had one on her chest of drawers and Annie had a small album full of poly-photos.

Before my marriage to John, she'd given me some of the photos she'd taken of me when I was four. She'd been given a Brownie Box camera for her twelfth birthday. The photos were small and had crinkly edges. I was a solemn looking child. The only photos where I was smiling were at Charles and Ruby's. I left the photos in Hunstanton. Annie brought them with her, on her first visit.

"You forgot these," she'd said.

As soon as she'd gone, I'd torn them up and thrown them in the bin. "You controlled my childhood, you're not going to control my marriage." I'd told the fragments as they fell into the detritus of daily living. But of course she tried.

"Aunty Ruby shows me pictures of you when we go to her house. She has one in a frame in her bedroom. She has one of Uncle Charles and one of me as a baby. She doesn't have one of Annie, or Pearl or that other lady. What's her name?"

"Amethyst."

"Is she a jewel?"

"Yes."

"What colour jewel?"

"Mauve."

"I don't like mauve. Does Aunty Ruby hate Annie like we do?"

"No, Aunty Ruby doesn't hate Annie, and we don't either."

"I do. I hate her as much as I hate Carl."

"Who's Carl?"

"A boy in our school; there are two Carls, Carl Evans and Carl Williams. Carl Evans is good. Carl Williams is naughty. He says rude words and Miss says, 'Why can't you be good like Carl Evans?' Guess what Mummy? Sometimes he kicks us. Emma and I kick him back. Emma's my best friend."

"I thought Jade was your best friend."

"She was, but she likes Paula now and I like Emma."

"You and Emma oughtn't to kick Carl."

"We have to. We're being like David with that giant. You have to stop giants, Mummy."

"Yes, of course you do." I should stop feeling anxious when I leave Claire at school. I couldn't imagine her ever being bullied by anyone. She knew how to stick up for herself. She had no need of a spider.

"Can we go and see Aunty Ruby and Uncle Charles soon? I love them best after you and Emma and Nana and Granddad."

"Yes, I think we should. In fact, I've had an idea. I'm going to talk to Daddy about it, later."

"Will I go to the funeral?"

"Shall," said John, coming into the room.

"Do you want to go?" I asked. I couldn't help frowning at John.

She pursed her lips. "I don't know."

"You can tell me nearer the day." My thought was that, if she decided she wanted to go to the funeral, maybe she could stay with Charles and Ruby, and we could stay with Annie.

"Shall I ask Nana and Granddad if you can stay with them, just in case?"

"Yes please. They're my real grandparents, aren't they?"

No warning. The tears I'd pushed down into the well of lost causes, rose and swam about in my eyes. I got up and went over to the cooker to stir the chicken casserole that didn't need stirring.

"I'd forgotten, Einna, I've a meeting at the rugby club, so I won't need a meal this evening," said John. "You'll be okay?"

It was nice of him to ask. "Yes, thank you." John seemed to have a lot of rugby club meetings these days. It didn't bother me, because I liked having the house and my daughter to myself. When he came home, he smelt of beer, cigarette smoke and chips.

He kissed Claire. "Be a good girl for Mummy."

"I always am," said Claire, rubbing her face. "You ought to shave before you go, Daddy. Your face is all scratchy."

He laughed and, silently now he had his trainers on, left. The atmosphere was so different when he was relaxed. I wished... no point wishing.

"Can we have egg and chips, Mummy?" asked Claire.

"Yes, and you can have loads of tomato ketchup." The casserole could cool down and keep in the fridge for the following day.

Claire chattered about the photos as I peeled potatoes. I didn't need to interact as she was in narrative, not questioning, mode. I couldn't help thinking about Pearl and death. Would her death free me from bitterness? Would I be able to talk about her as my mother? Would I be able to wear the gold earrings? Perhaps mercurial time would tell.

Chapter Eight
Persil Tickets

A weekend in London
of laughter and fun.
But the train has been cancelled.
It's not going to run.
I have to get on a coach.
How will Maggie know?
What are you like British Rail?
This is not going to
encourage us to fly free, let go.

I was sitting on a bench at Lime Street station, wondering why no platform number for the London train had appeared on the departures board. Just as I was thinking I would have to make enquiries, the tannoy crackled into life. I thought I heard, for as with most station tannoys the voice was almost indecipherable, that I was to make my way to the entrance where a coach would be waiting to transport me to Crewe. There I'd be able to pick up the Manchester to London train. Along with other passengers, I hurried to the information desk to see if we'd interpreted the crackles correctly. What a mess! How would Maggie know I'd be arriving on a coach? If she hadn't decided to visit her childhood friend, Leila, we'd be facing British Rail turmoil together.

John's words snapped at my heels as I made my way to the entrance. "You're irresponsible. You're selfish. You're irresponsible. You're selfish." And I couldn't help thinking that he had put a blight on the trip. *Trip, trip years colliding but this time, the word was so apposite. I'm going on a trip, jaunt, break, with Maggie. John has tripped us up. Can I bring this into the rhyme? Oh, no time. I think our coach has arrived.*

Since Pearl's death and the brief, slightly odd conversation we'd had when I went to find Claire's baby photos, John and I had been amicably at odds. Was that a contradiction? If so, it was one of many.

John had given up the pretence of wanting to have sex. Part of me would have liked another baby, but I wasn't unhappy that I didn't have to put up with 'it' any more. I had come to the conclusion that he didn't enjoy having sex with me; I couldn't call it 'making love'. Perhaps he ought to have been a monk? His parents were catholic. Sometimes I wondered if it was my fault, but I usually came to the conclusion that it wasn't. I'd tried to interest him in sex that wasn't just about penetration, but he had been vehemently resistant. Then, after Claire was born, it was as though producing an heir had been the marital accomplishment he'd strived for and he could relax into a sexless marriage; he had done his manly duty.

There was no flame for me to rekindle, either. Looking back, I realised that so much of my life had been bound up with surviving the crocodile and the Pearl Queen, I had forced John into the role of knight errant. He wasn't a knight errant. I'd tried to tell Annie about my doubts and she had storm clouded them away. Claire and Emma may have been Davids fighting Goliath, I wasn't bold enough to stand my ground against a crocodile.

So, John and I lived together like a couple who didn't belong. I, in what used to be our bedroom; he in the spare room, his den. We told Claire that we disturbed each other, which wasn't a fib. I usually went to bed at about ten, John later. I got up early. John on the dot of seven-thirty. Whenever Annie came to stay, he moved back in with me. We lay in bed as though a bolster were between us.

It worked well enough. Claire seemed like a well adjusted child. We still attended some social events together; we were often at our best with friends. And we went to stay with Uncle Charles and Aunty Ruby. They had their own bedrooms and didn't find it strange that we wanted the same arrangement, even though we were much younger than them. Charles and John got on in a, *men who like sport*, fashion.

Time continued to play tricks on me, for suddenly Claire was on the cusp of adolescence and demanding more independence. She continued to share much of her life with me, but I suspected she had secrets for the ears of her friends alone, and I was constantly reminding myself that this was normal. Maggie and Debbie were going through similar scenes in their homes. Jacob and Sophie, vociferously; Stuart, who had been the noisiest of the toddlers, quietly. He was a studious boy with his eyes already fixed on medicine as a career. Claire changed her mind every week, or so it seemed. I couldn't keep up with her. At present, she wanted to be a lawyer, because, to use her own words, they made loads of money. Last week she had wanted to run her own restaurant. The week before, to be an air-hostess.

My circle of acquaintances had inevitably widened; college and work had seen to that. At the teachers' centre I enjoyed the company of a woman called Lena, my boss's personal assistant, but so far it remained a work relationship, and the women I was still closest to were my friends in the gang; according to Trevor we were as monstrous as ever. I loved each woman in a different way, but I guess I was most fond of Maggie; perhaps because she was the first friend I'd made in Liverpool. Maggie still had the ability to transform me into a giggling school girl in a matter of seconds, which was one of the many reasons why I was so excited about our proposed weekend away in London; the Persil tickets weekend. Laughter is good for us and there was little of that around John.

The saga had begun on a day in February when fill dyke blues had penetrated my soul. As I shivered my way down the hall, the phone rang. John wasn't home yet; a parents' evening, he'd said. Claire was doing her homework, so I answered it.

"They've come." It was Maggie.

"What have come?"

"Oh Einna, I know you've just got in from work, but do get your head into gear. What have we been waiting for?"

"It's a wonder I can hold the phone, my hands are so cold, let alone use my brain. The Persil tickets?"

"Yes. Why haven't you... I don't need to ask... Scrooge."

"Whatever the weather, the heating doesn't kick in until six. Claire does her homework wrapped up in my black baa-lamb coat."

"In winter, I insist on a four o'clock start. Now, do you want the good news or the bad?"

"Bad?"

"Saturday evening's performance of *Once A Catholic* is full, so I've booked for Friday which means we'll need the afternoon off work. We can't catch a train after five, that'll get us to London in time to leave our cases at Abercrombie Mansions, freshen up, and make the show. Can you ring your aunt and uncle to confirm that it's still okay for us to use the flat that weekend, and give me a bell when you've spoken to them. Abercrombie Mansions, near Fortnum and Masons, posh or what?"

"Okay, but what's the good news?"

"That we're going. Bye-ee."

My wonderful Aunt Ruby had verbal diarrhoea. I have no memory of her incessant chatter when I was young. I think it's something that developed as she got older. I loved the bones of her, as they said in Liverpool, but her conversations were like going on an *Alice in Wonderland* journey. Feeling mean and disloyal, I hoped my uncle would answer the phone.

"Darling, you must be psychic. I've been thinking about you such a lot recently, and here you are ringing me. I thought you were the man about pruning the wisteria. I've told your uncle we should wait until after it's bloomed, but he's convinced that if we leave it, it will be in through our bedroom window by the summer. It really isn't the sort of weather to go climbing ladders. I'm sure wisteria ought to be pruned in July.

"Are you coming to see us soon? I do hope so. The last time we saw you, I taught Claire to play canasta. Does she still do ballet?

"I wish your uncle would come with me to see you, but he's developed this irrational fear of Liverpool. He thinks there are gangs waiting to steal the wheels off his Daimler. He never used to think that. Why, when you and John were first married we came to see you lots of times, didn't we?"

Here we go, down the rabbit hole. "Claire's into synchronised swimming now, Ruby."

"Darling, you've grown up. You called me, Ruby. I'm so thrilled. Charles, Einna's grown up. She feels able to call us Ruby and Charles, at last. Isn't it wonderful? Oh, and she's just told me that Claire's doing some odd swimming thing instead of ballet."

I heard a muttering in the background. My aunt liked to have three way conversations on the phone.

"It's like line dancing in water," I said.

"Oh that. We've seen something like that on the television, haven't we, Charles? They put pegs on their noses, don't they? Frightfully uncomfortable I should think.

"Einna, I must tell you about the kitchen. We're having it decorated and about time too, it's been cream and beige forever, hasn't it? We've decided on dark green and white, but I'm beginning to have doubts. What do you think? Is it too adventurous for two staid people like us?"

"I'd never call you and Charles staid, Ruby. I'm sure it'll look lovely."

"That nice man from Vivienne's shop is going to do it Do you remember him? He has a slight squint in his left eye. It doesn't prevent him from being a good decorator. What's that Charles? Oh yes, the calendar."

"I was wondering if we could come for half term?"

"This one? Super. It's soon, isn't it? Now, why do I know that? Ah, Audrey, my lovely woman who does, can't come then. She has to look after her grand-daughter. I don't know, the country would fall apart if it weren't for grandparents. Oh darling, I'm so sorry. I shouldn't have said that. Pearl was a useless grandmother and a useless mother, but one shouldn't speak ill of the dead, should one?"

I didn't want to open the Pearl box. "It starts the weekend of Friday the thirteenth," I said.

"Oh, you can't come that day. I wouldn't know a moment's peace if you were travelling on Friday the thirteenth."

"We wouldn't be able to come on the Friday. John and I are at work, and Claire's at school. Won't it be too much trouble for you without Audrey?"

"No. Audrey can make up the beds before she doesn't come, if you see what I mean, and we can all go out for lots of meals. Oh, Charles has reminded me that he's got a game of golf on Sunday morning, but John could go with him, couldn't he? I'll book The Fire Station. It did use to be one, you know. The food there is super, but I expect you remember that, we've taken you there before."

"Lovely. I'll put the date on our calendar. Claire will be thrilled."

"I suppose she'll want to do all the things we usually do. Children are such pattern people, aren't they? I'm not sure croquet will be possible. It's not really the month for it. You used to love croquet when you were a tot.

"I don't know about you, sweetheart, patterns help me to remember what I'm supposed to be doing. On Tuesdays, I go to the hairdressers. On Wednesdays I pop in to see Betty in Oak Vale. That really is a very good sort of Residential Home. On Thursdays… bugger, the pattern's not working. What do I do on Thursdays, Charles?" There was more muttering. "Oh of course, I stay at home because we play bridge in the evening with Philip and Betty. On Fridays, it's market day and I meet the girls for coffee. Mind you, that's all going to have to change soon. The lovely couple who own our sweet little café have been told it needs a Ladies *and* a Gents. Bloody stupid law if you ask me. They can't afford to have one put in, so they've been forced to sell up. There are lots of splendid things about Europe but the laws aren't one. Heaven alone knows where we're going to meet now. Philip has suggested we go to The Almonry. It is nice there, but—"

There was more muttering.

"In a mo, Charles. We haven't been talking for ten minutes yet. Now, where was I?"

'With the Mad Hatter', I was tempted to say.

"Ah yes, my pattern. It's when other things crop up and interrupt it that I get really confused, like last weekend. Charles suggested we go to our local for lunch. Philip had told him it was under new management, and that the roast beef was very good. Anyway, we were just about to go out the door when the phone rang.

"'Where are you?' a voice said. It was Amethyst. 'You said you'd be here by twelve.'"

The line went dead. This was a tactic of my uncle's to save my phone bill. I waited. Just as I expected, it rang immediately.

"Charles cut me off. He said I'd been talking for fifteen minutes and it would cost you an arm and a leg. 'We shall be with you in two shakes of a duck's tail,' I said. 'Not if you obey the speed limit. It's a good thing I've done a casserole.' Your uncle was so disappointed. He's decided to take control of the calendar, now. I'm waiting to see what a mess he makes of it. It was a lovely casserole. I think they're better if they're left standing for a while."

"Would it be possible to have a word with Charles, please?"

"Of course, darling, if I can find him. You know men. They're always under your feet if you're trying to do a job, and never there when you want them."

"I thought—"

"He went out. I'll call him. He's either in the garden bothering Sid, or he's gone up to his office. He's trying to persuade his nephew to have some Highland Cattle in his meadow. I'm not sure why. I think he misses the market. There's nothing wrong, darling, is there? You'd tell me if there were, wouldn't you?"

"No, there's nothing wrong. Do you remember I asked you and Charles if Maggie and I could borrow the flat, the third weekend in March?"

"Of course. Maggie's that nice woman you brought to stay with us in October, isn't she? Lovely red hair and an amazing Liverpool accent."

I laughed. "Yes, she's a scouser through and through. Claire's got a scouse accent now."

"Scouse?"

"Liverpudlian."

"Ah, how frightfully sweet. I couldn't help noticing how well Maggie's son Stuart got on with Claire. I wonder if they'll... no, I'm romanticising again. I'll go and find Charles. You'll certainly need him where dates for the flat are concerned. I'm not privy to flat comings and goings." I heard her feet tapping away, court shoes on terracotta tiles.

"Where were you?" I asked when Charles answered.

"Out in the garden. I was picking some New Zealand Spinach for lunch. Your aunt's getting very forgetful. She asked me to pick some just before you rang."

In no time at all, my uncle told me our visit had been set in stone ever since I'd first mentioned it.

By the time John got in, Claire was in bed and I was preparing the next day's lessons. He went up to say goodnight to her.

"I spoke to Charles and Ruby earlier," I said when he came down.

"I know. Claire told me. I suppose you've planned something without consulting me?"

"Sort of. I rang up for a chat, and Ruby asked if we could manage a visit at half term."

"That's what Claire said. As it happens, I haven't got anything planned."

Checking up, cleverly disguised so Claire wouldn't know what he was up to. I didn't tell him about the rest of the conversation: that could wait. However, as I was preparing Claire's and my packed lunch, the phone rang.

"Who the hell's that, at this time of night?" said John.

"It's only ten thirty."

"I might have been in bed."

"You're never in bed before eleven."

"But I could have been."

I turned my back on him to answer it. "You were going to ring me," said Maggie.

"Who is it?" asked John.

Spider lie or truth? "Maggie," I said.

He gave me a look and disappeared upstairs.

"What was all that about?"

"Just John complaining about the late hour for a phone call. Sorry I didn't ring you back, I got immersed in preparation and then he started interrogating me about Ruby and Charles."

"Grunt and Groan. Other women don't have Grunts and Groans for husbands."

"I bet some do, and I bet some husbands have Grunts and Groans for wives. Look at your mother and Annie."

"Annie isn't married. You can't count her. And I don't want to think about either of them. They'll spoil my idea of our London trip. I think my dad died to escape Edith."

"Maggie!"

"What? We do shoulder burdens, don't we? No wonder we need wet-knickers' sessions. What did the Roly Polies say?"

"That the weekend we want the flat is fine."

"Fabby. How are they?"

"Ruby, as scatty as ever; Charles, still trying to keep her feet on the ground."

"They remind me of characters in a Dornford Yates novel. I keep expecting Charles to talk about Ruby's fine grey eyes and dainty feet."

"He seems a little worried about her memory, but she's always been scatty. Anyway, I'd better ring off or…"

"Groan will moan. Am I a poet or what? Trevor's already queried my decision to take Friday off. I'm owed, Einna, all the after school stuff I do. I'm going to see Leila. I haven't seen her since she moved to Crewe. It seems too good an opportunity to miss."

"You don't have to swamp me with reasons, friend. Is Trevor okay about looking after Stuart?"

"I haven't mentioned it yet. I suspect Stuart will have footy matches on both Saturday and Sunday, so he'll be out quite a bit. He might go to stay with Katy and Molly."

I wondered how John would react. He wouldn't want to look after Claire. He'd probably be playing rugby all weekend. *Should I broach the subject now or tomorrow? Now. Get it over with.* I knocked and went into his room. The dark cloud in the bed didn't move. It seemed that John hadn't been able to put the ten-thirty phone-call into a box and shut the lid. Or, was it because it was Maggie? His mother sometimes rang us quite late. He wouldn't have dreamt of complaining about that.

"Maggie and I would like to go to London for the third weekend in March. I'm giving you—"

The cloud sat up. "You what? Are you mad?"

I was puzzled. I'd imagined he might quibble with regard to looking after Claire for the whole weekend, but mad? Why was I mad? "I don't expect you to look after Claire. I know there will be rugby matches."

"It's nothing to do with who will mind Claire. What about the bombs, Einna?"

"Bombs? They're bomb scares John, not bombs. You don't let bomb scares stop you going to Rugby Internationals."

"Rugby Internationals aren't in central London. You didn't ring up Charles and Ruby to see how they were. You rang to see if you could borrow their flat."

"Yes, I did. But I also rang for a chat and to arrange for us to go over to see them."

"Are you telling me you would have rung if you and your precious friend didn't want the flat?"

"I ring Charles and Ruby regularly, as you know, and I asked about the flat months ago."

"Huh! You know what I think? You're taking advantage of their good nature. What about Claire if you get caught up in an IRA attack?"

"Oh, don't be stupid, John, Why should that happen? Millions of people live and work in London. We can't let terrorists run our lives."

I couldn't believe he was really having this argument with me and I didn't want to continue it. At least I could get away to my own room.

When the trip weekend finally arrived, he left for work without saying goodbye. Claire had decided she wanted to stay with her friend, Emma; fortunately I hadn't mentioned anything to May and James, so they weren't disappointed. So, apart from a slight feeling of guilt about a pretend dentist's appointment, I caught the bus to Lime Street with merry elves dancing in my mind until the announcement.

I was one of the first to board as my weekend bag didn't need to go in the hold.

"You see that man over there," said a woman who plonked herself down on the seat next to me. She pointed to a man in a grey suit. "He was very rude to me just now. I was trying to tell him we ought to complain to British Rail, because they've a duty to get us to our destination on time, not send us all round Rosie on a bus. He mumbled something and stalked off."

"But we don't know we shall be late," I said

She snorted. "We're half an hour late already." I massaged my temples. "I don't wonder you've got a headache. My knees are playing up. They always do when I'm stressed. I've told Dr. Hardy it's not arthritis, but he won't listen. He keeps telling me I have to exercise. He's not living with the pain I have to put up with. And he's a hypocrite. You should see the weight his body has to bear."

I was beginning to understand why the grey suited man had been rude to her.

The coach came to a halt on Runcorn Bridge. I could see a road-works sign ahead.

"I'm going to find out what the driver's going to do about this," said the woman.

I couldn't imagine he'd be able to do anything, but when she returned she told me there was another change of plan. We were going to Runcorn station to catch the Manchester train, instead of all the way to Crewe by coach.

"I hope passengers at Crewe are being informed about what's going on," I said.

"Why?"

I told her about the Persil tickets and Maggie deciding she might as well take the whole day off work.

"No wonder teachers get a bad name for themselves," the woman said. "As if all those holidays aren't enough."

"Both Maggie and I do lots of extra-curricular activities we don't get paid for," I said.

"Yes, well." I could almost see the war going on in her mind. Ignore me or put up and shut up. I was a useful recipient for her grumbles.

At Crewe, I got off. I saw Maggie at the ticket barrier. I waved. The guard blew his whistle. She saw me and ran. I got back on. The guard prevented Maggie from boarding and the train departed. I was off to Euston with no friend and no ticket.

"What am I going to say to the ticket inspector?" I wailed as I plumped myself down in my seat. Did I expect sympathy?

"The truth," said my travelling companion. "I can see him in the next carriage."

"I have no information about this particular offer," he said, when he arrived at our seat and I told him of my plight. "I don't suppose you have a receipt, do you?"

"No, my friend organised everything."

"Well, you have to have a valid ticket to be on this train."

I could see my London budget flying into the coffers of British Rail, and it was their fault I was in this pickle. I reached for my bag.

"I can't tease you any longer. I saw what happened. The guard was well within his rights to stop your friend from boarding, she could have had an accident. He'll make sure she gets the next train. It gets in ten minutes after yours."

I wasn't sure whether I wanted to kiss him or shout at him.

Madame Grumble wasn't so reticent. "I shall be writing to British Rail to complain," she said. "The whole journey's been very stressful. I've—"

"You can pick up a form at any station, madam." He smiled at me and continued on down the carriage.

Maggie didn't arrive in ten minutes because Euston was awash with police. There was a bomb scare. *My husband's a bloody Cassandra.*

The passengers on the Manchester train weren't allowed off and other trains were being held up outside the station.

When we did meet, Maggie said, "I don't know whether I want a cup of tea, or alcohol. What a journey! I'll give Trevor a ring when we get to the flat, to tell him we're safe. He can ring John. Save you getting an, 'I told you so'."

"How will they know about it?"

"It's bound to be on the news. Shall we go for a cuppa?"

"Charles has put a bottle of champagne in the fridge for us."

"Then, why are you keeping me here talking? Let's go."

"Isn't it a bit naughty to indulge in alcohol this early? What does Ruby say? The sun has to be over the yardarm.'

"Frazzled Scousers don't have yardarms."

"I hope they have teaspoons in the flat. I'm not sure what's actually provided."

"What have teaspoons got to do with alcohol or yardarms? Of course they'll have teaspoons. MPs and civil servants not able to have a cuppa? Unthinkable! Why do you want a teaspoon?"

"To get rid of an excess of fizz. I love the taste of champagne, but the bubbles get up my nose and can give me hiccups."

"You're seriously weird, Einna. You can use a pen or pencil if there's no cutlery."

"Paddy might have some spoons. We have to have a chat with him before we go up, Ruby was most insistent about that."

"And who is Paddy that he demands conversation from delayed, bomb scared women in need of a rooster booster?"

"Haven't I told you about Paddy?"

"No."

"He's… I suppose he's a concierge."

"Liverpool flats don't have concierges. I knew it was a posh place as soon as you told me the name."

"Liverpool flats don't have lifts that work. We can have breakfast in bed, if we want."

"How will I be able to go back to a life of connie-onnie butties and Lambrusco?"

"Maggie, I don't want to wet my knickers in the tube."

"Why not, you wet them everywhere else?"

When we arrived at Abercrombie Mansions, we saw an elderly man in a grey uniform, standing on the pavement, looking anxious.

"Paddy?" I said.

"I was beginning to get worried, madam. Sir Charles told me you'd be arriving at three."

"Did I know Charles was a sir?"

"Probably not. I told my uncle we'd arrive around three, Paddy. I'm sorry if you've been anxious. We've been delayed because of a b…" *Whoops! Paddy's Irish. Better not mention bombs and the IRA.* "I'm Einna, and this is Maggie."

"I did wonder, madam. I heard it on the news. Will I take your cases for you?"

He picked them up in a way that could only be described as deferential and deposited them by the lift. "Now, all I need to know is what you'd like for breakfast, madam?"

"I don't think we'll bother with breakfast, Paddy," said Maggie.

"Sir Charles will be very disappointed, madam. He's paid for your breakfasts. Your aunt likes Fortnum and Mason's croissants."

"That sounds lovely," I said. "Oh, and coffee, please."

"Are we being spoilt, or what?" said Maggie as the lift door closed. "Champagne and Fortnum and Mason croissants. I shall buy your aunt and uncle a present. What do Sirs like?"

"I've no idea. Us to go to stay with them, probably. So they can spoil us some more—"

"And force feed us New Zealand spinach. Yuk! I shouldn't have mentioned that hideous vegetable. I've got a strong taste of iron in my mouth."

Giggling, we let ourselves into the flat which was definitely bijou. We both collapsed on the single beds in the one bedroom. "What is this place, Einna? I feel as though I'm in a time warp, if not Berry and Co., definitely Bertie Wooster? And why is one bed higher than the other?" Suddenly she sniggered. "I've got it."

"What?"

"Sir Charles' bed has to be higher than Ruby's, so he can roll on top for a bit of nookie. Is she Lady Albright?"

"I suppose so. I don't like to think about Uncle Charles and Aunty Ruby having nookie."

"I've always called them the Roly-Polies, now I know why, Sir Roly and Lady Poly."

Our laughter, like the champagne when the cork popped, bubbled over.

"Hey, Einna, can you hear a noise?"

"No."

"Shh. Listen."

There was a click and a whirr.

"Perhaps the flat's bugged," I said.

"Bugs don't make a noise. They're hidden and silent."

The whirring and clicking stopped. "I bet it's the central heating," said Maggie.

"How disappointing, I was rather taken with the idea of someone listening to our conversation."

"I'm glad we're going to a comedy. I couldn't cope with anything serious, I'd laugh in inappropriate places."

Laughter, like a yawn, is catching and that weekend, we laughed at everyone and everything. We even laughed when we missed two consecutive trains home.

"Are you going to wear your tart shoes and poppy earrings to work tomorrow?" Maggie asked

"I might. Claire and Groan will hate them."

"So will Grunt."

We were off again. We ached from laughing.

As we pulled into Lime Street, we rearranged our faces. Maggie put on lipstick. I wiped away smudged mascara with a spat-upon tissue.

Our Persil Ticket weekend in London was over.

Chapter Nine
A Brick Wall

The words are there.
They cannot be
thrown in the bin.
They hover in the air,
like a smog
a smothering blanket.

"I'm gay, Einna."

I'd always known. I'd never known. Now that the words were there, hanging in the air between us, I experienced such a powerful sense of relief. *It's not me; not my fault.* John wouldn't have fancied any woman. I went across to him to give him a hug. He must have thought I was going to hit him, for he stepped backwards, and I was left with my arms outstretched before me. I wanted to laugh, to cry, for it seemed to symbolise all of our, years ago, sexual life. Oh my god! Not just that, my need to be loved.

He moved in with his rugby mate, Tony. My lack of interest in John's comings and goings had given them plenty of opportunity to develop their relationship. And, how naïve had I been to imagine John would play rugby on a Saturday *and* a Sunday? Apparently, it was only Claire and the thought of what his father would say that had kept him with us for so long. I wondered what had tipped the balance into honesty.

I knew it wasn't just sex that had driven us apart. Our characters were at odds. Issues important to him, weren't important to me and vice-versa. We had contrived a polished surface and worked in a desultory fashion to keep it shiny.

We sold our Ferndale Road house and I bought a three bedroom terraced house in Ivydale Road, only a couple of roads away, so that Claire could continue at the same school. Karl Marx, Claire's cat moved with us.

What parent has ever found the adolescent years an easy ride? Mostly, Claire and I trotted along reasonably smoothly. Then an un looked-for hurdle loomed. We both fell.

Once upon our history together, John had called me a drama queen. Teenager Claire could be dramatic. Often I wanted to laugh at her histrionics, but I tried to keep the laughter gurgling inside, unlike knickers' wetting sessions with the gang.

> *Tick, tock, tick, tock, Thomas Gardner*
> *signals the passing of the years.*
> *Brick by brick, the words we hurl,*
> *create a barrier wide and tall*
> *as the Berlin wall.*
> *We frail mortals fall*
> *either side of the brawl.*

I stared at the coffee I wasn't drinking and at the poems I'd written the day before. I was going to push them both under Claire's bedroom door, but my courage, my stubbornness, whatever it was, was failing me.

I had been given advice by all my friends, and still I couldn't proceed. I was back on that railway platform in Ely, staring at the rail tracks. Karl Marx jumped up onto my lap and purred loudly as he kneaded my legs with sharp claws.

Aunty Ruby always said patterns helped her remember what she was supposed to be doing. She used the wrong word; she meant 'routines'. Patterns are different from routines. Claire and I enjoyed creating a pattern with my earrings when she was five. I enjoyed creating patterns in the sand when I was eight. Jean called them mazes. If I was upset, if I'd been punished, making those mazes used to carry me into a world of brave knights, beautiful princesses, angels and crocodiles. My monster in the heart of the maze was always a crocodile.

"Why is there an angel?" Jean had asked, the day I made the first maze.

"Because princesses need angels," I'd replied. "She's a guardian angel. She couldn't stop her going into the maze, but she can help her to choose the right path out."

"Your angel is a she, not a he, then?"

"Yes." I'd looked up at her for I'd wanted to say, "She's you."

I needed a hint as to the right path now.

I had three coping mechanisms: writing poems, playing my violin, and the earring board. None of them were managing to shut out the words; they continued to ricochet off the walls into my head.

"You are the adult in the situation, Einna," Debbie had said. "It's up to you to try and find a way through."

> *A way through.*
> *A way through the rubble.*
> *The rubble of our row.*

I screwed up the scribble and chucked it on the floor.

"If the Casablanca said no alcohol, they meant no alcohol," Maggie had added.

"I can't believe you allowed yourself to behave like that. It's not like you, Einna,"

Angela had shaken her head.

Fear. Incapacitating fear. Fear that was the history of my life. My friends couldn't empathasise with it. *Throw the earrings on the track, Einna.*

I picked up the two verses, leaving the screwed up third where it lay. *Go upstairs. Knock on her bedroom door and... and... wait. If you hear anything that might be an acknowledgement of your presence, go in.*

Claire was sitting on the bed, her rucksack, the rucksack I'd given her for her sixteenth birthday on the floor beside her. I summoned up the courage to tell her I was wrong, to tell her I didn't want her to leave. Of course she could go to The Casablanca. Help! Danger! The very word screamed danger. It ran round my brain, careered through my veins and jumped about in my stomach. *Come on, Einna. You can do this. You understand. Of course you understand; she and her friends must celebrate their GCSE triumphs. Oh... I don't want you to go, daughter.* There was such a big, *what if*, in my mind.

August the fifteenth. I doubted I would ever be able to forget the date when I failed to listen, failed to understand, failed as a parent: became a crocodile.

During the holidays, Claire was rarely up before ten, so I was surprised when she popped her head round my bedroom door at eight. She looked pale.

"What's up?" I asked. "Don't you feel well? Have you got your period?" She was one of nature's unfortunates where menstruation was concerned. Her pains incapacitated her.

"Mu-um, you've forgotten, haven't you? It's THE day."

THE day? What day? And then I remembered. How could I have forgotten? It was highlighted and ringed in red on the calendar, her O-level results.

"I haven't slept. Will you take me to school? I can't face going on my own."

"I thought they sent the results."

"I can't wait till whenever that is," she wailed. "If you won't take me I shall have to ring Emma and ask if I can go with her."

"Calm down. I didn't say I wouldn't take you, did I? I meant I thought they would arrive by post, today. Do you want some breakfast first?"

"I can't eat."

"I tell you what then, when you've picked up your results, we'll celebrate by having breakfast in Lark Lane. Would you like that?"

She looked at me as though I was mad. "I still won't be able to eat. I know I've failed everything."

"Of course you haven't."

"Even if I haven't failed, I won't have got As and Bs. I won't have done as well as Emma."

"You will have done as well as Claire, and that's all that matters. I bet Emma's mum's saying exactly the same thing to her."

"I doubt it." She looked at her watch. "Can you get ready, Mum? I need to go as soon as possible. At least then I'll know. If I fail everything, I'll have to go to the job centre or something this afternoon."

"Now you're being daft. If the worst comes to the worst, and it won't, you can always re-take in September."

"I'd die rather than do that."

I saw she didn't want to be mollified. I had a quick shower and got dressed. We drove to the school in a silence heavy with anticipation.

When we pulled up outside the gates, she said, "Don't forget, only cross the fingers of one hand." She took a deep breath and opened the car door.

I couldn't help feeling that she was enjoying dramatising the moment. Ten minutes later, she and Emma came out. They were arm in arm and laughing. I sighed with relief. The histrionics were over.

"Can Emma come with us to Lark Lane? Her mum's had to go to work."

"Of course. But you have to put me out of my misery first."

She grinned. "I got five As, three Bs, and one C. What did I get C in, Mum?"

"French."

"I knew you'd guess. Mum knows I hate French."

"You hate Madame Clarke," said Emma.

"No, she hates me. Emma did do better than me, Mum. I told you she would."

"I didn't do better than you, liar. I got four As and five Bs. That's not better, is it Einna?"

"You didn't get a C."

"I didn't get five As. That's well better."

"Are we going to sit here all day while you two argue about who did best or shall we eat?"

"I'm starving," said Claire.

"No you're not," said Emma. "You're very hungry."

"Pedantic or what?"

"Oooh, big word, or what? Who's swallowed a dictionary then? Proves your well cleverer than me."

Well better. Well cleverer. A flash memory of John. *"No wonder your speech is so slovenly, Claire. Your friends don't know how to speak properly."*

English breakfast. Sometimes words had you salivating. In my mind, I could smell the bacon. Lark Lane was still a favourite haunt of the gang's, but I'd never been to Keith's for breakfast before.

The girls chose a table in the window. I ordered at the bar. "The full monty, three times, please, and Bucks Fizz."

When I joined the girls, they were discussing what subjects they would take in the sixth form. They both wanted to do English Literature.

"Doctor King is such a laugh," Emma said. "I don't know why he didn't become an actor."

"Probably same reason Mum didn't become a professional musician; very good, but not good enough."

"She's right, Emma," I said. "As far as I'm concerned, anyway."

The breakfasts arrived and, for a few minutes, there was silence as we ate.

"We're going to do something special every day this week, Mum," said Claire. "We sort of planned it all before we started our revision, didn't we, Em?" Emma, her mouth full of fried bread and baked beans, nodded. "We didn't know that we'd be treated to an amazing breakfast, though. That's an extra."

"It's yummy. Ta, Einna," said Emma. "No more revising," she sang.

"No more bloody revising. Brill," said Claire. "Tell Mum what we've planned for Friday."

"Friday's going to be best the best day ever. A girly getting ready day, and then The Casa. I can't wait. What are you going to wear, Clairey?"

"Not sure. Probably that mini Mum bought for me…"

The rest of her sentence got lost in my desperate attempt not to choke on my fried egg. *Are you both out of your minds?* I wanted to scream at them.

They continued to chatter through the rest of breakfast; plans for the summer, plans for after the summer, their light voices, scouse ringing in my ears, as my breakfast turned to a gluey mess in my mouth, which the acid in the Buck's Fizz couldn't dissolve.

When we got back to Ivydale Road, Claire made straight for the kitchen.

"I'll phone Dad. I know he'll tell me I should have done better in French."

"Before you do, I need to have a word, love." It couldn't wait any longer. I hoped my voice didn't sound as anxious as I was feeling. Her hand hovered over the phone. "You can't go to The Casablanca, Claire. You've only just turned sixteen. It's a club; you have to be eighteen to go to a club. Fran won't let Emma go. I doubt whether any of your friends' parents will let them go."

The row began with those words. I tried to remain calm. Claire alternated between persuasive tactics, histrionics and threats. It was the, "I could be dead tomorrow and I'll never have known happiness," that burst my self control. I laughed. I couldn't help it.

Thus the first row of bricks were laid.

I looked at the abject person on the bed. She had her hand on the clasp of her rucksack, press click, press click, and there I was again, sucked into my past, a doleful figure sitting on a platform waiting for a train, hoping it would come, hoping it wouldn't.

'Go away,' I said to my teenage self. *'Go back into the box where I keep you.'* Claire's future wasn't to be damaged by my past. I knew there

would be a danger of history repeating itself unless I could change its course.

'Rush across the room, Einna, and take her in your arms.' No, that was precisely how Annie used to behave, punishment and cuddles later, like the torturer who offers a cigarette. *'Repeat after me, you are not Annie. You must remove the bricks from the wall, one at a time, and... Stop clinging to the door handle.'*

"Claire, I'm sorry I over-reacted the other day. But when you said you were going to The Casablanca, I—"

"I don't want to talk about it, Mum."

"Please, darling, let me finish. All through breakfast in Lark Lane, I saw dreadful things happening to you. Luckily, you and Emma were chattering nineteen to the dozen, so you didn't notice I left half my breakfast. I love you, poppet. I know I mustn't be overprotective. But it's hard, so hard. You won't know what it's like until you have children."

"I'm never going to have any kids. Why don't you trust me? Emma's mum trusts her."

"I know she does. I gave her a ring. But she's finding it hard as well. And I do trust you; it's other kids I don't trust, well some of them. I know I wasn't listening properly, the other day. I heard 'The Casa', and all I could think of was, drugs, alcohol abuse, kids being glassed, knifed, raped. I was terrified." *I still am.*

"I'm not an idiot, Mum. My friends and I know the score. In any case, I told you; it's a huge O-Level celebration. Kids from all over Liverpool will be going. There won't be any alcohol. I expect the most stimulating drink will be coke."

My lovely, naïve daughter. That's why it's other adolescents I don't trust, not you and your friends. Some will drink before they go and some will secrete pills about their person. I can't tell you any of this; we're talking not shouting.

At last I had the confidence to sit on the bed beside her. I still wanted to put my arms around her, love her, keep her safe.

"I don't want you to leave home."

"I don't want to leave." It's true; you do feel weak with relief. I wanted to cry "I bought you a pressie yesterday," she said.

"Yesterday?" Yesterday a brick wall had been between us.

"I thought I'd leave it on the kitchen table, with a note, and when you found it you'd be sorry I'd gone. But then I thought, if I found a way of giving it to you, we'd talk, and it'd be okay again. And we are talking, aren't we?"

"Yes."

"Oh, Mum, I do love you."

"I know. And I love you."

"But I have to grow up and go out into the big bad world, you know."

"Of course you do." *Why now? I'm not prepared. You're all I've got.* "I was being a wimp, wasn't I?"

"Sort of."

"Hey you, you're supposed to contradict me."

She smiled. "Oh, yeah?" Finally, she undid the clasp and took a paper bag out of one of the pockets. She handed it to me. Inside was a pair of parrot earrings. They were gaudy and cheerful. I wanted to cry. I knew I mustn't cry. But why not? Tears could be cathartic. Tears could heal. I cried, so did Claire. I cried for the woman who'd failed to listen. I cried for the wall we'd erected.

"They're wonderful, Claire." I wondered if she had any idea just how wonderful they were? As a toddler, she used to love my eccentric choice of earrings. She created the first earring board because she didn't like them all in a tangle, in a saucer, on my dressing table. Everything changed when she started secondary school. Suddenly, they were too wacky. She wanted a more conformist mum. "I'm going to try them on, and then we're going to have some croissants for breakfast. I've got some in the freezer." I hesitated. She noticed.

"Breakfast was the beginning, and breakfast is the end," she said. "Right?"

"Right." I got up, and went across to the mirror.

"They're you, Mum."

"They are, aren't they?"

"Why do you keep those?" She pointed to the Mona Lisa earrings I'd taken out. "I mean, Dad gave them to you, didn't he?"

"Whatever gave you that idea?"

"I'm sure you told me. You often used to tell me the stories of your earrings."

"I can't have told you he gave me the earrings. I bought them when we went to Paris. It was the first time you made your feelings about Annie, known."

"I was two when you went to Paris, wasn't I?"

"Yes. Why?"

"And I let you know I didn't like Annie?"

"Your dad said Annie could come to look after you while we were away. You said, 'No Annie'."

Claire laughed. "Precocious or what?"

"You stayed with Granny May and Granddad James. Anyway, your dad got food poisoning and had to stay in bed, in the hotel, so I had two days in Paris, on my own." I didn't tell her how wonderful it was. "I bought them in a souvenir shop on the rue de Rivoli after I'd seen the picture in The Louvre. The moment he saw them he told me they were tacky. Which reminds me, you know when we were yelling at each other and I told you, you were like your dad—"

"Yeah, I know. We both think your earrings are tacky."

"Yes you do, but it wasn't that. I didn't mean it."

"I know you didn't. People just say that sort of thing in rows, don't they?"

"Yes, and they shouldn't. It was unfair of me. Of course you're like your dad, in some ways; it would be odd if you weren't, after all, you have half his genes. John has lots of admirable qualities."

"And a lot of shit ones."

"Claire!"

"Well he has. You know he has."

"We all have."

"He has more than most. Before he told me I'd done okay in my exams, he said that I ought to have worked harder at French. I knew he would."

"He didn't!" But of course he did. That was John.

One day when I was staying with Uncle Charles and Aunty Ruby, my uncle said, "One of the most important pieces of advice I can give you is, 'engage brain before opening mouth'." John would have benefited from that advice, especially where his daughter was concerned.

"He did. He never seems glad to see me, you know."

"Of course he is. He's just no good at saying it. Few men are good at expressing feelings. Surely you remember how he idolised you when you were a little girl, don't you? You were the most beautiful girl in the world."

"He's short sighted, Mum."

How contrary we humans are. We remember insults and forget compliments. We're all too complex for our own good.

"Did you tell Dad about The Casa?"

"No."

I knew what he would have said if I had: *'You give her far too much freedom; you always have. You have no standards, Einna.'*

I didn't think I would ever forget the rows that resounded around the house.

'Mum, tell him.'

'John, couldn't we…?'

'Standards Einna, there have to be standards; what does, 'I'll lend it off me friend' mean? It's not grammatical.'

'Oh come off it Dad. You know full well what it means. You're just getting at me again. I do have standards. They're me own standards, not yours. Yours are sad.'

'Go to your room and don't come down until you can apologise. You ought to back me up, Einna.'

'No she shouldn't, not if you're being unfair. And I won't want to come down. Who wants to see your meffy face, anyway?'

'Get out, now!'

The slammed doors. That was how it always ended, one downstairs and one upstairs. My days were full of slams.

When John told me he was gay and that he wanted to go and live with his lover, my first thought was, *how can you be gay? We've had sex. You have a daughter.* My second thought was, *the gay men I know are so much nicer, more accepting, than you.* My third was, *sometimes, Einna, you are so naïve; yes, you had sex, humping sex. And after Claire was born, hardly ever and then not at all.* And my fourth thought was, *peace. I shall have a peaceful home with no slams.* Ha-ha!

"Mu-um, would you and Dad have stayed together if he hadn't met Tony?"

"I doubt it. But there's a good reason I'm glad I married John, you know."

She grinned. "Me?"

"Yes, you." I couldn't bear the thought of a world without her.

"You're too nice, Mum."

"I wasn't too nice, two days ago, was I?" Mentally, I crossed my fingers. "About Friday evening, Claire." I put my hand over hers. "You can go; of course you can go. But I've got a request, is that okay?"

"You're not going to ask me if you can pick me up, are you?"

"No." With every cell in my body, I wanted to. "Please don't go off anywhere on your own. I know it's an O-Level only, night, but there are some pretty scary sixteen and seventeen year olds out there."

"I reckon you watch too much TV, Mum. You're such an old worry guts. Emma and I never do anything on our own, do we?"

"So, that's okay then?"

"Well, sort of."

"What do you mean, 'sort of'?"

"If a fit lad asks me to dance, I'm not going to say, 'can Emma come too,' am I?"

I smiled. "I guess not. What time does it end?"

"I don't know. I'll find out before Friday, promise. Is that sorted then?"

It was and it wasn't. Nothing was going to prevent an evening of anxiety, and there would be more. Claire was at the adolescent/adult crossroads. But whatever nail biting stress lay before me, I would try to muzzle my anxiety, and I wouldn't ever greet my daughter with a face to frighten ogres, if she was a quarter of an hour late. I touched the parrot earrings.

Chapter Ten

The Cold Heart is More Precious Than Diamonds

Why do you think we walked to your house?
I fancied you.
I thought we'd stroll along the river,
you in your curly black coat,
the collar framing your face
and I'd kiss you in the moonlight.

I walk down the empty street and stop outside the house where once I loved. The lightless windows stare back at me. They seem to say, 'go now, don't be a ghost haunting these rooms. Take your memories, gently by the hand, and…'

The tears were dripping onto the paper turning it into blue pulp. Trying to write the hurt away wasn't working. Had it ever worked? And it wasn't even real; it was something I imagined doing because I wanted to take the memories in my hands and transform them into a positive… *How could I have ever been so stupid? I wish Claire… No I don't. I don't want her to see me like this. She worries about me as it is.* I screwed the paper into a ball and chucked it into the bin but Michael didn't sink into the kitchen detritus. *I wish I'd never met you, you shit.* Who was it who said, *'if we don't ever suffer pain, we don't know what happiness is?'* Well I'd had enough pain in my life… *Crap, Einna. You're not in the middle of a bloody war like the people of Iran and Iraq, are you? Women in those countries, both of them, repressed and worse, now losing people they love.*

But chiding myself didn't help either. Pain, all pain, is relative.

I met Michael, the man who enticed me into a beautiful room and then kicked me out, at a concert. He betrayed me. Was it a betrayal? It felt like a betrayal. He certainly misled me.

I'd been getting ready to go to a concert at the Philharmonic Hall when the phone rang.

"Einna, Sophie's ill, I can't go tonight." It was Debbie.

"Poor sweetheart. I hope it's not serious."

"I don't think so. I suspect it's a twenty-four hour virus, but—"

"Can't Bill look after her?"

"I was just going to say Bill can't look after her, he's working late. It's that time of year, you know, pricking out etc. She's been sick twice on the landing, so it's not fair to leave her with the baby-sitter."

Bugger! Debbie and I had booked to go to this concert months ago.

"It's not just the concert. I really can't afford to take time off work at the mo. The school's being inspected next week."

I had to add to Debbie's troubles. "I doubt I'll be able to get rid of the ticket, Debbie, but I will try."

"I realise that, thanks anyway. I've rung Maggie and Angela. They're both busy."

When I put down the phone, I wondered if I should ring May. I started to punch in her number, then decided against it. She didn't like leaving James, not after his stroke.

'You'll have to go on your own, Mum. Pity I'm not here to go with you.' Claire's voice was as clear as if she were by my side instead of in Manchester where she was studying law.

Go on my own? Not a prospect I relished, but I did want to experience *The Alpine Symphony* played live. *Don't be a wuss, Einna.*

As I was handing in Debbie's ticket at the box office, a woman accosted me. "Will you sell me your spare ticket? I didn't realise this concert would be so popular."

I was delighted. I would be able to give Debbie back her money.

The first item on the programme was Steve Reich's *Music for Eighteen Musicians.*

It was clever. I could appreciate the skill of the players, but, for me, the composition was too repetitive; a bit like Trevor's *plink-plonk*.

I didn't attempt the bar during the first interval, reasoning that maybe less people would seek drinks in the second. Mistake. I ought to have ordered a drink before I went to my seat, but forgot because of time: having to queue at the box office to see if they would take back Debbie's ticket, the transaction with the woman, leaving my coat in the cloakroom, a visit to the Ladies.

I enjoyed the Berlioz, and was looking forward to a glass of wine to whet my appetite for the unashamedly romantic music of Richard Strauss, but the queue stretched out the door. Want was replaced by need. I needed a glass of wine. *How bloody pathetic, Einna.*

Queues often have a hypnotic effect on me and it was through a haze, therefore, that I became aware of someone talking. I turned round. "Did you speak to me?" I asked the man with long fair hair tied in a ponytail, muttering words I couldn't hear.

"I wasn't addressing anyone in particular, the walls and ceiling, maybe? What I said was 'you could die of thirst before you got a drink in this place'."

"I forgot to pre-order mine."

We inched forward. "So did I. My own fault. Did you enjoy the Steve Reich? You don't look the Steve Reich type, somehow."

I frowned. "What does a, Steve Reich type, look like then? You?"

He was dressed in navy Chinos, a cream cotton shirt open at the neck and a cream linen jacket. I was wearing black. I like myself in black, black with a splash of a different colour somewhere on my body. Tonight I'd chosen my Biba, poppy earrings, red sandals and a red, patent leather belt. My black baa-lamb coat, as Claire called it, was in the cloakroom.

"I didn't mean to offend you, it's just that..." He shrugged

"My outfit's Straussarian? I found *The Music for Eighteen Musicians...* interesting, but—"

"I use the word 'interesting' when I don't like something but don't want to offend."

I smiled. "I prefer Richard Strauss, Beethoven, Rachmaninov; I could go through a whole list. I've always wanted to hear *The Alpine Symphony* live."

"Ah, I haven't. I may well leave after I've had a drink. If I ever get one."

"I don't see the point of that. You could go to a pub if you're not going back in."

"But I haven't decided."

I know from experience, that time plays tricks. Waiting in that queue seemed longer than the interval, but only a few more minutes passed before it was the man's turn at the bar. He bought two white wines.

"This is for you," he said. "It's to say sorry I stereotyped you. I think I can see a space over there, come on." He walked off.

I'm to follow? I'm to trot after him, as meek as Mary's lamb, trit, trot, trit, trot across the deep pile Wilton carpet. I followed.

"Do you like contemporary art?" he asked when I caught up with him.

"Some, when I can see the skill. That goes for all the arts."

"You can't see any skill in Steve Reich's composition?"

"Yes, I can see skill, but not a huge amount by comparison with, say, Wagner. It's very repetitive."

"How dismissive."

"Maybe, but I've given you a reason. I want to be amazed by art. When I see a Turner, I know I couldn't have painted it. If I listen to Strauss, or Sibelius, I know I couldn't have composed the music."

"What about the challenge of a piece like *Music for Eighteen Musicians?*"

"Okay. Perhaps there is a challenge, especially if you're new to atonal music. I'm not. I've experienced and rejected."

"I think that's patronising."

"And I think that's the second time you've been rude to me."

"I didn't mean to be. This is just a conversation."

"Do you always come out with what you think in a conversation, no matter the effect?"

"Depends if I believe the person I'm talking to can take it."

"And that's a compliment, I suppose?"

He held my gaze. It was at this moment I knew I wanted to go to bed with him, and without realising it I was being drawn towards a land of melting landscapes, through which I would dance until I arrived at a beautiful room where I would want to stay forever.

I took a last gulp of wine and looked for somewhere to put down my glass. It was then I noticed that we were alone in the bar. "I don't believe it, we've missed the bell for the start of the second half," I wailed.

"I know. But I told you I wasn't sure if I'd bother with the Richard Strauss. I'm surprised you didn't see everyone going back to their seats."

"Why didn't you warn me? I told you how much I was looking forward to it. I can't believe I've done this. Bloody hell, that's two mistakes in one evening. Whatever's the third going to be?"

"Saying no to going for a walk with me. I bet you've got a recording of *The Alpine Symphony*. We could stroll back to yours for coffee and listen to it in comfort, if you don't live too far from the centre, or did you bring your car?"

"No, I didn't. I live near Sefton Park, and I came in by bus. This is all beside the point. I told you I wanted to hear it live. You really are..." Are what? The first man I've been attracted to since Adrian. Interesting... Adrian, not John, popped into my mind. Was I never attracted to John? I have often thought that he was just a gate to freedom. "I didn't pay good money for a ticket to listen to it at—" I was prevented from finishing the sentence, for he grabbed my hand and dragged me off. *Not true, Einna, you skipped out of The Philharmonic Hall thinking lustful thoughts.* "I warn you, I've a sharp clawed rapacious cat at home."

When we got to my house, we sat on the floor, he on the Chinese rug, with Karl Marx on his knee, me on a beanbag, which didn't have enough polystyrene bits in it, so amoebaed into a blob, and if you happened to have a mug of tea or coffee, you got wet, possibly scalded. I had its measure, no one else did. It was my secret weapon for unwanted guests.

We drank herbal teas. We listened to Richard Strauss's *Alpine Symphony*, the recording conducted by Sir John Barbaroli, and all the while I was conscious of Michael studying me in a way I found disconcerting.

He'd told me his name was Michael during our walk, and he was the first person I'd met not to comment on my name. At the time, it was such a relief not to have to explain. Later I believed it was because he wasn't interested in me.

When the music finished, he stretched, stood up and said, "Let me put you to bed, Einna."

"What?" I gasped

"I want to put you to bed. Trust me." He held out his hand.

I was confused. Was this his way of saying he wanted to have sex with me? I'd had so little experience of sexual communication.

He led me upstairs.

"This is the sort of bedroom I imagined you would have," he said, as we stood in the doorway.

"Is that like assuming I don't like Steve Reich?"

"No, it's your choice of decoration and your furniture, coupled with your love of romantic music."

"The furniture's my choice. I haven't got round to decorating yet."

"I couldn't live with anything I found aesthetically displeasing."

I shrugged. "I've had more important things to sort out, like a divorce and my daughter going to Uni."

"Ah!"

What did 'ah' mean? That he had suddenly realised the gap in our ages?

He undressed me. I pretended not to mind. He walked around me. He tilted my chin. He stroked my shoulder. I wanted to hide my stretch marks. I wanted to get into bed with him. The thought of him naked beside me, touching me, skin to skin; it was an entirely new experience and nothing like my teenage infatuation for Adrian, or my wish to feel something sensual, erotic with John. It was like my Paris dream that I'd then brought to fruition. I groaned.

"I'm cold." I said to cover it up.

"Shh…" He put a finger on my lips. "When you sit for me, you're going to have to put up with being a bit cold."

Sit for him? Who had said anything about sitting for him? "I'm not going to sit for you." *Come to bed with me. Warm me. Make love to my forty year old body… my forty…* my age cooled my desire. How old was Michael?

"You will."

"You are the most arrogant—"

Michael placed a finger on my lips. I wanted to suck it. He picked me up and put me into bed, covering me with the duvet.

"So, you're a prude?"

"No… God no. My body embarrasses me." My breasts were no longer young; they drooped slightly and I had stretch marks.

"What have you got to be embarrassed about? You've got a beautiful body." He didn't add, 'for a woman of your age'. "I shall paint you, Einna, sometime."

Had my breasts become perky with desire? Had my stretch marks vanished with yoga? I didn't make a habit of studying my body. I knew I wouldn't let him draw or paint me. I kept seeing Lucian Freud portraits.

The next day, Debbie rang to see if I'd enjoyed the concert. I told her about Michael and how he had deliberately prevented me from going back in to listen to *The Alpine Symphony.*

"Deliberately? How deliberately?"

"He didn't tell me that the interval was over."

"But why didn't you know?"

I understood why Debbie was confused. I was confused. Why hadn't I noticed? Okay, I had my back to the crowd in the bar, looking at a pillar, looking at a man whose chestnut, yes *chestnut* brown eyes were pulling me towards thralldom. "I was too busy being attracted."

"So, when are you going to see him again?"

"We didn't make any arrangements."

"What? I can't believe you. Really, Einna!"

"He said he wanted to paint me. If that's true, he'll have to contact me."

"In six months? You duffer."

I rang Maggie. Trevor answered. "Hi Trevor, is Maggie in?"

"Yes she is. I saw you at the Phil yesterday evening, Einna. I was hoping to catch you at the end to see what you thought of *Music for Eighteen Musicians?*"

"I…" I didn't want a discussion about Steve Reich. I wanted to tell Maggie about my experience. "It was challenging." Consciously I used the word I'd half-heartedly used when I was discussing the piece with Michael.

"Well that's an improvement on 'plink plonk'. Unfortunately, I can't quiz you at the moment as I'm about to go to the library to borrow some new CDs. I want to order the Steve Reich, and Harrison Birtwhistle's *Gawain*. I think even you and Maggie might like that. I'll call her."

"I've met a man," I said, when she came to the phone.

"Since yesterday?" I was at Maggie's school, yesterday.

"Yes, at the concert." I told her everything.

"He sounds like a weirdo."

"A very attractive weirdo, but I must be at least thirteen years his senior."

"So? I think you've forgotten how attractive you are."

Am I? I didn't feel attractive, not sexually. I hadn't flirted with a man since John, in Hunstanton, and look how that had turned out. Besides, it was more usual for men to be attracted to younger women, not older ones.

The poem arrived two weeks after the aborted concert, and the… the what?

Why do you think we walked to your house?
I fancied you.
I thought we would stroll by the river,
you in your curly black coat,
the collar framing your face,
and I would kiss you in the moonlight.

Why do you think we walked to your house?
I fancied you.
I thought we would sit by the fire,
you in your black skirt,
the hem framing your ankles
and I would caress you in the lamplight

Why do you think we walked to your house?
I fancied you.
I thought I would take off all your clothes,
put you to bed,
and your loosened hair would fan out on the pillow...

It isn't finished.

The only other words on the sheet of paper were, *Ring me on this number 702 7338.* Thus I began my journey across the treacherous landscape.

We become part-time lovers. Satisfactory for him; he held the strings that manoeuvred me. Where had the concert night woman gone? She was feisty. Could I only be witty and assertive with a stranger? Stranger danger, but I was used to being hurt by those close to me, so what was the danger? It wasn't the man. It was me. I allowed him to make me his puppet. He took me out of the toy box when he wanted to play, and put me back when he'd had enough. I never knew when he would lift the lid again. Even in the sexual act itself, he was controlling.

"No, Einna, I'll come too quickly if you, ooh, suck my cock like that." And he would pull me up his body and, with one finger, then the tip of his tongue open the door to the beautiful room.

I sang romantic songs all the way to his studio-flat, and sad ones after we'd said goodbye. I knew, *Puppet On A String*, off by heart. I forgot about the Mona Lisa's smile. Puppets don't masturbate.

My friends tolerated my obsession, but couldn't help giving me advise which I ignored. We do, don't we, when we don't want to listen?

Maggie: "I told you he was a weirdo. Get rid of him, Einna. He's using you."

I couldn't.

Angela: "You've lost weight. It suits you. But I agree with Maggie, he's using you. Tell him to take a running jump."

I couldn't.

Debbie: "I don't agree with Maggie's and Angela's advice, but he's not making you happy, Einna. You do need to have a long talk with him."

I couldn't.

Six months into the fragmented relationship, I got a phone call.

"How do you fancy a weekend in Lincoln? The Usher wants to talk to me about an exhibition. I'd like you to come along."

"Usher?"

"Usher Art Gallery."

Lincoln was Michael's home town.

"Sounds lovely." My heart was yo-yoing. *Michael wants me to go to Lincoln with him. A whole weekend together. We've never slept a whole night together. Shit, do I snore? Shit, do I fart when I wake up? Does Michael snore? Does he fart when he wakes up?*

In films, making love, waking up with a new love, it's all romantic as though the director has ordered rose tinted camera lenses. I wanted rose tinted everything for Lincoln.

"Have you ever been to Lincoln?"

"No."

"I'll show you the cathedral and, while I'm in my meeting, you can visit the castle, the Magna Carta, the Jew's House, Stoke's coffee house. No leave Stoke's for us to do together."

I was struck by deja-vu. I heard John's voice echoing Michael's. *"We have to go up the Eiffel Tower, Einna."* Difference? I would trail after Michael round thousands of cathedrals, just to be with him.

We set off early, knowing it would take about three hours to get to Lincoln. As we drew up outside the hotel, he said, "I told them I was coming with my mum, so I'd need two single rooms."

Shock can smog you, clog you. You feel as though you're choking. I needed air. I opened the car door, and got out. Michael had turned away to get his jacket off the back seat. *Breathe slowly, Einna; in one, two, three, now walk away.* My mind was full of betrayal.

In a street called The Bailgate I saw a hotel. I veered inside, looking for the women's toilets. They were empty. I could howl without embarrassing or being embarrassed.

What was I? A red eyed, unlovely, older woman with saggy breasts and stretch marks, who ought to have known better. I wanted to plunge my head in a basin of cool water; water to stop water, water to soothe watery red eyes, but there was no plug and the tap allowed but a timed gush. I balled pieces of lavatory paper; soaked and pressed, soaked and pressed. I put mascara on my eyes, blusher on my cheeks and lipstick on my lips, red for brazen, red for anger. I told the painted puppet to get on a train back to Liverpool. She didn't need a man who wanted to pass her off as his mother. I picked up a street map in reception.

Michael and I met on the steep street they call The Strait. He was walking up, I was walking down.

"It was a joke, Einna. I'm sorry."

Red lips screamed, "Joke! You're the joke, Michael Pritchard." Red rimmed eyes, red cheeks, red mouth whispered, *"Ha! I'm the joke. I'm the jerked puppet."*

He held out his hand in supplication. I shoved both of mine into my jeans' pockets in case one of them betrayed me.

"I'm starving, Einna. Let's go and get something to eat." He smiled. I melted. He noticed. "I am really sorry. It was in bad taste." He took my arm. I didn't withdraw it.

After we'd eaten, we went into the Cathedral. He showed me the imp and told me one of the stories associated with it.

"The imp was wicked. He created havoc and misery wherever he went. So God told the North Wind to punish him. The North Wind blew the imp into the cathedral, up onto a pillar and petrified him. Tourists have fun looking for him."

"You didn't let me look for him."

"I knew you wouldn't be able to find him."

"I might have."

"But there's still so much I want to show you. We haven't got that much time together. My meeting's tomorrow morning. I'll jot down other bits and pieces you could look at while—"

"I am capable of discovering things for myself, you know."

"But you don't know Lincoln. I do."

I stared at him just to make sure he hadn't been transformed into John; Lincoln imp magic and no north wind to help. No. He was studying me, as though willing me to agree. I sighed; not a sigh he would have been able to hear; a sigh for my ears alone. I would accept his jottings with puppet gratitude and wander where I chose. *Hello Arry.* If he quizzed me? Oh well, at least Michael's Lincoln would be an aesthetic tour, not a rugby club one.

That night he made love to me as though he were the enraged wind who was going to fix me to a pillar.

Two weeks after we returned to Liverpool, he gave me a pair of silver, Lincoln Imp earrings. With the gift, was a sketch of me looking up at the imp; on the back was a poem.

I want to melt in you.
I want to drown in you.
I want to fill up all your hollow spaces.
I want to lead you through melting landscapes
to a beautiful room
where we can stay forever,
whatever forever is, or time allows.
Told you I'd draw you! Michael Pritchard.

He continued to take me out and put me back in the toy box for nine months. Then, just like that, he dropped the strings and closed the lid for good. If Annie had known about Michael, she would have said I was getting my just deserts for behaving like a tart.

The day he told me his days as my puppet master were over, we were driving across Runcorn Bridge. We had been to see a play at The Royal Exchange in Manchester.

"I'm not coming to yours tonight," he said.

"You've got to work?"

"No. These past nine months have been very special, Einna, but... we always knew our affair wasn't going to be a forever thing, didn't we?"

What did he say? Did he just say...?

"This is the right time to end our relationship."

End our relationship? What has happened to melting landscapes? But I knew the answer, didn't I? It was just poetry, Einna.

Melt in you, forever, forgive, forget, mother, mother, mother, fuck, fuck, age.

"Why?"

"I don't want to fall in love with you. I can't contemplate that sort of relationship right now. My work has to come first."

"I don't interfere with your work. When have I ever interfered with your work?"

"You haven't, but you would if you became too important to me. Surely you can see that? I hope we shall always be friends, but when the time's right, I want to fall in love with someone my own age."

There. He'd said it. My teeth began to chatter and the little imps in my ears danced along to the rhythm. I braked. "Get out, Michael."

"Be reasonable, Einna. If you're upset, I'll drive."

"Upset? Why should I be fucking upset? I get dumped every day. You can walk home. It's only a couple of miles."

"I thought you'd understand."

"You what? You shit! I don't understand."

"But you said I could borrow your car tomorrow. Mine's off the road, isn't it?"

There's always a straw, isn't there? I flew at him, maybe hoping he'd grab my wrists, pull me to him, hold and kiss me better, say, like he did in Lincoln, *'It's a joke, Einna. Can't you take a joke?'*. He hoisted his denim jacket off the back seat and got out.

I never saw him again.

Chapter Eleven
Fred

The police are shits.
They accuse before they know.
They harass black people.
They hound young people.
They are racist, sexist and homophobic.

I know a fat old policeman,
He's always...

Only he wasn't old. Fat, jolly, always laughing unless the job called for him to be serious. Fred looked kindly on everyone no matter their skin colour, gender or sexual orientation.

"There are people in this world you're going to like, get on with... and there are people you won't like or get on with. There are nice people and people who haven't got a nice bone in their bodies." That was how Fred viewed humanity.

Time is a healer. It's a cliché, but it's true. Some people heal quickly, others don't. But there's almost always a scar, and those who pretend otherwise, lie to themselves. If we're wise, we don't pick at it.

The steady ticking time of Thomas Gardner told me that the days, weeks and months were passing. I recovered. I imagined that my friends in the gang sighed with relief, as did Lena, a friend who worked at the Teachers' Centre.

I was a burden to them while the affair with Michael lasted, and a burden when it was over. They didn't tell me they were glad I'd returned to their world, but I knew they were. Sometimes we can't hide what we feel; face, body language, a hug too many.

My work also helped. No one at The Teachers' Centre where the peripatetic teams were based, knew about Michael, except for Lena and Lena, like Jean, could keep a confidence.

Our boss was a man called Philip Davies. Because of his enthusiasm for his and our work, I could almost forgive his inconsiderate behaviour where our time commitment was concerned. His life seemed to revolve around music in schools and the youth orchestra. He found it difficult to accept that others didn't feel the same way. I pitied his wife but – and here was a thought – maybe she was grateful to all the musical activities that kept him from being with her; like I used to be with John and rugby.

Philip was an eccentric who wouldn't have known what time of day it was if it hadn't been for Lena. She was his personal assistant. In Liverpool's reorganisation, her title was changed to Administrative Officer.

"I'm just a bleeding PA," she said. "Administrative Officer's too grand for what I do."

All four of us gang women loved the bones of Lena, as they say here in Liverpool. I knew her best because The Teachers' Centre was my work home. Debbie, Maggie and Angela attended meetings and workshops there and thus knew what it was to be embraced by her welcome. She was often the buffer between the team and Philip. Lena is, was, married to Fred, a policeman. Do people say, 'is' or 'was', when their partner dies?

"Maggie?"

"No it's Stuart."

"Sorry, Stuart. I wasn't expecting it to be you. I was thinking you'd be still at Uni, but of course you're home. It's the hols, Claire's home. And, you don't sound anything like your mum. Is she there?" Grief was making me babble.

"That's okay, and yes she is. Mu-um, it's Einna."

"Fred's dead isn't he?" Maggie said when she came to the phone.

"Yes, he died last night. Josie's just rung. The funeral's next Monday." Josie was Fred and Lena's daughter.

Grief doesn't depend on knowledge. I knew Fred was dying and yet still there was that knot of air that arrived inside my ribcage as soon as Josie told me he was dead. I first felt that knot when I was nine, the day I heard Jean had died. After that it was Pearl. The knot of air then was for the loss of the possibility of reconciliation, the loss of the possibility of love.

"How's Lena?"

"Being strong for everyone. But then what else would you expect?"

Lena had become a surrogate mother for Maggie and I. Yes, the gang women had each other, but unlike Debbie and Angela who had parents they could turn to for elder statesman advice and support, we had no one. Edith was still alive and I was still friendly with May but neither of them, for different reasons, could be consulted. My wonderful Aunt and Uncle? Wonderful yes, but not people who had ever advised me. Advice wasn't in the nature of our relationship. Support, yes. And unquestioning love.

"If you'd asked me a few years ago whether I'd know and like a policeman, and then be… What a bloody idiot the man was. He knew he was at risk, what with his family history," said Maggie.

"Was he an alcoholic, or someone who drank too much?"

"Is there a difference?"

"Don't know. Fred didn't drink on duty, he was a social drinker."

"Do you know what he told Lena when they took him into hospital? 'Don't forget you're to have a party, Queen. No morbid funeral. I want everyone to get bladdered and tell outrageous stories about me.'

"She told him not to be daft, said he'd be coming home soon. Apparently he just smiled at her. I think he knew he had cirrhosis of the liver. 'Play that disc with all my favourites on it, okay? And tell the girls… And tell the girls to wear their most outrageous earrings'."

Fred always called us, 'the girls', never 'the gang'. Gangs had an unpleasant connotation for him. Gangs could cause trouble. But then I sometimes thought that was why Trevor had chosen the word. Together, we spelled trouble for our men.

Maggie and I were silent for a moment or two. I imagined we were sharing similar thoughts: grief that Fred had died and joy that we'd known him.

"Josie told me that Lena's going to take him at his word about the burial being a party," I said.

I was the first gang member to meet Fred. Lena engineered it. One Friday afternoon, she called me into the office as I was about to go home.

"You have," she said.

"Have what?"

"Got on the Mona Lisas again."

I touched my ear. I'd worn them every day, since Michael. They were to remind me I could have good sex without a man. I'd told Lena their story.

"You look done-in, sweetheart. I hope you're going straight home?"

"No. I've got to go to the supermarket." Normally I shopped on a Thursday to avoid the Friday crush, but our inconsiderate boss had called an extra youth orchestra rehearsal the previous day.

"Large gin and tonic when you get home."

"White wine. I can see it in the fridge."

"I thought you preferred red?"

"I do. Claire prefers white."

"What we do for our kids! Fred promised Josie he'd take her to an Ultravox concert this evening, now he can't go, so I've got to do it."

"That wouldn't be a punishment for me. I love Ultravox."

"They're alright. Truth is, I switched off after the sixties. See you Monday."

The supermarket was heaving and, by the time I got home, all I wanted was that glass of wine and a long soak in the bath.

"Claire," I called, as I struggled in with the shopping. "Can you come and help me please?" There was no reply.

"Daughters," I hissed at my reflection in the hall mirror. "Never there when you want them."

I plonked the bags down on the hall floor and gave my arms a vigorous rub to get the circulation going again. "Well, Queen," I said in what I believed to be a passable imitation of a scouse accent and what Claire would call my, *Bread*, voice. "You look like a mef. Your hair needs washing, your face is like an old connie-buttie, and you're wearing the Monas again. Anyone would think you didn't have any other earrings."

"So?"

"You're mad, you know, talking to yourself."

"I'm not mad. I'm the only person worth talking to."

"Not true. Claire's worth talking to, Maggie's worth…"

"You're not going to go through the whole list, are yer?"

Karl Marx raced down the stairs and pretended he was practising maypole dancing, round my legs.

"Stop it, nuisance."

He ceased his, *hello woman who feeds me* greeting and attacked my school bag.

"What is it with you and that bag, you stupid cat? Get off!" The *stupid* cat, his teeth fixed on the handle, his feet pummelling the side of the bag, took no notice. "Bog off, menace." I nudged him with my foot: bad move, he turned his attention to the front door. I leapt over the bags to close it, tripped and banged my elbow. "Ow!" I yelled. My return home was fast turning into an imitation of *The Brick Layer's Story*.

"What on earth have you eaten today? You're hyper." I bent down to pick him up. He nipped my hand and shot off up the stairs. "I saved you, you ungrateful wretch. You were due to be drowned, you fat, hairy mog!"

I opened the living room door and picked up the bags of shopping. Karl Marx dashed through my legs, jumped onto the windowsill and started washing his paws as though he were a normal, comfy cat.

Claire appeared from the kitchen, carrying two mugs. "Hi, Mum. I didn't hear you come in." She put the mugs on the coffee table. "Let me help you with those." She took the bags.

"If you didn't hear me, who's the other tea for? Oh!" It was at this moment I noticed the large policeman sitting in one of the armchairs. I raised my eyebrows at Claire. She shrugged.

The policeman smiled. "What's the fat hairy mog's name?" Obviously he'd heard me. Had I said anything worse than, 'bog off'?

"It changes according to his behaviour," said Claire. "Officially, it's Karl Marx. When he's in an evil mood, like today, it's Satan, or fat hairy mog. If he's behaving nicely it's Marxy."

Karl Marx, as though he knew he was the topic of conversation, paused mid lick, and in one leap, landed on the policeman's lap.

"Chuck him off if you don't want him to molest you," she said.

"I think I can put up with him as long as he doesn't dig his claws in. I can't get up to shake hands though," he said to me.

There followed one of those silences where the air is full of questions.

Claire broke it. "Do you want a cuppa, Mum?"

"That would be nice." It wasn't, but I realised the bath and the glass of wine would have to wait. Claire handed me the tea she'd made for herself and went back into the kitchen. "Er. have you popped in for any particular reason?" I asked.

"Well…"

A flash. "Bloody hell! It isn't about my burglary, is it? I'd given up hope of hearing anything about that."

"I don't know anything about a burglary, sorry."

I slumped onto the beanbag forgetting my rule: approach with caution. It metamorphosed into an amoeba, depositing me on my back and slopping tea all over my skirt and the floor.

"Shi-er, blow," I said, struggling to get up. "Claire, can you grab me some kitchen tow…" I froze mid word. "I haven't been burgled again, have I?"

"Don't be daft, Mum," said Claire, coming in with a wad of towels. "I've been here all day. I think I'd have noticed if there'd been a burglary. After I'd phoned the police, I might have rung you at The Teachers' Centre."

"And," said the policeman, "I'd have mentioned it earlier."

"Is it my missing license then? Have you traced its whereabouts at last?"

The policeman looked blank. Six months previously, I'd been caught speeding. I'd admitted my fault and taken the required articles to the police station on Allerton Road. In due course, I paid the fine. However, that was the last I'd seen of my driving license. Several letters flew between my house, the police station and DVLA, but my license remained in some administrative black hole.

"I'm sorry," said the policeman. "I don't know anything about a missing license, but I can chase it up for you, if you like."

"I doubt it will do any good, but thanks anyway. I carry the receipt, given to me by the desk sergeant, in the glove compartment of the car in case I'm stopped in the future."

There was another long pause, broken only by Karl Marx's purrs. My Friday wilt was worsening. When would this policeman get to the point of his visit?

Claire went back into the kitchen and returned with her mug of tea and a plate of biscuits.

"Chocolate shortbread. I shouldn't," he said, taking two.

"Made by me," said Claire.

"They're yummy."

"Is this just a community police call then?" I asked, also taking a shortbread.

"Sort of." He looked embarrassed. "Look, there's no easy way to say this, so I'll be blunt. It's your neighbours."

I frowned. "Our neighbours?"

"Our neighbours?" Claire echoed.

"Yes. There's been a complaint."

"A complaint? But I don't really know any of my neighbours, except for Mary, next door that side." I pointed. "I've had one conversation with a woman called, Sadie. She lives at the top of the street. She stopped me one day, when I was on my way to the paper shop and told me that my neighbour, on the other side, had murdered his wife."

"Well, as far as I know there hasn't been a suspicious death reported. We don't know which of your neighbours complained," said the policeman. "An anonymous letter was sent to the station. We have to follow it up."

"Is it about noise? Has someone complained that we're noisy? It is a very quiet street. I don't think I make much noise, except when I shout at Karl Marx. We don't play loud music, do we Claire?" She shook her head.

"Perhaps they don't like the name," said Claire.

"What name?"

"My cat's name. You said not to call him that, people might think we were Commies."

"It's not about noise, or your cat's name. It's about visitors. Apparently you have lots of visitors and they're always male."

"You're having me on. You have to be having me on. Male visitors? It's a crime to have male visitors?"

"They're not always male. We have loads of female friends, in fact we have more female visitors than we do male," said Claire. "It's a wind-up, isn't it?"

"The problem is, we don't know if it's a wind-up, or not. As I said, we have to follow up complaints."

"But this is crazy. What did the letter actually say?"

"Well—"

Suddenly it was all too much for me, I burst into hysterical laughter. My neighbours thought I was running a brothel?

"It didn't just mention men, it mentioned drugs."

My laughter froze. Claire's face froze.

"Drugs? I don't do drugs; I never have. You can ask anyone. I have a glass or two of wine occasionally, no, if I'm honest, every evening." *Like now. I could really do with one now. Go away fat policeman with your absurd accusations, and let me open the bottle of Muscadet that's cooling in the fridge.*

"And I don't do drugs either," said Claire. "I bet they think it's me. Do they think it's me? After all, I'm a student. All students do drugs, don't they?"

"Claire, sweetheart, not even Sadie would think something like that, would she? Is it Sadie? I reckon she could be a right busybody." I was babbling. Why did I babble when I was stressed? Then I caught a glimpse of the fat policeman's face. He was trying not to laugh.

"What's so funny?"

"You are," he gasped, then let out one of the biggest laughs I'd ever heard. He howled with laughter.

Karl Marx leapt from his lap in high dudgeon, flew across the room, jumped onto the windowsill again, and washed every part of his body he could reach.

"There haven't been any complaints. I made it up. At least my wife and I made it up. She's Philip's secretary, you and she... Your astute daughter almost got it, didn't she? What a wind-up! My name's Fred, by the way."

"Lena's your wife?"

"Yes." A tidal wave of laughter engulfed him once more.

"So that's why she told me to get off home. I'll kill her."

"Please don't do that, I'm rather fond of her. Your boss might be upset as well. It seems he can't drink a coffee without her help. I told her yesterday, I'd been relocated to Allerton Road. She said you lived close by, and if you were at home, you'd give me a cuppa. Then we hatched this joke. I'm sorry... no I'm not... your faces. I couldn't have some of that kitchen roll, could I? I always end up crying when I laugh."

Memories, mother to daughter. I looked at Claire to see if we were having the same thought. How old had she been, four, five?

"Mum does too," she said. "She and her friends in the gang are always crying with laughter. They wet their knickers as well."

"Too much info, daughter," I said.

It was at this moment we heard a shout for help. Fred jumped up and ran for the door; for a big man, he moved quickly.

"That's Mary," I said. "Oh God, I hope she's okay."

She was, but on the pavement outside her house lay an inert figure, his head at a funny angle. It was Mr. Costello, the man Sadie told me had murdered his wife.

"I was just coming back from the shops and I saw these two lads attacking him with… I'm not sure what with, exactly… sticks, baseball bats maybe? I ought to have done something, but I froze," said Mary.

"You certainly didn't ought to have done anything," said Fred. "If you had, you might also be lying on the pavement." Fred knelt down beside the body and put his fingers on Mr. Costello's neck to check for a pulse. "He's dead."

"Are you okay, Mary?" I asked. I didn't put my arm round her shoulders. Mary didn't enjoy physical contact; this had become clear at our second meeting when I tried to give her a hug. She was as stiff as a wooden doll. She'd lived too long on her own, I guessed.

"Don't touch anything," Fred ordered, no longer the laughing policeman. He got in his car and phoned the station. "Have you noticed any lads hanging about over the last few days?" he asked when he'd finished.

We looked at each other, then shook our heads.

"The twins and their dad had a row last weekend," said Mary. "Remember, Einna? Claire was out, and you came round to escape the noise. You said how unusual it was, as you never heard them, as a rule."

"That's right. Then one of the twins flew past the window screaming, 'You shit! I'm out of here'."

"You don't think it was a deliberate attack, do you?" asked Claire.

"I can't say, at the moment," said Fred. "The only facts I know are, the man's dead, and you saw him being attacked by two youths. Are you sure they were lads?"

"I think so," said Mary. "I was at the end of the street, so I can't be positive. They scrambled over that wall." She pointed to the end of the cul de sac. On the other side of it was the post-office depot.

"The CID team will be here at any moment, and forensics. They'll want to talk to you, Mary. Einna, would you mind if we used your house?"

"Of course not. I think we could all do with a drink, and I don't mean tea. Is that okay, Fred?"

"You go ahead. Wish I could join you. My boozing will have to wait till I get home. I'm on lates, this week. I was supposed to take Josie to an Ultravox concert tonight."

"I know, Lena told me." I gave him a look.

"I'll open that bottle of wine, shall I?" said Claire. "I've never seen a dead body before let alone a murdered one."

"It could be manslaughter," said Fred. "A mugging gone wrong. All I can be sure of is, it wasn't an accident. Mr Costello hasn't died from natural causes."

Claire, Mary and I sat, staring into glasses of Muscadet as though hoping the wine would provide answers. One minute you're having a laugh at a joke against yourself and the next...

Before he left, I told Fred to pop in whenever he wanted.

"I will," he grinned. "If nothing else, to see more of the collection."

"The what?"

"Those." He pointed at my earrings. "They're—"

"Bizarre?" said Claire.

I touched my Monas. "They have a story," I said.

"What is it?"

"Ask Lena. She knows."

"Mum's always worn weird earrings. It's a gang badge, like wetting knickers through laughter."

Fred burst out laughing again. "Bloody good thing men don't wet theirs. I'd be in trouble wouldn't I?"

"I do wish you'd stop talking about me wetting my knickers, you treacherous girl, you'll get me arrested for incontinence. We don't all wear gaudy earrings; Debbie doesn't like them, she's our earth mouse. I have to stop by the office every morning so Lena can inspect the day's choice, not mine, theirs."

"What?" said Fred.

"Mum has this delusion that her earrings tell her which ones to wear. She has an earring collage in her bedroom. I started it when I was..." Claire looked at me.

"When you were five. And it's not a delusion. They do choose me. I catch a… it's almost like a wink, blink, and those are the ones demanding to be worn." Except over the past months, since Michael, I'd worn my Monas every day. I suddenly realised Fred had helped me to find a way through the fog. Laughter is a healer. Tonight, I'd be able to put the Monas back on their pin, and tomorrow see which other earrings opted to go to work with me.

"I like Einna's earrings," said Mary. "I wish I had the courage to be that colourful."

"Your style's right for you," I said.

"You mean boring?"

"You know I don't mean that."

"When I was a teenager, I used to wish Mum would dress more like a normal person. Then when I became more confident with who I was, I realised it didn't matter," said Claire.

For some reason, Mary blushed. "Better be going," she said.

"Me too," said Fred. "Lena will be wanting a full report when she gets back from the concert."

"Do you forgive me?" Lena called as I passed her office the next morning.

"I'll think about it."

"Good actor, isn't he?"

"Up to the point where he couldn't contain his laughter."

Lena smiled. "That laugh. I think that's why I agreed to marry him. He was just like—""

"The laughing policeman." I finished her sentence for her.

Chapter Twelve

How Can You Lose Yourself If You've Never Been Found?

Diddle, diddle dumpling my man Tom,
Tick, tick, tick, he's a ticking bomb.

But I didn't know that, in the beginning. How was I going to be able to make a decision when I felt so fragmented? Was it mad to say 'yes' to moving in with a man I'd known for six months?

When I was with Tom, moving in was what I wanted. When I wasn't with him I was full of doubts. Perhaps it was because he had long hair. Michael had long hair. John had short hair. It was stupid to make a decision based on hair.

Tom was an 'edge' man. I did see something of the crocodile in him, occasionally, in those first few months. A little snap, but it seemed to be more to do with tension than nastiness; there was very little that was relaxed about Tom, a taut wire was how Maggie described him. I saw him as a man of spurts. Silent for long periods, then spurting words as though he'd been storing them up; full of furious energy, then exhausted.

I wasn't a puppet in a toy-box, like I'd been with Michael. I wasn't a social necessity, like I was with John. But what was I? Could I work it out through writing? If, for example, I wrote about our holiday in The Lake District, when we were away from Liverpool, away from our lives there; together twenty four hours, for seven days, would it show me what Tom was? What I was to him? If we were compatible enough to live together?

The man walks down to the lake. He's a tall man, slim, with long, iron-grey hair caught into a low ponytail. He moves with stop-start caution, not wanting to disturb the flora and fauna. Over his shoulder is slung a pair of binoculars.

The woman walks down to the lake. She is of average height, slim, with salt and pepper, flyaway hair. She carries a notebook and pencil. She walks softly on plimsoll feet until she arrives at the place where she likes to sit.

Their chosen spot, a secluded glade, by the water's edge, is shaded from the afternoon sun by tall silver birches. It's far enough away from the man-made beach, for them to feel protected from endless activity and noise. Most days throughout the holiday season, it throbs with people and dogs.

The man sits with his back against a tree. He looks out across the water, which is like a sheet of glass in the still air. The trees surrounding the lake are mirrored and held within it, a stippled tapestry.

The woman sits on a rock. She opens her book, her pencil poised, ready to capture sights and sounds. Through the trees, she sees great shafts of light with dust particles suspended in them like dancing fireflies.

The man looks at a heron on the far shore through his binoculars; a stone sculpture waiting to scoop up a fish.

They both watch an Alsatian pestering its owner to throw sticks. It bounces through the water, barking and splashing.

The sound of a child's cries catches their attention. People on the beach don't seem to notice the colourful tapestry being frayed by misery. Adults by her are deep in conversation, oblivious to the noise. A girl, a few years older than the screaming toddler, the burden of motherhood already upon her, picks up the child, wraps her in her arms and sits on the beach, rocking and soothing. The crying gradually dwindles to hiccupping sobs, and ceases altogether when a sweet is proffered.

The moment of unease binding the man and the woman together is broken, and they continue side by side, yet apart.

"Cup of tea?" the man says. The woman jumps up, slipping her pad and pencil into her jeans' pocket. "I didn't know you wanted one that badly."

"I don't, but you do." She smiles.

The man takes her hand. No one on the beach notices them leaving the glade.

"It's so hot," says the woman. "You'd never think it was late September." She stops by one of the Durmast oaks, and picks a leaf. "Look, Tom. Isn't it beautiful? It's on the cusp of change. I love the colours of Autumn."

I was on the cusp of change, like the autumn leaves. But the end of their change is to fall to the ground, dead. I needed a better image than cusp, leaves. Lots of people leapt into relationships. *Yes, and look at your past leaps, Einna. That's why you're thinking fallen leaves.* As had happened all those years ago, in Paris, a film came to my aid. I saw Julie Andrews dancing down a lane, singing *'why am I so scared?'* Maria strode, rather than leapt into her new life. That's what I would do; head up, swinging my case with determination.

"You're an Autumn woman," he says.

"Will you help me pick some blackberries?" She fishes a freezer bag out of her pocket.

"You got the kitchen sink in there? I thought it was only men who filled their pockets with rubbish."

She laughs. "Not rubbish. Useful stuff. I suspect men's pockets have bits and pieces that are useful in them too. "

They gather a bag full of the sweet ripe fruit, then continue on down the lane.

"After you've put the kettle on, come into the garden."

"Why?" she asks.

The man taps his nose.

Help! Annie used to tap her nose. *Don't think Annie. Think Julie Andrews. Think Maria striding down the lane swinging her case and guitar. Guitar. She had a guitar you have a violin...*

The man taps his nose.

Intrigued, she does as he asks and sees he's rigged up a hosepipe over the branch of a tree. He strips down to his boxer shorts and stands under the cooling water.

"Get your clothes off," he orders.

She does and doesn't want to join him.

"Come on," the man says. "Don't be a baby."

"But it's September."

"So?"

She takes off her jeans and t-shirt, runs into the cold spray, screams and runs out again. It's horrible. It's wonderful. It's something she can't resist repeating.

"Stop screaming," says the man. "The whole village will think I'm assaulting you." He turns off the water.

"Assam or Earl Grey?" she asks as she drips back to the kitchen.

"Assam."

As she's putting out the tea things, she notices a small packet on the kitchen table. She meant to take it upstairs and pop it in her case, before they went to the lake. In it are some tiny, lake district pencil earrings. The man pulled a face when she bought them.

"They for your daughter?" he said.

"No, me. For my collection."

John thought my earrings were tacky. How often had he said things like, "I hope you don't wear those when you go out with me." Claire didn't like them, either. But she always put up with them. She even showed how much she loved me by giving me the parrots. Did Tom's reaction imply future struggles about how I chose to dress? *Oh god! What am I going to do? Think Maria.*

I met Tom while I was looking for the house of a pupil who'd left her violin at The Teachers' Centre. He was standing in his front garden, gazing up into the sky.

"Excuse me. You don't happen to know where Mia Sharpe lives, do you?" I said

"Have you ever seen a bird circus?" he replied

"Pardon?"

"Look." He pointed to a mass of starlings, wheeling about. "That's some murmuration for you."

"Murmuration?"

"The name. I don't know what I'm now going to tell you, it's an educated guess. The sound. The name must come from the sound of their wings as they're wheeling around."

It made sense. Their aerobatics were awesome. I must have seen the spectacle before but taken no notice. The Red Arrows would have been proud of such a display. We stood quite still, gazing at them, for several minutes.

"Who did you say you were looking for?" he asked, his eyes still on the whirling mass.

"Mia Sharpe."

He shook his head. "The name doesn't ring a bell."

"Would you mind if I used your phone to ring The Teachers' Centre? I left her address there."

"No problem. I was just about to make a brew. Would you like some tea?"

"Er…" Why not? "That would be nice, thank you. Mia left her violin at the centre I'm returning it."

As we went into the kitchen, I was almost overwhelmed by the scent of the honeysuckle trailing up a trellis by the door.

"Earl Grey or Assam? Cup or mug?"

"A mug of Assam, please. Er, where's your phone?"

"In the hall."

Luckily Lena was still in her office. "You've just caught me. I'll get the youth orchestra file. Here we are, Mia lives at thirty-four. You're not going out again, are you?"

"What?"

"Well you're not in a phone box: conclusion, you must be at home."

"Oh! No, I'm not at home. I'm having a cuppa with a man who introduced me to a bird circus. He said I could use his phone."

"You be careful. Stranger danger, Einna."

"He's a gardener."

"Safe as houses, then." She rang off.

The man came through to the hall with two mugs of tea in his hands. "I'm not a gardener. I love gardening but it's not my job. I'm a carpenter. Sorry. I wasn't deliberately listening."

"That's okay. My boss's PA was quizzing me. 'Stranger danger' she said. How much do I owe you?"

"I haven't heard that phrase since I was a kid. You don't owe me anything."

"Thank you. You've been very kind. I would have had to take the violin home otherwise. I didn't want Mia to get into trouble."

He stared at me for a moment. "I don't suppose... I mean, would you like to go out for a meal with me on Saturday? If we go to a pub in Frodsham, via the Runcorn Bridge, you might see a proper bird circus. The starlings create the most beautiful images in the sky."

Astonishment and curiosity bounced me into accepting the invitation.

"What time should I get here?"

"Half an hour before dusk. We can't stop on the bridge itself, but there's a road off just before it, that takes us near the river."

"Tell him all your friends know you're going out with him," said Maggie.

"As if. But I have, so if anything happens to me, you'll know where to send the police."

"That won't be any consolation if your body's floating about under The Runcorn Bridge."

Odd. Why was she concerned when I wasn't? There had been nothing about the man I'd met to alarm me.

When we were watching the murmuration, I experienced the same sense of awe as I had in the Sainte Chappelle in Paris, when Claire was two. Then, I was surrounded by coloured glass light on stone walls. I believe such experiences only happen infrequently in our small lives, if at all. Perhaps it was that, and the gratitude for it, that threw me into Tom's arms and his bed on our second date.

But, I must have been anxious about leaping for I mentioned it to each member of the gang in phone conversations. "Why wait?"

Was it because I wasn't entirely happy with their reactions that I repeated, "Why wait?" to Lena. "I'm forty six. How many more good sex years have I got? I've started having hot flushes as it is."

"Bloody hell, girl, sex doesn't stop with the menopause," said Lena. "For an intelligent woman, you're not very clued up about your body."

"You're not thinking of retiring, are you?"

"What's that got to do with sex?"

"Nothing," I said, and for some reason burst into tears.

"Hey sweetheart. Come on. Having sex with someone you fancy's not something to cry about."

"It's not that. I just feel so vulnerable, you know after—"

"John?" I shook my head. "Michael then." I nodded. "Going to bed with a man isn't a commitment, Einna. Enjoy it. After all, we've fought to have the same rights as men. As for retiring, what would Philip do without me? Can you imagine some air-head scouser being able to sort him out?"

Six months later, in a dither of yes, no, for my holiday scribbles hadn't pushed me in any direction, I put a different, 'why wait?' question to Lena, adding: "Love... I want to know what love is between a man and a woman? Love like you and Fred had."

She laughed. "Bloody difficult. Fred was no saint. I'm not sure about giving advice, girl. It's always better to ask questions that help the person who wants the advice, to make up their own mind. Advice can rebound on the adviser. 'You told me to x, y, or z and look what's happened.' So, what do you want to do?"

"I don't know."

"Can Tom wait until you do?"

"It's usually men who have a problem committing, isn't it?"

"But this is to do with your experience of living with John, isn't it? Tom isn't John."

Lena was right. But at that moment I also realised that it was to do with living alone; no one to criticise me, control me. Why would I want to change that? But I could see Tom's point of view. We enjoyed being together.

Okay, Einna. The holiday, a whole week, no problems, decisions made together, good sex… He rarely initiates sex. Oh for god's sake! Does that matter? Women have fought for the right to initiate all sorts of things, including sex. Perhaps he doesn't want to be pushy, sexually; force his attentions on a woman who may not be in the mood? Perhaps he's fearful of sexual rejection? But someone has to face that; make the first move.

"That's how it is with Trevor and me now," said Maggie, wistfully, in one of our 'Tom' conversations.

"It could be that Tom hasn't got a huge sex drive. Dave hasn't." Angela had rung me from France, where she and Dave now lived.

What had John said to me on our honeymoon? "I'm not like most men, Einna." And he'd turned out to be gay. *Tom, gay? I don't think so. But then you hadn't suspected John was gay, had you? You're older and wiser now, Einna, at least I hope you are.*

"You still thinking about whether to move in with him, or not?" said Angela.

"No. Yes. Tom wants it, but…"

"What do you want?"

"What do you want?" said Debbie.

"What do you want?" said Maggie.

"What do you want, Mum?" said Claire. "I knew I wanted to live with Andy."

A plate-full of 'what do I want?'. I didn't know what I wanted and I picked at my dilemma like a child picked at food he or she didn't like.

Then I got a phone call from Aunty Ruby that changed everything. Uncle Charles had suffered a stroke, a severe one.

"They've told me there will be damage," she said. "I shall need help. Fortunately, your uncle, well you know what he's like, has made provision for something like this happening. We've got places reserved in Oak Vale."

"Where Betty was?"

"Yes. I can't look after him. Bless him, he wouldn't want it. But we can be together there. G and T's before luncheon. Wine with every meal. Brandy afterwards, if you want. We shall be in clover, sweetheart. Everything we have here, without the work."

Bless her, what work? "So you'll sell up?"

"Yes."

I dropped everything and drove to Ely to be with her. Tom was sympathetic. "I'll be here when you get back," he said. "Give me a bell to let me know you've arrived safely."

It felt so nice, so unusual having a man care that I arrived safely somewhere. John's explosions about IRA bombs in London, hadn't made me feel cared for; there was too much history of attempted control.

I helped Ruby put the house up for sale and move into Oak Vale. Charles's nephew came over to see them, and promised Ruby he would make sure the estate agents did their job. In any case, they would have been foolish not to, the house was on the market for a considerable sum.

On my way back to Liverpool, I made a decision. Why wait? Why wait? Tom was in his sixties. We might not have many years together before… My shillyshallying was stupid.

"Glass of champagne?" Tom said, as he put down the cases. "I've got a bottle cooling in the fridge. We'll make the bed up later. I thought we'd use this room as it's at the back of the house. Less noisy." 'This room' was his parents' room.

"Champagne would be lovely, Tom." I couldn't help staring at the stained mattress. *Skin scales. Urine? I can't sleep on it. Careful Einna, this is his childhood home. You need to spin a web. I thought you weren't going to need to… just this once. I don't want to rock the boat on our first night of actually living together.* Deliberately, I sat on the bed. "There's a slight problem, Tom. I'm used to an orthopedic mattress. It helps my back." *'Spots!'* the crocodile snapped. I banished her. "I'll treat us to a new one." I smiled.

He frowned. "Your back?"

"My back."

"I didn't know you suffered from a back problem. You've never mentioned it before."

"I'm not the kind of person to go on about aches and pains, am I? I've been to an Osteopath and a chiropractor. It was an Alexander Technique practitioner who really helped. She taught me how to walk, go up and down stairs; you know stuff like that. But the best piece of advice was a firm mattress." This was true. For a while I'd accompanied Angela to Alexander Technique classes, but it was she who had the bad back, not I.

"Well, I shan't throw this one away. I'll put it in the spare room. It's better than the one in there."

Oh god! I never thought to inspect the mattress in there. It was always made up. The number of times we've had sex in that bed. Then my dismay turned to glee. In all probability, Annie would be our only guest; how delicious. Annie on a skin scaly, stained mattress. If Angela came home on a visit, she would stay with her parents.

We went downstairs. My grandfather clock, violin, and treasure box were in the hall. I didn't bring the earring board. I needed a new, bigger one. My earring collection had outgrown my previous one. Tom's house overflowed with furniture, much of it Victorian, solid oak and mahogany. Thomas Gardner already looked at home here, even though he was older, truly a grandfather.

Tom stroked the clock's case. "Beautiful wood and workmanship," he said.

"Did his chimes annoy you when you stayed at mine?"

He shrugged. "A bit."

"We ought to put him in the dining room then. It's not under our bedroom, is it?" I picked up my violin. "I'll pop this in there, shall I? It seems sensible as your mum's piano's in there."

He walked away. "I'm going to uncork that bottle."

His voice had changed. "Have I said something to upset you?"

"Can't you just relax? Does everything have to be done immediately?"

"Sorry."

"Come and sit down." He popped open the bottle and poured out two glasses. "To us."

The champagne bubbles tickled my nose. I sneezed. "Where are your teaspoons, Tom?"

"What do you want a spoon for?"

"To stir my champagne. It disperses the bubbles."

"What? Bubbles are the point, aren't they?"

He found a spoon. I stirred, I sipped, I didn't sneeze. "Lovely," I said.

There were two shadowy figures by the dresser. They were laughing. I heard the woman say, "You'll learn, my girl." I blinked and they were gone.

"Tomorrow, I'd like to make an earring collage in our bedroom like the one I had at my house." Maybe I was hoping that Thomas's steady tick, my violin by the piano and a new earring collage, would help me to feel that I belonged here.

Tom didn't reply. He drank down his champagne, put on his jacket, the one with the leather patches on the elbows and said, "I'm going to fetch the take-away."

Later, after we'd drunk all the champagne and eaten more than was good for us, we made love on his parents' stained mattress. I pretended an orgasm, for I saw ghosts pointing and sniggering. They were the figures I'd seen by the kitchen dresser.

The following day, on my way home from work, I ordered a new mattress and bought a large cork notice board. I was in the middle of putting it up when Tom charged into the room. I didn't know he was home.

"What the fuck are you doing, Einna? Couldn't you wait? I thought you were going to bring the whole house down with your banging."

I was so shocked I nearly fell off the chair. "I've hung pictures before, Tom. I'm sorry, I didn't realise I was making a noise. I've only tapped the nail once."

"That's not the point. You should have asked."

Tom had never spoken to me like this before. "I mentioned it last night."

He pointed at the picture-hook and pin. "I hope that's strong enough. It probably needs a fucking Rawl plug, the amount of earrings you've got. Here, let me do it." He held out his hand for the hammer. "I suppose you've been in my shed?"

What? "No. It's my hammer."

He looked at it. "Oh yes." He balanced it in his hand. "It's a good hammer. There, that's done. Now you can be arty-farty. I reckon you ought to put Claire's parrots in the corner, there." He picked up a red headed pin, stuck it in the cork and hung the parrot earrings on it.

I felt invaded. This was Claire's and my collage. I wanted him to go. *Oh God, I've only been in the house for twenty four hours and… Stop it Einna. You are both in an entirely new situation. This was Tom's parents' house. Now it is Tom's house. Yes he wants you here, but nevertheless… nevertheless what? You have to feel at home or… or what's the point?*

"I'm going to pick some runner beans for our meal. I'll cook this evening. Okay with you? Don't do any more hammering while I'm in the garden."

Why did he say that? Why do I need to do more hammering? I stared at the blank board, trying to visualise the new picture. The microcosmic scene had thrown me out of kilter and it took some time for an image to materialise. As I put the last pair of earrings in place, I knew the picture was right except for the parrots. I moved them to the middle.

Tonight was the beginning of our first weekend together. We had a pleasant evening. When we went to bed, Tom didn't comment on the relocated parrot earrings. I suggested we made love and, despite sniggering ghosts, I didn't have to fake an orgasm.

The following morning, he told me he had jobs to do in the garden. "Call me for coffee," he said. "You know where everything is." This seemed like it could be weekend normality. I decided to clean the kitchen. It was domestic chores that had made me feel comfortable in the first house I lived in, in Liverpool. This kitchen had that greasy look kitchens could acquire over years of neglect. There were objects on every surface. I suspected they hadn't been dusted since Tom's mother died. On the windowsill, there was a vase containing faded, plastic flowers. They were filthy. I wrapped them in newspaper, and put the vase in the sink to be washed. "Go away," I said to the tutting figures hovering by my shoulder. I dusted, washed paintwork, mopped the floor and it was eleven, coffee time, before I knew it. I found the cafetiere, the coffee and two china mugs. They were stained so I scoured them, then put the kettle on.

"Coffee's ready in five," I called out the back door.

When Tom came in, he went over to the sink to wash his hands. "Where are my mother's flowers?" he asked.

"Over there." I pointed. "We ought to throw them—"

Two seconds, three, he was toe to toe. I couldn't move. My back was against the unit.

"You don't throw anything out, understand?" He stabbed his finger in my chest.

Stress, tension, hot flush. He dumped his mug of coffee in the sink, turned and slammed out the door. Jelly legged, I sank onto a chair.

I struggled against a prickle-band headache all morning. The prickles marched across my scalp, growing in numbers until they fused together. I went into the lounge, sank into an armchair and closed my eyes. Moments, hours, later, I woke to the sound of Tom singing.

"Hey diddle- diddle the cat and the fiddle,

The cow jumped over the moon."

When did I fall asleep? How long had I slept? I had never heard Tom sing... hum, yes; always the same two lines, no more, no less. *'Do do do doo'*, a rising scale. *'Do do do doo'*, a descending scale.

I got up and ran my fingers through my hair. The prickle band headache seemed to have gone. Tom came into the lounge. "Oh you're in here," he said. "Close your eyes and hold out your hand." He placed a small, square object in my palm. "You can look now." It was a blue box; the kind you get from a jewellers. "Are you going to stare at it all day?"

I opened it. Inside was a pair of silver violin earrings. I took one out. It looked so real that had I an elfin bow I could have played a tune.

"They're exquisite Tom."

He put his arms round me. "I saw them when I went into town the other day. They're a moving in present."

A moving in present after what happened earlier? And what music would they play, I wondered? My head was full of scratchy noises.

"Aren't you going to put them on? I've always thought of you as a cat, you know, a cat who plays a violin."

I did know. It was one of the first things he said to me. But I wasn't a cat. I was a spider who spun webs. I kissed him. He rubbed his mouth and nose.

"That hair of yours," he said. "Champagne make you sneeze. Your hair makes me feel as though I'm going to sneeze." He'd never mentioned that before.

I took out the fan earrings Angela had given me and popped them on the draining board.

"Don't put them there." He mimed sweeping them into the sink. "Here, give them to me." He put them in his pocket.

My hands were shaking so much I couldn't find the holes. I turned to him. "Can you…?"

"Oh for fuck's sake, you'll want me to wipe your bum for you next. Come here."

Tom poked the wires through the holes in my ears, and stood back. "They look as though they were made for you, violin earrings for a violin teacher. Go and look at yourself in the mirror."

I held out my still jittery hand. "I'll put the others back on the earring board."

He shoved them at me.

In the bedroom, I sat on the bed. What had I done? I felt as though I'd wandered into a mine field. Where had the man I fell in love with gone? I didn't recognise this man.

As we were eating our evening meal, I said, "Tom, why are you being so aggressive towards me? Are you thinking it's a mistake—"

"What on earth are you talking about?"

"You never used to swear at me."

"You swear."

"Not at you."

"Well, if it's the swearing that bothers you, I'll try not to do it, okay? They're only words, Einna."

Words that did damage; especially when accompanied by facial and body language, "Did you swear in front of your parents?"

"Yes. No, I don't know. Does it matter?"

I bet you didn't, anymore than you've sworn in front of my friends. It was just me, and only since I moved in.

We struggled on, me tiptoeing, Tom ricocheting. I couldn't bring myself to tell anyone what was happening and how I was feeling, not even Lena. Then, both Tom's and my worlds were turned upside down. Tom retired and I was made redundant. The Education Authority was being forced to make sweeping cuts, all peripatetic teams were axed. My colleagues were re-deployed in schools. I couldn't face a school-based post.

"Be careful not to lose yourself," Lena said.

I shivered. *Lose myself? How can I lose what I've never found?*

Chapter Thirteen
The Mouse

Tiptoe through the minefield,
For the minefield is where I'll be.
Come tiptoe through the minefield with me.

Tom adjusted to retirement quickly. He seemed calmer, altogether less volcanic, as though it had been his work that had made him stressed. Perhaps there were pressures he hadn't talked about, or maybe it was the daily drive in rush hour traffic through the tunnel.

I, however, needed something to replace the solid ground of employment. I felt out of kilter, without purpose, but out of kilter with what? How can someone who has never really known who she is, be out of kilter?

LIST:
Abused child.
Wife, but not a wife.
Mother. Yes, definitely a mother.
Friend. Yes, I was a friend and I had friends. You even had friends when
  you were a child, Einna.
A partner. Yes, I was Tom's partner.
Early retired and purposeless. Help!

It was Maggie who came up with the idea of private coaching. It seemed like a path I could travel down, and I felt sure Tom would agree. It all made sense. I broached the subject as we were getting ready for bed. Tom, Mr. Calm, disappeared.

"You want to do what?" He interrupted so abruptly, I jumped. I'd been lulled into thinking Tom really was the man I'd first met, the starling murmuration man and it had just been an adjustment to living with another person, two agendas, that had made him so volatile.

"I thought I might give violin lessons in the dining room, Tom. We hardly ever use it and with the piano being there—"

"Are you out of your fucking mind? I'm not having a load of screaming kids rampaging around my house." The flash anger ricocheted off the walls, crashing into the 'my house'. Was it ever going to be, 'our' house?

"I'm not talking about loads, Tom. Private coaching involves one pupil at a time."

"Don't patronise me."

"I didn't think I was."

"You don't think, that's the fucking trouble. If you did, you'd know that giving private violin lessons here is out of the question."

"Why?"

"You don't know who the fucking kids will be. How do you know that one of them won't steal something? How do you know they won't run riot? You don't do a police check on them, do you? If you're so keen to work, why don't you take one of the posts that was offered to you?"

"I'm not a classroom teacher, Tom. Even if I were, I couldn't go back to that sort of work now, I haven't got the energy." *You zap my energy.*

"You could have fooled me. You never sit down. You want your cake and eat it, Einna."

Clichés and insults. It seemed that my whole life had been spent listening to clichés and insults. I turned away.

"Going now are you? Not prepared to listen?"

"It's not that, Tom. You've made up your mind, haven't you?"

He stabbed his finger at me. "You're always so concerned about looking after your own interests, you haven't even considered the effect it'll have on me. It's bad enough having to listen to you, scratching away at that old fiddle, without the addition of snotty nosed kids who can't tell one end of a bow from the other."

In the spitting of a phrase I was whisked back to my teenage years and Pearl, who had used exactly those words; words designed to hurt, to belittle, to control.

I walked over to the door; Tom was there before me, barring my way. "Just where do you think you're going? You'll stay here until I've finished what I want to say. I won't be dismissed like that. Who the fuck do you think you are?"

Tip-toeing across the minefield, I sank onto the stool by the dressing table. Without looking at it, I could see the crack in the door, evidence of a former explosion. My hand crept towards my ear and a violin earring; rub, tug, rub, tug.

'We told you,' said the ghosts by the door. *'But you thought you knew best.'* They sniggered and melted out into the corridor.

"You can use the dining room at ours," said Maggie. "There's a piano in there."

I'd told her Tom wasn't keen, but not mentioned his aggressive reaction.

"What about Trevor? I wouldn't want him to feel his space was being invaded."

"I'll ask him."

Problem solved. But only after a few days of prickle band headaches as I wrestled with how I was going to tell Tom what I was going to do. I didn't need to ask Lena how to approach him. *"Facts,"* I heard her say. *'Present him with the cold, bare facts.'* So I did.

"Two evenings a week, Tom. So on those days it will be sensible to eat our main meal at lunchtime. The whole thing's a good compromise." I didn't elaborate. Tom didn't explode.

In my thirties and forties, my body alarm clock woke me at seven. Now, in my fifties it had pushed the hour back to six. Tom rarely woke before eight. I had two hours to myself every day.

I would open my eyes, stare at the ceiling for a minute or two until my mind adjusted to being awake. I knew, without looking at the clock that it was six. Time to be myself. Time for myself. I'd stretch, very gently, then slide out of bed, making sure that the duvet stayed where it was. I'd tiptoe to the door and, millimetre by millimetre, turn the nob. I could do it without a sound. Then I'd creep downstairs, avoiding the creaks and say, "Done it." Day after day I'd say, "Done it," and Thomas Gardner would smile at me as I breathed in the sweet scent of silence.

If Tom happened to be awake, well then, it would depend on how I felt. Sometimes I'd just lie there until a quarter to eight. At other times I'd say, "I'm getting up now, Tom," and wait for the reaction. A grunt would signify acquiescence.

I always left my clothes in the bathroom. In Spring and Summer and Autumn, if it was a fine day, I would strip wash and dress so that I was ready to go into the garden. In winter or on inclement days, I wouldn't bother to dress.

On the morning of my grandson, Zak's, birthday, as I tiptoed down the hall, I saw the sun shining through a gap in the curtains in the sitting room. It created a golden pathway on the carpet, like the yellow brick road but without the Emerald City at its end. What would my Emerald City have been? Peace. Whole days of feeling like this. I walked along it to a morning of sun before seven. As I drew the curtains, I saw the lawn covered with a dewy haze.

'I can hear everything you do when you get up.'

Calmly I looked up at the ceiling and whispered, "Get out of my head, Tom. You aren't going to spoil this moment. You can't hear me. The ghosts can't hear me. Not even I can hear me."

I put some water in a small pan on the hob because I didn't use the kettle: too noisy. Today, barefoot, I took my mug of tea out into the garden where the peace would be enhanced by birdsong.

The early morning garden reminded me of a line in one of my favourite poems, *Upon Westminster Bridge*, by Wordsworth. *"This garden now doth like a garment wear the beauty of the morning."* I whispered to the honeysuckle, trailing around the door. I didn't think Wordsworth would have minded my altering one word. The honeysuckle was in bud. The kitchen would be filled with its scent later in the month. Oh, that the scent could be a conduit to the before. That was how I saw my present life; before and after removal day. No sweet scent to welcome me then. Only the honeysuckle's small clusters of black berries.

I wriggled my toes in the soft, wet grass. Baths are wonderful, so are showers, but they couldn't compare to the sensuality of this dew bathing my feet. I would have liked to take off all my clothes and roll in it.

Come downstairs Tom.
Roll in the dew with me,
no one to hear us, no one to see.

Taking a last sip of tea, I put the mug down on the doorstep and fished my notebook and pencil out of my jeans' pocket. I jotted down the three lines which might, might not be turned into something later.

I was in charge of pots. Rather like the house, the garden was Tom's, but he had no interest in pots for the patio. I thought of the patio, which was more like a terrace, as it was large and flagged with York stone, as an experimental garden. I took great pride in it, sewing seeds rather than buying plants. To my surprise, Tom loaned me the smaller of the two greenhouses and, this year, I'd sewn various squash and ornamental gourds, as well as annuals. If any of the squash bore fruit which ripened, it would be a bonus: spicy squash soup, roasted squash. My mouth watered. I would have to give the soup an exotic name, for I was fairly sure Tom wouldn't try it if he knew it was squash, not if the previous Autumn's outburst was anything to go by.

"Tom, do you like squashes?"

"I don't know. I don't like pumpkins. Why?"

"I wondered if we could grow some. They have beautiful, sun yellow flowers and they taste good."

"They won't ripen here, Einna."

"But you grow marrows."

"Marrows are a British vegetable, squashes aren't."

"But aren't they the same family? I thought if we could grow marrows, we could grow squashes." I ought to have stopped there. "Debbie makes a great pasta dish with squash, pine nuts and feta cheese. She fries the squash cubes in olive oil and nutmeg."

"I am not growing fucking squashes, Einna."

He slammed out. He always slammed out. It was one too many slams that had caused the split in the bedroom door.

Why was I thinking minefields? This was peace time. You aren't allowed to invade my peace time, Tom. But it's not your fault that you have. I've conjured you up. If I walk through the grass to my greenhouse, I should be able to banish you. I wish I didn't have to banish you. I wish…

'No use wishing, Einna. You've made your bed, lie in it.'

Bloody hell, two to banish. Go away Annie. No! Prickles. I don't want prickles today.

Prickles would start to gather on my scalp if I became tense or anxious; gardening, writing my problem as a poem, playing my violin or rearranging my earrings into a new collage could help. I didn't often play my violin, now; Tom talking about it as 'screeching away on that old fiddle' hadn't helped. Perhaps we gang women had metamorphosed into different beings. Maggie didn't direct plays, not since Bozo, her name for diverticulitis. Debbie didn't go on protest marches. Angela? Angela had pupated into an imago who lived in France and we didn't know the ins and outs of her daily life.

Gang jaunts were things of the past. Yes, the three of us who still lived in Liverpool did meet occasionally, but it wasn't the same. We no longer laughed until we wet our knickers; time, cares we couldn't reconcile, had put paid to unbridled mirth.

In my teens and early twenties, I would never have imagined being able to enjoy carefree laughter. In my thirties and forties, toppling into laughter became an event I was accustomed to, but I'd never have imagined being excited about seedlings poking their pale green heads through the soil. Now it was a joy I couldn't imagine living without.

I'm not a gardener who wears gloves. I love the feel of soil on my hands, between my fingers, especially if it's humus rich. In some odd way, it brings back memories of sand between my toes as Jean and I, shrimping nets over our shoulders, made our way down to the shallow, low tide sea.

As I opened the greenhouse door, I noticed the Glory Vine seeds had germinated. I could visualise a pot by the back door with an Eccremorcarpus, to give the plant its botanical name, winding up through the honeysuckle. Glory Vine was a far more evocative name than, Eccremorcarpus: a squash plant beside it to trail over the side and some French Marigolds and Nasturtiums in the front; companion planting, just like all the gardeners on *Gardeners' Question Time* and *Gardeners' World* suggested. I was addicted to gardening programmes and often imagined having a garden or part of a garden of my own to care for, not just pots. This particular pot would be a tribute to the sun, pale yellow through gold to orange. I would have to keep on top of the black fly and afterwards the cabbage white butterflies. Both pests honed in on Nasturtiums. Tom called them large whites. I stuck to my childhood name. It reminded me of Ruby; she was forever exhorting their gardener to watch out for cabbage whites on the Brassicas. I had no idea what Brassicas were then. For the Black Fly, I employed an ecological method of pest control: squidge or spray with a solution of eco-friendly washing up liquid and water.

I was so entranced by the Glory Vine shoots, I failed to notice what was waiting for me further on. The emerging squashes and gourds looked as though they'd been mistaken for targets in a war zone. Pots were lying broken on the floor. There were half eaten seeds, bitten off shoots, and soil everywhere.

The morning peace vanished in the mess. As I swept up, I noticed mouse droppings. The vandal! How the bloody hell had it, or they, got in? I was always very careful to close the door. Would Tom have popped in for a look and forgotten to close it? *Don't be daft, Einna. Tom is more careful than you about things like that.* Everything was pristine yesterday. I looked at my watch. It was five past seven, fifty-five minutes to breakfast, not enough time to find out how the mouse or mice got in and sort out a way of protecting my plants from further forays. But it was Tom's morning for the library. I could wait until he was gone and then prepare the defences for my propagation world. I added, 'MAKE SECURE', in big capital letters to my list of jobs. I knew what I was like when I gardened. Even though my gardening world was tiny, the least thing could deflect me from the job in hand, for one task merely illuminated others. Scrubbing the pots was one job I'd thought to do today. This would entail tipping out all the soil onto a large plastic sheet and, after the pots were clean and dry, replacing it with the addition of peat free humus and some horse manure so they were ready for planting.

What's the date? Oh come on, Einna, April the fifteenth, Zac's birthday. There was still time to sew more squash and gourd seeds. The now milder weather should help them to germinate quicker.

I don't know where this love of gardening came from, perhaps the father I never knew. He had a garden shed. Neither Pearl nor Annie were gardeners. Charles and Ruby had a lovely garden, but they could afford a gardener. The Hunstanton garden comprised of one pear tree, a long concrete path down to a fence and grass which was cut every ten days by Pearl. When I was old enough, it was one of the jobs I had to do for my pocket money. It was a job I enjoyed doing. I called the lawn mower Push-Me Pull-You, after the odd llama in Dr. Dolittle.

For half an hour, I re-sewed seeds; I had just about enough seed compost left. Then I made my way back to the house via the bins. I left the bag with all the debris from the mouse raid on the ground. I'd have to take it to the tip.

The silence in the house greeted me like an old friend. It was a comfortable silence which I knew would become edgy as the minutes ticked by.

'You were like a fucking elephant when you got up this morning. Why can't you stay in bed like me?'

'This coffee's shit. Have you bought a different brand?'

Pathetic, I'm pathetic. Tom isn't always explosive. Why do I let one burst of anger affect me so? Yesterday was a good day, wasn't it? Accentuate the positive. Where did that phrase hale from? A song?

At breakfast, he'd talked about a blackbird which had alighted on the handle of his spade. "I could almost believe it would come on my hand. I know they say the songbird population's decreasing, Einna, but we certainly help with our feeders and nesting boxes. I saw House Sparrows, Dunnocks, Blue Tits, Coal Tits, Long Tailed Tits, Great Tits, Green Finches and Gold Finches, all in the space of quarter of an hour." Not a swear word. Not one swear word.

Before lunch, he'd come into the kitchen with one of his hands behind his back. "Close your eyes, and open your mouth," he'd said and popped a small, round grainy fruit into it. It was sweet, with a sharp edge. "Well, what do you think?"

"Yummy."

"You know I didn't mean that. What is it?"

"A strawberry."

"The first of the greenhouse ones. I don't think they're as good as the ones in the garden, but they're not bad."

I'd leant over to give him a kiss. He'd brushed it away. He always brushed it away. "That hair of yours," he'd said. "You should get it cut."

"Maybe we..." *Don't make suggestions, Einna.*

"Maybe what?"

Don't say, 'nothing'. "Maybe we could have a few for our evening meal if there's enough?" I'd been going to say, maybe we could take some with us to Zac's birthday tea.

"We could. I'll have to leave picking them to you. England's playing a friendly."

But that was yesterday and the only certainty about living with Tom was uncertainty. As I laid the table, I heard the phone ringing. It was Claire, reminding me of Zak's birthday tea that afternoon.

"Did you really think I'd forget?"

"No. But I was wondering if you could do me a favour?"

"Of course, what is it?"

"Could you make one of your coffee and walnut cakes? When we were in the supermarket yesterday, I asked Zac to choose his birthday cake. He stared at them, shook his head and then looked away. It's his new, I'm ignoring you, trick.

"There were loads of different cakes to choose from. I thought he'd go for a Thomas the Tank Engine one. 'What about this one, Zac?' I said.

"He turned round again and frowned. Oh, Mum, he looked so serious, I wanted to laugh. He said, 'I want a nana cake.' 'A nana cake?' 'Yes, that brown one with nuts.' He must mean your coffee and walnut one, mustn't he?"

"I expect so. The only other cake I make regularly is a fruitcake. That's dark brown, but I seem to remember he spat it out. Wow, I'm flattered."

"It'll make a change if he eats anything on his birthday. He didn't eat much last year, remember?"

I did remember, and the memory highlighted another 'Tom' problem. *Should I ask him if the toy box is ready, or should I say nothing?* I did have a 'just in case' present.

For the second day in a row, he came down in a jaunty mood.

"The library phoned me yesterday. They've got the woodcraft book I ordered. I shall be home for lunch, though; I've got to finish Zak's toy box. We can't go to his birthday tea without his present. I wonder if he's still got that old duck I made him last year. He loved it, didn't he?"

He did. After he unwrapped it, he wouldn't be parted from it. He trundled it backwards and forwards across the living room shouting, 'quack'. The floor was ideal for his trundle, as Claire and Andy had stripped and varnished the floorboards. When it was time for tea, he refused to be put into his high chair, or be parted from the duck.

"No tea," he kept saying. "Quack, Tom's quack," and off he would toddle again.

I suggested they left him; it was his birthday, after all. But Claire decided otherwise. "He'll get overtired, Mum. You know what he's like then." She picked him up. Charmer two year old turned into monster two year old. He screamed. He kicked. He tried to bite.

"I can't hear myself think," Andy said.

Nor could I.

To her credit, Claire remained calm. "I'll take him over to the window. He loves the bird feeders in the apple tree." They sat on the wide sill and she started counting. "Look Zac, there's one sparrow, two, three, four…" Gradually he stopped trying to throw himself about and joined in. When they reached ten, the screams subsided to an odd hiccup.

He looked up at her. "Where Zac go?" he said.

I felt like crying.

Tom got up. "Now, young man, I think Quack's hungry. He needs to eat."

He took Zac from Claire, picked the duck off the floor where he'd been dropped and took them to the table. Zac made no further protests and was soon feeding egg sandwiches to the duck.

This year, Zac decided the toy-box Tom had made was a boat. Wisely, I thought, Claire and Andy allowed him to have his tea in it. I was so busy watching him select favourite toys to take with him on his voyage, that I failed to notice a small packet by my plate. There was a packet by Tom's plate as well. It was a custom of Andy's family.

"I got a present for Dad too," said Claire. "He and Tony can't come. They've got a golf match." She pulled a face. "They're going to try and pop in tomorrow when the kiddy gang are here."

The kiddy gang were Zac's friends from nursery. I was coming to help. Tom wasn't.

Now John had retired, he'd given up rugby in favour of golf. The 'face' told me that Claire had been hurt that he'd put a match before his grandson's family birthday celebration. Perhaps people never get used to feeling rejected. Too strong a word? My word. John hadn't rejected Claire, but he had often put himself first; Paris, my need to phone May to check Claire was alright, his need for food.

I opened the packet. Inside was a pair of earrings, enameled ones in the shape of Zs. They were black, pink, green and red.

"They're gorgeous," I said. "Every time I wear them I shall think of you, Zac."

Zac, who loved tuna rice salad, his choice of food for his birthday tea as well as my coffee and walnut cake, was stuffing spoonfuls into his mouth. "Now you open your present, Tom," he said, spraying Quack with rice.

Tom looked astonished. "What do I get a present for?"

"Zac insisted," said Andy. Tom unwrapped it. It was a garden almanac. "I thought it might come in handy."

"It will. Thank you, Zac."

"Put your earrings on, Mum? I'd like to see what they look like."

As I took the silver violins out of my ears, I wondered if Claire had noticed they were the only earrings I wore now. Recently, I'd been thinking it was time to spin an earring web. The winks and glints from the earrings on the board seemed to accuse me of neglect. But an image of Tom's lowering face had, so far, prevented me from succumbing to their enticements. I wasn't sure what the problem was; that the earrings on the board had been part of a life without him? Whatever it was, my need for earring independence was growing.

Tom noticed the struggle I was having to find the holes in my ears. "Here," he said. "I'll help. Did you choose them Zak?"

Zak looked up and nodded. "Yes," he said, spraying his toys with more rice. He picked up Quack and shook him clean. Tom handed me the violins. "Put these in your make-up purse." There was a pause, not long enough for anyone but me to notice. Had he read my mind? He smiled. "They'll be safe there." It was impossible to know what the smile meant.

When we got home, he said, "I don't know about you, but I don't like those earrings, I think they look cheap."

Tiptoe, Einna. "I like the colours," I said. "But mainly I like them because Zak chose them."

He pinched his eyebrow. A sign. I'd learnt to recognise signs. Sadly? Stupidly? Somethingly? I didn't always pay heed to them.

That night, when we got ready for bed, I put the earrings on the board. The violins would be back in my ears the following morning.

Chapter Fourteen
The Battlefield

Head in the sand, waiting
for the next fusillade of fury,
the next salvo of sarcasm,
the next bout of bullying,
the next,
the next…
In the silence I surface
and shake sand from my eyes.

I don't know how many poems I've written through my adult life, as an attempt to reconcile what I couldn't alter, for once written, I popped them in my treasure box which now lives in the drawer with my jumpers. I doubted that Tom would do a room search for a box full of childhood memorabilia; after all, I hadn't talked to him about the technique of writing down problems in order to help solve, rationalise, or ameliorate them. I never really knew if it helped. It became a habit; something I had to do. I wrote the one I'd just placed in the box because I didn't know how I'd arrived in this no man's land of a war. No, that wasn't quite true. In a physical sense, I knew how it had happened, but in a deserving sense I kept thinking, *why me?*

I had just about got accustomed to tiptoeing through the minefield that was living with Tom, when Annie retired and moved to Hunts Cross to be nearer to me.

"There's nothing to keep me in Hunstanton," she said. "Hunts Cross isn't far from you, is it? We can have nice days out together."

Annie talking about 'a nice day out' was astonishing. It made me anxious about what she might expect of me.

It didn't take long for me to realise what the expression, 'between a rock and a hard place' meant. The gaps between the prickle-band headaches lessened and I began to suffer with night sweats again. Was the menopause never ending?

I woke up gasping for breath. Sweat running down between my breasts. I wanted to throw off the duvet but I couldn't; it would wake Tom. I checked my clock. It was five thirty; too early to get up, too late to try and go back to sleep. All this anxiety because I was meeting Annie for a cup of tea? But it wasn't just about Annie; it was Annie and Tom.

If Tom was a minefield, Annie was a constant barrage and when the two were together, they were a war. In the beginning, they'd made a pretence at peace, but the season of goodwill on earth put paid to that, and Annie hasn't set foot in Tom's house since.

Deck the halls with boughs of holly, tra-la-la-la-la-la-la-la-la.
'Tis the season to be jolly, tra-la-la-la-la-la-la-la-la.

Musak, churned out in supermarkets from October on, seduced shoppers into frenzies of spending. Carols exhorted us to be kind and charitable to each other, but surface niceness was what so many people were about. Annie and Tom didn't understand surface niceness.

I'd gone over to Hunts Cross to pick up Annie on Christmas Eve. She seemed to be in a reasonable mood and didn't complain when I told her that I wouldn't be accompanying her to church the following morning.

"You know where it is, don't you?" I said.

"The one John and I used to go to?"

I didn't rise. "Yes, that one."

When I'd got dressed that morning, I'd considered exchanging the violin earrings, for the Annie, pearl ones. I'd looked at them, gleaming coldly, on their white headed pin.

Pearls, Mummy. Pearls, tears; a memory I couldn't shake off.

The devil I did. The devil I didn't. I used to wear them to try to please Annie, because I hoped it would save me from tongue lashings. But I was told they'd cost an arm and a leg and should be kept for best. I was told I'd lose them because I was careless. When I didn't wear them, I was an ungrateful wretch who didn't deserve presents. Whatever I did would displease either Annie or Tom. Of the two I'd rather displease Annie. I was distanced from her moods.

Christmas Eve continued amicably enough. She and I watched festive offerings on the television. Tom read the newspaper, looking up occasionally to see why we were laughing. I began to relax. I almost rang Maggie to see how she was faring and tell her my fears hadn't been justified.

We had a leisurely start to Christmas morning. Annie enjoyed the bagels, smoked salmon and cream cheese we had for breakfast. We decided to leave present giving until the afternoon as she wanted to have a shower and get ready for the ten-thirty service. She arrived back from church as I was preparing lunch. I heard her and Tom talking about the unseasonably mild weather. Their small talk encouraged me to hope that the rest of the day would pass off without incident.

"Let there be peace on the earth," I sang, not realising she had come into the kitchen.

"And, let it begin with me.
For peace is born on the earth,
So let it begin with me.
Let there be peace in your heart today."

"I don't know that carol," she said, making me jump.

"It's not a carol. It's a song I composed for the youth orchestra and choir."

"It's quite nice." Praise indeed. She stared at the swede I was cutting up. "Swede with turkey?" The look on her face suggested disbelief.

"Yes, mashed with lots of butter and black pepper. It's delicious."

"Would you like a sherry, Annie? Or a glass of white wine?" Tom said.

"A small, medium sherry, please."

"Einna?"

"As it's Christmas day, I think I'll have a G and T."

"G and T? You never used to drink G and Ts. As for swede with turkey, I've never heard the like. Brussels sprouts, that's what you should have. I hope we're having brussels. It's not a proper Christmas meal without brussels."

"I agree. We're also having carrots and roast parsnips. Tom and I like lots of veg, don't we Tom?"

Whatever goodwill may have been floating about, flew out the window with those words, or tried to but, as it was closed, smashed against the pane and fell to the floor.

"Tom and I, eh? What I'd like doesn't count."

Prickles began their march over my scalp, to a band playing, *'Tis the season to be jolly*.

"I didn't say that. I said we were going to have brussels—"

"You didn't have to. When you were married to John—"

Tom intervened. "No need for that, Annie. We've had a nice time so far, haven't we? Let's carry on trying to be polite to each other, shall we?"

"Polite? Ha! And who said I'd had a nice time?"

"Did you say, 'Ha'?"

"You heard."

I dug a hole in the sand, hoping that if I shoved my head in deep enough, I wouldn't hear the jolly music changing into the thud of bullets and the explosion of mines.

"You are a selfish, ignorant man who doesn't know the meaning of the word 'polite'. A polite man wouldn't have buried his head in the newspaper all yesterday evening. A polite man would have accompanied me to church, like John used to do. John may be a queer, but he's a gentleman."

"That's it. Pack your bags and get out." Annie didn't move. Tom took a step towards her. "Did you hear me? Get out of my house."

"It's Einna's house too. I'm not going unless she tells me to go."

"No, Annie, it's *my* house. Fucking misery, that's all you've ever brought me."

"Me, me, me. That's all that concerns you, doesn't it, Tom Emmerson?"

And what about you, Annie? What about you? She rounded on me. Had she read my thoughts?

"Are you going to stand there like a long streak of nothing, and let him speak to me like that?"

They were looking at me, waiting for a response. Oh god! I was their real enemy, kneeling in no-man's land, head in sand, arms in air, mute by choice.

Simultaneously, they turned and walked away; Tom towards the back door, Annie up the stairs. Muffled by the sand in my mouth, I sang words they wouldn't hear.

'Let there be peace on the earth,
And let it begin with me…'

Of course, I had to drive her back to her house and suffer the tirade which ended with *what did I think she was going to do about food?* She didn't have a big freezer, not like some people. I'd foreseen that this might have been a problem and put some groceries into a carrier bag.

"That's nice, isn't it? A tin of soup and a cold turkey sandwich for my Christmas lunch. Tramps who go to the Salvation Army hostel get a proper Christmas dinner."

That I didn't shout, *'Well bloody go there then, see if they can put up with your rudeness?'* was a Christmas miracle.

Since that day, once a fortnight, I'd driven to the centre of Liverpool to meet her for a cup of tea, a piece of cake and moans.

I slipped out of bed. The cool air in the room turned my perspiration cold. I shivered. That's what the menopause was like, one minute in the tropics, the next in Antarctica. If God did exist, what better proof was there that he was male? No self-respecting goddess would have given her own sex so much to endure; the pains of menstruation, accompanied by volatile mood swings, the agony of giving birth, the sweaty menopause, more mood swings. I cried at the drop of a Tom temper, or an Annie tantrum.

In the kitchen, I made myself a chamomile tea. No caffeine this morning. I needed to be gentle with myself.

As I drew back the curtains, I saw dawn breaking into a gloomy morning. The grey skies threatened rain. It wasn't a morning to take my drink outside. I grabbed a blanket from the chest in the hall, and went into the lounge. I would read until breakfast time. I'd got a new biography on Sir John Barbaroli, which Maggie had lent me.

The morning brought no surprises, no conflict. By two o'clock, when it was time for me to go out, it was pouring with rain. I took my umbrella out of the box seat of the hall stand, where it lay, stubby and black, among the boots and shoes. I opened the lounge door to say goodbye to Tom. He looked up from his newspaper, took in my outdoor clothes and said, "You're going out to see that fucking sister of yours, in this?"

My mind leapt about like the grasshoppers before my flying feet on the heath at Hunstanton, all those years ago. He knew. How?

"Don't ever apply to MI5 for a job. Fucking stupid code in your diary. 'A at B, 4'. Why B, not L, this week?"

Tom has read my diary? What else…? Has he found my treasure box and all my scribbling's? No, my treasure box is safe underneath my jumpers, and I'm pretty sure they haven't been moved. Why has he read my diary? I wouldn't read his diary. Tom doesn't have a diary.

I said, as calmly as I could, "I shall be late if I don't go now, Tom. Let's talk about it when I get in this evening; it'll keep, won't it?"

"No, it won't keep. I know what you're doing. You're playing fucking counselling games with me. We'll talk now, or not at all."

Not a game, Tom. A survival technique. "You don't like being late for appointments, do you? Well, neither do I. I'll see you this evening."

"Appointment? Having tea with your sister's an appointment? It's disloyalty."

I walked out, closing the door quietly behind me. There was no rush to prevent me going, no expletives. Perhaps he'd said all he wanted to.

Sometimes, like John, the barrage of words ended the rage and it would be followed by a period of calm. Tom would go about his business as though nothing had happened.

With part of my early retirement lump sum, I'd bought a newish, second hand KA. My Deux Chevaux, Brigitte, which had been lovingly serviced by a friend of Bill's, for many years, had finally gone to Deux Chevaux heaven. I didn't love KA as I'd loved Brigitte. But she was reliable. I called her Prunella because she was plum coloured.

Tom's car lived in the garage, mine in a cul-de-sac, near us. It was the only way to avoid the stress of having to move it every time he wanted to use his, or vice-versa.

On days like today, even the short walk meant battling with an umbrella that insisted on turning itself inside out in the blustery rain. I was going to be soaked as well as late, only a matter of a few minutes, but enough for the Annie grumbles to start. She wasn't in when I rang to suggest a change of café, so I left a message on her answer phone. Before the row with Tom, she used to leave me messages, almost every day, and she ticked me off for not listening to them. Not having to listen to interminable Annie messages was one positive outcome of the row.

I parked in a cul de sac behind Hope Street and before I got out I went through the earring ritual; silver violins into my make-up purse, Annie pearls into my ears. Why I didn't wear my Monas, for courage, I don't know; habit, Annie habit. As I was doing the swap, I noticed a cobweb between the wing mirror and the side of the car; it glittered with raindrops. It had travelled through the storm without being damaged. I needed a web that strong for why I was late. I couldn't give Annie the real reason.

As I opened the door, a pearl earring fell into my lap. I hadn't pushed the butterfly on far enough.

She was sitting with her back to the wall, staring at the stairs. "I was beginning to think you weren't going to turn up. You're over a quarter of an hour late," she said, her face screwing into punishment mode.

"The traffic's dreadful today, I don't know why."

"Most people take traffic into consideration when they're meeting someone. How was I to know if this was the right café? I've never been here before. I bet you didn't think about that when you decided to change the venue."

'Don't think, stupid, liar, I shall have to punish you.' Childhood abuse flickered around me. *'Be assertive,'* I heard my counsellor say.

"I'm sure I said, 'The Everyman Bistro, Hope Street,' Annie. There is only one. And it really isn't my fault I'm late." Would my hurriedly spun web hold? A thought struck me. I ought to buy spiders' web, earrings and wear them instead of the pearls, instead of the violins, instead of any of the earrings on the board.

"I'm sure it wasn't. I bet it was the fault of that man."

"No, it wasn't."

'You'll get spots on the tongue if you lie, Einna.'

I won't, Annie. It's a myth, a fairy tale, an old wife's tale, untrue… untrue… a lie. A lie you've told me all my life.

"And how was I supposed to know how to get here? You seem to forget I don't know Liverpool like you do. I had to ask someone where Hope Street was. We always meet in Lewis's café. I know how to get there. I got soaked coming all the way up here."

"Why didn't you take a taxi?"

"I'm not made of money. What did you want to go and change things for? That's what I want to know. I like Lewis's café. They do a nice teatime special, and it's a good price. I bet this arty-farty place is expensive." She sniffed. "So, what made you decide to alter our meeting place then?"

"Well, I was talking to Maggie, the other day…"

"And she suggested The Bistro, did she?"

"Yes."

"And you have to do everything Maggie says? I shan't be surprised if she turns up to stir the sugar in your tea, one day."

I resisted saying that I didn't take sugar. It would have only be greeted by, *'sarcasm is the lowest form of wit and the highest form of vulgarity.'* "I thought that you might like this place for a change."

"You oughtn't to discuss me with your friends. They should learn to mind theirs." She tapped the side of her nose.

Tom and Annie, Annie and Tom.
As alike as two peas
when they carry on.
But I wish I had
an enormous gong
to drown out their discordant song.

It seemed a long time ago that I'd made up that ditty.

"I don't suppose that man's ready to apologise?"

"I've told you before, Annie, Tom won't apologise." Tom thought he was in the right. You thought you were in the right: impasse. We know two wrongs don't make a right, but sometimes two rights don't make a right. I knew what she was going to say next; she always did.

"I don't know why you moved in with that man. Lots of women live on their own and they manage perfectly well. But not you, after you divorced John, you had to jump into bed with the first man who crooked his little finger."

It wasn't worth saying that I didn't divorce John. We divorced each other. I'd said it countless times before. I looked down at my wet shoes. Umbrellas, even those that didn't flip inside out, didn't protect shoes from blustery storms. *Well Einna, it's a good thing she knows nothing about Michael.*

"He'd have had you back, you know? He thought the world of you."

I looked up. This was a new, totally off the wall, tack. "John left me for Tony, Annie. He's gay."

She snorted. "Men aren't born queer, Einna. Something happens to make them want to do things with men. You didn't make him happy, so that Tony person was able to prey on him."

Oh for god's sake. "Tony didn't prey on him. They met, regularly at the rugby club and fell in love." Her face crunched up in disgust. "I don't see the point of rehashing all this. It's not relevant."

"Yes it is. It's why we meet in cafés. I hope I haven't caught a cold, that's all. What you don't know is, I waited outside in the rain. That way, I thought, I wouldn't make a fool of myself going into the wrong place. While I was waiting, I heard an ambulance go past. I thought you'd had an accident. I was worried sick. I came over all dizzy. I had to sit down. That's why I came in. I wouldn't have otherwise. I nearly fell down the steps. What do they want to have a café in a cellar for?"

"I don't know, and I don't understand why you were concerned. I may not be the best driver in the world, but I've never had an accident."

"More by luck than judgment."

"You don't drive, so how can you judge my driving?"

"You don't have to drive to know if someone's a safe driver. You're a harum-scarum person, all over the place."

A 'harum-scarum' person. A new tack, now a new insult. *Liar, thief, drama queen, coward,* those were the adjectives I was used to. Annie hadn't been worried sick. Bristling with annoyance, more like. *I am not going to say sorry.*

"And do stop that."

"Stop what?"

"That." She pointed to my earrings. I was twisting one in my ear. "They were quite expensive, you know. You oughtn't to wear them every day. You didn't used to. You wore those cheap, silver things that man gave you. You've lost them, I suppose."

"No, I haven't lost them. I don't wear these every day. I wore them today because you gave them to me. I always wear them on the days we meet."

"You didn't wear them when that man threw me out of the house."

Circles. Our conversations always went in circles. Did she hope that the second time around would bring a different outcome?

"Shall we go and order?"

Annie made no move to get up. "I hope they do a nice cup of tea here. I don't want coffee. I only drink coffee in the mornings. I don't sleep if I have it after midday. I bet you didn't think of that when you and your friend decided a change would be good for us. Do they do a special here, like they do in Lewis's? It's very good value, there."

Nice cup of tea. 'Would you like a nice cup of tea?' 'I could do with a nice cup of tea.' Who would want a nasty cup of tea? I could have done with a herbal tea and a headache tablet.

"They have real leaf tea here, Annie, and they make scrumptious cakes. I never know which one to chose. I'd like to try them all, really. I usually have coffee, but if I have tea, I have Assam."

"I don't like Assam. I always have Ceylon. I'm sure they do Ceylon tea with their special, at Lewis's. It's served in china cups. Tea should always be drunk out of a china cup."

I'm going to scream if she mentions Lewis's again. Anyone would think she had shares in the place.

"I got puffed out, getting here. It's uphill all the way. I'm sure my blood pressure went sky high."

"I'm sorry." There I'd done it. I'd given her the apology she was looking to throw away. "We won't ever come here again."

"It's no use being sorry now. People with cars never consider pedestrians."

"I got wet too, but you probably didn't notice."

"You wouldn't have got wet if we'd met at Lewis's, and neither would I. I know how to walk to Lewis's from the bus station so that I stay under cover."

"Have you looked at the cakes?"

"Of course I haven't. For crying out loud, stop fiddling with your earrings."

"Sorry, Annie." Bloody hell, the sorries were spilling out of me like an overflowing gutter.

"What are you sorry for? A silly habit; being late; or not standing up to that pig you live with? If you weren't such a wimp, we wouldn't be wet through, nor would we be forced to pay for having a cup of tea together. I'll never get over it, being thrown out of my sister's house."

Tom's house, Annie, not mine. "He didn't throw you out. He asked you to leave." *Round and round we go.*

"Asked? That's rich. I'm not going to repeat what he said, but if that's asking, then I'm a Dutchman. He threatened me. I was terrified."

"I don't remember you being terrified, Annie." If anyone was terrified, it was me. "You were as angry as Tom." *How many times have I said that in the course of our café meetings?*

"I didn't swear. I never swear."

And that makes you a better person, does it? That makes you less of a bully? At least Tom has never beaten me.

"I'm going to get a drink. Are you coming?" I didn't look to see if she was following me to the counter.

"I don't suppose you have any teacakes," she said to the person who served us. "They do a nice cup of Ceylon and a teacake for one ninety-five in Lewis's."

When I got home, before I went into the house, I did the earring swap. It was then I noticed that one of my pearl earrings was missing.

Chapter Fifteen
Enigma

Why? Why am I attracted to this man?
He uses me. He is callous.
He is angry. He is insecure.
He takes my love and
throws it back in my face.
He gives me pain in stormy scenes
when I need soothing words.
He accepts my gift of love
as though he deserves it
and offers me the tattered remains
of his fractured feelings.
He appears to enjoy his power
and I collude.

All my life I have colluded. Why? Why did I stay with Tom? Why did I continue to see Annie? Was I cursed with an oversized duty of care bundle? Whatever Annie had done to me when I was a child, however she behaved towards me now, I couldn't abandon her, nor could I abandon Tom. They had no-one else. Oh my god, was that it, that they had no-one else?

But where was love in all this? As I told John, many years ago, love is complicated.

Prickles, prickles on my scalp increasing, merging and forming into a tight band around my head. *I can't breathe. Calm down, Einna. You know what to do, breathe slowly, in, one two three; out, one two three. There, that's better, isn't it? Do it again: in, one two three; out, one two three. Now, lift your shoulders up. Go on, crunch them up. Hold, release.*

Sing? Toni told me that singing was therapeutic. It did work, sometimes. I enjoyed singing. I didn't have a good singing voice; luckily it wasn't necessary for teaching the violin.

I sang, *Please Don't Let Me Be Misunderstood*, on the way to my counselling session. On the way back I was too drained to sing.

I liked my counsellor. Her name was Toni. When I first phoned for an appointment, I thought I would be seeing a man. I was relieved to discover my thought was wrong, I wasn't sure why. Perhaps because I felt women understood emotions more than men.

In our first session, she told me that anything I said was in strict confidence.

I wish my partner was dead. I wish he would go away and never come back. I wish I'd never met him. The wishes leapfrogged over each other in their effort to escape. Then the guilt flooded in. I didn't wish Tom dead. I didn't wish he would go away. I didn't wish I'd never met him. So often we had lovely times together. What I wished was… that he would react differently; be my starling murmuration man, all the time. A tear trickled down my cheek.

When I was a child, I got used to wishing Annie and Pearl would die so that I could go to live with Aunty Ruby and Uncle Charles. Children can be forgiven bad thoughts, especially if they are being ill-treated. Adults can't. They are supposed to put away childish things. I thanked her. She asked me why I felt I needed counselling. Interesting that, *need* not *want*. Words are so important. Did I need counselling to help me get rid of bad thoughts? If I were stronger, would the good times swamp the bad?

"Strategies to help me to be stronger so I can deal with my partner's anger, and my sister's continued attempts to bully me. I have panic attacks."

"I'll come to the panic attacks in a moment. Tom doesn't abuse you, does he?"

Abuse. What is abuse? I felt as though I'd been abused all my life: Pearl, Annie, John, Michael, Tom. I colluded in the abuse for I rarely stood up to the abusers; I pretended I was a spider and built webs to survive.

"My sister's the only one who's abused me physically."

"She abused you, how?"

"Oh, Annie had a variety of punishments for different, so called, sins. She beat me with my hairbrush, she boxed my ears, she slapped my face… but… and it will probably seem odd to you, the worst thing she did was give my teddy bears to a Salvation Army jumble sale when I was six." I got a tissue out of the box on the table. "It's a long story."

"We've plenty of time. It'll be helpful for both of us."

"But will it be true? I know we can have false memories." Why did I say that? It was written down and safe in my treasure box, along with the poems and Lake District story. "When I was a child, I made friends with an angel. She suggested that writing about the abuse might help. I kept it all. I can let you read it, if you want?"

"It might be useful."

"My angel, Jean, was the owner of Matilda, the last hut along Hunstanton beach. She befriended me, one day, when I was eight years old. I was hiding under Matilda, crying for the abuse I'd suffered at the hands of Annie. Jean died of cancer when I was nine, and I didn't know how to deal with my grief. A few years ago, I wrote 'grief is a knot of air'. Air, because it floated about, like a grey cloud, inside me. 'Knot', because all my feelings were tangled together inside it. Did you know that clouds weigh hundreds, if not thousands of tons? My knot of air made me feel as though I couldn't lift my head from the pillow, couldn't put one foot in front of the other."

"You say you made friends with an angel?"

"Yes. I'm not being fey. Not a real angel, a figurative angel, my guardian angel for a while. Even though Annie still punished me and Pearl neglected me, I felt safer, somehow, knowing Jean existed, knowing she had offered me sanctuary."

"Tell me about your childhood."

I told Toni everything I felt was relevant, everything that I could remember. I didn't know whether counsellors were supposed to maintain neutral expressions when they were listening to clients. I imagined they were. I thought I saw sadness in Toni's eyes when I told her about the treatment I'd received from Pearl and Annie, and a fire of anger and bitterness consumed me. I hadn't deserved that abuse. No child, no adult deserves abuse. The session was eaten up with anger. She said it was okay to be angry.

"But I did have other guardian angels who helped." I told her about Uncle Charles, Aunty Ruby and Thomas Gardner.

"I'm glad there were some figurative angels in your life," she said. "I find it interesting that 'angels' is how you describe them but I like it. We all need angels."

"I'm not religious. But I've always loved the idea of angels. I know some are described as avenging angels, but others look after people. But none of my angels are alive now. Thomas Gardner does still help provide a rhythm.

"So your aunt and uncle are dead?"

"Yes some time ago. My uncle, not long after Tom asked me to move in with him. And my aunt, pretty soon after that. Gradually, through my middle-age, I saw less and less of them: distance, work, but we spoke once a week on the phone, and remained close.

"I want to understand why I'm so weak and wobbly. I'm fifty nine and I still can't deal with Annie and Tom. It was a friend who suggested counselling. I've got to stop being so pathetic."

"You're not pathetic. You're sensible. You've realised it's never too late to get help."

In session two, after I'd handed her my childhood scribbles and she'd asked how I'd been and I'd told her that it depended on the day and how Tom was, and whether I was due to see Annie, she said, "Tell me about your relationship with Tom."

"I care about him."

"Not love?"

"Isn't caring love? I think there are many kinds of love. I love my daughter and my grandson. I love my friends. I get a pain, mental and physical when I think about Tom not being in my life. That has to be love, doesn't it? It's just so hard living with him."

"Do you mind if I jot down the odd note?"

"No, of course not." I told her about John, Claire, Michael, and Tom. I told her about the gang. I told her about Lena and Fred. Another dam burst. I don't know what she made of the flood, but she didn't look as though she was drowning. Again, I used up the whole session in talk.

"I'm sorry."

"What for?"

"Talking non-stop. It must be exhausting having to listen; concentrate on people's splurges."

"It's what I've chosen to do. You needed to 'splurge', as you call it and it's been useful for me. Next time we'll discuss strategies. Creating webs isn't bad, per se, Einna. It's been your coping mechanism to date. You may still need it as one of your strategies. Religion has much to answer for in its attitude to lying. We all lie, almost every day."

"Do we?"

"Yes. Here's a Scenario. The alarm goes. X hears it, but for whatever reasons, doesn't react. Waking too late, the person realises he or she is going to be late for work. X blames travel conditions. This lie hurts no other person."

"I see."

"Just one thing before you go, Could you persuade Tom to come to counselling with you?"

"I doubt it."

"I thought you might say that."

In session three, we discussed strategies. One of the ones I knew I would practise was connected to breathing. When we become stressed, our breathing pattern quickens up. It's this that leads to a panic attack We need to learn to control the air in and out of the body. Slowing it down helps us to keep calm and stay focused.

I told her how difficult it was to engage in any conversations with Tom because they were so convoluted, I always got lost. "Conversations are almost always bound to give me a prickle-band headache."

"Prickle-band headache?"

"I get this sensation that feels like prickles creeping across my scalp until they form into a tightening band."

"Have you been to see a doctor?"

I knew what she was thinking: *brain tumour.* "Yes. And I've had a scan. It was clear. The doctor suggested it was stress."

"Have you talked to Tom about it?"

"No. It sounds so daft. When I tried to talk to him about our relationship, he said I ought to know that there were ups and downs in all relationships. Of course I know that, but…" There was a longish pause as though Toni was waiting for more. But I didn't know how to continue. "Knowing doesn't help the stress, or how it affects me," I finally said.

"Is sex okay for you?"

"It's always wrapped up in how he is. Isn't that the case for most people? Isn't everything I'm telling you what other people deal with as well? You know, normal life?"

"Other people didn't have your childhood."

"To be honest, nowadays, sex is more out of duty than want."

"Duty features a lot in your conversation, Einna."

"I know, I'm sorry."

"Why did you feel the need to say sorry?"

"I don't know. I say sorry a lot. I think it's a trait of women to apologise. If someone barges into a woman, she'll apologise."

We were silent again for a few seconds. There, in that safe room, I felt so relaxed. I glanced at the clock. The session was over. When I got home I looked at the notes I'd made and wondered if I'd ever deploy them. The breathing… I'd make an effort to breathe properly.

I liked the last one. *Make sure you have treats.* A treat could be anything from a glass of red wine with a morsel of grainy cheddar, or a square of dark, silky chocolate, to a day out with Maggie. It is only her and I now, with Angela in France and Debbie in Ireland. Sometimes I wondered if Bill's betrayal hit Maggie, me and Angela almost as hard as Debbie? *No, don't be stupid Einna. It hit us hard because we'd put him on a pedestal.* He was Maggie's role model man; for me an angel, now a fallen angel, for Angela? I never really knew what Angela thought of Bill.

"An affair?" I almost collapsed when Maggie told me. "No, not Bill."

"Yes, Bill. I've just got back from being with Debbie. She's... 'distraught' isn't the right word. Her world has collapsed. And it's not just an affair. He's gone to live with the other woman. She's a colleague. It's so cruel, Einna."

I couldn't get my head around it. They were *the* rock solid marriage. But no, they weren't. So, no relationship was... and it couldn't have been appearances, could it? I know we weren't there for the ins and outs of their marriage, but... how did one ever know? How could one ever be sure? If Bill and Debbie weren't a forever relationship, no marriage was.

About three months later, Debbie disappeared. Her note said that she couldn't bear to be in the same city as the man she'd loved, and who'd betrayed her... 'betrayed' was her word. I wondered if she would ever feel that it was better to have loved and lost, than never to have loved at all?

One morning, as Tom and I were having breakfast, the phone rang.
"It won't be for me," he said, his mouth full of toast.

It was Claire. "Mum, Zak's ill."

"Poor sweetheart. What is it?"

"A stomach bug, I think."

"I'll be over as soon as I've thrown some things in a bag."

"You're an angel, Mum."

No, just a granny.

"Zak's ill and you're whizzing over there to look after him," said Tom when I returned to the table.

"How did you know?"

"You haven't got a quiet voice, Einna."

"But I... Do you want to come with me?"

"What would I want to do that for? I don't want to catch whatever virus Zak's got, and I don't want you bringing it home. Anyway, I've things to do."

"Have you?" I realised I didn't know what was on the calendar this week.

"I've a doctor's appointment, and... Oh, it doesn't matter."

I kicked myself. "Do you want me to go with you?"

"No, but that's not the point. I don't have a say, do I? You're going to go, whatever I want. The fact that I think your daughter and her husband are being fucking inconsiderate is by the by. Surely Zak's old enough to be left on his own, isn't he?"

Again I was on the spot. Tom liked Claire, Andy and Zac. Why was he angry? *Which strategy, Einna? One, slow your breathing down, two, super nanny technique? Nothing really works, does it? Except for the breathing. In one, two three. Out one, two, three.* "He's poorly, Tom and he's only eight. You can't leave a child alone at that age. I don't think she or Andy are being inconsiderate. I'm glad they feel they can ask for my help. You do have a choice. You can come with me, or stay at home." *Wow! That was assertive, wasn't it? Toni would have been proud.*

"They're his parents. One of them should stay with him. It's not as though you'll be gone for just a day, is it? Oh do what you fucking want, you always do."

Unfair. But that was Tom. I went upstairs, packed a bag and left. In the car I sang:

"I'm just a woman whose intentions are good.
Oh Tom, please don't let me be misunderstood."

Had Tom been neglected when he was a child, or spoiled ? Either scenario could have produced this person who found it difficult to think outside his own box.

Treats. Zak and I need treats. As I drove through the Liverpool suburbs, I planned them: the latest film on DVD, suitable for an eight year old, invite Maggie round for lunch. I knew Claire and Andy wouldn't mind.

Read to Zak. He enjoys fantasy books. I'd popped *The Weirdstone of Brisingamen* into my bag.

I rang Tom every evening. He seemed quite cheerful. He told me he'd changed his books at the library, watched sport on the television, and kept his appointment at the doctors. His voice was my starling murmuration man voice.

"What did he say, Tom?"

"I'll tell you when you get home."

"Is something wrong?"

"Stop fussing."

Driving home wasn't a singing, journey. I did try to sing whenever I went back to Roby Road. But today I felt guilty, and anxious about Tom's health. *Why guilty, Einna? You're a granny, Tom isn't. He loves Zac. Does he love Zac? Or when he's with him, does he make a good show of loving him? Zac is taken in. Zac thinks the world of Tom.*

"You're back," he said as I walked through the front door. He was sitting at the kitchen table, an empty bowl in front of him.

"Yes." I put down my case and leant forward to give him a kiss.

"That hair." He rubbed his cheek.

"You okay?" I asked

"Why wouldn't I be?"

"I just wondered. You said you'd tell me how you got on at the doctor's."

"You've only just walked through the door, Einna. Don't you want to take your coat off before you start interrogating me?"

"I'm not interrogating you Tom. I care."

"If you cared so much, why did you fuck off and leave me?"

Stupid. You laid yourself open there, Einna. I took off my coat, poured myself a glass of red wine and sat down. *Deep breath, don't answer the question.* "I'd really like to know what the doctor said."

"I'm anaemic, and I have polymyalgia. We suspected the first, and knew the second. The visit was a waste of time."

"If he's put you on iron tablets, it's not a waste of time, surely."

He frowned. "I'll decide that."

"Is he keeping you on the steroids for the polymyalgia?"

"Yes. I shall be fucking rattling soon. Have you eaten? I've made some soup, but I've had mine. Why are you so late? You know I like to watch the news at seven."

"I had to wait for Claire or Andy to get back from work. No, I haven't eaten."

"I'm glad you're back. I'm tired of getting my own meals. You're in the driving seat now."

These words aren't threatening, Einna. Come on now, breathe slowly. Tom's going to watch the news; there's not enough time for an outburst.

He glanced at the clock, and hurried from the room. I put the soup back on the hot plate, took a sip of wine and cut a slice of bread.

One minute and he was back. "The fucking clock must be fast; the news isn't on yet. Have you altered it?"

"Did you watch the news yesterday?"

"Why don't you answer the question?"

"Because if you did, the clock was right yesterday."

"I… oh never mind. Before I forget, the kitchen sink's filthy, and we've run out of cleaner."

"I'll get some tomorrow." *Deep breaths. More wine. Why couldn't he buy some cleaner?* "I'm going to make a cuppa after I've eaten. Do you want one?"

"That would be nice, coffee please. Are you going to join me?"

It was the last thing I wanted to do. The news was always so depressing. I couldn't change what was happening: wars, torture, abuse. All the news did was make me feel more impotent. The news, for Tom was one more vehicle for his anger. He'd spent a lot of time in the lounge watching the television, since polymyalgia and anaemia.

"He and Trevor could be twins," Maggie had said, in one conversation about the idiosyncrasies of our respective partners. "They're both super-glued to inactivity aren't they?"

"Tom didn't use to be idle. It's the combination of—"

"Neither did Trevor. It must be us, Einna." She'd laughed. It hadn't been a knickers' wetting laugh.

"Trevor doesn't get angry."

"Trevor's too idle to get angry."

"Tom must have had anger issues before I met him. I still can't work out how he managed to hide them when we weren't living together."

"We did try to warn you about his body language. All his gestures were jerky. I've often wondered if he's bipolar?"

Yes, his gestures were, still are, jerky... bipolar? I didn't know enough about the condition. "My counsellor suggested he might be on the autistic spectrum."

"I think Trevor must be on that spectrum too. 'What would I want to socialise with your friends for, Maggie? They've nothing important to say.' But then perhaps we're all on that spectrum."

I was nodding as I thought of my earring collages, and how I'd know if any were moved.

We hugged each other for support, and for the men we'd met, loved and lost, or in my case, the man who never was. I also thought the hug was because Maggie had lost herself and I hadn't found myself.

I poured the soup into a bowl, and took it over to the table. Tom glanced at the clock, and rubbed his hip. "Don't look at me like that, Einna. Your face is so transparent. I know what you're thinking. Take the pain killers, and walk."

"I wasn't thinking that."

"You don't lie well, you know."

"I—"

"Don't interrupt. I do walk. I walk every fucking day."

I hid a gasp, by putting a spoonful of soup in my mouth. Walk? Walk where? Tom walked about the house. Sometimes he took a stroll in the garden, more often than not to grumble about what I was doing, because he had given up gardening. He had given up everything connected to being active.

"You know what you ought to do, and what you can manage." I said. He snorted and left the room. I heard him muttering but I couldn't catch what he was saying.

I finished my soup, drank up my wine and ate two pieces of chocolate. When I took the drinks through to the lounge, Tom said, "Gas is going up, electricity will follow. Arseholes."

"We could always change companies."

He gave me his, *you stupid woman*, look. "You don't think the others will follow suit? And if you want to change fucking companies, you do it."

"I…"

"By the way, Doreen called while you were away. She stayed for over an hour."

"That was nice."

"It wasn't. She was being nosey. Did you put her up to it?" I hesitated. I couldn't find the words. "You're not answering. I imagine that's a yes then."

"No, it isn't." Doreen was one of our neighbours, a pleasant woman, but not someone I would choose as a close friend; she has verbal diarrhoea. "I expect she came to see me about something. What was she being nosey about?"

"Why you were away, for one thing; she gave me the third degree and she talked at me for over an hour."

"She's lonely."

"Well, there are things she can do about it, like join some clubs."

Why does Tom suggest things for others he would never do himself?

"Look at that. They want wasting, fucking twats."

I wanted to cringe at the swearing, but I'd always suspected that was what Tom wanted. He only swore when he was with me. I told him, in the first couple of days after I moved in, the effect it had on me. Mistake. I finished my tea, put the mugs on the tray and got up.

"That didn't take you long. You haven't been home above half an hour, and you can't spend five minutes with me."

"It's not that Tom, you're watching the news and—"

"So, why can't you watch it with me for once?"

"You know I don't like watching it."

"And you won't do anything you don't like, will you?"

"I do…" No. This was the moment to leave the room, before the finger stabbing began.

"I'll have to think about that. I don't expect many people do things they don't want to do, unless it's necessary." I walked, deliberately slowly, towards the door.

"You're playing counselling games again, aren't you, Einna? You're no actor; not like that friend of yours, Maggie. She's a right little drama queen."

Why had Maggie crept into the conversation? I paused, hand on knob.

"And before you ask, she came round as well, so don't try to tell me you didn't alert all of Liverpool that your socially inept husband was going to be on his own for a few days." He tapped the side of his nose. "You should learn to mind this."

Maggie must have popped in after having lunch with me, meaning to be kind, to help me.

That night, I dreamt I placed marbles all the way down the stairs.

'You can have them, Mum. I don't need them any more. I play croquet now, don't I?'

'Thank you, sweetheart. Aunty Ruby tells me you're getting so good at the game, you've even beaten Uncle Charles once.'

'I did, and I beat him at marbles. You were wrong, you know. Marbles is a game for everyone Put them in the pocket of your dressing gown for safe keeping...'

'Claire, Claire, where are you? You hiding? Didn't Daddy tell you it's rude to leave before a conversation's ended?'

'But you've made up your mind, Mum. Nothing I can say will make any difference.'

'I only want a bit of peace. Concussion, hospital. Don't forget...'

'Don't forget to put the marbles back in my pocket before the ambulance arrives. I know.'

And make sure Tom's asleep before I put them on the stairs. I stare at him. Even breathing, good. I slide out of bed, tiptoe to the door, open it and avoiding the stair creaks, put one marble here, another there, all the way down...

I jolted awake. A noise, a thud, something had disturbed my sleep. Sometimes, when a person is woken suddenly, he or she remains in the dream. As I was wondering what I would discover at the bottom of the stairs, I heard a groan. Tom wasn't a crumpled heap in the hall. He'd fallen out of bed, and was struggling to get up.

"The room's at forty five degrees," he said. "I can't get up and if I don't I shall piss myself."

I helped him to the bathroom then back to bed. In the morning I rang the surgery and told the receptionist that Tom needed a home visit. A Doctor Patel arrived at midday. She gave him a thorough examination. Transient vertigo was her diagnosis. I had suspected it was something like that.

Later that day, as I was tidying our room, I found myself staring at the earring board.

'You need punishing, my girl. I'll punish you for having wicked thoughts, and even more wicked dreams. I'll dismantle your collage, and throw away all your earrings.'

My thoughts, Annie's voice. It wouldn't be a punishment, though, it would be a relief. I'd be shedding a burden. I mean, how fey, how stupid was it to stand and stare at an earring collage and imagine the earrings forcing me to choose them, pulling me into their stories?

I reached up to start stripping the board. I couldn't do it.

Later, I came to believe the vertigo was some kind of trigger, for Tom's health deteriorated from that day and, in due course, we learnt he had leukaemia.

Chapter Sixteen
Fairground Rides

We're climbing to the top.
of the Roller Coaster.
Whizzing down.
I fear we'll hit the ground.
I want to get off.

I never liked fairground rides. They always made me feel sick and scared. You weren't allowed off until your time was up, and the music stopped. That's how I felt when Dr. Jones told us about the results of Tom's blood tests.

"You have leukaemia, Tom," he said. "I'm going to send you to see a specialist at The Royal." Doctor Jones didn't believe in wrapping up bad news in euphemisms.

I heard my screams as the White Knuckle Ride took off. *Leukaemia, what does it mean? Not leukaemia, surely. Tom is anaemic. Leukaemia?*

"The symptoms of anaemia and leukaemia are very similar, which is why I asked the nurse to take another blood sample when you came in a couple of weeks ago. If you ring the surgery this afternoon, the receptionist should be able to tell you when your appointment at the oncology clinic is. The leukaemia could be why you had that bout of transient vertigo."

"What's the prognosis?" Tom asked.

"I can't say. I have very little experience with leukaemia. A GP can't know everything. That's why there are specialists. Mr. Ashton is one of the foremost specialists where leukaemia is concerned. He'll give you all the information you need."

On the day of his appointment, I drove Tom to hospital. The combination of the polymyalgia, anaemia, and leukaemia meant that driving had become uncomfortable for him. Tom usually commented on mine and other people's driving. Today he was silent.

The Oncology Clinic was heaving with bodies. Tom had always been irritated by queues. I waited for the explosion, prepared to pretend I wasn't with the bundle of anger at my side. *What am I thinking? Stupid woman! He's not going to explode. No, Einna, not stupid woman. You are not a stupid woman.* An explosion was no more likely now, than comments about driving. He hadn't the energy to explode, not any longer. And suddenly, Tom not exploding seemed like a matter for crying. I pretended to blow my nose to hide the threatening tears.

He took a number from a box at the reception desk and we sat down. A nurse came out of a room, facing us.

"Twenty seven," she called

Tom's number was fifty-six. I picked up a magazine and sat down. It looked as though we were in for a long wait.

Why do people in waiting rooms look at magazines that are years old? I didn't want to read the one I'd chosen. I didn't want to read any magazine. I leafed through it, pretending an interest I didn't feel. It was something to do. It masked anxiety. Tom stared straight ahead. I had no idea what he was thinking or feeling. Even if I'd asked, he wouldn't have told me.

I looked at the clock on the wall, knowing that when I looked at it again, the hands would have barely moved. Time has always puzzled me. It seems to have a will of its own, for it can go quickly or slowly, and is rarely how you want it to be. When you want something to end, like waiting, or to happen, like getting in to see the doctor, it crawls. If you are enjoying yourself, it whizzes along.

From time to time, I glanced about me. People were blank-faced, like commuters on the Underground. The difference? I didn't imagine many people travelling on the tube were hoping for good news, but expecting bad.

It was three quarters of an hour, that seemed like five, before Tom's number was called.

"You're lucky," said the man sitting next to us. "Last time we came we had to wait three hours before we saw the consultant."

"Do you want me to come in with you, Tom?" I asked.

"Please yourself. I'm quite capable of going in on my own."

"I'd like to come," I said. I needed to know everything about this disease. Leukaemia, cancer, words that caused anxiety, words that tolled a bell.

There were two nurses in the room, but no doctors. One of the nurses was already dealing with another patient, taking blood from her arm. I was puzzled. Where was Mr. Ashton? We were here to see Mr. Ashton.

"Can you roll up your sleeve please, Mr. Emerson?" said the nurse who had called us in.

"Why?" asked Tom.

"I have to take a blood sample."

"There's been a mistake," I said.

Tom frowned. His body, his disease. "I've come to see Dr. Ashton. I've already had blood tests at our surgery, and the results."

The nurse looked at Tom's notes. "There's no mistake, Mr. Emerson. We need to do a more comprehensive test, so we can check the composition of your blood now. There are different forms of leukaemia. We need to know which one you have."

"Does that mean I won't see Dr. Ashton today?"

"Oh, no. We analyse this test right away. It takes about fifteen to twenty minutes, usually."

Bloody hell, more waiting, but better than being told we have to make another appointment.

Tom rolled up his sleeve. Half an hour later, we were in Dr. Ashton's consulting room. He asked us to sit down.

"Tom," he said, looking at him over his glasses.

Interesting, the nurse had called Tom, 'Mr. Emmerson'.

"You have acute myeloblastic leukaemia."

Myelo what? Why didn't diseases have simple names like 'cold'? Everyone knows what having a cold signifies.

"It's a form of myeloid leukaemia."

As if that makes a difference to my understanding of the first word.

"With a disease like myeloblastic leukaemia, it's almost impossible to predict how it's going to progress, so," he paused, "no one can tell you what your life expectancy will be. Some people live with the disease for several years." He paused again. "With others, it's just a matter of months. Whichever it turns out to be, we'll try to give you as good a quality of life as possible." He smiled.

I stared at a painting of poplar trees. It was an Alfred Sisley print. It was the same picture as the one in the lounge of my childhood home, in Hunstanton. Annie now had it in her flat in Hunts Cross. I hate the picture. I always have. It was of a cold, flat landscape, and had seemed to embody the lack of warmth or love in that house. As I stared at it, the glass splintered and the trees swayed with the words 'years', 'months'.

Dr. Ashton continued, "We're going to manage your illness in this way, with your permission, of course."

Manage Tom's illness? Has the world gone mad? Is Myeloblastic leukaemia a firm? Is it a football club? I glanced at Tom's face. At the moment he was giving nothing away.

Dr. Ashton took off his glasses. "Your notes seem to suggest you're in favour of natural remedies, wherever possible. So I think we're ruling out any form of aggressive medicine as far as dealing with the leukaemia, aren't we?"

Aggressive medicine? Does that mean months, or years? What is aggressive medicine? Radiotherapy? Chemotherapy? Myeloblastic Leukaemia. How are we going to cope?

"You will have to have some drugs. But to begin with, I'm going to admit you to the oncology ward for a few days. You need to have several blood transfusions, and we have to monitor you in between.

Transfusions place a strain on body organs, and for an older person, that can be a risk. I don't want to keep you in hospital any longer than is necessary. We don't have a big problem with MRSA here, but…"

We waited. *But what? MRSA could kill Tom? Acute, myeloblastic, leukaemia, is going to kill Tom. Months? Years? It sounds like some form of explosive. Perhaps that's its meaning. Perhaps it explodes in the blood?*

"But you need three units of blood, one today, one Wednesday, and one Friday. That means you can go home on Sunday morning. You should feel much better by then. You'll be surprised how a transfusion will perk you up." He beamed at us.

"That's not a few days, that's seven," said Tom.

The smile froze on Dr. Ashton's face.

Something was tickling my neck. A thread from the sleeve of my jumper had caught in one of my earrings. I took it out. When I looked at it I was astonished to see how tarnished it had become.

"I don't think there'll be a problem getting you a bed on Darwin ward. They always keep one or two free for emergencies. Jenny, can you come in here a minute."

Jenny was 'Jenny'. Tom was 'Tom'. Dr. Ashton was 'Dr. Ashton'. Who was I?

The nurse who'd taken Tom's blood sample appeared round the door.

"Give Darwin ward a bell, will you? Tell them I'm sending a patient over." He turned back to us. "Any questions?"

I waited to see if Tom asked any. He was silent.

"How often will you want to see Tom?" I wanted to know what the future pattern of our lives would look like. *Months? Years?* This time Tom didn't frown at me. I looked across at him. His eyes were blank. What was he thinking?

Michael. I was back on the Runcorn bridge, hearing words that shocked, that clogged the mind and refused to allow other words, thoughts, to enter. Tom looked as I'd felt then. Different sentences but both devastating to the recipient. He, however, didn't become frenzied, as I had then. He remained still.

"Every two weeks," said Dr. Ashton.

"Every two weeks?" said Tom, coming back from wherever he had been. "You're not serious, are you?"

"Certainly I am. When you leave Darwin ward on Sunday, I want you to come to reception here and make another appointment to see me." He consulted the calendar on his computer. "On the twelfth. You'll have to have another blood test then. Like today, it will be checked right away, and then I'll decide whether or not you need another transfusion. As I said before, you're going to be surprised at the difference a unit or two of blood will make. You'll feel the benefit almost immediately. Your appetite will increase and you'll have more energy."

Tom pinched his eyebrow. "You mean I have to be admitted to fucking hospital every two weeks and stay for a week?"

No Tom, don't swear. Don't get angry. This doctor holds your myeloblastic leukaemia in his hands.

Dr. Ashton didn't react to the swear word. "I'm sorry," he said. "I wasn't very clear was I? No, if the blood test shows that you need a unit or two of blood, you'll attend the outpatient's clinic of Darwin ward. It's a day's procedure, no more."

"Then why do I have to stay in this time?"

"You've never had a blood transfusion before, have you, Tom? Transfusions give respite from the disease, but as I said, they also put the body under great stress, and we need to monitor that the first time. Any more questions?"

I shook my head. Tom continued to pinch his eyebrow. I wondered if consultants were trained to read body language?

"There's no reason why you shouldn't live a pretty normal life. I'm going to ask Tracey, the Macmillan nurse, to have a word with you during your stay in Darwin ward. The time will come when you need to decide if you're going to stay at home, or go into a hospice. Tracey has the expertise to help you with that."

"Of course I'm going to stay at home," Tom said.

"In that case you'll need support."

"What sort of support? Einna's all the support I'll need."

I was and wasn't astonished, pleased. It was a sort of compliment.

"I won't have strangers in my house."

Ah. Of course. My house.

"Yes, well. Let me put it like this. You don't live in a bungalow, do you Tom?"

"No."

"There will come a time when you can't manage the stairs. Tracey has the list of organisations that will be able to help, like social services. They would construct a second stair rail if one were needed, for example. Also, the hospice at home team is wonderful. But I'll let her tell you all about what's on offer." He looked at me. "You will need help, Mrs. Emerson.

Tom is 'Tom'. I am 'Mrs. Emerson'. Except I'm not Mrs. Emerson. Tom and I aren't married.

He stood up. We stood up. He held out his hand. "I'll see you on the oncology ward." We were dismissed. *Our months, our years, are no longer important. Why should they be? He might have to tell the next patient he, or she, has only a few weeks to live.*

"I'll have to go back to the house and fetch your pyjamas, and washing things," I said, as we waited at the desk for directions to Darwin ward. "Is there anything else you'd like?"

"My book, and that magazine Andy lent me, the one on wood turning. Who knows, I may get back into woodcraft this winter."

Months? Years? Oh Tom, even before the myeloblastic leukaemia, you had ideas, which you didn't follow through. *Months? Years?* I couldn't stop thinking about how Dr. Ashton talked of managing the illness for whatever time Tom had left.

"Leave him."

"I can't." He has to leave me. Help! Why had I ever allowed that thought? *You know why, Einna. Because you have never understood Tom's need to explode.*

We had coped with the polymyalgia, the anaemia; Tom doing less, me doing more. But this disease that sounded like a bomb, with diffusion being blood transfusions and tablets; how were we going to cope with it?

"If this is the gentle way to deal with fucking leukaemia, whatever's the aggressive way?" Tom said when he saw the number of tablets he was expected to take, every day.

One tablet made him constipated. Lactulose was added to the daily dose. Another made his skin dry. I didn't bother the doctor with this. I bought a moisturising bath wash and body cream. Sometimes, at night, he was convinced he was going to fall out of bed, and no amount of reassurance convinced him he was safe.

He developed an ulcer on his leg. A district nurse came every day to change the dressing. Like it or not, Tom's house was being invaded.

In the beginning, he railed at the disease, his body, the doctors and me. "Bloody witchdoctors. If I go to the surgery again, I'll be given another drug. I'm fucking rattling as it is. I thought all this," he swept the boxes of tablets onto the floor, "was supposed to give me a reasonable quality of life."

Then apathy set in and nothing seemed to matter. I could have stripped the house of his parents' possessions and I don't think he would have cared. He was swaddled in this debilitating Myeloblastic Leukaemia and, by association, so was I.

"Why was I such a bloody coward when he was well? If I had been braver, I could have… we could…" I wailed to the birds, the flowers, the fruit and vegetables in the garden. I dared not wail to my friends. I felt too ashamed. Claire, Andy and Zac visited, so did Maggie, and Lena. Sometimes Tom perked up when we had visitors.

Every fortnight, we trailed up to the hospital until the day arrived when Mr. Ashton told us that there were no leukaemia cells in Tom's blood. It was clear. No leukaemia cells. Tom was in remission. He needed antibiotics for the bronchitis he'd contracted but… years not months? I sang, 'Tomorrow', all the way home, in my head. Being a coward was too ingrained to risk singing aloud.

But then his appetite dwindled. He could barely make it from bed to armchair, to table, to lavatory, and back to bed and I couldn't cope. It was Dr. Jones who persuaded Tom that we needed help.

"I'm going to refer you to the hospice at home team, Tom. We don't want Einna to be ill as well as you, do we? And I'm going to prescribe—"

"I'm fucking rattling as it is," said Tom.

"Not more, just an increase in the dosage. May I use your phone? I'd like to get regular visits set up immediately."

As Dr. Ashton and Tracey had told us, they were wonderful. They even persuaded Tom of the wisdom of attending the day-care centre once a week, where they offered tempting meals and encouraged patients to have an alcoholic drink, if they would like one. It was also designed to give me respite. After his first visit, Tom told me he'd had a bottle of beer. The following week he didn't feel up to going.

On midsummer's eve Claire rang. "Mum, Zac's going to Quasar with his friends on Saturday but we're free on Sunday and I was wondering if we could come to lunch. We haven't seen you for ages. I'll bring the food."

"That would be lovely. It will be good for both of us. If Tom's having a bad day, I'll ring you. I never know how it's going to be, love." That was how we left it.

On the Sunday, Tom enjoyed a reasonable breakfast and seemed to be looking forward to seeing them. He ate his helping of seafood lasagne. Claire had used one of Angela's recipes. It had single cream in it, instead of a béchamel sauce.

"I thought you might enjoy it, Tom ," Claire said. She grinned "You need to put on weight. Andy, Mum and I don't, so you and Zac can have seconds if you want."

Throughout the meal, Zac kept taking surreptitious glances at Tom. He hadn't seen him for a few weeks, and I could tell, from the look on his face, how much Tom had altered. They left about five, and soon after Tom asked me to help him to bed.

In the first few months, after the blood transfusions, Tom had no problem climbing the stairs. Social services did put in a second stair rail so he could use both hands. More recently, they'd installed a stair lift. I slept in the spare room. I bought a baby alarm so that Tom could contact me if he needed help. My sleep was fragmented, just like it used to be when Claire was a baby, because I heard every sound Tom made.

"I enjoyed today," he said, as I folded up his clothes. His voice sounded younger, somehow. "I don't need a fucking sleeping pill. I think I'll be okay tonight."

He didn't fret about his pillows and he went to sleep straight away. Perhaps he was finally on the road to a long remission.

It was a beautiful evening. Feeling more hopeful than I had for weeks, I poured myself a glass of Shiraz and took it out onto the patio. I pictured Tom, sitting here, as I dead headed roses. "Be careful," I heard him say. "Don't yank the fucking heads off. Twist them."

Tom woke three hours later needing to go to the lavatory. He didn't manage to get there in time. Hope was sucked down the pan. I helped him to have a shower. After he was back in bed, I put on a wash, cleaned the hall and bathroom floors, then went into the bedroom to see if he'd managed to drop off again. He was sitting on the edge of the bed.

"It's no fucking good," he said. "I need some pain killers and my sleeping tablets."

I fetched them for him. "How about we watch TV?" I said. "There's a drama on at nine."

But he wasn't at ease in his chair, either. I helped him back to bed. Immediately, the vertigo overcame him. And that's how it was for the rest of the night. In his chair he rocked. In his bed he rolled. Despite sleeping pills, Ibuprofen, and paracetemol, neither of us got any sleep.

The next day, a long day, a short day, a day when the unexpected, expected happened.

I rang Anita, our district nurse, to see if she could make us one of her first calls. When she arrived I saw how shocked she was by Tom's appearance.

"You were great yesterday, weren't you? " I said. "I really thought…" I couldn't go on.

"I know you wanted to stay at home, Tom, but I think you need the special help of the hospice team. They know about pain relief. Shall I give them a ring?"

Tom nodded. Was I surprised? Four months ago I would have been… now? The man who had said 'no' to outside help, 'no' to going into the hospice had been worn down by this myeloblastic leukaemia.

When the ambulance arrived, the paramedics helped Tom into a wheelchair and out of the house. I didn't know where the hospice was, so I followed in my car. By the time I parked and found my way to reception, a doctor was already attending to him.

"My name's Rosie. We don't use titles here," she said and smiled. She scanned the note from Anita. "I'd like to insert a catheter, and then give you an injection of morphine, Tom. Is that okay?"

Tom, whose eyes were closed, nodded. I had to look away.

Rosie must have noticed for she said, "The procedure doesn't hurt, Einna."

She didn't understand. How could she understand? It wasn't to do with hurting Tom. It was the indignity… a catheter.

"Einna can stay with you, hold your hand."

You don't know Tom, Rosie; his body, his illness but… I held his hand.

The insertion of the catheter was effected quickly, and as Rosie administered the injection, I saw Tom close his eyes, and slip into a place of no pain, or at least, that was how it seemed. The sheet rose and fell to the rhythm of his morphine breathing. I wondered if he was dreaming? In some ways his whole illness had had the quality of a dream. From the beginning I'd felt as though we were on a nightmarish fairground ride we couldn't get off.

Now the roller-coaster was whizzing down the last slope, and the knot of air had taken up residence in my chest once again. Would it burst as we landed?

Chapter Seventeen
The Knot of Air

Knots of air
don't burst. They twist
and tangle, filling every
space in the chest
with a grief that
has nowhere to go.
Like clouds they loom,
lowering in the mind.
And every kind word
Only serves to remind
Me of the pain.

I was standing at the window, my head leaning against the warm glass, my eyes closed. I don't know how long I'd been standing there, but when I turned round, I knew Tom was dead. Was it the silence in the room?

I felt as though a knot of air was twisting in my chest. *How am I going to live without…? Without stress? Without tiptoeing through a minefield? Without Tom, my mercurial, starling, murmuration man? Is that what love is? Do I finally understand what love is?*

My feet wouldn't move. I had to move, to walk to the bed, press the red button.

"I need to go home for a little while." I'd told Sandra, one of the nurses, earlier in the day. "A few things to sort out." *Phone calls, Claire, Maggie, Debbie, Angela, Lena, not Annie.*

"That's fine. We'll ring you if there's any change."

Change? Does she mean when Tom wakes up?

When I got back to his house, I was so tired, I couldn't face ringing anyone. I couldn't face all the questions. Is he... Are you... Do you questions. Come on, Einna. Pull yourself together. At least ring Claire. Ask her to ring the others. But what to say? Do I know, really know what's happening? Pain relief or...?

"Do you want me to come?" she said.

"No, darling. I'm okay, really." I had to do this on my own. I couldn't face the responsibility of another person. "I'll let you know if there's a change." I used almost the same words the nurse had used. "I'm going to try and have a nap. Neither Tom nor I slept last night."

The phone woke me. Feeling as though I was struggling upwards through grey clouds, I answered it. It was the doctor, Rosie.

"We're moving Tom into a room on his own, Einna."

"Oh." The 'oh' went on inside my head for a long time. "I'll come back immediately." I thought I sounded drunk.

I grabbed some cheese and an apple, to eat in the car. *I don't understand. Why is Tom dying?* That's what she meant, didn't she? Room on his own. No cancer cells in his blood. We'd both heard Dr. Ashton say it.

As soon as I arrived at the hospice... *was it only ten hours ago when Tom was admitted?* I went to the Nurses' station and asked to speak to Rosie.

"I'm confused," I said. "I thought Tom had come in for pain assessment. That's what Anita told us, and now..." I couldn't say the words. Left unsaid they might not have been fact.

"He did," said Rosie. "Anita realised Tom was in a lot of pain; the sort of pain standard analgesics can't help. That's why she asked him if he'd be willing to come in. But when someone has been coping with pain for some time, and then they get relief, they can let go. They don't want to face the struggle any longer. I believe that's what's happened to Tom. We see it so often." She took hold of my hand.

"But why did Dr. Ashton tell us his blood was clear of cancer cells?"

"Because it was, then."

I wanted to scream. *Deep breath, Einna, now exhale slowly.* "Then why is he dyi...?" I still couldn't get the word out.

"It's not easy to understand everything connected to this form of cancer. I'm sure Dr. Ashton told you we can't always predict how leukaemia's going to behave."

"He did." *Months, years.* "But—"

"Just because the blood's clear of the cells doesn't mean Leukaemia goes away. The cells stay hidden in the bone marrow."

"Bone marrow? No one has ever mentioned bone marrow to us." *Leukaemia doesn't go away, it hides in the bone marrow.* My confusion and anger didn't go away but I had to box them up for... when? When was I going to be able to let them out? It wasn't Rosie's fault. But I wanted someone to blame. I was angry, so angry, heat behind the eyes angry. I would have behaved differently during these last two weeks. Instead of trying to get Tom to eat, to sleep, to stay in bed at night, I would have sought the morphine road earlier, saved him from some of the pain and discomfort. Then, maybe... If I'd known. If I'd known. Why weren't we told? Now it was too late. He'd gone somewhere beyond my reach and I couldn't say sorry.

How was I going to deal with this? I mean, had I enjoyed those months of increasing control? Was I somewhere in that iceberg of abuse? Had the abused become an abuser?

Not an Annie abuser; I would never have hit Tom, any more than I would have hit Claire when she was in a sixteen year old tantrum because she couldn't go to a night club. A nagger, that's what I'd been. But I did always say please. "Please Tom, try to eat, to drink, to take your pills, to let me help you get washed..." Could you be an abuser if you said 'please'?

I couldn't cry. Crying demanded energy. "Which room is Tom's, please?"

"I'll show you."

The room had a window overlooking the garden. The curtains hadn't been drawn and I saw a midnight blue/black sky with bright, glinting stars and a crescent moon. It was a Pierrot sky, a sad clown sky.

Once upon a time, I knew another sad clown. She had smudged mascara eyes and a red gash for a mouth.

"I'd like you to press the red button there," she pointed to a button on the wall above the bedhead. "If you're anxious about anything. You may notice Tom's breathing changes. That's a sign he's dying."

"Changes how?" I asked.

"Becomes shallow, fluttery."

"Shallow, fluttery." As I repeated her words my thoughts fluttered away from Tom, leukaemia, and death, to Matilda, the last hut along the beach at Old Hunstanton, and the sea that trickled in shallow ripples over the sand, and the little blue butterflies that fluttered above the heathland behind the dunes. Matilda, my childhood sanctuary, which had been destroyed by the nineteen fifty-three storms and tides. But death had trickled in across the sand there, too. For Jean, who had owned Matilda, and helped me survive Annie and Pearl for one year, had died; another cancer.

"Would you like one of our nurses to be with you?"

"No, thank you." I didn't mean to sound ungrateful but I wanted to be alone with Tom, to say sorry, tell him I loved him. I couldn't do that in front of a stranger.

"What about a cup of tea?"

Tea, the English panacea. Hot strong tea with plenty of sugar, a drink for shock. Would I shock Rosie if I told her that what I really wanted was a glass of dark, red wine, tasting of berries and terracotta earth? That *beaker full of the warm south* which would numb… Tea was… Tea was not what I wanted just now, indeed it made me feel nauseous thinking of it.

"I don't think so, not at the moment, thank you."

"Later perhaps?"

"Perhaps."

"Don't be alone if you need support."

"I won't."

Rosie left the room. She walked without making a sound. The whole hospice was quiet, not at all like a hospital. It was a peaceful quiet, and yet I was slightly unnerved by it. Doctors and nurses seemed to glide everywhere, about an inch off the floor. They reminded me of the Deputy Head at one of the schools I used to visit. She had been the eyes and ears of the Head, and as like a spook as anyone I'd ever met. She had glided about the school corridors; no one knew where she would materialise next.

One day, when I'd been taking an orchestra rehearsal, I heard a quiet voice in my ear. I jumped. I'd neither heard, nor seen her come in.

"You haven't noticed that Tracey's chewing gum, Lorraine's wearing training shoes, and Carl has his coat on, Einna."

I'd looked at her in astonishment. She was right, I hadn't noticed. What I had noticed was that the pupils were absorbed in what we'd been doing.

She hadn't stopped the rehearsal to demand the offences be pointed out to the offenders. She'd merely nodded, and left. Later she'd said, "I know you're not a teacher in our school, but I think it's important for everyone to be aware of school rules. You won't let it happen again, will you?" I remember thinking how clever it was to ask a question at the end of a telling off, however mild. What could you do but agree, or have an argument and get into trouble?

Trouble. I think I've always been scared of getting into trouble. Annie used to punish me for nothing, then when I was too big to hit, box, clip, there were sanctions. When I got married they metamorphosed into tirades. Annie tirades, John tirades, Tom...

Does any of this matter now, Einna? In the face of death, nothing really matters. That's the song I want played at my funeral, Bohemian Rhapsody. 'Mama, just killed...'

Leukaemia was killing a man, my man.

"Don't Mum," Claire said, when I told her what I wanted. "You know I can't bear to think of you dying."

However uncomfortable, we should discuss death and all things related to it. After all, birth followed by death is, perhaps, the only universal truth. We aren't very good at death in England. All that stiff upper lip stuff. Isn't it better to wail and gnash teeth, have a proper wake?

A friend of Maggie and Trevor's had sent out invitations to a death café. She and I had been intending to go before this myeloblastic leukaemia. It might have helped me to know what to do.

Music, Tom. What music would you like played at your funeral? Richard Strauss? You loved his darkly romantic music, didn't you? The Alpine Symphony *maybe?*

What was I saying? I couldn't play that particular piece at Tom's funeral. It would be disrespectful. I wouldn't be able to concentrate on him. I'd be whisked back into a world where I danced like a puppet to the tune of alpine horns.

Will Debbie remember? She might think it very odd, if she does. I could play Thus Sprak Zarathustra. *No, I'll play* Go Now. *It will be more appropriate. Tom likes the music of the sixties and The Moody Blues is one of his favourite bands. Is it 'is', or 'was'? Hot tears, hot anger. Does the body know the difference?*

Debbie might not be able to come. It's a long way from the Beara Peninsular to Liverpool. It's a long way from The Maine et Loire for Angela and Dave, too.

I suspected that, of the gang, it would be only Maggie and I who would be there to say, *Go Now*, to my mercurial man.

What's the legal process? What do I have to do? I know there's a lot of business connected to dying, the funeral, the death certificate, the will, stuff like that. Stuff, stuff, I don't know what to do about the stuff. I sniffed, but the heat threatening tears still lingered.

I knew Tom had left a will. He told me it was with his solicitor and there was a copy in the bureau drawer in the lounge. I didn't ask what was in it. I didn't even think about asking. He was such a private person in so many ways. He hated nosiness. Nose tapping to signify, stop being nosy.

I'd never been actively involved in anyone's death. I'd attended funerals, paid my respects, but not helped to organise. Annie dealt with Pearl. Ruby and the Oak Vale staff dealt with Charles. And when Ruby died, they rang me, but said it was all in hand; Ruby had left clear instructions for her funeral and burial. It might have been the only clear, concise instructions she ever gave; unless Charles had done it all before his stroke.

I sat down on the chair by the bed. "Shall I hold your hand, Tom?" I knew he wouldn't answer, but I felt that holding Tom's hand might help centre me, help me to get my thoughts straight. Why? Holding hands had never played a part in our relationship. What had? What physical aspects had been 'us'?

"I'm drowning, Tom. I need the touch of your warm hand to pull me up through this knot of air, that like weeds in a pond, are holding me under the water."

I picked it up, cradled it in mine. It was warm. Why had I expected it to be cool?

"Do you care what music's played at your funeral?" I asked him.

"Play what you want," I heard.

Suddenly the tears water-falled down my cheeks and I could feel my body shaking with sobs. I tried to stifle them, keep still; I didn't want to wake him. Could external noise, movement wake someone who was in a poppy-infused sleep? I touched his cheek. It felt prickly. Tom was a twice-a-day shaver. He wouldn't be shaving any more. Sometimes, during the months of the myeloblastic leukaemia, I'd shaved him. He hadn't had the energy to stand at the basin, and he couldn't bear electric razors. Social services had provided us with a bathroom chair and a shower stool.

"Want me to do it today?" I'd say, and I'd wait to hear, "Mind you're careful. I know what you're like."

I know what you're like. You didn't say it, you thought it. I knew it was the illness that made you accept my help without commenting. Pre myeloblastic leukaemia you used to claim you knew what I was like, oh about so many different things. Pearl, Annie, John, Tom, you'd all claimed to know me, but you didn't. You had imposed an image you'd dreamt up, on me. I was a figment of your imaginations.

As I massaged my chest where the pain was greatest; where the knot of air was tangled. I saw a small brown bird, flitting through trees in a wood. I saw a young man waiting, waiting to hear its inimitable song

224

so he could pass out of this world to one that was pain free. Tom had been given a dulling opiate, perhaps not the one the poet had described, and I felt as though I could have done with one too. I wanted to escape what was happening.

There was a wet patch on the sheet from the tears dripping off my nose. I got up, walked across to the basin, splashed my face with cold water and patted it dry with paper towels. *Where is panda Einna? She's as dead as Tom will be. Water to cool watery red eyes. Oh how different the scenario. You can't be a panda without mascara, Einna.* I hadn't worn make-up in ages.

It was at this moment I noticed the label. My blouse was inside out, and no-one here had drawn my attention to it. As tears had welled, so now did laughter. *Don't wake Tom, Einna.* I couldn't stop. *Whoops, no spare knickers in your bag.* For, woken by the telephone, I'd hurriedly washed and changed my clothes, as the ones I'd had on were sleep crumpled. I didn't know how long being in a separate room meant: minutes, hours, days?

I took the blouse off and turned it the right way. This simple action seemed to calm me more than the water. Then I heard, *"I don't know where you'd be without me to check you over."* Tom had often tucked in labels, checked to see that my clothes weren't inside out, and popped wires through the holes in my ears. The knot of air grabbed me once again. How was I going to manage without…

'Don't be such a wimp, Einna. You were always a wimp. You never stood up for yourself. That's why Pearl couldn't stand you. You made me abuse you because you were such a wimp.'

'Go away, Annie.'

'You managed before you got into bed with that man. You'll manage again.'

I wasn't married to Tom. I was what's called, a common-law wife. What rights did I have? I would ask Andy; he was a solicitor. I wouldn't be able to ask anyone anything if I couldn't stop crying.

In the mirror, I saw the sun dipping in the sky. Was today the longest day? Or was it yesterday when Claire, Andy and Zac had come for lunch? The peas would soon be swelling in their pods, and after them, the French beans. In August, there might be a melon or two; in

September, squashes. Last year, Tom had enjoyed the squash soup I made.

"This is an unusual carrot soup," he'd said. "But I like it."

"It's the nutmeg." A small spider's web.

This year I'd kept the mouse, the slugs and the snails at bay, but Tom wouldn't be there to enjoy any of the harvest. Nor would he be there to pick the first strawberry, tell me to close my eyes, hold out my hand, and guess what he had placed in it.

I walked across to the window, leant my head on the warm glass and closed my eyes. *Oh god, all I want to do is sleep.*

Was it that the pane of glass was growing cooler? Certainly the room was growing darker. Or was it that I could hear only my breathing? I drew the curtains, turned away from the window, and glanced across at Tom. Was he still poppy sleeping? I held my breath. Silence. *One foot in front of… Come on Einna.* Almost tiptoeing, I walked back to the bed, and reached for his hand. It was still warm. I tried to find a pulse. I couldn't. I pressed the red button. Rosie and a nurse came in. I stepped away from the bed, to give them space. Rosie knew without checking, but went through the process because, legally, she was obliged to do so.

"Would you like to help us wash him?" she asked.

I didn't know what to say.

"You don't have to. Some people feel it helps them to say goodbye."

My teeth were chattering, but I wasn't cold. The silver violin earrings danced in my ears. "It's not that. I've helped Tom to wash and dress for the past month. But, I'm used to doing it on my own, not with… strangers. Do we have to dress him now, for his funeral? I haven't thought about clothes. We never discussed his funeral. Tom is…wasn't religious."

Rosie took my hands, held them; the shaking gradually lessened, then stopped. My teeth ached. "There," she said. "That's better. You don't have to make any decision about a funeral at the moment."

"May I ring my daughter?" Claire might know what to do. Andy would know what to do.

"Of course you may. You can do it from the nurses' station. And you must have that cup of tea. It would help if you had a spoonful of sugar."

Just a spoonful of sugar… It wouldn't help.

Claire said she would go to Tom's house and bring over some of his clothes; no formal suit, no collar and tie; his tweed jacket with the leather patches on the elbows, his Vyella checked shirt, and his corduroy trousers; clothes he was fond of, clothes he was comfortable in. She knew they were his favourites.

She had a spare key. I never told Tom I'd given her one. But I needed to know that she and Andy could get in, in case I needed help. Before Tom started to lose weight, he was almost too heavy for me to lift. I had a terrible job getting him up, when he fell out of bed, especially the first time, the vertigo time.

When she arrived, I saw she had been crying. We hugged, and the physical contact released more tears.

"Andy will see to all the legal stuff for you," she said, when she could speak. "Do you want me to stay, Mum?"

"No, it's okay, sweetheart. I'm going to help wash Tom now, then I'll go…" I couldn't say, 'back to Tom's house'.

"Come to ours. You can stay the night, stay as long as you like."

Tom's house and memories, or the bed I used when I stayed at theirs? "Thank you, I will."

"Have you eaten today?"

"I had some porridge this morning and a bit of cheese and apple after I had a sleep, this afternoon."

"I'll heat up some soup." She kissed me, stroked Tom's hand and left.

Closure, the fashionable word for coming to terms with death. Washing Tom helped me to say goodbye to his body. When I washed his face, I gave him a kiss. I heard, no one else did, *"That hair of yours."*

I would have liked to leave then, but it seemed to be expected that I would want to stay, for Rosie and the nurse left the room on their angel-winged feet. Ten minutes, Tom? Would it be considered odd, unfeeling, if I left in ten minutes? Whispers filled the room, '*Do what you want. Can't stay the course. You can't even watch a…*' I put my hands over my ears. "Tom," I cried. "I've hardly left your side in…" *Why do I do this? Why can't I think about all the good, the great times? Why can't I dwell on Tom, the starling murmuration man?*

Nothing of what had happened during the past few hours seemed real. Real was being with Tom, listening for sounds not associated with sleep. Real was getting out of bed to help him walk to the lavatory, cleaning him up if we didn't get there in time. Real was giving him oxygen. Real was helping him to the lounge where, for a little while, he was comfortable in his chair. Real was encouraging him to have some Horlicks, trying to get him to eat.

I thought about taking out my silver violin earrings and putting them in the breast pocket of Tom's jacket, but my hands froze by my ears.

Chapter Eighteen
The Earring Board

With a glint. With a giggle.
With a squint. With a frown.
They call, 'Us. Choose us. Our turn.
We want to come down.'

On the bedroom wall of Tom's house was a collage of earrings. Every time I looked at it, I saw bits of my life hanging on pins. Claire grabbed a handful of earrings off the board. Ooof! I felt as though she'd punched me in the stomach.

"Don't put those on the reject pile please, darling." I was surprised I still had air in my lungs.

"I thought we agreed to get rid of all the stuff you don't want."

Stuff? Thought we agreed? I hadn't agreed, had I? Surely silence doesn't mean agreement? "I need my earrings, sweetheart." *Need, not want.*

"You hardly ever wear them, Mum. It's not a criticism, but you really only wear the ones Tom gave you."

"I know, but…" I touched one of the violins in my ears. It seemed to burn my fingers. I couldn't let it go.

'Silver violins for a violin teacher.'

His voice was so loud, I wondered that Claire didn't hear it. The ghosts by the door tittered.

'But the circumstances, Tom. A moving in present after you'd hurled abuse at me for…' For what?

'Words, Einna. Only fucking words.'

Words that hurt. Words that made me wonder what I was doing; when in the beginning, I'd thought we dovetailed like the joints in the furniture you made.

"Did you hear what I said, Mum?"

"Yes, I did. I'm sorry, I was thinking about something else."

"What are you like? Do you realise I've been here all afternoon, and all we've got to show for it are these piles of clobber." She sighed. "I know it's hard, Mum, but we have to get through this. You move tomorrow."

A Tom pile and two Einna piles. A pile to pack into cardboard boxes and a case; they are to take. Then two piles to put in bin bags. Tom and Einna into bin bags. Sell them in a charity shop.

Stuff, grot, clobber, junk, clutter. Harsh sounding words for personal belongings that brought comfort. I looked at my charity shop pile to make sure my treasure box wasn't on it. *Stupid me. Why would it be? We haven't tackled my bedside cabinet yet. Not stupid, Einna. Stupid thought, because the box had lived in the drawer where your jumpers were, when Tom was alive. You put it in the bedside cabinet, after Tom died, so that you could read the poems without having to get out of bed.*

Claire put the earrings on the dressing table. She walked across to the clobber and picked up a pair of scarlet, patent leather sandals, with yellow flowers on the toes. The heels were four inches high. They were on the charity shop pile.

"However did you manage to walk in these?"

"I didn't. They killed me. Your dad called them tart shoes."

"They are tart shoes."

"Maggie bought a pair as well. She wore hers until they fell apart."

"I was jealous of Maggie. I thought you loved her more than me."

"So did your dad." *He was right. You were wrong.*

"You and Maggie were always chatting, and giggling."

"Yes. But you and I did lots of that as well."

"I don't remember. I do remember you telling me there were different kinds of love. I didn't understand that until I met Andy. He was jealous of my friendship with Emma. Perhaps he still is, he just doesn't mention it any more."

What slippery tricks memory can play.

"I bet you and Maggie bought earrings to match the sandals, didn't you? Don't tell me which they are, let me guess." She looked at those left on board. "Are they here, or in the pile on the dressing table?"

"On the board."

She pointed to a pair of huge red poppies with black centres. "Those?"

"Uh-huh. Do you remember me wearing them?"

"Mum, you wore different earrings each day. How could I possibly remember them all? I know I hated most of them."

"You did, didn't you? You wanted me to dress like Emma's mum."

She shook her head. "It wasn't as simple as that. I did and I didn't. I didn't like you being different and yet I was proud of you. I mean, look at those tart shoes, they're outrageous. Shall I try them on? I bet I won't be able to walk in them." She took off her training shoes and put on the sandals. "Bloody hell, they're like stilts. I need lessons in managing them. They can't be good for your feet. You put them on, Mum. Show me how to do it."

The Carnaby Street sandals pinched my toes. As I grimaced about the room, I wondered why we women treated our bodies so badly. I sank onto the bed, and pulled them off. "Ow! I need a foot massage."

Claire laughed. "I wonder if I'd have disowned you if you'd come to school in them."

"I expect so. Do you remember when you told your teacher you were fostered?"

"Emma and I thought we were being so cool. Luckily Mrs. Adams had a sense of humour. Does that shop in Carnaby Street still exist?"

"I've no idea."

"The owners ought to have been prosecuted for deforming women's feet."

"Oh, come on, sweetheart. You wanted to wear wedges when you were eleven."

"I don't remember that. Did you let me?"

"No." I wanted to hug her. Instead I leant over to open the door of my bedside cupboard, and pulled out piles of sheet music. "I don't need these any more," I said.

"Do you know, I didn't catch the moment when you changed into a butterfly. How did you leap from Carnaby Street and shoes to sheet music?"

"*These Boots Are Made For Walking.* Most of the shops had music blaring out. I don't remember the name but I do remember the music. In the shop we found the sandals, they were playing sixties' songs, and when we were trying on the shoes, it was Nancy Sinatra."

"But why do you want to give the sheet music away?"

Tom's face, crunched and angry, thrust itself in front of my eyes. I almost fell onto the bed in shock.

"Mum! Mum! Are you okay?" Claire's voice interrupted the harsh music of the silver violins. "You've gone white."

"Yes, fine, I…" *What lie must I spin, spider? Age, tell the age lie.* "I don't feel comfortable when I play now. I've got a bit of arthritis in my hands, so I thought I might give my violin to Zac. I don't want to sell it; as you know, it was your great-grandfather's." My wilful tongue slid across my palate.

'*Spots on the tongue. Liars are beaten. Liars burn in hell.*'

'*No they don't, Annie.*'

'*We all lie, Einna. Remember the person who is late for work.*'

'*Thank you, Toni.*'

"When I didn't go to college—"

"I don't understand. You did go, when I started school."

"Yes, but I was supposed to go when I was eighteen. Annie prevented me from going. No, I suppose that's not fair. I can't have wanted it enough to overcome Annie and Pearl. I believed she would control me from Hunstanton. After I'd made the decision, I realised I didn't trust Annie or Pearl not to sell the violin or give it away, as they had my bears, so I thought I would ask Ruby and Charles to look after it. But I couldn't. It would have meant that I'd have had to tell them why. It was bad enough telling them I wasn't going to college. I pretended that I was deferring."

"How did you protect your violin?"

"By auditioning for and being accepted by the local chamber orchestra."

"You did defer then."

"Yes I did, just a little bit longer than I said."

"But why give it to Zac? He doesn't play the violin."

"He told me he'd like to learn."

"You know what teenagers are like, Mum. I bet he and his friends have talked about forming a band. Zac's very like I was at his age, into one thing one moment, and abandoning it the next."

"You did do a fair bit of flitting, didn't you?"

"They call it sampling now. Were you very upset that I didn't want to learn the violin?"

I looked at her in amazement. "No, not in the least."

"I just wondered. I mean, with Great Granddad having played professionally, and you teaching the violin. I wish you'd made me stick at something, Mum. I'm no good at anything."

"And there was I thinking I'd been a liberal mum, allowing her daughter freedom of choice."

"You were. You did. Oh God, that came out all wrong. I'm sorry, Mum. I know I could have stuck at things if I'd wanted to. Emma did. And I'd have hated it if you were authoritarian like Dad. But it would have been nice to excel in one thing, like you and Great Granddad."

"I wasn't that good on the violin."

"But Great Granddad played for the Bournemouth Symphony Orchestra, didn't he? I've always thought that was amazing,"

"If he hadn't died in the First World War, he might have been first or second violin."

"I'd forgotten he'd died in the First World War. I knew my granddad died in the second one. I've only just thought. Pearl was a single parent."

"Yes, she was." It didn't excuse her neglect of me. Would things have turned out differently if those men had lived? My dad wouldn't have let Pearl give me to Annie, would he? What would Annie have been like if she'd had a living father?

"I can't remember Pearl, Mum. I never liked Annie. I still don't, but I'm sorry for her."

"Me too. Do you remember when your dad and I went to Paris?"

"Sort of. You bought these. You told me that when I was sixteen, remember?" She held up my Mona Lisa earrings.

"Yes." Of course I remembered. How could I have forgotten the Berlin wall? "You were two. Your dad suggested we asked Annie to look after you. 'No Annie,' you said, echoing my thoughts. I told you that too, didn't I? Poor Annie."

"I'm not sure, maybe. I hope that 'poor Annie' doesn't mean you'll have her to live with you."

I shuddered at the thought. "No. Whatever gave you that idea?"

"I know what you're like, Mum."

How many more people were going to tell me that they knew what I was like? I wasn't sure what she meant. I was too tender hearted, soft, easily persuaded? Still under my sister's thumb?

"I've never told you this, but she used to ring me up and complain about the way Tom treated her. She said the most dreadful things. I know Tom wasn't an easy man, but she made him out to be some kind of monster. Trouble is, when she's in full flow, it's difficult to get a word in."

Edgeways, vertically, horizontally, any which way with Annie, and Tom. I closed my eyes. There was no Tom, not now. I'd told Annie not to come to his funeral. She'd replied that she wouldn't have come even if she'd been invited, because I wasn't giving 'that man' a Christian burial. Pointless to have said, "Tom wasn't a believer, Annie." Pointless to have said, "Christian? Where are your Christian values?"

Claire was still talking. "When I could speak, I told her I didn't think Tom was very different from any other man of my acquaintance, except for Andy. I don't know where he came from, Mum, but he's certainly not a Martian." She paused, frowned. "He's not from Venus either. I liked Tom. So did Andy and Zac. Why did Tom throw Annie out the house that Christmas?"

Why indeed? "It was six of one and... She was very rude to both of us." Then I became their victim. Tears like a millpond behind my eyes were ruffled by memories.

Claire sat on the bed and put her arm round my shoulders. I grabbed a tissue out of my pocket. "I'm sorry. I don't seem to be able get used to any of it. I'm okay one minute, then I'm stepping on broken glass the next. I'll be all right in a moment. I'm being stupid."

"No you're not." She held me, stroked my hair. "Have you considered bereavement counselling?"

"I don't think I can cope with any more counselling. Tom and I were offered some after we saw the oncology specialist. I accepted. Tom refused." The counsellor was okay, but not as good as Toni. Claire didn't know about Toni.

"He was in denial. He told Andy he didn't want any fuss. He'd be as right as rain after the last blood transfusion... It's going to be great having you live near us. Zac says he's looking forward to popping in on his way home from school. I know the bungalow isn't like this house, but it'll be cosy."

"I hate this house, Claire. I'm not sorry to be leaving it. I never felt at home here. It was Tom's parents' house. It never became ours. He couldn't let them go." Too many uncomfortable memories, and the sniggering ghosts. "It's harder to leave the garden. I love gardening." Luckily the bungalow had a large, under-developed garden. I blew my nose, then rubbed my eyes, gently at first then harder, harder; I wanted to rub the ache away. "I've got to have a pee. Do I look like a panda?"

"Yes."

"Bloody mascara, you'd think by now, they'd have invented one that's rub proof as well as water proof, wouldn't you?"

"The trick is to dust a little translucent powder on your eyelids and beneath your eyes, for the waterproof bit, anyway. I don't think anything works if you insist on trying to gouge your eyes out." She gave my head a little pat.

Pat, pat. She was sitting on my knee, patting my head, trying to comfort me when Annie told me that Pearl had died. She pointed to the board. "I see you've still got the parrot earrings, even though you don't wear them."

"Of course I've got them; they're one of my favourite pairs." *I hope I shall wear them, now.* Tom was hovering near the pile of stuff. He was smiling. The smile didn't reach his eyes. *'You thought I hadn't noticed you'd moved them. I noticed everything, Einna.'*

'No you didn't, Tom, you didn't. Mina Lobata climbing up the hedge. I planted it. It wasn't bird sewn, before… before the leukaemia with the name like gunpowder. That quickly? Have I forgotten it's full name that quickly? Myel… something.'

"I never knew if I loved it when you wore them, or if I was embarrassed."

"Embarrassed, I expect. You were always telling me what to wear. You'd rifle through my cupboards wailing, 'You don't have any normal clothes'."

"You didn't."

We were laughing now, laughter mingling with tears. "That's it. I need clean knickers. I hate getting old."

"What do you mean, getting old? I've never known you not to wet your knickers when you laugh. It's a gang badge, isn't it?"

A gang badge. Not any more. Not with Angela in France, Maggie coping with Bozo, and Debbie in Alihies. "It used to be. We're not a gang any more. Perhaps we're too old to be a gang."

"I'm going to make us a coffee while you sort yourself out," Claire said.

When she returned, I saw she'd found the packet of chocolate digestives I'd bought for a mid-morning break on removal day. Chocolate digestives. Throughout my life chocolate digestives have been comfort food.

"Better?"

"Yes."

The silence in the room was comfortable, as though our laughter had chased away any malign spirits who haunted this place.

"Mu-um, you haven't still got your baa-lamb coat have you?"

"Of course I've got it."

"I haven't seen you wearing it, not since you moved in with Tom."

I didn't tell her I couldn't put it on again after Michael had dumped me.

Why do you think we walked here?

I fancied you.

I thought we would stroll by the river,

you in your curly black coat…

"I think you were the last person to wear it. It was your Russian Countess outfit for protection against Ivydale, Siberian winters."

"That house was cold."

"Yes, but you were a typical radiator hugging, teenage girl. Mind you, you weren't a teenager when you came home for the hols from Uni. I remember you, slumped on the beanbag in the baa-lamb coat then."

"All teenage girls are cold, except when they go out at night, then vanity warms them. Emma and I weren't proper teenagers, though. Vanity never warmed us. We always wore coats in winter, wherever we went. Are you going to put it in the reject pile?"

"I don't know. I might wear it again. I used to work out how I could save it, my earring board, my violin and Thomas Gardner, if there were a fire."

"What about me?"

"You weren't a thing, daughter. You first." *Always you first.*

"I'd have saved Fred Bear."

Fred Bear who is now threadbare and sits… where does he sit? He used to sit in the nursing chair in her's and Andy's bedroom. "Where is he? I don't remember seeing him the last time I was at yours?"

"Zac's pinched him. He's put all his soft toys on top of his wardrobe except for Fred Bear and Quack."

Quack, Tom's run-along duck. Tom lifting Quack and Zac into his highchair.

'You see, Einna? A lovely day, a fucking lovely day. We had plenty of those. Why dwell on the few bad ones?'

Claire took a sip of coffee. "What are you going to do with all these, Mum?"

"Make a new collage in the bungalow, I expect. I may even…" We had come round in a full circle. Could I help her to understand that my earrings were different from all the rest of my belongings. Earrings for pierced ears so intimately penetrate the flesh that I felt as though the memory was part of me. How could I put it so she saw what I saw? "The parrots, sweetheart; they're you and they're me. They're a memory of a mother who forgot what being a teenager was like; who hurt as she'd been hurt but then changed the ending."

"Ye-es. What I don't understand is why you want all the memories, like the Annie and Pearl ones, for example."

"They help me to understand who I am."

"But other objects can do that. I mean, Thomas Gardner is Charles and Ruby."

"You're right. Of course, you're right. But Thomas Gardner's external to me. An earring becomes part of your body, doesn't it?"

"I suppose. Have you finished your coffee?"

She doesn't understand. I handed her the mug. We went downstairs.

"Make sure you eat something, Mum, and try to get a good night's sleep. It's going to be a tiring day tomorrow. Have you still got those sleeping tablets the doctor gave you?"

"No, I threw them away. They made me feel so ghastly in the morning. I've got plenty of tisanes."

She hugged and kissed me, then rushed off to her world of Zac and Andy. I thought about getting something to eat, but found myself drifting back to the bedroom. I'd told Claire I'd bag up the stuff, grot, clobber, and ring the hospice charity shop to see if they would collect it. I couldn't face selling bits of my life at a car boot sale.

A snatch of colour caught my eye. A poppy earring was hooked onto the strap of a Biba sandal. I extricated it. In one of the dressing table drawers was a jewellery box. A pair at a time, I put all the earrings in it, removed the pins from the board and lifted it off the wall.

"You were wrong, Tom," I said. "The hook held." I waited for an answer. The house resounded with silence, not even broken by the tittering of ghosts or the ticking of Thomas Gardner.

Despite what I'd said to Claire about tisanes, I couldn't sleep. I gnawed at what I ought to have done to make Tom's last weeks more bearable and no amount of telling myself that I didn't know he was dying, helped.

'*Good god woman. Can't you let it go? I've been dead for nine months.*'

'*I know, Tom. But if—*'

'*Enough, Einna. We can't change what happened... I knew you'd sell my house. You never felt...*'

'*Of course I didn't Tom. You couldn't share the house with me. Your ghosts wouldn't let you.*'

When I did drop off, my sleep was in fits and starts and I woke with a head full of sludge. I managed to tick off the morning's items on Claire's *to do* list and was standing at the dressing table, staring in the mirror, when I heard a voice; it was Zac.

"Nana, Nana, we're here with the van, and so are the people from the charity shop."

The only reason we needed a van was for Thomas. I was glad the people from the hospice were here. It meant that I didn't have to wait in the house after the others had gone.

My gaze shifted from my reflection to the space on the wall where the earring board used to hang. "I'm..."

"Nana, Mum says you have to come down now. She says you'll want to organise things."

I doubted that. Claire, Andy and Zac were quite capable of doing what was necessary. The crockery set I'd bought, plus bits and pieces of kitchen equipment were boxed up and in the hall by Thomas Gardner. I wasn't taking any furniture apart from him. None of it felt as though it belonged to me. A new single bed had been delivered to the bungalow two days ago. Andy and Claire had constructed it. They had lent me their pasting table and a kitchen chair as a temporary measure. I would choose other bits of furniture when I saw pieces I liked.

In the beginning, there was one bed for Tom and I, then there were two. In the beginning... my hand crept up my body like a little mouse after food. I touched one of the silver violin earrings. "I'll never forget you, Tom."

'Have you ever seen a bird circus?'

Zac came into the bedroom. "Nana?"

"I'm coming, Zak. I'm just saying goodbye to this room, to Tom. Tell your mum I'll be down in a minute. Oh, and tell the hospice people they can start up here. Everything's labelled."

"Will do, Nan." He hesitated. "I liked Tom. He was funny."

"Yes he was. I'm glad you liked him. As you're here could you carry—"

"Of course, Nan." He grabbed the cases. I heard his feet thumping down the stairs.

"I didn't always like you Tom, but I loved you, and I will remember the good times."

Chapter Nineteen
Knickers Wetting Laughter

We were a gang,
a monstrous regiment
of giggling women.
We laughed at our husbands,
our colleagues,
our children
and ourselves.

The bungalow is silent except for the steady ticking of Thomas Gardner. I'm used to silence. I like it. Some people seem to need constant noise. They chat to each other and visitors over programmes on the television or the radio. I've come to believe that they don't know the particular appliance is on. It is a first thing in the morning habit, like cleaning their teeth.

There are downsides to ticking silence. I jump at unexpected sounds, like the doorbell. I've replaced it with a knocker in the shape of an angel. I have several angels about the bungalow, including the earrings Zac gave me for Christmas, last year. Their wings are made from soft white feathers, the downy kind; they caressed my cheeks when I tried them on.

I hung them on the earring board, on separate, pearl headed pins. Angels, shouldn't be crowded; they'd never be able to take off. I thought carefully about where they should be placed and finally decided that it might be sensible to put them next to the space I've left for Tom's violin earrings. I've a feeling they may want me to wear them today. They don't wink and blink, but I'm sure I've seen their wings moving.

"Claptrap."

I whirl round. "Tom?" Nothing. *Don't be stupid, Einna. Tom didn't come with you when you moved. He's not a ghost. It's all in your mind. Will you stop calling yourself stupid.* But is it the violin earrings in my ears that are conjuring ghosts?

Zac teases me about my penchant for angels. I like being teased by my grandson.

I've given him his own key. Claire said he'd lose it. But he hasn't, not yet anyway. He often comes to see me on his way home from school. I'm surprised, pleased. What can a teenager find interesting in the conversation of a sad, elderly woman who wishes angels existed, who talks to her dead partner, and thinks her earrings demand to be worn? I suspect it's the jam tarts and cakes. All he gets at home is an empty house and a bowl of cereal. But then modern children are used to being on their own. Sometimes he brings Sean with him. I like Sean. He makes me laugh. He says he wants me to teach him to make a coffee and walnut cake so he can surprise his mum.

The last time Zac visited me, he told me I ought to change the ring tone on my new smart phone as it's the theme tune for the film, *The Exorcist.* I saw the film years ago. I don't remember the theme tune. When I asked him how he knew, he said, "Gran, it's an iconic film," a big word for a thirteen year old. I haven't changed it. If he's so bothered, he can do it the next time he pops in.

I'm going out with the gang today. Ought I to think, *gang?* It will be the four of us, so yes, perhaps. Look out Chester, here come the gang of monstrous women who tipple-topple into laughter at the drop of a story, an irreverence, a joke; laughter to make us cry; laughter to make us wet our knickers; well, we used to. I don't need laughter, these days, to make me wet my knickers. A cough can do it. Remembering to use any convenient toilet, *'Lavatory Einna. Toilet is a vulgar word,'* should be etched into elderly people's brains.

I don't know what time I'll be back. I shall leave some chocolate digestive biscuits by the kettle, just in case Zac forgets I'm not going to be here. No jam tarts or flapjacks today; I haven't had time to make any. But Zac loves chocolate digestives as much as I do. They are good memories of East Anglia, Jean, Aunty Ruby and Uncle Charles. I wish Zac had known them.

If I hadn't been consumed by Tom and that myel-something leukaemia, would I have been able to help Debbie more than I did? *Enough.* She's here now, for a few days. I hope Ireland has helped to heal her wounds.

Men. We four women have been negatively affected by men. But is that true of Angela? Maybe I'm not being fair on Dave? Angela always told us that it was a mutual decision to emigrate to France. They're back in Britain now; necessity rather than choice, so I can say she's been negatively affected by a man; her father was diagnosed with senile dementia and her mother could no longer cope. He'd tried to beat her with his walking stick, because she wouldn't get up at four in the morning to make his breakfast. Is there always a funny side to tragedy? Maybe tragedy is too strong a word. Shakespeare always had a comic character or two in his tragedies, like the grave digger in Hamlet. It was to give the audience some moments of light relief before the full impact of the tragedy weighed down on them. The funny side in the walking stick scene was that Harold had appeared at Mona's bedside demanding to know what clothes he ought to put on. He was holding up two of her dresses for inspection.

Today, I don't jump when the phone rings. "703 8431, no... oh bugger! Hello Maggie, if it's anyone else, sorry I don't know my new number yet."

"You'll have to write it on a post it and stick it on the wall by the phone. How are you? Becoming a bungalow person? Did I just say that? What the hell is, a bungalow person? Debbie hasn't changed a bit; well in character anyway. Obviously she looks older, but still beautiful. We're all beautiful."

"Are we?"

"We are."

There is such positivity in her voice, I daren't gainsay her. But I look in the mirror and I don't see beauty. Why don't I see beauty? Why can't the elderly be beautiful?

"I don't know about beautiful, but I'm looking forward to our jaunt."

"So am I. Remember our song, *Time Off For Good Behaviour*?"

"How could I forget? But that was after Rock Follies became the show we had to watch, wasn't it? Before that, it was, *These Boots Are Made For Walking*, because of our trip to London." I bought the sheet music. I'm not sure why, now. I never did play it.

"While Debbie's here, we're going to have lots of that, time off, I mean. She's in love, by the way."

"I am not." I hear Debbie shout. "I shall never fall in love again. Love's for naïve idiots. Once bitten… I'm in lust and like, and that's enough for anyone.

"That's brazen," says Maggie. "Einna, I'm a beautiful woman who needs a favour. Could you drive? My knee's playing up."

Ah! Mentally I replace the knickers in the drawer. I wait for the catalogue of ailments. This has been our relationship for quite a few years now. But a catalogue doesn't fit today. Her voice is too light for an ailment moan.

"Are you still there?"

"Yes, I thought… oh it doesn't matter. Of course I don't mind driving. What time shall I pick you up?"

"Angela's coming for ten."

"Is Trevor in the attic?"

Maggie laughs; a shared joke. "No, he's talking to Debbie. He's quite animated for Trevor. He's been grunting less and less since daffodil day."

Daffodil day was Maggie's *Road to Damascus* experience. Apparently she was heading home after buying some furnishing fabric and did a detour via Sefton Park to see if the swathes of daffodils were out. Whilst sitting in her car staring at their wind bobbing heads, she realised she was heading for a nervous breakdown, might already be having one. In a golden trumpet flash, she knew she had to grab Trevor and Ian by their horns and tell them they had to help her sort out Edith. She also decided to tell Trevor they couldn't carry on as they were; they had to sell The Old Vicarage and work on their marriage or split up. "There are no grey daffodils," she told him.

"I think all men need Super Nannies for partners. J.M.Barrie was right. They're all Peter Pans, Mr. Darlings, Captain Hooks, or a mixture of all three."

"I hope I've helped Stuart to grow up."

"You'll have to ask Beth that."

"Maybe I will, one day. I do hope Beth and Stuart stay together. She is such a darling.

"It's going to be wonderful, us four together again, isn't it? We're going to try to persuade Debbie to come back so we can reform the knickers wetting gang."

"I don't think you can recreate the past successfully. Too much water has flowed; too many pairs of saturated knickers."

"Even if I could come back to betrayal city, Mitey would never leave his farm." Debbie calls.

"You would want Mitey to come? It must be serious then," says Maggie.

"Perhaps we should have another reunion in Ireland, in six months time?" says Debbie, not rising to Maggie's question. "You'll be able to see why I love The Beara Peninsula."

"Ye-es, yes, we could." There is doubt in Maggie's voice. I understand why. Daffodil day only happened recently. She and I are *one day at a time* people for now.

After I put the phone down, I think about our proposed day out; a day that will entail a wander, a bite to eat, comforting chatter, perhaps laughter. I'm looking forward to it. This is progress.

I wonder what to wear. I haven't been much interested in my appearance for... for years. My black jersey-cotton skirt? I still have it, but will Michael upset me all day? *How many years, Einna? Too much water,*

Einna. It's odd that he came into my mind. I do sometimes wonder where he is, if he's a successful artist? Is he is married now? Does he have children? *Oh, put it on.* With? With? I need warm, but not too warm. Layers, think layers. Black, long-sleeved t-shirt, my long grey and black striped, sleeveless jumper, my patchwork waistcoat and a red belt. Decision made. I shan't need a coat, the local weather forecast promises a fine day.

"Where's the belt? You're hiding, aren't you? Come out, come out, wherever you are."

I wonder how many people talk to themselves out loud? Is it just people who live alone? I started talking to things when I was a child. I talked to my bears. I still talk to Cocoa. He sits on my pillow. I also talk to objects in the house, and plants in the garden. I'm a believer in plant therapy. I think they thrive if you talk to them.

It was the garden that drew me into purchasing the bungalow. It was a blank canvas. As soon as the risk of frosts is over, I'm going to create a cottage garden overflowing with perennials like lupins. Next weekend, Andy and Zac are laying a patio so I'll be able to eat outside. I don't really like the word 'patio', but 'terrace' is too grand for what they are planning.

I seem to have green fingers where garden plants are concerned. Indoor ones don't survive. I kill them, with kindness or neglect. Vases of dried flowers and grasses work best for me. They don't die; they just fade in an interesting way. I've learnt a trick about how to keep synthetic or dried flowers free from dust. Pop the vase by an open window and give them a blow with the hair dryer. It doesn't work on kitchen greasy ones, though. I left the vase and the plastic flowers in Tom's house for the new owners to dispose of. It and they were too disgusting to give to the hospice charity shop. I wonder if a ghost will shout at them?

I find the belt hidden under a pile of scarves and bags in a wicker basket. I pull it and a black bag out. Inside the bag are tissues and a five pound note. What a piece of luck. I shall put it towards treating the gang to coffee.

I try on the belt and look at myself in the mirror. No, not waspy… loose, a medieval look. I suppose I'm thin enough to wear waspy. I lost weight looking after Tom, but I prefer loose.

Now, which shoes are more comfortable, the black or red ones? I toss the two pairs in my mind. Relevant question: are we going to be doing a lot of walking? I doubt it. We will probably mooch round the shops, have a bite to eat, and all the while we'll chatter and laugh. The latter isn't certain, not like in gang outings of the seventies and eighties. Then it was almost de rigour to wet our knickers.

"Get em off!"

For a few seconds, seventies' ghosts float round the bungalow. I smile at them.

I sweep my, once dark brown, now grey hair into an unstructured bun, mascara my eyes, and draw a line round my mouth with a neutral wax pencil because red lipstick can bleed into the fine lines around older mouths. I used to wear foundation and blusher, but living with Tom put a stop to all that. He didn't approve of make-up and I didn't want more confrontation.

What am I going to do about earrings? I don't need to touch my ear lobes to know I have on the silver violins. Will Tom's ghost swear at me if I take them out? Oh stop being daft. Which ones? I wait. The angels; their wings are fluttering. I remove the violins. Nothing. I choose a black-headed pin, and hang them on the board in the space that has always been there. It is their first hanging.

The phone rings as I'm about to leave the house. "Don't forget the spare knickers." It's Debbie.

"As if I would." I don't tell her they've been in and out of my bag, mentally, several times. Laughter bubbles, although for some contrary reason, I also feel like crying.

When I pull into the drive, I hoot to let them know I've arrived. As they come out of the house, I can't help thinking of brightly coloured Macaws, except for our brown mouse, Debbie. I see she still favours earth colours.

"You sit in the front, Maggie, as your knee's playing up," says Angela.

"What about your back?" I say.

"What are we like? Courageous Crocks, not a monstrous regiment, any longer," says Debbie.

"Crocks? How dare you? I'm not a crock, courageous or otherwise," says Angela. She stretches up to the sky and stoops over to touch her toes without bending her legs. "You're still pretending to be a Scouser, then?" she adds, looking at Debbie through her knees.

We all laugh. It isn't knickers' wetting laughter, yet.

In the car, the gang, the once monstrous regiment of women, put the world to rights. We decide how tax money should be spent and what laws should be changed. We would make the country a better, safer place for women. We wouldn't send young men off to wars we believe to be wrong. We deplore the example set to children and adolescents by devious politicians, crooked bankers and badly behaved football stars.

"Why are they allowed to get away with it?" cries Maggie.

"And why do we have to foot the bill for those who are prosecuted and sent to prison?" says Angela. "They ought to be made to pay."

"It's greed," I say. "Money rules. Once upon a time a million was a sum up in Cloud Cuckoo Land as far as most people were concerned. Now it's a billion. Look at the amount you can win on the Euro Millions. The bonuses given to fat cat bankers, and heads of organisations is obscene, as are the transfer fees and wages paid to footballers."

"Not all footballers get paid silly money," says Angela. "Only those in the Premier League."

"And it's not just them. Any sports person nowadays can earn ridiculous sums," says Maggie.

"I'd like to scrap how footy's organised," says Debbie.

"Just in the UK?" I ask.

"No, world wide. How can a Spanish player be loyal to Liverpool, or West Ham, for example? The only players, today, who are loyal to LFC are those like Gerrard and Carragher. We should grow our own players. So should towns, cities, counties all round the world."

"Well, it won't happen," says Angela. "We just have to accept what's going on now. That is the way the world works."

"Doesn't make it a good place to live in, does it?" I say.

"How can really rich people, like Abramovich, justify their extraordinary wealth to themselves?"

We ponder the question. "Angela's right," I say despondently.

"Do you know what puzzles me?" says Debbie. "All the people we're talking about have, or will have, children and grandchildren. This money-ridden society is making the world spin faster and faster towards catastrophe, because of consumption, greenhouse gasses and depletion of the world's resources. And they don't care. If they did, they'd change things. But firms aren't allowed to stand still. A bigger profit has to be made each year. Shareholders, bonuses and on and on. Do they hope their grandchildren will escape to another planet?"

"Maybe," says Angela. "Then they can ruin that one."

"We're never going to wet our knickers if we carry on like this," says Maggie. "We should have stuck to what men think we talk about… them."

"Then we'd be in danger of committing suicide," I say.

"Never," says Maggie. "We have to beat the buggers." This is the Maggie we used to know. It's heartening.

"No general election changes anything, does it?" says Debbie. "If it weren't for my grandmother fighting for women to get the vote, I wouldn't bother to apply for a postal one, next time."

"Next time? You're staying in Ireland for a few more years then?"

"Who knows? Day to day is all I can cope with. Are you impressed by New Labour?"

"New Labour, as a party, is so close to the Tories, it doesn't much matter who wins. The poverty gap in this country has increased," says Maggie.

"Come and live in Allihies," says Debbie.

"Are there Freds in Southern Ireland?" asks Maggie.

"Fred wasn't on the beat, was he?" I say.

"Almost as good as."

"No, not really," says Debbie. "I suspect Bobbies on the beat are a thing of our past."

"It would be good if they weren't. They knew everyone," says Maggie.

"Mitey's nephew Charlie, is a guarda cadet. He's the kind of man you think ought to try for another profession, because he's gentle. He told me, in front of Mitey, he was glad his uncle had met someone special, someone who might be able to keep him in order. You should have seen the look on Mitey's face. He was grinning from ear to ear. I half expected him to start clapping."

"Why?" asks Angela.

"Because he's considered the black sheep of the family."

"No, why are you smiling now?"

"At Charlie saying I was special. He's only nineteen. Teenagers aren't known for saying things like that, are they?" The smile disappears. "What I felt like replying was, 'You don't know me, Charlie. I'm not special. If I were special…' But that was then."

"You are special, a special nut-case," says Angela.

"A special Woolyback," I add. "Like Angela and me."

"Victims seem to have a tendency to feel they're to blame," says Maggie. It sounds heartfelt.

"In bleak moments, I did wonder if you lot thought I was to blame. After all, you often said I fed Bill on too many pulses." Debbie blows a raspberry, then laughs.

We laugh with her, but the laughter is tinged with sadness.

"Mitey wants me to move in with him. Trouble is, I've got used to a bit of space. I like it, even though the space is just a caravan. And there's the other thing." She pauses. "Mitey likes to wear women's clothes."

"Oh my god!" says Angela.

"I found out the first time we had sex."

"What on earth did you say?" says Maggie.

"Something daft: 'I knew there was something odd about you when you accosted me on the ferry and asked me to go to a wedding with you.' He replied, 'Does it turn you off?' I thought about it and said. 'I don't think so. Let's find out.' A casual sex basis is one thing. Living with a closet transvestite is another. It might be too weird."

"I can see that," says Angela.

We nod in agreement. We all know what it feels like to want to push walls and people away, but I can't imagine what I'd feel like if I'd found out that any of the men with whom I've had sexual relations were transvestites. But I wasn't shocked when I discovered John was gay. Would I have wanted to continue to live with him? Not a question I was asked to consider, and I'm not sure there would have been any point. We had very little to talk about.

"Not all teenagers grunt," says Maggie.

"You've butterflied again," says Angela.

"No I haven't. I've just gone back to what we were talking about before Mitey. I don't think Ben grunts. Stuart had a calm adolescence. I didn't grunt when I was a teenager. The gorgon wouldn't have allowed grunting. Any sign of a grunt and I'd have been given the basilisk stare, followed by a clip round the ear."

"Claire had a dramatic adolescence. There were a lot of slammed doors. Daughter and Father. John never grew out of being a teenager."

"I saw him the other day," says Maggie. "He's put on a lot of weight. He would have passed me by if I hadn't grabbed his arm. He said he didn't recognise me. He's got to have a hip replacement operation."

I don't know this. Why don't I know? Did Claire tell me? Does she know?

"Trevor wasn't doing much grunting this morning. I was almost flattened by his civility," says Debbie.

"Since daffodil day, I can almost see the man I married."

"Did I tell you, Lena's moving in with her daughter?" I say.

"What's that got to do with Trevor?"

"Trevor Grunt. Edith Dragon."

"What?" Angela and Debbie speak at the same time.

"Edith and Ian's suggestion she should move in with us? I don't want to spoil our jaunt by talking about Edith. It might provoke Bozo. I'm going to butterfly deliberately. How are you getting on at Saint Benedict's, Angela?"

"God it was dreadful. I wish I knew why I have to fill in for absent language teachers, just because I've lived in France? On the form I put that I was prepared to teach English and at a push, drama."

"There's a shortage of language, science and maths teachers," says Maggie.

"I know that. But surely knowing a subject's important, isn't it?"

"You know a lot more French than most people," Debbie points out.

"I don't feel as though I do. I gabbled away to my friends, but my French was far from grammatical. No one ever corrected me. They knew what I was saying, even if I got the gender or ending of a word wrong. I would have thought it had to be correct for schoolwork."

She's right, but supply teachers are expected to cover for whoever's away.

"Did I tell you what happened last week? First lesson, I was down to sub for was fourth year French. I went to the classroom and waited for the end of registration. I looked at the work the teacher had left, mostly games, and puzzles, like word searches. The bell went. Two minutes later, the door was flung open, bags were hurled in, followed by lads. They were like a pack of hounds after a fox, jumping chair and desk hurdles to get to their quarry: the back row. The girls slouched in. The whole class ignored me. I almost pinched myself to see if I existed.

"'That's not the way you're supposed to come into a lesson,' I said. No one took any notice. 'That's not the way you're supposed to come into a lesson,' I shouted. 'Now, please go out, line up, and come in quietly.'

"'Fuck off,' one lad said. He grabbed his bag. The rest of the lads grabbed theirs and they left in the same way they'd entered. That was the last I saw of them. Most of the girls sat there, smirking. I asked them to choose a work sheet while I popped next door to tell the Head of Languages what had happened.

"'They always do this, Miss,' said one girl. 'It's not you.'

"'Don't worry,' said the Head of Languages. 'I'm afraid it's par for the course. They'll turn up at some point.'

"I could hardly believe it. I'm sure my mouth was imitating a fish. I wanted to tell him that education had gone down the drain, along with the manners of young people. I've told the Education Authority I'm only prepared to do supply in the primary sector from now on, and I've told them why."

We're travelling down the M56 at sixty miles an hour. Vehicles pass us doing over seventy, most of them driven by people much younger than us; another example of lack of care about the world for their children and grandchildren? Maybe they don't believe the warnings? However, I think it's, part of the, *I do it because I can*, society. There seem to be too many toads poop-pooping their way through life for me to believe otherwise.

"I couldn't teach now," says Maggie. "Not even in the primary sector."

I'm reminded of one heated discussion with Tom, when I suggested giving violin lessons in the dining room at Roby Road.

"If I wanted to earn some pennies, teaching, in Castletown Bere, I'd have to pass an exam in Irish."

"It was the same for me in France," says Angela. "So much for let or hindrance."

"What?" says Maggie.

"European law. A European citizen can work in any of the EU countries, without let or hindrance. Mind you, the EU's just a theory according to Madame Tatry."

"Madame Tatry?" we echo.

"One of the bureaucrats at CPAM where we had to go to get our cartes sociale. She said we couldn't have them without cartes de sejours. It's bollocks."

"I see France hasn't improved your use of language," says Debbie.

"Okay, Miss Prude. You didn't use to be, did you?"

"No, and I'm not now. I was trying to be ironic. Why are you doing supply? You're past retirement age. You have your work and state pension, don't you?"

"We do. Dave and I need an excuse to be out the house so we don't feel overwhelmed by Mum and Dad. Does that sound cruel?"

"No, it doesn't sound at all cruel," I say. "Are you looking for your own place?"

"Yes, but it has to be near them. The whole idea of coming home was so we could help... be there in case of emergencies. Mum can't lift Dad."

A Tom flash. At the beginning of the myel-something road, I found it difficult to lift him.

"Have they considered sheltered accommodation?" says Maggie. "Ian and Trevor have managed to persuade Edith to move to Stowe Lodge. The one and two bedroomed bungalows are lovely. The one Edith's having looks out onto a duck pond. At the back is a large, communal courtyard, with beds of flowers, tubs and benches to sit on."

"We daren't even mention it. It will come to that."

We're silent for a while, perhaps remembering the women we used to be, the life we used to have, the world as it was when we were young married women laughing until we wet our knickers. I think about life's ironies. I didn't love John, but because of these women, I loved my life. I did love Tom, but these women weren't in my life then, in the way that they used to be. And living with him was like tiptoeing through a minefield. Whatever the silence is about, no hint of a smile touches our lips, let alone laughter which brings tears and wet knickers.

Chapter Twenty
The Mirror In The Cathedral

We laughed and laughed
Until we wet our knickers
Our knickers,
Our… 'get em off knickers.'
Our… in the bag knickers.
Pretty, lacy knickers.
Once upon a time.

Once upon a time there was a gang of women, a monstrous regiment, who… If I hadn't been driving I would have shaken my head. It was foolish to put spare knickers in my bag. We are different from the cackling hags of our thirties and forties, and no amount of wishing will change that. Still, the spark that always lit our fuses might still be there, buried deep maybe, but reachable? Who am I to say 'not possible'?

We arrive at the Park and Ride. I remember, only too well, how difficult it used to be to find a parking space in this historic city with its Roman walls, sandstone cathedral and rows. It attracts flocks of tourists throughout the year, so I'm glad we all agreed it was best to park there.

Angela struggles to get out the car. "I wish you had a four door car, Einna. I'm stuck. I was alright getting in."

"Perhaps you, Maggie and I should sign up for a Pilates class," I say.

"I signed up for a Pilates class as soon as I set foot on Liverpool soil," says Angela. "You could sign up for it too. I don't think Amy's list is full."

"I'm not sure Bozo would allow me to do one," says Maggie.

"I've never asked you why you call the diverticulitis, Bozo, Maggie?" says Angela.

"Dr. Clarke suggested that giving it a name, like Bozo, might help me to deal with the pain. I could talk to it, swear at it if I felt like it. I thought I might as well adopt that name. It sounded like a cartoon monster."

I would like to suggest she tries Pilates and sees how Bozo reacts, but I'm not sure she will listen, yet. I can see there are changes in her morale since daffodil day but... Maybe today, the four of us together, will be a door opening onto a more hopeful future? Saying 'perhaps we should sign up' isn't something I'd planned to say. But once the words are floating in the sunshine I feel hopeful. Pilates would be a weekly commitment with the possibility of a coffee and a natter afterwards, maybe some new friends. I shall look into it. There's bound to be information online. If I get in a muddle, Zac will help me. There's a gentle irony in the possibility. It was an ante-natal class that brought me the friendship of these three women.

Debbie helps Angela out of the car. They both stretch. It's an unconscious movement.

"Are we fit?" Maggie asks.

I wonder if that's comic, or tragic irony.

"Fit for anything," says Debbie.

"You speak for yourself," I say.

"Your appearance is at odds with your words," says Angela. "Brazen, sexy lips, and as for those mad, angel earrings."

Brazen, sexy? Is that really how Angela sees red lipstick, sees me? "I've been partial to red lipstick for, well almost ever. Since I escaped the clutches of my sister, certainly. John couldn't have cared less about... except when I turned myself into a panda. Michael liked my red lips." I pause while I think about what I've just said. *Odd that, John never commenting on my make-up. Perhaps it was because he didn't see me, or didn't want to keep facing the mistake he'd made. But even if homosexuality had been legalised in the early sixties, there was still his father and the teaching profession to contend with. Both hurdles too high for John to jump over.* I touch the soft wings of the angels. Why hadn't he been bothered about my make-up, but been critical of my earrings. He hated most of them. The number of times he said, "I hope you're not going to come out with me in those. Why don't you wear the pearl ones Annie gave you, or your gold hoops?"

"These are my Zac earrings. I'm in the process of putting together a new Einna."

"We rather liked the old one," says Debbie.

"I hope to be that person but more assertive." I cross my fingers, just in case there are any ghosts travelling with me, wagging fingers, shouting abuse. Then I shake the thought out of my head. Annie isn't a ghost. John isn't a ghost. Michael? I hope not. I've forgiven Michael the garden path. *'Makes you look wanton,'* he used to say when I arrived at his flat with scarlet lips. 'Makes me want to eat you.' Bloody hell, my vaginal muscles are clenching. I haven't felt a sexual frisson like this since… the first time I went to bed with Tom. Ah Tom! I wish… No, go away Tom, go away Michael.

Two little dickey birds holding a bomb.
One named Michael. One named Tom.
Go away Michael. Go away Tom.
Einna has diffused the bomb.

Or my body has.

I don't write about relationship problems any more. I don't have any. I write about the ageing process. My body has chosen to diffuse the sexual bomb. I am drying up. To be crude, my cunt is dry. Before Tom died, but after he became ill with the explosive sounding leukaemia, when sex was no longer possible, I masturbated. It felt good, but as soon as I began to use my dildo, it hurt; even with the KY jelly, it hurt. Full adult circle, I thought. No climaxes for you, anymore, my girl. Not only has my cunt become dry, so has my mouth; not all the time, just at night. At first I thought it was the red wine, so I switched to white. It made no difference. I stopped drinking wine for a few weeks, still no difference. Then my hygienist told me that some of my saliva glands were blocked. I have a gel for my mouth now, instead of my cunt. Well, well. No Annie threatening punishment? Am I having a daffodil day? Oh my god, I've just had a thought. Once we're on the bus, I'll ask the others.

The invisible line that used to link the women in the gang must still have strength in its fibres, for Maggie links arms with me, Debbie with her, and Angela with Debbie and we sashay across to the waiting bus. We don't care if other park and riders think we're crazy. There are smiles on all of our faces.

"I haven't been to Chester since I emigrated to Ireland," says Debbie as she sits down. "Does Annie Grizzle still live here?"

"She never did, Debbie. Don't you remember?" Silly question. Debbie was in hell when Annie moved across country. "She decided that the bungalow on the outskirts of Chester was too expensive. She bought a flat in Hunts Cross. It's very nice, though to hear her talk you wouldn't think so. It's in a Housing Association complex for the over fifties."

"It wasn't just the expense, Einna. Chester was too far away to be able to bully you," says Maggie. "She was in a cleft stick: live in vulgar Merseyside and be able to bully, or live in a city with social clout, and not be able to bully."

"She doesn't bully me any more. She's realised it has no effect."

Maggie raises her eyebrows. "There's bullying, and bullying."

I sigh. "You're wrong, Maggie. Annie's a sad, lonely woman who's one pleasure is grumbling. When we see each other, all she seems to do is moan about the children who catch the bus to school, outside the flats. Do you know what she said to me the other day? 'They throw sweet papers into the garden. When I asked them how they would feel if I were to go to their house and do the same. They said, 'whatever!' What kind of a response is that?' I told her that all teenagers say, '*whatever*'. She didn't believe me."

"We shan't risk bumping into her then," says Debbie. "That's good. Sorry, Einna, but seeing Annie would spoil the gang outing."

Why does Debbie feel the need to say, sorry? I agree with her. I change the subject. "Have you lot noticed any physical changes in your bodies over the last few years, apart from lines and age spots?"

"Not sure what you mean," says Angela.

"Well, I take ages to have a pee, now. I think I've finished and then more dribbles out."

"That's me," says Debbie.

"I haven't noticed it," says Angela.

"My body seems to have let me down every which way," says Maggie. "But no more. I am in control."

"I'm making a list, so that when I'm senile, Claire will be able to give it to the home."

"A. Why do you think you'll end up in a home? B. I don't know why you think you're going to suffer from senile dementia. And C... if my dad's anything to go by, the dementia changes your personality, so if the list includes likes and dislikes it won't be any good," says Angela.

"Annie told me that my maternal gran went senile and my great grandmother, so genetically, it is possible. I shall be in a home because I don't want to spoil Claire and Andy's late middle age."

"She probably told you that to upset you. It's the only way she has of punishing you, now," says Maggie.

"How has the dementia changed your dad's personality?" asks Debbie.

"If you remember, he was a very gentle soul. He had a wonderful sense of humour. Now, he's often aggressive and never jokes. He doesn't like things he used to like, for example sausages. He says he doesn't know what they are. When we persuaded him to taste one, he said it was disgusting, and spat it out. If he makes a cup of tea, he always leaves the tea-bag in the mug and gets angry if you suggest removing it."

"We do so much now with technology, but we still haven't got to grips with diseases like dementia and Alzheimer's," I say.

"Nor with arthritis. What's the point of living to a grand old age if your mind's gone and you're in pain?" says Maggie.

"That's what I always think when I see pictures of celebrities who've had endless nips and tucks and botox. The various old age pains will still affect them," I say.

There is a mutual sigh. "Come on gang women," says Angela. "Enough of this. New challenges, that's what we all need. They say it keeps the brain healthy."

Tom kept me healthy; always on my toes. Now I don't have him, I need something else, like Pilates. That will be my first new challenge, Angela's class.

We shop. We lunch. We talk. We laugh. We agree that Chester is no longer the interesting shopping experience it used to be. Gone are many of the little, one-off, shops. The rows are full of the chain stores you find in any high street. We don't buy anything, and by the time we leave, all the spare knickers are still in our bags.

On the bus back to the park and ride, Maggie says, "It's only two. There's an exhibition of contemporary, stained glass in Paddy's Wigwam. Shall we go? We could have a cuppa and a cake in The Bistro, afterwards."

Angela and I readily agree. Debbie is less enthusiastic. "I haven't quite forgiven Liverpool yet. She didn't treat me well when we first moved, later Allie was killed, then I broke my ankle and got involved with a rat."

"Yes, but some of that was before the gang got together, wasn't it?" says Maggie.

"True"

"And Bill kept his ratty characteristics well hidden, didn't he?"

"They all do," I say.

"Neither John, Trevor, Dave or Tom were rats in the way Bill was a rat. He betrayed the trust I had in him."

I agree. Although John had been unfaithful, he hadn't seemed like a rat because my heart wasn't in the marriage and therefore couldn't be broken by infidelity. Michael wasn't a rat in that sense either. He was a… what animal was Michael? I always saw him as a boy with a toy-box, or a puppeteer.

"Would you prefer not to risk Liverpool?" says Maggie.

"Yes, but I can't. I'm seeing Sophie tomorrow. Anyway it's stupid. I'm being stupid. It's people not a place. I shan't bump into Bill, his new partner, the girls who tormented me, or the man who killed Allie, and I shall be able to enjoy a scrummy cake."

"Okay," I say and hold out my arm to be linked. "I've read about the exhibition in The Echo. There's an angel window."

"What is it with you and angels?" asks Angela.

"I like the idea of them. I don't believe in God, but I'd like it if angels were real. In stories and films they're always helping people."

"Some angels are vengeful. Michael was a warrior angel."

"I wonder if he's the angel in Epstein's sculpture?" I say.

"That angel doesn't tell Jacob his name. Did you know that Jews won't eat the sinew of the thigh because the angel in the story put Jacob's hip out of joint when he couldn't beat him," says Angela.

"Yuk!" Debbie pulls a face. "Who'd want to eat sinew anyway? Who wants to eat meat?"

"We do," we say.

She laughs. "Mitey can't understand my vegan ways. He's a real beef eater. But then his farm is a cattle and sheep farm, so I guess it's understandable. A beef eater who loves dressing up in women's clothes. What a conundrum! Do you know, a couple of weeks after I'd met him, he asked if I'd mind if he used my car to transport his sheep, one at a time, to be dipped? His truck was off the road. You can imagine what my response was. It almost made me run to another county; prospective meat and God alone knows what chemicals in my car. What a chat-up line! Is it any wonder the bra and panties were a shock?"

The rugged farmer in bra and panties does make us giggle, but not to the point of crying with laughter, nor wetting our knickers. *Am I becoming obsessed with knickers' wetting laughter?*

"He can't have thrown an Irish paddy or you two wouldn't have got together," Angela says.

Debbie looks thoughtful. "No, he didn't. Mitey's not like that. He was abjectly apologetic. So much so, I had to shout at him to stop."

"You? Shout?" I say.

"I've changed quite a bit since Bill. I was more assertive before I met him, wasn't I? Anyway, Ben—"

"Ben?" asks Angela.

"Didn't I mention Ben in any emails?"

"You did to me," I say.

"And me," echoes Maggie.

"I can't remember a Ben. Describe him," says Angela.

"He's a her," Debbie says as we pile into Prunella." Her full name's Benedetta. She has a, nearly new shop in Castletown Bere, with a café attached. She's a fantastic cook."

"*That* Ben. You sent me her apple amber recipe. I used it on the Committee des Fêtes. They loved it and then said, 'Ah!' when I told them it was an Irish recipe, as though that explained everything. Not English, you see. The fact that I was English, and I'd cooked it, didn't enter their heads."

"How are you getting on with your book?"

"Slowly. France, and all my experiences there, are too close to me. I feel as though I've got to put them in a box, for a while. Then, maybe, I'll be able to look at them dispassionately."

"I wish I could view Mitey dispassionately," says Debbie. "I understand why it would be good to live together; our age, for one thing. But, even if the cross dressing didn't phase me, meat being cooked and eaten in a kitchen we shared would."

"Is his house big enough for two kitchens?" says Maggie.

We laugh. "That's ridiculous. It is ridiculous, isn't it?"

"Two cookers, then," I say.

"No. It's the smell. I'm not sure I could ever get used to the smell and Mitey would never consider becoming a vegan."

I don't know whether I don't blame him, or whether I think his desire for Debbie isn't strong enough. "There's another thing to consider. Will you get your underwear mixed up?"

Debbie laughs. "Have I emailed you a photo of Mitey, Einna?"

"I don't know. I don't think so."

"He's six feet one and chunky. I'm a thirty-four B cup. And I take size twelve knickers. Mitey's possibly a size forty? The cup size doesn't matter, does it? Knickers? Well his trousers are size thirty six."

"I hope there isn't a strong smell of incense in Paddy's wigwam," I say. "It makes me nauseous."

"Now you've butterflied," says Angela.

"Yes." I'd wanted to change the subject. Not because the idea of Mitey in underwear shocks or perturbs me, but because we aren't dominoing into laughter.

"Most things to do with religion make me nauseous," says Maggie. "Especially the hypocrisy of some church goers. They're every 'ist' under the sun."

"Not just church. I bet that applies to any religion you can name. Some believers are inspirational," says Debbie. "Sometimes I wish I did believe. There's comfort in talking to God, asking for help."

"The other day Zac asked me if I believed in God. I said, 'No, do you?'

"'You have to be joking, Nana,' he said. 'Believe in someone so cruel? I mean, what if Dad were God, and one day he said to Mum, 'Claire, people are evil. They murder each other. They rape, they torture, they make war. They're greedy for power and money. Tell you what I'm going to do, I'm going to send Zac to earth and let them arrest, torture and kill him. That'll be bound to make them better, won't it.' Talk about out of the mouths."

We're silent for a few minutes, then Angela says, "Tea and cake sounds fabby. Is the food as good as ever in The Bistro?"

"Yes," Maggie and I chorus, although why I'm so vociferous, I don't know. I haven't been to The Bistro since Annie and I met there, three years ago. She was full of grumbles then, and invective against Tom.

"I'm not sure I'll be allowed in Paddy's Wigwam. I'm a lapsed catholic," says Debbie.

"Edith always said she'd be excommunicated if she put one foot inside," says Maggie.

"I took Claire and Annie, once, some time ago. Claire was three or four. It was probably on one of Annie's Christmas visits. As we were looking around, a nun appeared out of a chapel. Claire took one look at her and started screaming. Annie told me I ought to smack her if she didn't stop. I can hear her now: 'You spoil that child, Einna. She'll never know what's right or wrong if you don't punish her. This maybe a Catholic church, but it's still a place of God, and Claire should be taught to be respectful.' 'She's scared of something,' I replied. 'Children don't cry for nothing.' Later I discovered Claire thought the nun was the Hooded Claw."

The exhibition is wonderful. And fortune smiles on us as the sun is shining, so all the stained glass reflects coloured lights onto the walls and floor. My one disappointment is the angel window; all I can see are wing shapes.

"It's a perfect day for looking at stained glass," says Angela. "But my neck's beginning to ache."

"Look, in front of the choir, there's a mirror, for little old ladies," says Maggie.

"Enough of the *old*," snaps Angela.

"Enough of the *ladies*," says Debbie. "I may be little but I'm not a lady and men get sore necks too."

We step up to look in the mirror and, as one, step back as if repelled by what we see. The sagging flesh, the bags and the wrinkles that are symbolic of the march of time, all clearly visible in our reflections.

"The windows will retain their beauty, whereas we must turn to dust," says Debbie.

"Then, let's have a cup of tea before we do," says Maggie.

"A nice cup of tea," says Angela.

"Oh, I think I'd prefer a nasty one," I say. "The real question is, meringue roulade, chocolate orange mousse, almond and orange cake, or… ?"

"Oh god, I can feel my belly expanding and Bozo… No. No Bozo today." She smiles. "Bozo will not control me any more. I shall control him."

"Tomorrow?" says Angela.

Maggie looks puzzled. "I thought I—"

"Sorry, Maggie. I mean what are we doing tomorrow? I've told the agency I'm not available for work this week."

"Debbie's going to see Sophie tomorrow."

"Ah yes. I forgot. Isn't she working?"

"She's taken the day off."

"The day after tomorrow?"

"How about Knutsford?" I say.

"Good idea. After lunch we could always have a walk in Tatton Park. I bet the daffs are beautiful there."

"Snowdrops, daffs, they've all become seasonal features of gardens now. There are so many snowdrop walks in February, it's difficult to know which one to choose."

"Ten-thirty at yours, Maggie?"

"I'll drive if I'm up to it. Stop the, *if*, Maggie. You will be up to it."

"Bozo isn't connected to your knee."

Maggie grimaces. "I've been a wreck, haven't I?"

"Yes," says Angela. "We should have had you put down."

Back at Maggie's, Angela phones Dave to collect her. I'd offered her a lift but she'd refused as she and Dave were continuing time off for good behaviour, and going to see *Sin City*. We kiss. We hug. I depart.

The angel door knocker greets my return home. "You may not have had a knickers wetting day, but that's okay," it seems to tell me. And I realise it's right. It doesn't matter that the monstrous regiment of women are no longer a cackling, knickers wetting gang. Nor does it matter that lads we met then, wouldn't shout, *'get em off!'* now, for I feel that I can move forward. I have asked the right questions and found answers. Because of Pearl and Annie, it was difficult to appreciate all the good moments in my relationship with Tom, and to some extent John. I dwelt on the bad. I could apologise to John. I can't apologise to Tom. I shan't apologise to John. He doesn't need my apology. He is content in his relationship with Tony. I can apologise to myself. I can forgive myself and say aloud, "Leave the bad behind. Dwell on the good. Close your eyes and think of the first strawberry."

CPSIA information can be obtained
at www.ICGtesting.com
Printed in the USA
LVOW04s1535061215
465638LV00031B/1055/P